G

Gala Days

SALZWASSER VERLAG

Gail Hamilton

Gala Days

Reprint of the original, first published in 1863.

1st Edition 2022 | ISBN: 978-3-37500-692-1

Verlag (Publisher): Salzwasser Verlag GmbH, Zeilweg 44, 60439 Frankfurt, Deutschland
Vertretungsberechtigt (Authorized to represent): E. Roepke, Zeilweg 44, 60439 Frankfurt, Deutschland
Druck (Print): Books on Demand GmbH, In de Tarpen 42, 22848 Norderstedt, Deutschland

GALA-DAYS

BY

GAIL HAMILTON

BOSTON

1863

CONTENTS.

GALA-DAYS.

GALA-DAYS.

I.

ONCE there was a great noise in our house, — a thumping and battering and grating. It was my own self dragging my big trunk down from the garret. I did it myself because I wanted it done. If I had said, "Halicarnassus, will you fetch my trunk down?" he would have asked me what trunk? and what did I want of it? and would not the other one be better? and could n't I wait till after dinner? — and so the trunk would probably have had a three-days journey from garret to basement. Now I am strong in the wrists and weak in the temper; therefore I used the one and spared the other, and got the trunk down-stairs myself. Halicarnassus heard the uproar. He must have been deaf not to hear it; for the old ark banged and bounced, and scraped the paint off the stairs, and pitched head-foremost into the wall, and gouged out the plastering, and dinted the mop-board, and was the most stupid, awkward, uncompromising, unmanageable thing I ever got hold of in my life.

By the time I had zigzagged it into the back chamber, Halicarnassus loomed up the back stairs. I stood hot and panting, with the inside of my fingers tortured into burning leather, the skin rubbed off three knuckles, and a bruise on the back of my right hand, where the trunk had crushed it against a sharp edge of the doorway.

"Now, then?" said Halicarnassus interrogatively.

"To be sure," I replied affirmatively.

He said no more, but went and looked up the garret-stairs. They bore traces of a severe encounter, that must be confessed.

"Do you wish me to give you a bit of advice?" he asked.

"No!" I answered promptly.

"Well, then, here it is. The next time you design to bring a trunk down-stairs, you would better cut away the underpinning, and knock out the beams, and let the garret down into the cellar. It will make less uproar, and not take so much to repair damages."

He intended to be severe. His words passed by me as the idle wind. I perched on my trunk, took a pasteboard box-cover and fanned myself. I was very warm. Halicarnassus sat down on the lowest stair and remained silent several minutes, expecting a meek explanation, but not getting it, swallowed a bountiful piece of what is called in homely talk, "humble-pie," and said, —

"I should like to know what 's in the wind now."

I make it a principle always to resent an insult and to welcome repentance with equal alacrity. If people thrust out their horns at me wantonly, they very soon run against a stone-wall; but the moment they show signs of contrition, I soften. It is the best way. Don't insist that people shall grovel at your feet before you accept their apology. That is not magnanimous. Let mercy temper justice. It is a hard thing at best for human nature to go down into the Valley of Humiliation; and although, when circumstances arise which make it the only fit place for a person, I insist upon his going, still no sooner does he actually begin the descent than my sense of justice is appeased, my natural sweetness of disposition resumes sway, and I trip along by his side chatting as gayly as if I did not perceive it was the Valley of Humiliation at all, but fancied it the Delectable Mountains. So, upon the first symptoms of placability, I answered cordially, —

"Halicarnassus, it has been the ambition of my life to write a book of travels. But to write a book of travels, one must first have travelled."

"Not at all," he responded. "With an atlas and an encyclopædia one can travel around the world in his arm-chair."

"But one cannot have personal adventures," I said. "You can, indeed, sit in your arm-chair and describe the crater of Vesuvius; but you cannot tumble into the crater of Vesuvius from your arm-chair."

"I have never heard that it was necessary to tumble in, in order to have a good view of the mountain."

"But it is necessary to do it, if one would make a readable book."

"Then I should let the book slide,—rather than slide myself."

"If you would do me the honor to listen," I said, scornful of his paltry attempt at wit, "you would see that the book is the object of my travelling. I travel to write. I do not write because I have travelled. I am not going to subordinate my book to my adventures. My adventures are going to be arranged beforehand with a view to my book."

"A most original way of getting up a book!"

"Not in the least. It is the most common thing in the world. Look at our dear British cousins."

"And see them make guys of themselves. They visit a magnificent country that is trying the experiment of the world, and write about their shaving-soap and their babies' nurses."

"Just where they are right. Just why I like the race, from Trollope down. They give you something to take hold of. I tell you, Halicarnassus, it is the personality of the writer, and not the nature of the scenery or of the institutions, that makes the interest. It stands to reason. If it were not so, one book would be all that ever need be written, and that book would be a census report. For a republic is a republic, and Niagara is Niagara forever; but tell how you stood on the chain-bridge at Niagara — if there is one there — and bought a cake of shaving-soap from a tribe of Indians at a fabulous price, or how your baby jumped from the arms of the careless nurse into the Falls, and immediately your own individuality is thrown around the scenery, and it acquires a human interest. It is always five miles from one place to another, but that is mere almanac and statistics. Let a poet walk the five miles, and narrate his experience with birds and bees and flowers and grasses and water and sky, and it becomes literature. And let me tell you further, sir, a book of travels is just as interesting as the person who writes it is interesting. It is not the countries, but the persons, that are 'shown up.' You go to France and write a dull book. I go to France and write a lively book. But France is the same. The difference is in ourselves."

Halicarnassus glowered at me. I think I am not using strained or extravagant language when I say that he glowered at me. Then he growled out, —

"So your book of travels is just to put yourself into pickle."

"Say, rather," I answered, with sweet humility, — "say, rather, it is to shrine myself in amber. As the insignificant fly, encompassed with molten glory, passes into a crystallized immortality, his own littleness uplifted into loveliness by the beauty in which he is imprisoned, so I, wrapped around by the glory of my land, may find myself niched into a fame which my unattended and naked merit could never have claimed."

Halicarnassus was a little stunned, but presently recovering himself, suggested that I had travelled enough already to make out a quite sizable book.

"Travelled!" I said, looking him steadily in the face, — "travelled! I went once up to Tudiz huckleberrying; and once, when there was a freshet, you took a superannuated broom and paddled me around the orchard in a leaky pig's-trough!"

He could not deny it; so he laughed, and said, —

"Ah, well! — ah, well! Suit yourself. Take your trunk and pitch into Vesuvius, if you like. I won't stand in your way."

His acquiescence was ungraciously, and I believe I may say ambiguously, expressed; but it mattered little, for I gathered up my goods and chattels, strapped them into my trunk, and waited for the summer to send us on our way rejoicing, — the gentle and gracious young summer, that had come by the calendar, but had lost her way on the thermometer. O these delaying Springs, that mock the merry-making of ancestral England! Is the world grown so old and stricken in years, that, like King David, it gets no heat? Why loiters, where lingers, the beautiful, balm-breathing June? Rosebuds are bound in her trailing hair, and the sweep of her garments always used to waft a scented gale over the happy hills.

> "Here she was wont to go! and here! and here!
> Just where the daisies, pinks, and violets grow;
> Her treading would not bend a blade of grass,
> Or shake the downy blow-ball from his stalk!
> But like the soft west-wind she shot along;
> And where she went the flowers took thickest root,
> As she had sowed them with her odorous foot."

So sang a rough-handed, silver-voiced, sturdy old fellow, harping unconsciously the notes of my lament, and the tones of his sorrow wail through the green boughs to-day, though he has been lying now these two hundred years in England's Sleeping Palace, among silent kings and queens. Fair and fresh and always young is my lost maiden, and "beautiful exceedingly." Her habit was to wreathe her garland with the May, and everywhere she found most hearty welcome; but May has come and gone, and June is still missing. I look longingly afar, but there is no flutter of her gossamer robes over the distant hills. No white cloud floats down the blue heavens, a chariot of state, bringing her royally from the court of the King. The earth is mourning her absence. A blight has fallen upon the roses, and the leaves are gone gray and mottled. The buds started up to meet and greet their queen, but her golden sceptre was not held forth, and they are faint and stunned with terror. The censer which they would have swung on the breezes, to gladden her heart, is hidden away out of sight, and their own hearts are smothered with the incense. The beans and the peas and the tasselled corn are struck with surprise, as if an eclipse had staggered them, and are waiting to see what will turn up, determined it shall not be themselves, unless something happens pretty soon. The tomatoes are thinking, with homesick regret, of the smiling Italian gardens, where the sun ripened them to mellow beauty, with many a bold caress, and they hug their ruddy fruit to their own bosoms, and Frost, the cormorant, will grab it all, since June disdains the proffered gift, and will not touch them with her tender lips. The money-plants are growing pale, and biting off their finger-tips with impatience. The marigold whispers his suspicion over to the balsam-buds, and neither ventures to make a move, quite sure there is something wrong. The scarlet tassel-flower utterly refuses to unfold his brave plumes. The

Zinnias look up a moment, shuddering with cold chills, conclude there is no good in hurrying, and then just pull their brown blankets around them, turn over in their beds, and go to sleep again. The morning-glories rub their eyes, and are but half awake, for all their royal name. The Canterbury-bells may be chiming velvet peals down in their dark cathedrals, but no clash nor clangor nor faintest echo ripples up into my Garden World. Not a bee drones his drowsy song among the flowers, for there are no flowers there. One venturesome little phlox dared the cold winds, and popped up his audacious head, but his pale, puny face shows how near he is to being frozen to death. The poor birds are shivering in their nests. They sing a little, just to keep up their spirits, and hop about to preserve their circulation, and capture a bewildered bug or two, but I don't believe there is an egg anywhere round. Not only the owl, but the red-breast, and the oriole, and the blue-jay, for all his feathers, is a-cold. Nothing flourishes but witch-grass and canker-worms. Where is June? — the bright and beautiful, the warm and clear and balm-breathing June, with her matchless, deep, intense sky, and her sunshine, that cleaves into your heart, and breaks up all the winter there? What are these sleety fogs about? Go back into the January thaw, where you belong! What have the chill rains, and the raw winds, and the dismal, leaden clouds, and all these flannels and furs to do with June, — the perfect June of hope and beauty and utter joy? Where is the June? Has she lost her way among the narrow, interminable defiles of your crooked old city streets? Go out and find her! You do not want her there. No blade nor blossom will spring from your dingy brick, nor your dull, dead stone, though you prison her there for a thousand years of wandering. Take her by the hand tenderly, and bid her forth into the waiting country, which will give her a queenly reception, and laurels worth the wearing. Have you fallen in love with her on the Potomac, O soldiers? Are you wooing her with honeyed words on the bloody soil of Virginia? Is she tranced by your glittering sword-shine in ransomed Tennessee? Is she floating on a lotus-leaf in Florida lagoons? Has she drunk Nepenthe in the orange-groves? Is she chasing golden apples under the magnolias? Are you toying with the tangles of her hair in the bright sea-foam? O, rouse her from her trance, loose the fetters from her lovely limbs, and speed her to our Northern skies, that moan her long delay.

Or is she frightened by the thunders of the cannonade sounding from shore to shore, and wakening the wild echoes? Does she fear to breast our bristling bayonets? Is she stifled by the smoke of powder? Is she crouching down by the Caribbean shores, terror-stricken and pallid? Sweet June, fear not! The flash of loyal steel will only light you along your Northern road. Beauty and innocence have nothing to dread from the sword a patriot wields. The storm that rends the heavens will make earth doubly fair. Your pathway shall lie over Delectable Mountains, and through vinelands of Beulah. Come quickly, tread softly, and from your bountiful bosom scatter seeds as you come, that daisies and violets may softly shine, and sweetly twine with the amaranth and immortelle that spring already from heroes' hearts buried in soldiers' graves.

"But there is no use in placarding her," said Halicarnassus. "We shall have no warm weather till the eclipse is over."

"So ho!" I said. "Having exhausted every other pretext for delay, you bring out an eclipse! and pray when is this famous affair to come off?"

"To-morrow if the weather prove favorable, if not, on the first fair night."

Then indeed I set my house in order. Here was something definite and trustworthy. First an eclipse, then a book, and yet I pitied the moon as I walked home that night. She came up the heavens so round and radiant, so glorious in her majesty, so confident in her strength, so sure of a triumphal march across the shining sky; not knowing that a great black shadow loomed right athwart her path to swallow her up. She never dreamed that all her royal beauty should pass behind a pall, that all her glory should be demeaned by pitiless eclipse, and her dome of delight become the valley of humiliation! Is there no help? I said. Can no hand lead her gently another way? Can no voice warn her of the black shadow that lies in ambuscade? None. Just as the young girl leaves her tender home, and goes fearless to her future, — to the future which brings sadness for her smiling, and patience for her hope, and pain for her bloom, and the cold requital of kindness, or the unrequital of coldness for her warmth of love, so goes the moon, unconscious and serene, to meet her fate. But at least I will watch with her. Trundle up to the window here, old lounge! you are almost as good as a grandmother. Steady there! broken-legged table. You have gone limping ever since I knew you; don't fail me to-night. Shine softly, Kerosena, next of kin to the sun, true monarch of mundane lights! calmly superior to the flickering of all the fluids, and the ghastliness of all the gases, though it must be confessed you don't hold out half as long as you used when first your yellow banner was unfurled. Shine softly to-night, and light my happy feet through the Walden woods, along the Walden shores, where a philosopher sits in solitary state. He shall keep me awake by the Walden shore till the moon and the shadow meet. How tranquil sits the philosopher, how grandly rings the man! Here, in his homespun house, the squirrels click under his feet, the woodchucks devour his beans, and the loon laughs on the lake. Here rich men come, and cannot hide their lankness and their poverty. Here poor men come, and their gold shines through their rags. Hither comes the poet, and the house is too narrow for their thoughts, and the rough walls ring with lusty laughter. O happy Walden wood and woodland lake, did you thrill through all your luminous aisles and all your listening shores for the man that wandered there?

Is it begun? Not yet. The kitchen clock has but just struck eleven, and my watch lacks ten minutes of that. What if the astronomers made a mistake in their calculations, and the almanacs are wrong, and the eclipse shall not come off? Would it be strange? Would it not be stranger if it were not so? How can a being, standing on one little ball, spinning forever around and around among millions of other balls larger and smaller, whirling breathlessly the same endless waltz,— how can he trace out their paths, and foretell their conjunctions? How can a puny creature fastened down to one world, able to lift himself but a few paltry feet above, to dig but a few paltry feet below its surface, utterly unable to divine what shall happen to himself in the next moment,— how can he thrust out his hand into inconceivable space, and anticipate the silent future? How can his feeble eye detect the quiver of a world? How can his slender strength weigh the mountains in scales, and the hills in a balance? And yet it is. Wonderful is the Power that framed all these spheres, and sent them on their great errands; but more wonderful still the Power that gave to finite mind its power, to stand on one little point, and sweep the whole circle of the skies. Almost as marvellous is it that man, being man, can divine the universe, as that God, being God, could devise it. Cycles of years go by. Suns and moons and stars tread their mysterious rounds, but steady eyes are following them into the awful distances, steady hands are marking their eternal courses. Their multiplied motions shall yet be resolved into harmony, and so the music of the spheres shall chime with the angels' song, "Glory to God in the highest!"

Is it begun? Not yet.

No wonder that eclipses were a terror to men before Science came queening it through the universe, compelling all these fearful sights and great signs into her triumphal train, and commanding us to be no longer afraid of our own shadow. The sure and steadfast Moon, shuddering from the fulness of her splendor into wild and ghostly darkness, might well wake strange apprehensions She is reeling in convulsive agony. She is sickening and swooning in the death-struggle. The principalities and powers of darkness, the eternal foes of men, are working their baleful spell with terrible success to cast the sweet Moon from her beautiful path, and force her to work woe and disaster upon the earth. Some fell monster, roaming through the heavens, seeking whom he may devour,—some dragon, "monstrous, horrible, and vaste," whom no Redcrosse Knight shall pierce with his trenchand blade, is swallowing with giant gulps the writhing victim. Blow shrill and loud your bugle blasts! Beat with fierce clangor your brazen cymbals! Push up wild shrieks, and groans, and horrid cries,

> "That all the woods may answer, and your echoes ring,"

and the foul fiend perchance be scared away by deafening din.

O, sad for those who lived before the ghouls were disinherited; for whom the woods and waters, and the deep places, were peopled with mighty, mysterious foes; who saw evil spirits in the earth forces, and turned her gold into consuming fire. For us, later born, Science has dived into the caverns, and scaled the heights, and fathomed the depths, forcing from coy yet willing Nature the solution of her own problems, and showing us everywhere, GOD. We are not the children of fate, trembling at the frown of fairies and witches and gnomes, but the children of our Father. If we ascend up into heaven, he is there. If we take the wings of the morning, and dwell in the uttermost parts of the sea, even there shall his hand lead, and his right hand hold.

Is it begun? Not — well, I don't know, though. Something seems to be happening up in the northwest corner. Certainly, a bit of that round disk has been shaved off. I will wait five minutes. Yes, the battle is begun. The shadow advances. The moon yields. But there are watchers in the heaven as well as in the earth. There is sympathy in the skies. Up floats an argosy of compassionate clouds, and fling their fleecy veil around the pallid moon, and bear her softly on their snowy bosoms. But she moves on, impelled. She sweeps beyond the sad clouds. Deeper and deeper into the darkness. Closer and closer the Shadow clutches her in his inexorable arms. Wan and weird becomes her face, wrathful and wild the astonished winds; and for all her science and her faith, the Earth trembles in the night, and a hush of awe quivers through the angry, agitated air. On, still on, till the fair and smiling moon is but a dull and tawny orb, with no beauty to be desired; on, still on, till even that cold, coppery light wanes into sullen darkness. Whether it is a cloud kindly hiding the humbled queen, or whether the queen is indeed merged in the abyss of the Shadow, I cannot tell, and it is dismal waiting to see. The wildness is gone with the moon, and there is nothing left but a dark night. I wonder how long before she will reappear? Are the people in the moon staring through an eclipse of the sun? I should like to see her come out again, and clothe herself in splendor. I think I will go back to Walden. Ah! even my philosopher, aping Homer, nods. It shimmers a little, on the lake, among the mountains — of the moon.

I declare! I believe I have been asleep. What of it? It is just as well. I have no doubt the moon will come out again all right, — which is more than I shall do if I go on in this way. I feel already as if the top of my head was coming off. Once I was very unhappy, and I sat up all night to make the most of it. It was many hundred years ago, when I was younger than I am now, and did not know that misery was not a thing to be caressed and cosseted and coddled, but a thing to be taken, neck and heels, and turned out doors. So I sat up to revel in the ecstasy of woe. I went along swimmingly into the little hours, but by two o'clock there was a great sameness about it, and I grew desperately sleepy. I was not going to give it up, however, so I shocked myself into a torpid animation with a cold bath, it being mid-winter, and betwixt bath and bathos, managed to keep agoing till daylight. Once since then I was very happy, and could not keep my eyes shut. Those are the only two times I ever sat up all night, and, on the whole, I think I will go to bed; wherefore, O people on the earth, marking eagerly the moon's eclipse, and O people on the moon, crowding your craggy hills to see an eclipse of the sun, Good night!

Then the lost June came back. Frost melted out of the air, summer melted in, and my book beckoned me onward with a commanding gesture. Consequently I took my trunk, Halicarnassus his cane, and we started on our travels. But the shadow of the eclipse hung over us still. An evil omen came in the beginning. Just as I was stepping into the car, I observed a violent smoke issuing from under it. I started back in alarm.

"They are only getting up steam," said Halicarnassus. "Always do, when they start."

"I know better!" I answered briskly, for there was no time to be circumlocutional. "They don't get up steam under the cars."

"Why not? Bet a sixpence you could n't get Uncle Cain's Dobbin out of his jog-trot without building a fire under him."

"I know that wheel is on fire," I said, not to be turned from the direct and certain line of assertion into the winding ways of argument.

"No matter," replied Halicarnassus, conceding everything, "we are insured."

Upon the strength of which consolatory information I went in. By and by a man entered and took a seat in front of us. "The box is all afire," chuckled he to his neighbor, as if it were a fine joke. By and by several people who had been looking out of the windows drew in their heads, rose, and went into the next car.

"What do you suppose they did that for?" I asked Halicarnassus.

"More aristocratical. Belong to old families. This is a new car, don't you see? We are *parvenus*."

"Nothing of the sort," I rejoined. "This car is on fire, and they have gone into the next one so as not to be burned up."

"They are not going to write books, and can afford to run away from adventures."

"But suppose I am burned up in my adventure?"

"Obviously, then, your book will end in smoke."

I ceased to talk, for I was provoked at his indifference. I leave every impartial mind to judge for itself whether the circumstances were such as to warrant composure. To be sure, somebody said the car was to be left at Jeru; but Jeru was eight miles away, and any quantity of mischief might be done before we reached it,—if indeed we were not prevented from reaching it altogether. It was a mere question of dynamics. Would dry wood be able to hold its own against a raging fire for half an hour? Of course the conductor thought it would; but even conductors are not infallible; and you may imagine how comfortable it was to sit and know that a fire was in full blast beneath you, and to look down every few minutes expecting to see the flames forking up under your feet. I confess I was not without something like a hope that one tongue of the devouring element would flare up far enough to give Halicarnassus a start; but it did not. No casualty occurred. We reached Jeru in safety; but that does not prove that there was no danger, or that indifference was anything but the most foolish hardihood. If our burning car had been in mid-ocean, serenity would have been sublimity, but to stay in the midst of peril when two steps would take one out of it is idiocy. And that there was peril is conclusively shown by the fact that the very next day the Eastern Railroad Depot took fire and was burned to the ground. I have in my own mind no doubt that it was a continuation of the same fire, and if we had stayed in the car much longer, we should have shared the same fate.

We found Jeru to be a pleasant city, with only one fault: the inhabitants will crowd into a car before passengers can get out; consequently the heads of the two columns collide near the car-door, and there is a general choke. Otherwise Jeru is a delightful city. It is famous for its beautiful women. Its railroad-station is a magnificent piece of architecture. Its men are retired East-India merchants. Everybody in Jeru is rich and has real estate. The houses in Jeru are three stories high and face on the Common. People in Jeru are well-dressed and well-bred, and they all came over in the Mayflower.

We stopped in Jeru five minutes.

When we were ready to continue our travels, Halicarnassus seceded into the smoking-car, and while the engine was shrieking off its inertia, a small boy, laboring under great agitation, hurried in, darted up to me, and, thrusting a pinchbeck ring with a pink glass in it into my face, exclaimed, in a hoarse whisper, —

"A beautiful ring, ma'am! I 've just picked it up. Can't stop to find the owner. Worth a dollar, ma'am; but if you 'll give me fifty cents — "

"Boy!"

I rose fiercely, convulsively, in my seat, drew one long breath, but whether he thought I was going to kill him, — I dare say I looked it, — or whether he saw a sheriff behind, or a phantom gallows before, I know not; but without waiting for the thunderbolt to strike, he rushed from the car as precipitately as he had rushed in. I *was* angry, — not because I was to have been cheated, for I have been repeatedly and atrociously cheated and only smiled, but because the rascal dared attempt on me such a threadbare, ragged, shoddy trick as that. Do I *look* like a rough-hewn, unseasoned backwoodsman? Have I the air of never having read a newspaper? Is there a patent innocence of eye-teeth in my demeanor? O Jeru! Jeru! Somewhere in your virtuous bosom you are nourishing a viper, for I have felt his fangs. Woe unto you, if you do not strangle him before he develops into mature anacondaism! In point of natural history I am not sure that vipers do grow up anacondas, but for the purposes of moral philosophy the development theory answers perfectly well.

In Boston we had three hours to spare; so we sent our luggage — that is, my trunk — to the Worcester Depot, and walked leisurely ourselves. I had a little shopping to do, to complete my outfit for the journey, — a very little shopping, — only a nightcap or two. Ordinarily such a thing is a matter of small moment, but in my case the subject had swollen into unnatural dimensions. Nightcaps are not generally considered healthy, — at least not by physicians. Nature has given to the head its sufficient and appropriate covering, the hair. Anything more than this injures the head, by confining the heat, preventing the soothing, cooling contact of air, and so deranging the circulation of the blood. Therefore I have always heeded the dictates of Nature, which I have supposed to be to brush out the hair thoroughly at night and let it fly. But there are serious disadvantages connected with this course. For Nature will be sure to whisk the hair away from your ears where you want it, and into your eyes where you don't want it, besides crowning you with magnificent disorder in the morning. But as I have always believed that no evil exists without its remedy, I had long been exercising my inventive genius in attempts to produce a head-gear which should at once protect the ears, confine the hair, and let the skull alone. I regret to say that my experiments were an utter failure, notwithstanding the amount of science and skill brought to bear upon them. One idea lay at the basis of all my endeavors. Every combination, however elaborate or intricate, resolved into its simplest elements, consisted of a pair of rosettes laterally to keep the ears warm, a bag posteriorly to put the hair into, and some kind of a string somewhere to hold the machine together. Every possible shape into which lace or muslin or sheeting could be cut or plaited or sewed or twisted, into which crewel or cord could be crocheted or netted or tatted, I make bold to declare was essayed, until things came to such a pass that every odd bit of dry goods lying round the house was, in the absence of any positive testimony on the subject, assumed to be one of my nightcaps, — an utterly baseless assumption, because my achievements never went so far as concrete capuality, but stopped short in the later stages of abstract idealism. However, prejudice is stronger than truth; and, as I said, every fragment of every fabric that could not give an account of itself was charged with being a nightcap till it was proved to be a dish-cloth or a cart-rope. I at length surrendered at discretion, and remembered that somewhere in my reading I had met with exquisite lace caps, and I did not know but that from the combined fineness and strength of their material they might answer the purpose, even if in form they should not be everything that was desirable, — and I determined to ascertain, if possible, whether such things existed anywhere out of poetry.

As you perceive, therefore, my Boston shopping was not every-day trading. It was to mark the abandonment of an old and the inauguration of a new line of policy. Thus it was with no ordinary interest that I looked carefully at all the shops, and when I found one that seemed to hold out a possibility of nightcaps, I went in. Halicarnassus obeyed the hint which I pricked into him with the point of my parasol, and stopped outside. The one place in the world where a man has no business to be is the inside of a dry-goods shop. He never looks and never is so big and bungling as there. A woman skips from silk to muslin, from muslin to ribbons, from ribbons to table-cloths, with the grace and agility of a bird. She glides in and out among crowds of her sex, steers sweepingly clear of all obstacles, and emerges triumphant. A man enters, and immediately becomes all boots and elbows. He needs as much room to turn round in as the English iron-clad Warrior, and it takes him about as long. He treads on all the flounces, runs against all the clerks, knocks over all the children, and is generally under-foot. If he gets an idea into his head, a Nims's battery cannot dislodge it. You thought of buying a shawl; but a thousand considerations, in the shape of raglans, cloaks, talmas, pea-jackets, induce you to modify your views. He stands by you. He hears all your inquiries and all the clerk's suggestions. The whole process of your reasoning is visible to his naked eye. He sees the sack or visite or cape put upon your shoulders and you walking off in it, and when you are half-way home, he will mutter, in stupid amazement, "I thought you were going to buy a shawl!" It is enough to drive one wild.

No! Halicarnassus is absurd and mulish in many things, but he knows I will not be hampered with him when I am shopping, and he obeys the smallest hint, and stops outside.

To be sure he puts my temper on the rack by standing with his hands in his pockets, or by looking meek, or likely as not peering into the shop-door after me with great staring eyes and parted lips; and this is the most provoking of all. If there is anything vulgar, slipshod, and shiftless, it is a man lounging about with his hands in his pockets. If you have paws, stow them away; but if you are endowed with hands, learn to carry them properly, or else cut them off. Nor can I abide a man's looking as if he were under control. I wish him to *be* submissive, but I don't wish him to *look* so. He shall do just as he is bidden, but he shall carry himself like the man and monarch he was made to be. Let him stay where he is put, yet not as if he were put there, but as if he had taken his position deliberately. But, of all things, to have a man act as if he were a clod just emerged for the first time from his own barnyard! Upon this occasion, however, I was too much absorbed in my errand to note anybody's demeanor, and I threaded straightway the crowd of customers, went up to the counter, and inquired in a clear voice, —

"Have you lace nightcaps?"

The clerk looked at me with a troubled, bewildered glance, and made no reply. I supposed he had not understood me, and repeated the question. Then he answered, dubiously, —

"We have breakfast-caps."

It was my turn to look bewildered. What had I to do with breakfast-caps? What connection was there between my question and his answer? What field was there for any further inquiry? "Have you ox-bows?" imagine a farmer to ask. "We have rainbows," says the shopman. "Have you cameo-pins?" inquires the elegant Mrs. Jenkins. "We have linchpins." "Have you young apple-trees?" asks the nursery-man. "We have whiffle-trees." If I had wanted breakfast-caps, should n't I have asked for breakfast-caps? Or do the Boston people take their breakfast at one o'clock in the morning? I concluded that the man was demented, and marched out of the shop. When I laid the matter before Halicarnassus, the following interesting colloquy took place.

I. "What do you suppose it meant?"

H. "He took you for a North American Indian."

I. "What do you mean?"

H. "He did not understand your *patois*."

I. "What *patois?*"

H. "Your squaw dialect. You should have asked for a *bonnet de nuit*."

I. "Why?"

H. "People never talk about nightcaps in good society."

I. "Oh!"

I was very warm, and Halicarnassus said he was tired; so he went into a restaurant and ordered strawberries, — that luscious fruit, quivering on the border-land of ambrosia and nectar.

"Doubtless," says honest, quaint, delightful Isaac, — and he never spoke a truer word, — "doubtless God might have made a better berry than a strawberry, but doubtless God never did."

The bill of fare rated their excellence at fifteen cents.

"Not unreasonable," I pantomimed.

"Not if I pay for them," replied Halicarnassus.

Then we sat and amused ourselves after the usual brilliant fashion of people who are waiting in hotel parlors, railroad-stations, and restaurants. We surveyed the gilding and the carpet and the mirrors and the curtains. We hazarded profound conjectures touching the people assembled. We studied the bill of fare as if it contained the secret of our army's delay upon the Potomac, and had just concluded that the first crop of strawberries was exhausted, and they were waiting for the second crop to grow, when Hebe hove in sight with her nectared ambrosia in a pair of cracked, browny-white saucers, with browny-green silver spoons. I poured out what professed to be cream, but proved very low-spirited milk, in which a few disheartened strawberries appeared *rari nantes.* I looked at them in dismay. Then curiosity smote me, and I counted them. Just fifteen.

"Cent a piece," said Halicarnassus.

I was not thinking of the cent, but I had promised myself a feast; and what is a feast, susceptible of enumeration? Cleopatra was right. "That love" — and the same is true of strawberries — "is beggarly which can be reckoned." Infinity alone is glory.

"Perhaps the quality will atone for the quantity," said Halicarnassus, scooping up at least half of his at one "arm-sweep."

"How do they taste?" I asked.

"Rather coppery," he answered.

"It is the spoons!" I exclaimed, in a fright. "They are German silver! You will be poisoned!" and knocked his out of his hand with such instinctive, sudden violence that it flew to the other side of the room, where an old gentleman sat over his newspaper and dinner.

He started, dropped his newspaper, and looked

around in a maze. Halicarnassus behaved beautifully, — I will give him the credit of it. He went on with my spoon and his strawberries as unconcernedly as if nothing had happened. I was conscious that I blushed, but my face was in the shade, and nobody else knew it; and to this day I have no doubt the old gentleman would have marvelled what sent that mysterious spoon rattling against his table and whizzing between his boots, had not Halicarnassus, when the uproar was over, conceived it his duty to go and pick up the spoon and apologize for the accident, lest the gentleman should fancy an intentional rudeness. Partly to reward him for his good behavior, partly because I never did think it worth while to make two bites of a cherry, and partly because I did not fancy being poisoned, I gave my fifteen berries to him. He devoured them with evident relish.

"Does my spoon taste as badly as yours?" I asked.

"My spoon?" inquired he, innocently.

"Yes. You said before that they tasted coppery."

"I don't think," replied this unprincipled man, — "I don't think it was the flavor of the spoon so much as of the coin which each berry represented."

If we could only have been at home!

I never made a more unsatisfactory investment in my life than the one I made in that restaurant.

I felt as if I had been swindled, and I said so to Halicarnassus. He remarked that there was plenty of cream and sugar. I answered curtly, that the cream was chiefly water, and the sugar chiefly flour; but if they had been Simon Pure himself, was it anything but an aggravation of the offence to have them with nothing to eat them on?

"You might do as they do in France, — carry away what you don't eat, seeing you pay for it."

"A pocketful of milk and water would be both delightful and serviceable; but I might take the sugar," I added, with a sudden thought, upsetting the sugar-bowl into a "Boston Journal" which we had bought in the train. "I can never use it, but it will be a consolation to reflect on."

Halicarnassus, who, though fertile in evil conceptions, lacks nerve to put them into execution, was somewhat startled at this sudden change of base. He had no idea that I should really act upon his suggestion, but I did. I bundled the sugar into my pocket with a grim satisfaction; and Halicarnassus paid his thirty cents, looking — and feeling, as he afterwards told me — as if a policeman's gripe were on his shoulders. If any restaurant in Boston recollects having been astonished at any time during the summer of 1862 by an unaccountably empty sugar-bowl, I take this occasion to explain the phenomenon. I gave the sugar afterwards to a little beggar-girl, with a dime for a brace of lemons, and shook off the dust of my feet against Boston at the "B. & W. R. R. D."

Boston is a beautiful city, situated on a peninsula at the head of Massachusetts Bay. It has three streets: Cornhill, Washington, and Beacon Streets. It has a Common and a Frog-pond, and many sprightly squirrels. Its streets are straight, and cross each other like lines on a chess-board. It has a state-house, which is the finest edifice in the world or out of it. It has one church, the Old South, which was built, as its name indicates, before the Proclamation of Emancipation was issued. It has one bookstore, a lofty and imposing pile, of the Egyptian style (and date) of architecture, on the corner of Washington and School Streets. It has one magazine, the "Atlantic Monthly," one daily newspaper, the "Boston Journal," one religious weekly, the "Congregationalist," and one orator, whose name is Train, a model of chaste, compact, and classic elegance. In politics, it was a Webster Whig, till Whig and Webster both went down, when it fell apart and waited for something to turn up, — which proved to be drafting. Boston is called the Athens of America. Its men are solid. Its women wear their bonnets to bed, their nightcaps to breakfast, and talk Greek at dinner. I spent two hours and a half in Boston, and I know.

We had a royal progress from Boston to Fontdale. Summer lay on the shining hills, and scattered benedictions. Plenty smiled up from a thousand fertile fields. Patient oxen, with their soft, deep eyes, trod heavily over mines of greater than Indian wealth. Kindly cows stood in the grateful shade of cathedral elms, and gave thanks to God in their dumb, fumbling way. Motherly, sleepy, stupid sheep lay on the plains, little lambs rollicked out their short-lived youth around them, and no premonition floated over from the adjoining pea-patch, nor any misgiving of approaching mutton marred their happy heyday. Straight through the piny forests, straight past the vocal orchards, right in among the robins and the jays and the startled thrushes, we dashed inexorable, and made harsh dissonance in the wild-wood orchestra; but not for that was the music hushed, nor did one color fade. Brooks leaped in headlong chase down the furrowed sides of gray old rocks, and glided whispering beneath the sorrowful willows. Old trees renewed their youth in the slight, tenacious grasp of many a tremulous tendril, and, leaping lightly above their topmost heights, vine laughed to vine, swaying dreamily in the summer air; and not a vine nor brook nor hill nor forest but sent up a sweet-smelling incense to its Maker. Not an ox or cow or lamb or bird living its own dim life but lent its charm of unconscious grace to the great picture that unfolded itself, mile after mile, in ever fresher loveliness to ever unsated eyes. Well might the morning stars sing together, and all the sons of God shout for joy, when first this grand and perfect world swung free from its moorings, flung out its spotless banner, and sailed majestic down the thronging skies. Yet, though but once God spoke the world to life, the miracle of creation is still incomplete. New every spring-time, fresh every summer, the earth comes forth as a bride adorned for her husband. Not only in the gray dawn of our history, but now in the full brightness of its noonday, may we hear the voice of the Lord walking in the garden. I look out upon the gray degraded fields left naked of the kindly snow, and inwardly ask, Can these dry bones live again? And while the question is yet trembling on my lips, lo! a Spirit breathes upon the earth, and beauty thrills into bloom. Who shall lack faith in man's redemption, when every year the earth is redeemed by unseen hands, and death is lost in resurrection?

To Fontdale sitting among her beautiful meadows we are borne swiftly on. There we must tarry for the night, for I will not travel in the dark when I can help it. I love it. There is no solitude in the world, or at least I have never felt any, like standing alone in the doorway of the rear car on a dark night, and rushing on through the darkness, — darkness, darkness everywhere, and if one could only be sure of rushing on till daylight doth appear! But with the frightful and not remote possibility of bringing up in a crash and being buried under a general huddle, one prefers daylight. You may not be able to get out of the huddle even by daylight; but you will at least know where you are, if there is anything of you left. So at Fontdale Halicarnassus branches off temporarily on a business errand, and I stop for the night a-cousining.

You object to this? Some people do. For my part, I like it. You say you will not turn your own house or your friend's house into a hotel. If people wish to see you, let them come and make a visit; if you wish to see them, you will go and make them one; but this touch and go, — what is it worth? O foolish Galatians! much every way. For don't you see, supposing the people are people you don't like, how much better it is to have them come and sleep or dine and be gone than to have them before your face and eyes for a week? An ill that is temporary is tolerable. You could entertain the Evil One himself, if you were sure he would go away after dinner. The trouble about him is not so much that he comes as that he won't go. He hangs around. If you once open your door to him, there is no getting rid of him; and some of his followers, it must be confessed, are just like him. You must resist them both, or they will never flee. But if they do flee after a day's tarry, do not complain. You protest against turning your house into a hotel. Why, the hotelry is the least irksome part of the whole business, when your guests are uninteresting. It is not the supper or the bed that costs, but keeping people going after supper is over and before bed-time is come. Never complain, if you have nothing worse to do than to feed or house your guests for a day or an hour.

On the other hand, if they are people you like, how much better to have them come so than not to come at all! People cannot often make long visits, — people that are worth anything, — people who use life; and they are the only ones that are worth anything. And if you cannot get your good things in the lump, are you going to refuse them altogether? By no means. You are going to take them by driblets, and if you will only be sensible and not pout, but keep your tin pan right side up, you will find that golden showers will drizzle through all your life. So, with never a nugget in your chest, you shall die rich. If you can stop over-night with your friend, you have no sand-grain, but a very respectable boulder. For a night is infinite. Daytime is well enough for business, but it is little worth for happiness. You sit down to a book, to a picture, to a friend, and the first you know it is time to get dinner, or time to eat it, or time for the train, or you must put out your dried apples, or set the bread to rising, or something breaks in impertinently and chokes you off at flood-tide. But the night has no end. Everything is done but that which you would be forever doing. The curtains are drawn, the lamp is lighted and veiled into exquisite soft shadowiness. All the world is far off. All its din and dole strike into the bank of darkness that envelops you and are lost to your tranced sense. In all the world are only your friend and you, and then you strike out your oars, silver-sounding, into the shoreless night.

But the night comes to an end, you say. No, it does not. It is you that come to an end. You grow sleepy, clod that you are. But as you don't think, when you begin, that you ever shall grow sleepy, it is just the same as if you never did. For you have no foreshadow of an inevitable termination to your rapture, and so practically your night has no limit. It is fastened at one end to the sunset, but the other end floats off into eternity. And there really is no abrupt termination. You roll down the inclined plane of your social happiness into the bosom of another happiness, — sleep. Sleep for the sleepy is bliss just as truly as society to the lonely. What in the distance would have seemed Purgatory, once reached, is Paradise, and your happiness is continuous. Just as it is in mending. Short-sighted, superficial, unreflecting people have a way — which in time fossilizes into a principle — of mending everything as soon as it comes up from the wash, — a very unthrifty, uneconomical habit, if you use the words thrift and economy in the only way in which they ought to be used, namely, as applied to what is worth economizing. Time, happiness, life, these are the only things to be thrifty about. But I see people working and worrying over quince-marmalade and tucked petticoats and embroidered chair-covers, things that perish with the using and leave the user worse than they found him. This I call waste and wicked prodigality. Life is too short to permit us to fret about matters of no importance. Where these things can minister to the mind and heart, they are a part of the soul's furniture; but where they only pamper the appetite or the vanity, or any foolish and hurtful lust, they are foolish and hurtful. Be thrifty of comfort. Never allow an opportunity for cheer, for pleasure, for intelligence, for benevolence, for any kind of good, to go unimproved. Consider seriously whether the syrup of your preserves or the juices of your own soul will do the most to serve your race. It may be that they are compatible,—that the concoction of the one shall provide the ascending sap of the other; but if it is not so, if one must be sacrificed, do not hesitate a moment as to which it shall be. If a peach does not become sweetmeat, it will become something, it will not stay a withered, unsightly peach; but for souls there is no transmigration out of fables. Once a soul, forever a soul,—mean or mighty, shrivelled or full, it is for you to say. Money, land, luxury, so far as they are money, land, and luxury, are worthless. It is only as fast and as far as they are turned into life that they acquire value.

So you are thriftless when you eagerly seize the first opportunity to fritter away your time over old clothes. You precipitate yourself unnecessarily against a disagreeable thing. For you are not going to put your stockings on. Perhaps you will not need your buttons for a week, and in a week you may have passed beyond the jurisdiction of buttons. But even if you should not, let the buttons and the holes alone all the same. For, first, the pleasant and profitable thing which you will do instead is a funded capital, which will roll you up a perpetual interest; and secondly, the disagreeable duty is forever abolished. I say forever, because, when you have gone without the button awhile, the inconvenience it occasions will reconcile you to the necessity of sewing it on, — will even go further, and make it a positive relief amounting to positive pleasure. Besides, every time you use it, for a long while after, you will have a delicious sense of satisfaction, such as accompanies the sudden complete cessation of a dull, continuous pain. Thus what was at best characterless routine, and most likely an exasperation, is turned into actual delight, and adds to the sum of life. This is thrift. This is economy. But, alas! few people understand the art of living. They strive after system, wholeness, buttons, and neglect the weightier matters of the higher law.

—— I wonder how I got here, or how I am to get back again. I started for Fontdale, and I find myself in a mending-basket. As I know no good in tracing the same road back, we may as well strike a bee-line and begin new at Fontdale.

We stopped at Fontdale a-cousining. I have a veil, a beautiful —— *have*, did I say? Alas! Troy *was*. But I must not anticipate —— a beautiful veil of brown tissue, none of your woolleny, gruff fabrics, fit only for penance, but a silken, gossamery cloud, soft as a baby's cheek. Yet everybody fleers at it. Everybody has a joke about it. Everybody looks at it, and holds it out at arms' length, and shakes it, and makes great eyes at it, and says, "What in the world —" and ends with a huge, bouncing laugh. Why? One is ashamed of human nature at being forced to confess. Because, to use a Gulliverism, it is longer by the breadth of my nail than any of its contemporaries. In fact, it is two yards long. That is all. Halicarnassus fired the first gun at it by saying that its length was to enable one end of it to remain at home while the other end went with me, so that neither of us should get lost. This is an allusion to a habit which I and my property have of finding ourselves individually and collectively left in the lurch. After this initial shot, everybody considered himself at liberty to let off his rusty old blunderbuss, and there was a constant peppering. But my veil never lowered its colors nor curtailed its resources. Alas! what ridicule and contumely failed to effect, destiny accomplished. Softness and plenitude are no shields against the shafts of fate.

I went into the station waiting-room to write a note. I laid my bonnet, my veil, my packages upon the table. I wrote my note. I went away. The next morning, when I would have arrayed myself to resume my journey, there was no veil. I remembered that I had taken it into the station the night before, and that I had not taken it out. At the station we inquired of the waiting-woman concerning it. It is as much as your life is worth to ask these people about lost articles. They take it for granted at the first blush that you mean to accuse them of stealing. "Have you seen a brown veil lying about anywhere?" asked Crene, her sweet bird-voice warbling out from her sweet rose-lips. "No, I 'a'n't seen nothin' of it," says Gnome, with magnificent indifference.

"It was lost here last night," continues Crene, in a soliloquizing undertone, pushing investigating glances beneath the sofas.

"I do' know nothin' about it. *I* 'a'n't took it"; and the Gnome tosses her head back defiantly. "I seen the lady when she was a-writin' of her letter, and when she went out ther' wa'n't nothin' left on the table but a hangkerchuf, and that wa'n't hern. I do' know nothin' about it, nor I 'a'n't seen nothin' of it."

O no, my Gnome, you knew nothing of it; you did not take it. But since no one accused you, or even suspected you, why could you not have been less aggressive and more sympathetic in your assertions? But we will plough no longer in that field. The ploughshare has struck against a rock and grits, denting its edge in vain. My veil is gone,—my ample, historic, heroic veil. There is a woman in Fontdale who breathes air filtered through—I will not say *stolen* tissue, but certainly through tissue which was obtained without rendering its owner any fair equivalent. Does not every breeze that softly stirs its fluttering folds say to her, "O friend, this veil is not yours, not yours," and still sighingly, "not yours! Up among the northern hills, yonder towards the sunset, sits the owner, sorrowful, weeping, wailing"? I believe I am wading out into the Sally Waters of Mother Goosery; but, prose or poetry, somewhere a woman,—and because nobody of taste could surreptitiously possess herself of my veil, I have no doubt that she cut it incontinently into two equal parts, and gave one to her sister, and that there are two women,—nay, since niggardly souls have no sense of grandeur, and will shave down to microscopic dimensions, it is every way probable that she divided it into three unequal parts, and took three quarters of a yard for herself, three quarters for her sister, and gave the remaining half-yard to her daughter, and that at this very moment there are two women and a little girl taking their walks abroad under the silken shadows of my veil! And yet there are people who profess to disbelieve in total depravity.

Nor did the veil walk away alone. My trunk became imbued with the spirit of adventure, and branched off on its own account up somewhere into Vermont. I suppose it would have kept on and reached perhaps the North Pole by this time, had not Crene's dark eyes, — so pretty to look at that one instinctively feels they ought not to be good for anything, if a just impartiality is to be maintained, but they are, — had not Crene's dark eyes seen it tilting into a baggage-crate, and trundling off towards the Green Mountains, but too late. Of course there was a formidable hitch in the programme. A court of justice was improvised on the car-steps. I was the plaintiff, Crene chief evidence, baggage-master both defendant and examining-counsel. The case did not admit of a doubt. There was the little insurmountable check, whose brazen lips could speak no lie.

"Keep hold of that," whispered Crene, and a yoke of oxen could not have drawn it from me.

"You are sure you had it marked for Fontdale," says Mr. Baggage-master.

I hold the impracticable check before his eyes in silence.

"Yes, well, it must have gone on to Albany."

"But it went away on that track," says Crene.

"Could n't have gone on that track. Of course they would n't have carried it away over there just to make it go wrong."

For me, I am easily persuaded and dissuaded. If he had told me that it must have gone in such a direction, that it was a moral and mental impossibility it should have gone in any other, and have said it times enough, with a certain confidence and contempt of any other contingency, I should gradually have lost faith in my own eyes, and said, "Well, I suppose it did." But Crene is not to be asserted into yielding one inch, and insists that the trunk went to Vermont and not to New York, and is thoroughly unmanageable. Then the baggage-master, in anguish of soul, trots out his subordinates, one after another, —

"Is this the man that wheeled the trunk away? Is this? Is this?"

The brawny-armed fellows hang back, and scowl, and muffle words in a very suspicious manner, and protest they won't be got into a scrape. But Crene has no scrape for them. She cannot swear to their identity. She had eyes only for the trunk.

"Well," says Baggage-man, at his wits' end, "you let me take your check, and I'll send the trunk on by express, when it comes."

I pity him, and relax my clutch.

"No," whispers Crene; "as long as you have your check, you as good as have your trunk; but when you give that up, you have nothing. Keep that till you see your trunk."

My clutch re-tightens.

"At any rate, you can wait till the next train, and see if does n't come back. You 'll get to your journey's end just as soon."

"Shall I? Well, I will," compliant as usual.

"No," interposes my good genius again. "Men are always saying that a woman never goes when she engages to go. She is always a train later or a train earlier, and you can't meet her."

Pliant to the last touch, I say aloud, —

"No, I must go in this train"; and so I go, trunkless and crestfallen, to meet Halicarnassus.

It is a dismal day, and Crene, to comfort me, puts into my hands two books as companions by the way. They are Coventry Patmore's "Angel in the House," "The Espousals and the Betrothal." I do not approve of reading in the cars; but without is a dense, white, unvarying fog, and within my heart it is not clear sunshine. So I turn to my books.

Did any one ever read them before? Somebody wrote a vile review of them once, and gave the idea of a very puerile, ridiculous, apron-stringy attempt at poetry. Whoever wrote that notice ought to be shot, for the books are charming, — pure and homely and householdy, yet not effeminate. Critics may sneer as much as they choose: it is such love as Vaughan's that Honorias value. Because a woman's nature is not proof against deterioration, because a large and long-continued infusion of gross blood, and perhaps even the monotonous pressure of rough, pitiless, degrading circumstances, may displace, eat out, rub off the delicacy of a soul, may change its texture to unnatural coarseness and scatter ashes for beauty, women do exist, victims rather than culprits, coarse against their nature, hard, material, grasping, the saddest sight humanity can see. Such a woman can accept coarse men. They may come courting on all fours, and she will not be shocked. But women in the natural state wish men to stand godlike erect, to tread majestically, and live delicately. Women do not often make an ado about this. They talk it over among themselves, and take men as they are. They quietly soften them down, and smooth them out, and polish them up, and make the best of them, and simply and sedulously shut their eyes and make believe there is n't any worst, or reason it away, — a great deal more than I should think they would. But if you would see the qualities that a woman spontaneously loves, the expression, the tone, the bearing that thoroughly satisfies her self-respect, that not only secures her acquiescence, but arouses her enthusiasm and commands her abdication, crucify the flesh, and read Coventry Patmore. Not that he is the world's great poet, nor Arthur Vaughan the ideal man ; but this I do mean : that the delicacy, the spirituality of his love, the scrupulous respectfulness of his demeanor, his unfeigned inward humility, as far removed from servility on the one side as from assumption on the other, and less the opponent than the offspring of self-respect, his thorough gentleness, guilelessness, deference, his manly, unselfish homage, are such qualities, and such alone, as lead womanhood captive. Listen to me, you rattling, roaring, rollicking Ralph Roister Doisters, you calm, inevitable Gradgrinds, as smooth, as sharp, as bright as steel, and as soulless, and you men, whoever, whatever, and wherever you are, with fibres of rope and nerves of wire, there is many and many a woman who tolerates you because she finds you, but there is nothing in her that ever goes out to seek you. Be not deceived by her placability. "Here he is," she says to herself, "and something must be done about it. Buried under Ossa and Pelion somewhere he must be supposed to have a soul, and the sooner he is dug into the sooner it will be exhumed." So she digs. She would never have made you, nor of her own free-will elected you; but being made, such as you are, and on her hands in one way or another, she carves and chisels, and strives to evoke from the block a breathing statue. She may succeed so far as that you shall become her Frankenstein, a great, sad, monstrous, incessant, inevitable caricature of her ideal, the monument at once of her success and her failure, the object of her compassion, the intimate sorrow of her soul, a vast and dreadful form into which her creative power can breathe

the breath of life, but not of sympathy. Perhaps she loves you with a remorseful, pitying, protesting love, and carries you on her shuddering shoulders to the grave. Probably, as she is good and wise, you will never find it out. A limpid brook ripples in beauty and bloom by the side of your muddy, stagnant self-complacence, and you discern no essential difference. "Water 's water," you say, with your broad, stupid generalization, and go oozing along contentedly through peat-bogs and meadow-ditches, mounting, perhaps, in moments of inspiration, to the moderate sublimity of a cranberry-meadow, but subsiding with entire satisfaction into a muck-puddle: and all the while the little brook that you patronize when you are full-fed, and snub when you are hungry, and look down upon always, — the little brook is singing its own melody through grove and orchard and sweet wild-wood, — singing with the birds and the blooms songs that you cannot hear; but they are heard by the silent stars, singing on and on into a broader and deeper destiny, till it pours, one day, its last earthly note, and becomes forevermore the unutterable sea.

And you are nothing but a ditch.

No, my friend, Lucy will drive with you, and talk to you, and sing your songs; she will take care of you, and pray for you, and cry when you go to the war; if she is not your daughter or your sister, she will, perhaps, in a moment of weakness or insanity, marry you; she will be a faithful wife, and float you to the end; but if you wish to be her love, her hero, her ideal, her delight, her spontaneity, her utter rest and ultimatum, you must attune your soul to fine issues, — you must bring out the angel in you, and keep the brute under. It is not that you shall stop making shoes, and begin to write poetry. That is just as much discrimination as you have. Tell you to be gentle, and you think we will have you dissolve into milk-and-water; tell you to be polite, and you infer hypocrisy; to be neat, and you leap over into dandyism, fancying all the while that bluster is manliness. No, sir. You may make shoes, you may run engines, you may carry coals; you may blow the huntsman's horn, hurl the base-ball, follow the plough, smite the anvil; your face may be brown, your veins knotted, your hands grimed; and yet you may be a hero. And, on the other hand, you may write verses and be a clown. It is not necessary to feed on ambrosia in order to become divine; nor shall one be accursed, though he drink of the ninefold Styx. The Israelites ate angels' food in the wilderness, and remained stiff-necked and uncircumcised in heart and ears. The white water-lily feeds on slime, and unfolds a heavenly glory. Come as the June morning comes. It has not picked its way daintily, passing only among the roses. It has breathed up the whole earth. It has blown through the fields and the barn-yards and all the common places of the land. It has shrunk from nothing. Its purity has breasted and overborne all things, and so mingled and harmonized all that it sweeps around your forehead and sinks into your heart as soft and sweet and pure as the fragrancy of Paradise. So come you, rough from the world's rough work, with all out-door airs blowing around you, and all your earth-smells clinging to you, but with a fine inward grace, so strong, so sweet, so salubrious that it meets and masters all things, blending every faintest or foulest odor of earthliness into the grateful incense of a pure and lofty life.

Thus I read and mused in the soft summer fog, and the first I knew the cars had stopped, I was standing on the platform, and Coventry and his knight were — where? Wandering up and down somewhere among the Berkshire hills. At some junction of roads, I suppose, I left them on the cushion, for I have never beheld them since. Tell me, O ye daughters of Berkshire! have you seen them, — a princely pair, sore weary in your mountain-land, but regal still, through all their travel-stain? I pray you, entreat them hospitably, for their mission is "not of an age, but for all time."

II.

THE descent from Patmore and poetry to New York is somewhat abrupt, not to say precipitous, but we made it in safety; and so shall you, if you will be agile.

New York is a pleasant little Dutch city, on a dot of island a few miles southwest of Massachusetts. For a city entirely unobtrusive and unpretending, it has really great attractions and solid merit; but the superior importance of other places will not permit me to tarry long within its hospitable walls. In fact, we only arrived late at night, and departed early the next morning; but even a six-hours sojourn gave me a solemn and "realizing sense" of its marked worth, — for, when, tired and listless, I asked for a servant to assist me, the waiter said he would send the housekeeper. Accordingly, when, a few moments after, it knocked at the door with light, light finger, (see De la Motte Fouquè,) I drawled, "Come in," and the Queen of Sheba stood before me, clad in purple and fine linen, with rings on her fingers and bells on her toes. I stared in dismay, and perceived myself rapidly transmigrating into a *ridiculus mus*. My gray and dingy travelling-dress grew abject, and burned into my soul like the tunic of Nessus. I should as soon have thought of asking Queen Victoria to brush out my hair as that fine lady in brocade silk and Mechlin lace. But she was good and gracious, and did not annihilate me on the spot, as she might easily have done, for which I shall thank her as long as I live.

"You sent for me?" she inquired, with the blandest accents imaginable. I can't tell a lie, pa, — you know I can't tell a lie; besides, I had not time to make up one, and I said, "Yes," and then, of all stupid devices that could filter into my soggy brain, I must needs stammer out that I should like a few matches! A pretty thing to bring a dowager duchess up nine pairs of stairs for!

"I will ring the bell," she said, with a tender, reproachful sweetness and dignity, which conveyed without unkindness the severest rebuke tempered by womanly pity, and proceeded to instruct me in the nature and uses of the bell-rope, as she would any little dairy-maid who had heard only the chime of cow-bells all the days of her life. Then she sailed out of the room, serene and majestic, like a seventy-four man-of-war, while I, a squalid, salt-hay gunlow, (Venetian blind-ed into *gondola,*) first sank down in confusion, and then rose up in fury and brushed all the hair out of my head.

"I declare," I said to Halicarnassus, when we were fairly beyond ear-shot of the city next morning, "I don't approve of sumptuary laws, and I like America to be the El Dorado of the poor man, and I go for the largest liberty of the individual; but I do think there ought to be a clause in the Constitution providing that servants shall not be dressed and educated and accomplished up to the point of making people uncomfortable."

"No," said Halicarnassus, sleepily; "perhaps it was n't a servant."

"Well," I said, having looked at it in that light silently for half an hour, and coming to the surface in another place, "if I could dress and carry myself like that, I would not keep tavern."

"Oh! eh?" yawning; "who does?"

"Mrs. Astor. Of course nobody less rich than Mrs. Astor could go up-stairs and down-stairs and in my lady's chamber in Shiraz silk and gold of Ophir. Why, Cleopatra was nothing to her. I make no doubt she uses gold-dust for sugar in her coffee every morning; and as for the three miserable little wherries that Isabella furnished Columbus, and historians have towed through their tomes ever since, if you know of anybody that has a continent he wishes to discover, send him to this housekeeper, and she can fit out a fleet of transports and Monitors for convoy with one of her bracelets."

"I don't," said Halicarnassus, rubbing his eyes.

"I only wish," I added, "that she would turn Rebel, so that government might confiscate her. Paper currency would go up at once from the sudden influx of gold, and the credit of the country receive a new lease of life. She must be a lineal descendant of Sir Roger de Coverley, for I am sure her finger sparkles with a hundred of his richest acres."

Before bidding a final farewell to New York, I shall venture to make a single remark. I regret to be forced to confess that I greatly fear even this virtuous little city has not escaped quite free, in the general deterioration of morals and manners. The New York hackmen, for instance, are very obliging and attentive; but if it would not seem ungrateful, I would hazard the statement that their attentions are unremitting to the degree of being almost embarrassing, and proffered to the verge of obtrusiveness. I think, in short, that they are hardly quite delicate in their politeness. They press their hospitality on you till you sigh for a little marked neglect. They are not content with simple statement. They offer you their hack, for instance. You decline with thanks. They say that they will carry you to any part of the city. Where is the pertinence of that, if you do not wish to go? But they not only say it, they repeat it, they dwell upon it as if it were a cardinal virtue. Now you have never expressed or entertained the remotest suspicion that they would not carry you to any part of the city. You have not the slightest intention or desire to discredit their assertion. The only trouble is, as I said before, you do not wish to go to any part of the city. Very few people have time to drive about in that general way; and surely, when you have once distinctly informed them that you do not design to inspect New York, they ought to see plainly that you cannot change your whole plan of operations out of gratitude to them, and that the part of true politeness is to withdraw. But they even go beyond a censurable urgency; for an old gentleman and lady, evidently unaccustomed to travelling, had given themselves in charge of a driver, who placed them in his coach, leaving the door open while he went back seeking whom he might devour. Presently a rival coachman came up and said to the aged and respectable couple, —

"Here 's a carriage all ready to start."

"But," replied the lady, "we have already told the gentleman who drives this coach that we would go with him."

"Catch me to go in that coach, if I was you!" responded the wicked coachman. "Why, that coach has had the small-pox in it."

The lady started up in horror. At that moment the first driver appeared again, and Satan entered into me, and I felt in my heart that I should like to see a fight; and then conscience stepped up and drove him away, but consoled me by the assurance that I should see the fight all the same, for such duplicity deserved the severest punishment, and it was my duty to make an *exposé* and vindicate helpless innocence imposed upon in the persons of that worthy pair. Accordingly I said to the driver, as he passed me, —

"Driver, that man in the gray coat is trying to frighten the old lady and gentleman away from your coach, by telling them it has had the small-pox."

Oh! but did not the fire flash into his honest eyes, and leap into his swarthy cheek, and nerve his brawny arm, and clinch his horny fist, as he marched straightway up to the doomed offender, fiercely denounced his dishonesty, and violently demanded redress? Ah! then and there was hurrying to and fro, and eagerness and delight on every countenance, and a ring formed, and the prospect of a lovely "row," — and I did it; but a police-officer sprang up, full-armed, from somewhere underground, and undid it all, and enforced a reluctant peace.

And so we are at Saratoga. Now, of all places to stay at in the summer-time, Saratoga is the very last one to choose. It may have attractions in winter; but, if one wishes to rest and change and root down and shoot up and branch out, he might as well take lodgings in the water-wheel of a saw-mill. The uniformity and variety will be much the same. It is all a noiseless kind of din, narrow and intense. There is nothing in Saratoga nor of Saratoga to see or to hear or to feel. They tell you of a lake. You jam into an omnibus and ride four miles. Then you step into a cockle-shell and circumnavigate a pond, so small that it almost makes you dizzy to sail around it. This is the lake, — a very nice thing as far as it goes; but when it has to be constantly on duty as the natural scenery of the whole surrounding country, it is putting altogether too fine a point on it. The picturesque people will inform you of an Indian encampment. You go to see it, thinking of the forest primeval, and expecting to be transported back to tomahawks, scalps, and forefathers; but you return without them, and that is all. I never heard of anybody's going anywhere. In fact there did not seem to be anywhere to go. Any suggestion of mine to strike out into the champaign was frowned down in the severest manner. As far as I could see, nobody ever did anything. There never was any plan on foot. Nothing was ever stirring. People sat on the piazza and sewed. They went to the springs, and the springs are dreadful. They bubble up salts and senna. I never knew anything that pretended to be water that was half as bad. It has no one redeeming quality. It is bitter. It is greasy. Every spring is worse than the last, whichever end you begin at. They told apocryphal stories of people's drinking sixteen glasses before breakfast; and yet it may have been true; for, if one could bring himself to the point of drinking one glass of it, I should suppose it would have taken such a force to enable him to do it that he might go on drinking indefinitely, from the mere action of the original impulse. I should think one dose of it would render a person permanently indifferent to savors, and make him, like Mithridates, poison-proof. Nevertheless, people go to the springs and drink. Then they go to the bowling-alleys and bowl. In the evening, if you are hilariously inclined, you can make the tour of the hotels. In each one you see a large and brilliantly lighted parlor, along the four sides of which are women sitting, solemn and stately, in rows three deep, with a man dropped in here and there, about as thick as periods on a page, very young or very old or in white cravats. A piano or a band or something that can make a noise makes it at intervals at one end of the room. They all look as if they were waiting for something, but nothing in particular happens. Sometimes, after the mountain has labored awhile, some little mouse of a boy and girl will get up, execute an antic or two and sit down again, when everything relapses into its original solemnity. At very long intervals somebody walks across the floor. There is a moderate fluttering of fans and an occasional whisper. Expectation interspersed with gimcracks seems to be the programme. The greater part of the dancing that I saw was done by boys and girls. It was pretty and painful. Nobody dances so well as children; no grace is equal to their grace; but to go into a hotel at ten o'clock at night, and see little things, eight, ten, twelve years old, who ought to be in bed and asleep, tricked out in flounces and ribbons and all the paraphernalia of ballet-girls, and dancing in the centre of a hollow square of strangers, — I call it murder in the first degree. What can mothers be thinking of to abuse their children so? Children are naturally healthy and simple; why should they be spoiled? They will have to plunge into the world full soon enough; why should the world be plunged into them? Physically, mentally, and morally, the innocents are massacred. Night after night I saw the same children led out to the slaughter, and as I looked I saw their round, red cheeks grow thin and white, their delicate nerves lose tone and tension, their brains become feeble and flabby, their minds flutter out weakly in muslin and ribbons, their vanity kindled by injudicious admiration, the sweet child-unconsciousness withering away in the glare of indiscriminate gazing, the innocence and simplicity and naturalness and childlikeness swallowed up in a seething whirlpool of artificialness, all the fine, golden butterfly-dust of modesty and delicacy and retiring girlhood ruthlessly rubbed off forever before girlhood had even reddened from the dim dawn of infancy. Oh! it is cruel to sacrifice children so. What can atone for a lost childhood? What can be given in recompense for the ethereal, spontaneous, sharply defined, new, delicious sensations of a sheltered, untainted, opening life?

Thoroughly worked into a white heat of indignation, we leave the babes in the wood to be despatched by their ruffian relatives, and go to another hotel. A larger parlor, larger rows, but still three deep and solemn. A tall man, with a face in which melancholy seems to be giving way to despair, a man most proper for an undertaker, but palpably out of place in a drawing-room, walks up and down incessantly, but noiselessly, in a persistent endeavor to bring out a dance. Now he fastens upon a newly arrived man. Now he plants himself before a bench of misses. You can hear the low rumble of his exhortation and the tittering replies. After a persevering course of entreaty and persuasion, a set is drafted, the music galvanizes, and the dance begins.

I like to see people do with their might whatsoever their hands or their tongues or their feet find to do. A half-and-half performance of the right is just about as mischievous as the perpetration of the wrong. It is vacillation, hesitation, lack of will, feebleness of purpose, imperfect execution, that works ill in all life. Be monarch of all you survey. If a woman decides to do her own housework, let her go in royally among her pots and kettles, and set everything a-stewing and baking and broiling and boiling, as a queen might. If she decides not to do housework, but to superintend its doing, let her say to her servant, "Go," and he goeth, to another, "Come," and he cometh, to a third, "Do this," and he doeth it, and not potter about. So, when girls get themselves up and go to Saratoga for a regular campaign, let their bearing be soldierly. Let them be gay with abandonment. Let them take hold of it as if they liked it. I do not affect the word flirtation, but the thing itself is not half so criminal as one would think from the animadversions visited upon it. Of course, a deliberate setting yourself to work to make some one fall in love with you, for the mere purpose of showing your power, is abominable,— or would be, if anybody ever did it; but I do not suppose it ever was done, except in fifth-rate novels. What I mean is, that it is entertaining, harmless, and beneficial for young people to amuse themselves with each other to the top of their bent, if their bent is a natural and right one. A few hearts may suffer accidental, transient injury; but hearts are like limbs, all the stronger for being broken. Besides, where one man or woman is injured by loving too much, nine hundred and ninety-nine die the death from not loving enough.

But these Saratoga girls did neither one thing nor another. They dressed themselves in their best, making a point of it, and failed. They assembled themselves together of set purpose to be lively, and they were infectiously dismal. They did not dress well: one looked rustic; another was dowdyish; a third was over-fine; a fourth was insignificant. Their bearing was not good, in the main. They danced, and whispered, and laughed, and looked like milkmaids. They had no style, no figure. Their shoulders were high, and their chests were flat, and they were one-sided, and they stooped, — all of which would have been of no account, if they had only been unconsciously enjoying themselves: but they consciously were not. It is possible that they thought they were happy, but I knew better. You are never happy, unless you are master of the situation; and they were not. They endeavored to appear at ease, — a thing which people who are at ease never do. They looked as if they had all their lives been meaning to go to Saratoga, and now they had got there and were determined not to betray any unwontedness. It was not the timid, eager, delighted, fascinating, graceful awkwardness of a new young girl; it was not the careless, hearty, whole-souled enjoyment of an experienced girl; it was not the natural, indifferent, imperial queening it of an acknowledged monarch: but something that caught hold of the hem of the garment of them all. It was they with the sheen damped off. So it was not imposing. I could pick you up a dozen girls straight along, right out of the pantries and the butteries, right up from the washing-tubs and the sewing-machines, who should be abundantly able to "hoe their row" with them anywhere. In short, I was extremely disappointed. I expected to see the high fashion, the very birth and breeding, the cream cheese of the country, and it was skim-milk. If that is birth, one can do quite as well without being born at all. Occasionally you would see a girl with gentle blood in her veins, whether it were butcher-blood or banker-blood, but she only made the prevailing plebsiness more striking. Now I maintain that a woman ought to be very handsome or very clever, or else she ought to go to work and do something. Beauty is of itself a divine gift and adequate. "Beauty is its own excuse for being" anywhere. It ought not to be fenced in or monopolized, any more than a statue or a mountain. It ought to be free and common, a benediction to all weary wayfarers. It can never be profaned; for it veils itself from the unappreciative eye, and shines only upon its worshippers. So a clever woman, whether she be a painter or a teacher or a dress-maker, — if she really has an object in life, a career, she is safe. She is a power. She commands a realm. She owns a world. She is bringing things to bear. Let her alone. But it is a very dangerous and a very melancholy thing for common women to be "lying on their oars" long at a time. Some of these were, I suppose, what Winthrop calls "business-women, fighting their way out of vulgarity into style." The process is rather uninteresting, but the result may be glorious. Yet a good many of them were good honest, kind, common girls, only demoralized by long lying around in a waiting posture. It had taken the fire and sparkle out of them. They were not in a healthy state. They were degraded, contracted, flaccid. They did not hold themselves high. They knew that in a marketable point of view there was a frightful glut of women. The usually small ratio of men was unusually diminished by the absence of those who had gone to the war, and of those who, as was currently reported, were ashamed that they had not gone. A few available men had it all their own way; the women were on the lookout for them, instead of being themselves looked out for. They talked about "gentlemen," and being "companionable to *gen*-tlemen," and who was "fascinating to *gen*-tlemen," till the "grand old name" became a nuisance. There was an under-current of unsated coquetry. I don't suppose they were any sillier than the rest of us; but when our silliness is mixed in with housekeeping and sewing and teaching and returning visits, it passes off harmless. When it is stripped of all these modifiers, however, and goes off exposed to Sáratoga, and melts in with a hundred other sillinesses, it makes a great show.

No, I don't like Saratoga. I don't think it is wholesome. No place can be healthy that keeps up such an unmitigated dressing.

"Where do you walk?" I asked an artless little lady.

"O, almost always on the long piazza. It is so clean there, and we don't like to soil our dresses."

Now I ask if girls could ever get into that state in the natural course of things! It is the result of bad habits. They cease to care for things which they ought to like to do, and they devote themselves to what ought to be only an incident. People dress in their best without break. They go to the springs before breakfast in shining raiment, and they go into the parlor after supper in shining raiment, and it is shine, shine, shine, all the way between, and a different shine each time. You may well suppose that I was like an owl among birds of Paradise, for what little finery I had was in my (eminently) travelling-trunk: yet, though it was but a dory, compared with the Noah's arks that drove up every day, I felt that, if I could only once get inside of it, I could make things fly to some purpose. Like poor Rabette, I would show the city that the country too could wear clothes! I never walked down Broadway without seeing a dozen white trunks, and every white trunk that I saw I was fully convinced was mine, if I could only get at it. By and by mine came, and I blossomed. I arrayed myself for morning, noon, and night, and everything else that came up, and was, as the poet says, —

> "Prodigious in change,
> And endless in range," —

for I would have scorned not to be as good as the best. The result was, that in three days I touched bottom. But then we went away, and my reputation was saved. I don't believe anybody ever did a larger business on a smaller capital; but I put a bold face on it. I cherish the hope that nobody suspected I could not go on in that ruinous way all summer, — I, who in three days had mustered into service every dress and sash and ribbon and rag that I had had in three years or expected to have in three more. But I never will, if I can help it, hold my head down where other people are holding their heads up.

I would not be understood as decrying or depreciating dress. It is a duty as well as a delight. Mrs. Madison is reported to have said that she would never forgive a young lady who did not dress to please, or one who seemed pleased with her dress. And not only young ladies, but old ladies and old gentlemen, and everybody, ought to make their dress a concord and not a discord. But Saratoga is pitched on a perpetual falsetto, and stuns you. One becomes sated with an interminable *pièce de résistance* of full dress. At the seaside you bathe; at the mountains you put on stout boots and coarse frocks and go a-fishing; but Saratoga never "lets up," — if I may be pardoned the phrase. Consequently, you see much of crinoline and little of character. You have to get at the human nature just as Thoreau used to get at bird-nature and fish-nature and turtle-nature, by sitting perfectly still in one place and waiting patiently till it comes out. You see more of the reality of people in a single day's tramp than in twenty days of guarded monotone. Now I cannot conceive of any reason why people should go to Saratoga, except to see people. True, as a general thing, they are the last objects you desire to see, when you are summering. But if one has been cooped up in the house or blocked up in the country during the nine months of our Northern winter, he may have a mighty hunger and thirst, when he is thawed out, to see human faces and hear human voices; but even then Saratoga is not the place to go to, on account of this very artificialness. By artificial I do not mean deceitful. I saw nobody but nice people there, smooth, kind, and polite. By artificial I mean wrought up. You don't get at the heart of things. Artificialness spreads and spans all with a crystal barrier, — invisible, but palpable. Nothing was left to grow and go at its own sweet will. The very springs were paved and pavilioned. For green fields and welling fountains and a possibility of brooks, which one expects from the name, you found a Greek temple, and a pleasure-ground, graded and grassed and pathed like a cemetery, wherein nymphs trod daintily in elaborate morning-costume. Everything took pattern and was elaborate. Nothing was left to the imagination, the taste, the curiosity. A bland, smooth, smiling surface baffled and blinded you, and threatened profanity. Now profanity is wicked and vulgar; but if you listen to the reeds next summer, I am not sure that you will not hear them whispering, "Thunder!"

For the restorative qualities of Saratoga I have nothing to say. I was well when I went there; nor did my experience ever furnish me with any disease that I should consider worse than an intermittent attack of her spring waters. But whatever it may do for the body, I do not believe it is good for the soul. I do not believe that such places, such scenes, such a fashion of life ever nourishes a vigorous womanhood or manhood. Taken homœopathically, it may be harmless; but if it become a habit, a necessity, it must vitiate, enervate, destroy. Men can stand it, for the sea-breezes and the mountain-breezes may have full sweep through their life; but women cannot, for they just go home and live air-tight.

If the railroad-men at Saratoga tell you that you can go straight from there to the foot of Lake George, don't you believe a word of it. Perhaps you can, and perhaps you cannot; but you are not any more likely to "can" for their saying so. We left Saratoga for Fort-William-Henry Hotel in full faith of an afternoon ride and a sunset arrival, based on repeated and unhesitating assurances to that effect. Instead of which, we went a few miles, and were then dumped into a blackberry-patch, where we were informed that we must wait seven hours. So much for the afternoon ride through summer fields and "Sunset on Lake George," from the top of a coach. But I made no unmanly laments, for we were out of Saratoga, and that was happiness. We were among cows and barns and homely rail-fences, and that was comfort; so we strolled contentedly through the pasture, found a river, — I believe it was the Hudson; at any rate, Halicarnassus said so, though I don't imagine he knew; but he would take oath it was Acheron rather than own up to ignorance on any point whatever, — watched the canal-boats and boatmen go down, marvelled at the arbor-vitæ trees growing wild along the river-banks, green, hale, stately, and symmetrical, against the dismal mental background of two little consumptive shoots bolstered up in our front yard at home, and dying daily, notwithstanding persistent and affectionate nursing with "flannels and rum," and then we went back to the blackberry-station and inquired whether there was nothing celebrated in the vicinity to which visitors of received Orthodox creed should dutifully pay their respects, and were gratified to learn that we were but a few miles from Jane McCrea and her Indian murderers. Was a carriage procurable? Well, yes, if the ladies would be willing to go in that. It was n't very smart, but it would take 'em safe, — as if "the ladies" would have raised any objections to going in a wheelbarrow, had it been necessary, and so we bundled in. The hills were steep, and our horse, the property of an adventitious by-stander, was of the Rosinante breed; but we were in no hurry, seeing that the only thing awaiting us this side the sunset was a blackberry-patch without any blackberries, and we walked up hill and scraped down, till we got into a lane which somebody told us led to the Fort, from which the village, Fort Edward, takes its name. But, instead of a fort, the lane ran full tilt against a pair of bars.

"Now we are lost," I said, sententiously.

"A gem of countless price," pursued Halicarnassus, who never quotes poetry except to destroy my equilibrium.

"How long will it be profitable to remain

here?" asked Grande, when we had sat immovable and speechless for the space of five minutes.

"There seems to be nowhere else to go. We have got to the end," said Halicarnassus, roaming as to his eyes over into the wheat-field beyond.

"We might turn," suggested the Anakim, looking bright.

"How can you turn a horse in this knitting-needle of a lane?" I demanded.

"I don't know," replied Halicarnassus, dubiously, "unless I take him up in my arms, and set him down with his head the other way," — and immediately turned him deftly in a corner about half as large as the wagon.

The next lane we came to was the right one, and being narrow, rocky, and rough, we left our carriage and walked.

A whole volume of the peaceful and prosperous history of our beloved country could be read in the fact that the once belligerent, life-saving, death-dealing fort was represented by a hen-coop; yet I was disappointed. I was hungry for a ruin, — some visible hint of the past. Such is human nature, — ever prone to be more impressed by a disappointment of its own momentary gratification than by the most obvious well-being of a nation; but, glad or sorry, of Fort Edward was not left one stone upon another. Several single stones lay about, promiscuous rather than belligerent. Flagstaff and palisades lived only in a few straggling bean-poles. For the heavy booming of cannon rose the "quauk!" of ducks and the cackling of hens. We went to the spot which tradition points out as the place where Jane McCrea met her death. River flowed, and raftsmen sang below; women stood at their washing-tubs, and white-headed children stared at us from above; nor from the unheeding river or the forgetful woods came shriek or cry or faintest wail of pain.

When we were little, and geography and history were but printed words on white paper, not places and events, Jane McCrea was to us no suffering woman, but a picture of a low-necked, long-skirted, scanty dress, long hair grasped by a half-naked Indian, and two unnatural-looking hands raised in entreaty. It was interesting as a picture, but it excited no pity, no horror, because it was only a picture. We never saw women dressed in that style. We knew that women did not take journeys through woods without bonnet or shawl, and we spread a veil of ignorant, indifferent incredulity over the whole. But as we grow up, printed words take on new life. The latent fire in them lights up and glows. The mystic words throb with vital heat, and burn down into our souls to an answering fire. As we stand, on this soft summer day, by the old tree which tradition declares to have witnessed that fateful scene, we go back into a summer long ago, but fair, and just like this. Jane McCrea is no longer a myth, but a young girl, blooming and beautiful with the roses of her seventeen years. Farther back still, we see an old man's darling, little Jenny of the Manse, a light-hearted child, with sturdy Scotch blood leaping in her young veins, — then a tender orphan, sheltered by a brother's care, — then a gentle maiden, light-hearted no longer, heavy-freighted, rather, but with a priceless burden, — a happy girl, to whom love calls with stronger voice than brother's blood, stronger even than life. Yonder in the woods lurk wily and wary foes. Death with unspeakable horrors lies in ambush there; but yonder also stands the soldier lover, and possible greeting, after long, weary absence, is there. What fear can master that overpowering hope? Estrangement of families, political disagreement, a separated loyalty, all melt away, are fused together in the warmth of girlish love. Taxes, representation, what things are these to come between two hearts? No Tory, no traitor is her lover, but her own brave hero and true knight. Woe! woe! the eager dream is broken by mad war-whoops! alas! to those fierce wild men, what is love, or loveliness? Pride, and passion, and the old accursed hunger for gold flame up in their savage breasts. Wrathful, loathsome fingers clutch the long, fair hair that even the fingers of love have caressed but with reverent half-touch, — and love and hope and life go out in one dread moment of horror and despair. Now, through the reverberations of more than fourscore years, through all the tempest-rage of a war more awful than that, and fraught, we hope, with a grander joy, a clear, young voice, made sharp with agony, rings through the shuddering woods, cleaves up through the summer sky, and wakens in every heart a thrill of speechless pain. Along these peaceful banks I see a bowed form walking, youth in his years, but deeper furrows in his face than age can plough, stricken down from the heights of his ambition and desire, all the vigor and fire of manhood crushed and quenched beneath the horror of one fearful memory.

Sweet summer sky, bending above us soft and saintly, beyond your blue depths is there not Heaven?

"We may as well give Dobbin his oats here," said Halicarnassus.

We had brought a few in a bag for luncheon, thinking it might help him over the hills. So the wagon was rummaged, the bag brought to light, and I was sent to one of the nearest houses to get something for him to eat out of. I did not think to ask what particular vessel to inquire for; but after I had knocked, I decided upon a meat-platter or a pudding-dish, and with the good woman's permission finally took both, that Halicarnassus might have his choice.

"Which is the best?" I asked, holding them up.

He surveyed them carefully, and then said,—

"Now run right back and get a tumbler for him to drink out of, and a teaspoon to feed him with."

I started in good faith, from a mere habit of unquestioning obedience, but with the fourth step my reason returned to me, and I returned to Halicarnassus and—kicked him. That sounds very dreadful and horrible, and it is, if you are thinking of a great, brutal, brogan kick, such as a stupid farmer gives to his patient oxen; but not, if you mean only a delicate, compact, penetrative nudge with the toe of a tight-fitting gaiter,—addressed rather to the conscience than the sole, to the sensibilities rather than the senses. The kick masculine is coarse, boorish, unmitigated, predicable only of Calibans. The kick feminine is expressive, suggestive, terse, electric,—an indispensable instrument in domestic discipline, as women will bear me witness, and not at all incompatible with beauty, grace, and amiability. But, right or wrong, after all this interval of rest and reflection, in full view of all the circumstances, my only regret is that I did not kick him harder.

"Now go and fetch your own tools!" I cried, shaking off the yoke of servitude. "I won't be your stable-boy any longer!"

Then, perforce, he gathered up the crockery, marched off in disgrace, and came back with a molasses-hogshead, or a wash-tub, or some such overgrown mastodon, to turn his sixpenny-worth of oats into.

Having fed our mettlesome steed, the next thing was to water him. The Anakim remembered to have seen a pump with a trough somewhere, and they proposed to reconnoitre while we should "wait *by* the wagon" their return. No, I said we would drive on to the pump, while they walked.

"You drive!" ejaculated Halicarnassus, contemptuously.

Now I do not, as a general thing, have an overweening respect for female teamsters. There is but one woman in the world to whose hands I confide the reins and my bones with entire equanimity; and she says, that, when she is driving, she dreads of all things to meet a driving woman. If a man said this, it might be set down to prejudice. I don't make any account of Halicarnassus's assertion, that, if two women walking in the road on a muddy day meet a carriage, they never keep together, but invariably one runs to the right and one to the left, so that the driver cannot favor them at all, but has to crowd between them, and drive both into the mud. That is palpably interested false witness. He thinks it is fine fun to push women into the mud, and frames such flimsy excuses. But as a woman's thoughts about women, this woman's utterances are deserving of attention; and she says that women are not to be depended upon. She is never sure that they will not turn out on the wrong side. They are nervous; they are timid; they are unreasoning; they are reckless. They will give a horse a disconnected, an utterly inconsequent "cut," making him spring, to the jeopardy of their own and others' safety. They are not concentrative, and they are not infallibly courteous, as men are. I remember I was driving with her once between Newburyport and Boston. It was getting late, and we were very desirous to reach our destination before nightfall. Ahead of us a woman and a girl were jogging along in a country wagon. As we wished to go much faster than they, we turned aside to pass them; but just as we were well abreast, the woman started up her horse, and he skimmed over the ground like a bird. We laughed, and followed, well content. But after he had gone perhaps an eighth of a mile, his speed slackened down to the former jog-trot. Three times we attempted to pass before we really comprehended the fact that that infamous woman was deliberately detaining and annoying us. The third time, when we had so nearly passed them that our horse was turning into the road again, she struck hers up so suddenly and unexpectedly that her wheels almost grazed ours. Of course, understanding her game, we ceased the attempt, having no taste for horse-racing; and nearly all the way from Newburyport to Rowley, she kept up that brigandry, jogging on, and forcing us to jog on, neither going ahead herself nor suffering us to do so, — a perfect and most provoking dog in a manger. Her girl-associate would look behind every now and then to take observations, and I mentally hoped that the frisky Bucephalus would frisk his mistress out of the cart and break her ne— arm, or at least put her shoulder out of joint. If he did, I had fully determined in my own mind to hasten to her assistance, and shame her to death with delicate and assiduous kindness. But fate lingered like all the rest of us. She reached Rowley in safety, and there our roads separated. Whether she stopped there, or drove into Ethiopian wastes beyond, I cannot say; but I have nó doubt that the milk which she carried into Newburyport to market was blue, the butter frowy, and the potatoes exceedingly small.

Now do you mean to tell me that any man would have been guilty of such a thing? I don't mean, would have committed such discourtesy to a woman? Of course not; but would a man ever do it to a man? Never. He might try it once or twice, just for fun, just to show off his horse, but he never would have persisted in it till a joke became an insult, not to say a possible injury.

Still, as I was about to say, when that Rowley jade interrupted me, though I have small faith in Di-Vernonism generally, and no large faith in my own personal prowess, I did feel myself equal to the task of holding the reins while our Rosinante walked along an open road to a pump. I therefore resented Halicarnassus's contemptuous tones, mounted the wagon with as much dignity as wagons allow, sat straight as an arrow on the driver's seat, took the reins in both hands, — as they used to tell me I must not, when I was a little girl, because that was women's way, but I find now that men have adopted it, so I suppose it is all right, — and proceeded to show, like Sam Patch, that some things can be done as well as others. Halicarnassus and the Anakim took up their position in line on the other side of the road, hat in hand, watching.

"Go fast, and shame them," whispered Grande, from the back-seat, and the suggestion jumped with my own mood. It was a moment of intense excitement. To be or not to be. I jerked the lines. Pegasus did not start.

"C-l-k-l-k!" No forward movement.

"Huddup!" Still waiting for reinforcements.

"H-w-e." (Attempt at a whistle. Dead failure.)

(*Sotto voce.*) "O you beast!" (*Pianissimo.*) "Gee! Haw! haw! haw!" with a terrible jerking of the reins.

A voice over the way, distinctly audible, utters the cabalistic words, "Two forty." Another voice, as audible, asks, "Which 'll you bet on?" It was not soothing. It did seem as if the imp of the perverse had taken possession of that terrible nag to go and make such a display at such a moment. But as his will rose, so did mine, and as my will went up, my whip went with it; but before it came down, Halicarnassus made shift to drone out, "Would n't Flora go faster, if she was untied?"

To be sure, I had forgotten to unfasten him, and there those two men had stood and known it all the time! I was in the wagon, so they were secure from personal violence, but I have a vague impression of some "pet names" flying wildly about in the air in that vicinity. Then we trundled safely down the lane. We were to go in the direction leading away from home, — the horse's. I don't think he perceived it at first, but as soon as he did snuff the fact, which happened when he had gone perhaps three rods, he quietly turned around and headed the other way, paying no more attention to my reins or my terrific "whoas!" than if I were a sleeping babe. A horse is none of your woman's-rights men. He is Pauline. He suffers not the woman to usurp authority over him. He never says anything nor votes anything, but declares himself unequivocally by taking things into his own hands, whenever he knows there is nobody but a woman behind him, — and somehow he always does know. After Halicarnassus had turned him back and set him going the right way, I took on a gruff, manny voice, to deceive. Nonsense! I could almost see him snap his fingers at me. He minded my whip no more than he did a fly, — not so much as he did some flies. Grande said she supposed his back was all callous. I acted upon the suggestion, knelt down in the bottom of the wagon, and leaned over the dasher to whip him on his belly, then climbed out on the shafts and snapped about his ears; but he stood it much better than I. Finally I found that by taking the small end of the wooden whip-handle, and sticking it into him, I could elicit a faint flash of light; so I did it with assiduity, but the moderate trot which even that produced was not enough to accomplish my design, which was to outstrip the two men and make them run or beg. The opposing forces arrived at the pump about the same time.

Halicarnassus took the handle, and gave about five jerks. Then the Anakim took it and gave five more. Then they both stopped and wiped their faces.

"What do you suppose this pump was put here for?" asked Halicarnassus.

"A milestone, probably," replied the Anakim.

Then they resumed their Herculean efforts till the water came, and then they got into the wagon, and we drove into the blackberries once more, where we arrived just in season to escape a thunder-shower, and pile merrily into one of several coaches waiting to convey passengers in various directions as soon as the train should come.

It is very selfish, but fine fun, to have secured your own chosen seat and bestowed your own luggage, and have nothing to do but witness the anxieties and efforts of other people. The exquisite pleasure we enjoyed for fifteen minutes, edified at the last by hearing one of our coachmen call out, "Here, Rosey, this way!"—whereupon a manly voice, in the darkness, near us, soliloquized, "Respectful way of addressing a judge of the Supreme Court!" and, being interrogated, the voice informed us that "Rosey" was the vulgate for Judge Rosecranz; whereupon Halicarnassus glossed over the rampant democracy by remarking that the diminutive was probably a term of endearment rather than familiarity; whereupon the manly voice—if I might say it—snickered audibly in the darkness, and we all relapsed into silence. But could anything be more characteristic of a certain phase of the manners of our great and glorious country? Where are the Trollopes? Where is Dickens? Where is Basil Hall?

It is but a dreary ride to Lake George on a dark and rainy evening, unless people like riding for its own sake, as I do. If there are suns and stars and skies, very well. If there are not, very well too: I like to ride all the same. I like everything in this world but Saratoga. Once or twice our monotony was broken up by short halts before country inns. At one an excitement was going on. "Had a casualty here this afternoon," remarked a fresh passenger, as soon as he was fairly seated. A casualty is a windfall to a country village. It is really worth while to have a head broken occasionally, for the wholesome stirring-up it gives to the heads that are not broken. On the whole, I question whether collisions and collusions do not cause as much good as harm. Certainly, people seem to take the most lively satisfaction in receiving and imparting all the details concerning them. Our passenger-friend opened his budget with as much complacence as ever did Mr. Gladstone or Disraeli, and with a confident air of knowing that he was going not only to enjoy a piece of good-fortune himself, but to administer a great gratification to us. Our "casualty" turned out to be the affair of a Catholic priest, of which our informer spoke only in dark hints and with significant shoulder-shrugs and eyebrow-elevations, because it was "not exactly the thing to get out, you know"; but if it was n't to get out, why did he let it out? and so from my dark corner I watched him as a cat does a mouse, and the lamp-light shone full upon him, and I understood every word and shrug, and I am going to tell it all to the world. I translated that the holy father had been "skylarking" in a boat, and in gay society had forgotten his vows of frugality and abstinence and general mortification of the flesh, and had become, not very drunk, but drunk enough to be dangerous, when he came ashore and took a horse in his hands, and so upset his carriage, and gashed his temporal artery, and came to grief, which is such a casualty as does not happen every day, and I don't blame people for making the most of it. Then the moral was pointed, the tale adorned, and the impression deepened, solemnized, and struck home by the fact that the very horse concerned in the "casualty" was to be fastened behind our coach, and the whole population came out with lanterns and umbrellas to tie him on,—all but one man, who was deaf, and stood on the piazza, anxious and eager to know everything that had been and was still occurring, and yet sorry to give trouble, and so compromising the matter and making it worse, as compromisers generally do, by questioning everybody with a deprecating, fawning air.

Item. We shall all, if we live long enough, be deaf, but we need not be meek about it. I for one am determined to walk up to people and demand what they are saying at the point of the bayonet. Deafness, if it must be so, but independence at any rate.

And when the fulness of time is come, we alight at Fort-William-Henry Hotel, and all night long through the sentient woods I hear the booming of Johnson's cannon, the rattle of Dieskau's guns, and that wild war-whoop, more terrible than all. Again old Monro watches from his fortress-walls the steadily approaching foe, and looks in vain for help, save to his own brave heart. I see the light of conquest shining in his foeman's eye, darkened by no shadow of the fate that waits his coming on a bleak Northern hill; but, generous in the hour of victory, he shall not be less noble in defeat, — for to generous hearts all generous hearts are friendly, whether they stand face to face or side by side.

Over the woods and the waves, when the morning breaks, like a bridegroom coming forth from his chamber, rejoicing as a strong man to run a race, comes up the sun in his might and crowns himself king. All the summer day, from morn to dewy eve, we sail over the lakes of Paradise. Blue waters, and blue sky, soft clouds and green islands, and fair, fruitful shores, sharp-pointed hills, long, gentle slopes and swells, and the lights and shadows of far-stretching woods; and over all the potence of the unseen past, the grand, historic past, — soft over all the invisible mantle which our fathers flung at their departing, — the mystic effluence of the spirits that trod these wilds and sailed these waters, — the courage and the fortitude, the hope that battled against hope, the comprehensive outlook, the sagacious purpose, the resolute will, the unhesitating self-sacrifice, the undaunted devotion which has made this heroic ground; cast these into your own glowing crucible, O gracious friend, and crystallize for yourself such a gem of days as shall worthily be set forever in your crown of the beatitudes.

III.

SOMETIMES I become disgusted with myself. Not very often, it is true, for I don't understand the self-abhorrence that I occasionally see long drawn out in the strictly private printed diaries of good dead people. A man's self-knowledge, as regards his Maker, is a matter that lies only between his Maker and himself, of which no printed or written (scarcely even spoken) words can give, or ought to give, a true transcript; but in respect of our relations to other people I suppose we may take tolerably accurate views, and state them without wickedness, if it comes in the way; and since the general trend of opinion seems to be towards excessive modesty, I will sacrifice myself to the good of society, and say that, in the main, I think I am a rather "nice" sort of person. Of course I do a great many things, and say a great many things, and think a great many things, that I ought not; but when I think of the sins that I don't commit, — the many times when I feel cross enough to "bite a ten-penny nail in two," and only bite my lips, — the sacrifices I make for other people, and don't mention it, and they themselves never know it, — the quiet cheerfulness I maintain when the fire goes out, or unexpected guests arrive and there is no bread in the house, or my manuscript is respectfully declined by that infatuated editor, — when I reflect upon these things, and a thousand others like unto them, I must say, I am lost in admiration of my own virtues. You may not like me, but that is a mere difference of taste. At any rate, I like myself very well, and find myself very good company. Many a laugh, and "lots" or "heaps" (according as you are a Northern or a Southern provincial) of conversation we have all alone, and are usually on exceeding good terms, which is a pleasure, even when other people like me, and an immense consolation when they don't. But as I was saying, I do sometimes fall out with myself, and with human nature in general (and, in fact, I rather think the secret of self-complacence lurks somewhere hereabouts, — in a mental assumption that our virtues are our own, but our faults belong to the race). But to think that we were so puny and puerile that we could not stand the beauty that breathed around us! I do not mean that it killed us, but it drained us. It did not cease to be beautiful, but we ceased to be overpowered. When the day began, eye and soul were filled with the light that never was on sea or shore. We spoke low and little, gazing with throbbing hearts, breathless, receptive, solemn, and before twelve o'clock we flatted out and made jests. This is humiliation, — that our dullard souls cannot keep up to the pitch of sublimity for two hours; that we could sail through Glory and Beauty, through Past and Present, and laugh. Low as I sank with the rest, though, I do believe I held out the longest: but what can one frail pebble do against a river? "How pretty cows look in a landscape," I said; for you know, even if you must come down, it is better to roll down an inclined plane than to drop over a precipice; and I thought, since I saw that descent was inevitable, I would at least engineer the party gently through æsthetics to puns. So I said, "How pretty cows look in a landscape, so calm and reflective, and sheep harmoniously happy in the summer-tide."

"Yes," said the Anakim, who is New Hampshire born; "but you ought to see the New Hampshire sheep, if you want the real article."

"I don't," I responded. "I only want the picture."

"Ever notice the difference between Vermont and New Hampshire sheep?" struck up Halicarnassus, who must always put in his oar.

"No," I said, "and I don't believe there is any."

"Pooh! Tell New Hampshire sheep as far off as you can see 'em," he persisted, "by their short legs and long noses. Short legs to bring 'em near the grass, and long noses to poke under the rocks and get it."

"Yes, my boy, yes," said the Anakim pleasantly. "I O U 1"

"He hath made everything beautiful in his time," murmured Grande, partly because, gazing at the distant prospect, she thought so, and partly as a praiseworthy attempt, in her turn, to pluck us out of the slough into which we had fallen.

"I have heard," said Halicarnassus, who is always lugging in little scraps of information apropos to everything, — "I have been told that Dr. Alexander was so great an admirer of the Proverbs of Solomon, that he used to read them over every three months."

"I beg your pardon," I interposed, glad of the opportunity to correct and humiliate him, "but that was not one of the Proverbs of Solomon."

"Who said it was?" asked the Grand Mogul, savagely.

"Nobody; but you thought it was when she said it," answered his antagonist, coolly.

"And whose proverb is it, my Lady Superior?"

"It is in Ecclesiastes," I said.

"Well, Ecclesiastes is next door to Solomon. It's all one." Halicarnassus can creep through the smallest knot-hole of any man of his size it has ever been my lot to meet, provided there is anything on the other side he wishes to get at. If there is not, and especially if anything is there which he wishes to shun, a four hundred and fifty pounder cannot crash a hole large enough for you to push him through. By such a pitiful chink as that did his Infallible Highness wriggle himself out of the range of my guns, and pursue his line of remark.

"But I really cannot say that I have been able to detect the excessive superiority of Solomon's proverbs. If it were not for the name of it, I think Sancho Panza's much better.

"*Taisez-vous.* Hold your tongue," I said, without mitigation. If there is anything I cannot away with, it is trivial apostasy. I tolerate latitudinarianism when it is hereditary. Where people's fathers and mothers before them have been Pagans, and Catholics, and Mohammedans, you don't blame *them* for being so. You regret their error, and strive to lead them back into the right path; only they are not inflammatory. But to have people go out from the faith of their fathers with malice aforethought and their eyes open — well, that is not exactly what I mean either. That is a sorrowful, but not necessarily an exasperating thing. What I mean is this: I see people Orthodox from their cradles, (and probably only from their cradles, certainly not from their brains,) who think it is something pretty to become Unitarianistic. They don't become Unitarians, as they never were Orthodox, because they have not thought enough or sense enough to become or to be anything; but they like to make a stir and attract attention. They seem to think it indicates great liberality of character, and great breadth of view, to be continually flinging out against their own faith, ridiculing this, that, and the other point held by their Church, and shocking devout and simple-minded Orthodox by their quasi-profanity. Now for good Orthodox Christians I have a great respect; and for good Unitarian Christians I have a great respect; and for sincere, sad seekers, who can find no rest for the sole of their foot, I have a great respect; but for these Border State men, who are neither here nor there, on whom you never can lay your hand, because they are twittering everywhere, I have a profound contempt. I wish people to be either one thing or another. I desire them to believe something, and know what it is, and stick to it. I have no patience with this modern outcry against creeds. You hear people inveigh against them, without for a moment thinking what they are. They talk as if creeds were the head and front of human offending, the infallible sign of bigotry and hypocrisy, incompatible alike with piety and wisdom. Do not these wise men know that the thinkers and doers of the earth, in overwhelming majority, have been creed men? Creeds may exist without religion, but neither religion, nor philosophy, nor politics, nor society, can exist without creeds. There must be a creed in the head, or there cannot be religion in the heart. You must believe that Deity exists, before you can reverence Deity. You must believe in the fact of humanity, or you cannot love your fellows. A creed is but the concentration, the crystallization, of belief. Truth is of but little worth till it is so crystallized. Truth lying dissolved in oceans of error and nonsense and ignorance makes but a feeble diluent. It swashes everywhere, but to deluge, not to benefit. Precipitate it, and you have the salt of the earth. Political opposition, inorganic, is but a blind, cumbrous, awkward, inefficient thing; but construct a platform, and immediately it becomes lithe, efficient, powerful. Even before they set foot on these rude shores, our forefathers made a compact, and a nation was born in that day. It is on creeds that strong men are nourished, and that which nourishes the leaders into eminence is necessary to keep the masses from sinking. A man who really thinks, will think his way into light. He may turn many a somersault, but he will come right side up at last. But people in general do not think, and if they refuse to be walled in by other people's thoughts, they inevitably flop and flounder into pitiable prostration. So important is it, that a poor creed is better than none at all. Truth, even adulterated as we get it, is a tonic. Bring forward something tangible, something positive, something that means something, and it will do. But this flowery, misty, dreamy humanitarianism, — I say humanitarianism, because I don't know what that is, and I don't know what the thing I am driving at is, so I put the two unknown quantities together in a mathematical hope that minus into minus may give plus, — this milk-and-watery muddle of dreary negations, that remits the world to its original fluidic state of chaos, I spew it out of my mouth. It was not on such pap our Cæsars fed that made them grow so great. I believe that the common people of early New England were such lusty men, because they strengthened themselves by gnawing at their tough old creeds. Give one something to believe, and he can get at it and believe it; but set out butting your head against nothing, and the chances are that you will break your neck. Take a good stout Christian, or a good sturdy Pagan, and you find something to bring up against; but with nebulous vapidists you are always slumping through and sprawling everywhere.

Of course, I do not mean that sincere and sensible people never change nor modify their faith. I wish to say, for its emphasis, if you will allow me, that they never do anything else; but generally the change is a gradual and natural one, a — growth, not a convulsion,—a reformation, not a revolution. When it is otherwise, it is a serious matter, not to be lightly done or flippantly discussed. If you really had a religious belief, it threw out roots and rootlets through all your life. It sucked in strength from every source. It intertwined itself through love and labor, through suffering and song, about every fibre of your soul. You cannot pull it up or dig it up, or in any way displace it, without setting the very foundations of your life a-quivering. True, it may be best that you should do this. If it was but a cumberer of the ground, tear it up, root and branch, and plant in its stead the seeds of that tree whose leaves are for the healing of the nations. But such things are done with circumspection,— not as unto man. If you are gay and jovial about it, if you feel no darts of torture flashing through the fastnesses of your life, do not flatter yourself that you are making radical changes. You are only pulling up pig-weed to set out smart-weed, and the less you say about it the better.

Now Halicarnassus is really just as Orthodox as I. He would not lie or steal any quicker than I. He would not willingly sacrifice one jot or tittle of his faith, and yet he is always startling you with small heresies. He is like a calf tied to a tree in the orchard by a long rope. In the exuberance of his glee Bossy starts from the post, tail up, in a hand gallop. You would think, from the way he sets out, that he was going to race around the whole orchard, and probably he thinks he is himself. But by the time he is fairly under full headway, his rope tightens up with a jerk, and away he goes heels over head. The only difference is, that Halicarnassus knows the length of his tether, and always fetches up in time to escape an overturn; but other people do not know it, and they imagine he is going pell-mell into infidelity. Now I was determined to have none of this trash in a steamboat. One has no desire to encounter superfluous risks in a country where life and limb are held on so uncertain a tenure as in this. There are quite chances enough of shipwreck without having any Jonahs aboard. Besides, in point of the fine arts, heterodoxy is worse than puns. So I headed him off at the first onset. But I should not have been so entirely successful in the attempt had I not been assisted by a pair of birds who came to distract his and our attention from a neighboring thicket. They wheeled — the gentle, graceful, sly, tantalizing things — in circles and ellipses, now skimming along the surface of the water, now swooping away in great smooth curves, then darting off in headlong flight and pursuit. "My kingdom for a gun!" exclaimed Halicarnassus with amateur ardor.

"I am glad you have no gun," said compassionate Grande. "Why should you kill them?"

"Do not be alarmed," I said, soothingly, "a distaff would be as deadly in his hands."

"Do you speak by the book, Omphale?" asked the Anakim, who still carried those New Hampshire sheep on his back.

"We went a-ducking once down in Swampshire," I answered.

"Did you catch any?" queried Grande.

"Duckings? no," said Halicarnassus.

"Nor ducks either," I added. "He made great ado with his guns, and his pouches, and his fanfaronade, and knocking me with his elbows and telling me to keep still, when no mouse could be more still than I, and after all he did not catch one."

"Only fired once or twice," said Halicarnassus, "just for fun, and to show her how to do it."

"How not to do it, you mean," said the Anakim.

"You fired forty times," I said quietly, but firmly, "and the ducks would come out and look at you as interested as could be. You know you did n't scare a little meadow-hen. They knew you could n't hit."

"Trade off your ducks against my sheep, and call it even?" chuckled the Anakim; and so, chatting and happy, we glided along, enjoying, not entranced, comfortable, but not sublime, content to drink in the sunny sweetness of the summer day, happy only from the pleasant sense of being, tangling each other in silly talk out of mere wantonness, purling up bubbles of airy nothings in sheer effervescence of animal delight; falling into periodic fits of useful knowledge, under the influence of which we consulted our maps and our watches in a conjoint and clamorous endeavor to locate ourselves, which would no sooner be satisfactorily accomplished than something would turn up and set our calculations and islands adrift, and we would have to begin new. Dome Island we made out by its shape, unquestionably; Whortleberry we hazarded on the strength of its bushes; "Hen and Chicks," by a biggish island brooding half a dozen little ones; Flea Island, from a certain snappishness of aspect; Half-Way Island, by our distance from dinner; Anthony's Nose, by its unlikeness to anything else, certainly not from its resemblance to noses in general, let alone the individual nose of Mark Antony, or Mad Anthony, or any Anthony between. And then we disembarked and posted ourselves on the coach-top for a six-mile ride to Champlain; and Grande said, her face still buried in the map, "Here on the left is 'Trout Brook' running into the lake, and a cross on it, and 'Ld. Howe fell, 1758.' That is worth seeing."

"Yes," I said, "America loved his brother."

"America loved *him*," howled Halicarnassus, thinking to correct me and avenge himself. Now I knew quite well that America loved him, and did not love his brother, but with the mention of his name came into my mind the tender, grieved surprise of that pathetic little appeal, and I just said it, — thought it aloud, — assuming historic knowledge enough in my listeners to prevent misconception. But to this day Halicarnassus persists in thinking, or at least in asserting, that I tripped over Lord Howe. As he does not often get such a chance, I let him comfort himself with it as much as he can; but that is the way with your whipper-snapper critics. They put on their "specs," and pounce down upon some microscopic mote, which they think to be ignorance, but which is really the diamond-dust of imagination. "But let us see the place," said Grande. "We must drive within sight of it."

"Yes," I said. "Halicarnassus, ask the driver to be sure to tell us where Lord Howe fell."

"Fell into the brook," said that Oracle, and sat as stiff as a post.

Ticonderoga, — up-hill and down-hill for six miles, white houses and dark, churches and shops, and playing children and loungers, and mills, and rough banks and haggard woods, just like any other somewhat straggling country village. O no! O no! There are few like this. *I* have seen no other. Churches and shops and all the paraphernalia of busy, bustling common life there may be, but we have no eyes for such. Yonder on the green high plain which we have already entered is a simple guide-post, guiding you, not on to Canada, to New York, to Boston, but back into the dead century that lived so fiercely and lies so still. We stand on ground over-fought by hosts of heroes. Here rise still the breastworks, grass-grown and harmless now, behind which men awaited bravely the shock of furious onset, before which men rushed as bravely to duty and to death. Slowly we wind among the little squares of intrenchments, whose deadliest occupants now are peaceful cows and sheep, slowly among tall trees, — ghouls that thrust out their slimy, cold fingers everywhere, battening on horrid banquets, — nay, sorrowful trees, not so. Your gentle, verdant vigor nourishes no lust of blood. Rather you sprang in pity from the cold ashes at your feet, that every breeze quivering through your mournful leaves may harp a requiem for Polydorus. Alighting at the landing-place we stroll up the hill and among the ruins of the old forts, and breast ourselves the surging battle-tide. For war is not to this generation what it has been. The rust of long disuse has been rubbed off by the iron hand of fate, — shall we not say, rather, by the good hand of our God upon us? — and the awful word stands forth once more, red-lettered and real. Marathon, Waterloo, Lexington, are no longer the conflict of numbers against numbers, nor merely of principles against principles, but of men against men. And as we stand on this silent hill, the prize of so many struggles, our own hearts swell with the hopes and sink with the fears that its green old bluffs have roused. Up from yon water-side came stealing the Green-Mountain Boys, with their grand and grandiloquent leader, and, at the very gateway where we stand, as tradition says, (*et potius Dii numine firment,*) he thundered out, with brave, barbaric voice, the imperious summons, "In the name of the great Jehovah and the Continental Congress." No wonder the startled, half-dressed commander is confounded, and "the pretty face of his wife peering over his shoulder" is filled with terror. Well may such a motley crew frighten the fair Europeanne. "Frenchmen I know, and Indians I know, but who are ye?" Ah! Sir Commander, so bravely bedight, these are the men whom your parliamentary knights are to sweep with their brooms into the Atlantic Ocean. Bring on your besoms, fair gentlemen; yonder is Champlain, and a lake is as good to drown in as an ocean. Look at them, my lords, and look many times before you leap. They are a rough set, roughly clad, a stout-limbed, stout-hearted race, insubordinate, independent, irrepressible, almost as troublesome to their friends as to their foes; but there is good stock in them,—brain and brawn, and brain and brawn will yet carry the day over court and crown, in the name of the right, which shall overpower all things. We clamber down into arched passages, choked with *débris*, over floors tangled with briers, and join in the wild wassail of the bold outlaw, fired by his victorious career. We clamber up the rugged sides and wind around to the headland. Brilliant in the "morning-shine," exultant in the pride and pomp of splendid preparation, ardent for conquest and glory, Abercrombie sails down the lovely inland sea, to sail back dismantled and disgraced. The retrieving fleet of Amherst follows, as brilliant and as eager, — to gain the victory of numbers over valor, but to lose its fruit, as many a blood-bought prize has since been lost, snatched from the conqueror's hand by the traitor, doubt. But this is only the prologue of our great drama. Allen leaps first upon the scene, bucklered as no warrior ever was since the days of Homer or before. Then Arnold comes flying in, wresting laurels from defeat, — Arnold, who died too late. Here Schuyler walks up at night, his military soul vexed within him by the sleeping guards and the intermittent sentinels, his gentle soul harried by the rustic ill-breeding of his hinds, his magnanimous soul cruelly tortured by the machinations of jealousy and envy and evil-browed ambition. Yonder on the hill Burgoyne's battery threatens death, and Lincoln avenges us of Burgoyne. Let the curtain fall; a bloodier scene shall follow.

* * * * *

And then we re-embark on Lake Champlain, and all the summer afternoon sail down through phantom fleets, under the frowning ramparts of phantom forts, past grim rows of deathful-throated cannon, through serried hosts of warriors, with bright swords gleaming and strong arms lifted and stern lips parted; but from lips of man or throat of cannon comes no sound. A thousand oars strike through the leaping waves, but not a plash breaks on the listening ear. A thousand white sails swell to the coming breeze, that brings glad greeting from the inland hills, but nothing breaks the silences of time.

And of all beautiful things that could have been thought of or hoped for, what should come to crown our queen of days but a thunder-storm, a most real and vivid thunder-storm, marshalling up from the west its grand, cumulose clouds; black, jagged, bulging with impatient, prisoned thunder biding their time, sharp and fierce against the brilliant sky, spreading swiftly over the heavens, fusing into one great gray pall, dropping a dim curtain of rain between us and the land, closing down upon us a hollow hemisphere pierced with shafts of fire and deafening with unseen thunders, wresting us off from the friendly skies and shores, wrapping us into an awful solitude. O Princess Rohan, come to me! come from the hidden caves, where you revel in magical glories, come up from your coralline caves in the mysterious sea, come from those Eastern lands of nightingale, roses, and bulbuls, where your tropical soul was born and rocked in the lap of the lotus! O sunny Southern beauty, lost amongst Northern snows, flush forth in your mystical splendor from the ruby wine of Hafiz, float down from your clouds of the sunset with shining garments of light, open the golden door of your palace domed in a lily, glide over these inky waves, O my queen of all waters, come to me wherever you are, with your pencil dipped in darkness, starry with diamond dews and spanned with the softness of rainbows, and set on this land-locked Neptune your cross of the Legion of Honor, assure to the angry god his bowl in Valhalla, that the thunder-vexed lake may be soothed with its immortality!

But the storm passes on, the clouds sweep magnificently away, and the glowing sky flings up its arch of promise. The lucent waters catch its gleam and spread in their depths a second arch as beautiful and bright. So, haloed with magnificence, an earth-born bark on fairy waters, completely circled by this glory of the skies and seas, we pass through our triumphal gateway "deep into the dying day," and are presently doused in the mud at Rouse's Point. Rouse's Point is undoubtedly a very good place, and they were good women there, and took good care of us; but Rouse's Point is a dreadful place to wake up in when you have been in Dream-Land, — especially when a circus is there, singing and shouting under your windows all night long. I wonder when circus-people sleep, or do they not sleep at all, but keep up a perpetual ground and lofty tumbling? From Rouse's Point through Northern New York, through endless woods and leagues of brilliant fire-weed, the spirit of the dead flames that raved through the woods, past corn-fields that look rather "skimpy," certainly not to be compared to a corn-field I wot of, whose owner has a monomania on the subject of corn and potatoes, and fertilizes his fields with his own blood and brain, — a snort, a rush, a shriek, and the hundred miles is accomplished, and we are at Ogdensburg, a smart little town, like all American towns, with handsome residences up, and handsomer ones going up, with haberdashers' shops, and lawyers' offices, and judges' robes, and most hospitable citizens, — one at least, — and all the implements and machinery of government and self-direction, not excepting a huge tent for political speaking and many political speeches, and everybody alert, public-spirited, and keyed up to the highest pitch. All this is interesting, but we have seen it ever since we were born, and we look away with wistful eyes to the north; for this broad, majestic river stretching sky-ward like the ocean, is the St. Lawrence. Up this river, on the day of St. Lawrence, three hundred years ago, came the mariner of St. Malo, — turning in from the sea till his straining eyes beheld on both sides land, — and planted the lilies of France. Now it is the boundary line of empires. Those green banks on the other side are a foreign country, and for the first time I am not monarch of all I survey. That fine little city, with stately trees towering from the midst of its steeples and gray roofs, is Prescott. At the right rise the ramparts of Fort Wellington, whence cannon-balls came hissing over to Ogdensburg some fifty years ago. We stand within a pretty range, suppose they should try it again! Farther on still is a plain, gray tower, where a handful of "patriots" intrenched and destroyed themselves with perverse martyrophobia in a foolish and fruitless endeavor. The afternoon is before us; suppose we row over; here is a boat, and doubtless a boatman, or the ferry-steamer will be here directly. By no means; a ferry-steamer is thoroughly commonplace; you can ferry-steam anywhere. Row, brothers, row, perhaps you will never have the chance again. Lightly, lightly row through the green waters of the great St. Lawrence, through the sedge and rank grass that wave still in his middle depths, over the mile and a half of great rushing billows that rock our little boat somewhat roughly: but I am not afraid, — for I can swim.

"You can, can you?" says the Anakim, incredulously.

"Indeed I can, can't I, Halicarnassus?" appealingly.

"Like a brick!" ejaculates that worthy, pulling away at the oars, and on we shoot, steadily nearing the rustic stone city that looks so attractive, so different from our hasty, brittle, shingly American half-minute houses, — massive, permanent, full of character and solid worth. And now our tiny craft buts against the pier, and we ascend from the Jesuit river and stand on British soil. No stars and stripes here, but Saint George and his dragon fight out their never-ending brawl. No war, no volunteering, no Congress here; but peace and a Parliament and a Queen, God bless her! and this is her realm, a kingdom. Now if it had been a year ago I do not know that I should not, like Columbus, have knelt to kiss these dingy stones, so much did I love and reverence England, and whatever bore the dear English name. But we — they, rather — have changed all that. Among the great gains of this memorable year, — among the devotions, the sacrifices, the heroisms, — all the mighty, noble, and ennobling deeds by which we stand enriched forevermore, — there broods the shadow of one irreparable loss, — the loss of England. Success or failure can make no difference there. English gold, English steel, English pluck, stand to-day as always; but English integrity, English stanchness, English love, where are they? Just where Prescott is, now that we have come to it; for the substantial stone city a mile and a half away turns out to be a miserable little dirty, hutty, smutty, stagnant owl-cote when you get into it. What we took for stone is stolidity. It is old, but its age is squalid, not picturesque.

We stumble through the alleys that answer for streets, and come to the "Dog and Duck," a dark, dingy ale-room, famous for its fine ale, we are told, or perhaps it was beer: I don't remember. It is not in male nature to go by on the other side of such a thing, and we enter, — they to test the beverage, Grande and I to make observation of the surroundings. We take position in the passage between the bar-room and parlor. A yellow-haired Saxon child, with bare legs and fair face, crawls out from some inner hollow to the door, and impends dangerous on the sill, throwing numerous scared backward glances over his shoulder. The parlor is taken bodily out of old English novels, a direct descendant, slightly furbished up and modernized, of the Village inn parlor of Goldsmith, — homely, clean, and comfortless. A cotton tidy over the rocking-chair bewrays, wrought into its crocheted gorgeousness, the name of Uncle Tom. This I cannot stand. Time may bring healing, but now the wound is still fresh. "O, you did Uncle-Tom it famously," I hurl out, doubling my fist at the British lion which glares at me from that cotton tidy. "I remember those days. O yes! you were rampant on Uncle Tom. You are a famous friend of Uncle Tom, with your Exeter Halls, and your Lord Shaftesburys, and your Duchess of Sutherlands! Cry your pretty eyes out over Uncle Tom, dear, tender-hearted British women. Write appealing letters to your sisters over the waters, affectionate, conscientious kindred; canonize your saint, our sin, in tidies, and chair-covers, and Christmas slippers, — we know how to take you now; we have found out what all that is worth; we can appraise your tears by the bottle — in pounds, shillings, and pence." But the beer-men curtail my harangue, so I shake my departing fist at the cowering lion, and, leaving this British institution, proceed to investigate another British institution, — the undaunted English army, in its development in Fort Wellington. A wall shuts the world out from those sacred premises; a stile lets the world in, — over which stile we step and stand on the fort grounds. A party of soldiers are making good cheer in a corner of the pasture, — perhaps I ought to say parade-ground. As no sentinel accosts us, we hunt up one, and inquire if the fort is accessible. He does not know, but inclines to the opinion that it is. We go up the hill, walk round the wall, and mark well her bulwarks, till we come to a great gate, but it refuses to turn. The walls are too high to scale, besides possible pickets on the other side. I have no doubt in the world that we could creep under, for the gate has shrunk since it was made, and needs to have a tuck let down; but what would become of dignity? Grande and the Anakim make a reconnoissance in force, to see if some unwary postern-gate may not permit entrance.

Halicarnassus fumbles in his pockets for edge-tools, as if Queen Victoria, who rules the waves, on whose dominions the sun never sets, whose morning drum-beat encircles the world, would leave the main gate of her main fort on one of the frontiers of her empire so insecurely defended that a single American can carry it with his fruit-knife. Such ideas I energetically enforce, till I am cut short by the slow retrogression of the massive gate on ponderous hinges turning.

"What about the fruit-knife?" inquires Halicarnassus as I pass in. The reconnoitring party return to report a bootless search, and are electrified to find the victory already gained.

"See the good of having been through college," exults Halicarnassus.

"How did you do it?" asks Grande, admiringly.

"By genius and assiduity," answers Halicarnassus.

"And lifting the latch," I append, for I have been examining the mechanism of the gate since I came in, and have made a discovery which dislodges my *savant* from his pinnacle; namely, that the only fastening on the gate is a huge wooden latch, which not one of us had sense enough to lift; but then who thinks of taking a fort by assault and battery on the latch? Halicarnassus hit upon it by mere accident, and I therefore remorselessly expose him. Then we saunter about the place, and, seeing a woman eying us suspiciously from an elevated window, we show the white feather and ask her if we may come in, which, seeing we have been in for some ten minutes, we undoubtedly may; and then we mount the ramparts and peer into Labrador and Hudson's Bay and the North Pole, and, turning to a softer sky, gaze from a "foreign clime" upon our own dear land, home of freedom, hope of the nations, eye-sore of the Devil, rent by one set of his minions, and ridiculed by another, but coming out of her furnace-fires, if God please and man will, heartier and holier, because freer and truer, than ever before. O my country, beautiful and beloved, my hope, my desire, my joy, and my crown of rejoicing, immeasurably dearer in the agony of your bloody sweat than in the high noon of your proud prosperity! standing for the first time beyond your borders, and looking upon you from afar, now and forevermore out of a full heart I breathe to you benedictions.

IV.

DOWN the St. Lawrence in a steamer, up the St. Lawrence on the maps, we sail through another day full of eager interest. Everything is fresh, new, novel. Is it because we are in high latitudes that the river and the country look so high? I could fancy that we are on a plateau, overlooking a continent. Now the water expands on all sides like an ocean meeting the sky, and now we are sailing through hay-fields and country orchards, as if the St. Lawrence had taken a turn into our back-yard. We hug the Canada shore, and thick woods come down the banks dipping their summer tresses in the cool Northern river, — broad pasture-lands stretch away, away from river to sky, — brown, dubious villages sail by at long intervals. On the distant southern shore America has stationed her outposts, and unfrequent spires attest a civilized, if remote life. In the sunny day all things are sunny, save when a Claude Lorraine glass lends a dark, rich mystery to every hill and cloud. The Claude

Lorraine glass is a *rara avis*, and not only gives new lights to the scenery, but brings out the human nature on board in great force. The Anakim tells us of one man who asked him in a confidential aside, if it was a show, whereat we all laugh. Even I laugh at the man's ignorance, — I, a thief, an assassin, a traitor, who six weeks ago had never heard of a Claude Lorraine glass; but nobody can tell who has not tried it how much credit one gets for extensive knowledge, if only he holds his tongue. In all my life I am afraid I shall never learn as much as I have been inferred to know simply because I kept still.

Down the St. Lawrence in an English steamer, where everything is not so much English as John Bull-y. The servants at the table are thoroughly and amusingly yellow-plush, — if that is the word I want, and if it is not that, it is another; for I am quite sure of my idea, though not of the name that belongs to it. The servants are smooth and sleek and intense. They serve as if it was their business, and a weighty business at that, demanding all the energies of a created being. Accordingly they give their minds to it. The chieftain yonder, in white choker and locks profusely oiled and brushed into a resplendent expanse, bears Atlas on his shoulders. His lips are compressed, his brow contracted, his eyes alert, his whole manner as absorbed as if it were a nation, and not a plum-pudding, that he is engineering through a crisis. Lord Palmerston is nothing to him, I venture to say. I know the only way to accomplish anything is to devote yourself to it; still I cannot conceive how anybody can give himself up so completely to a dinner, even if it is his business and duty. However, I have nothing to complain of in the results, for we are well served, only for a trifle too much obviousness. Order and system are undoubtedly good things, but I don't like to see an ado made about them. Our waiters stand behind, at given stations, with prophetic dishes in uplifted hands, and, at a certain signal from the arch-waiter, down they come like the clash of fate. Now I suppose this is all very well, but for me I never was fond of military life. Under my housekeeping we browse indiscriminately. When we have nothing else to do, we have a meal. If it is nearer noon than morning, we call it dinner. If it is nearer night than noon, we call it supper, unless we have fashionable friends with us, and then we call it dinner, and the other thing lunch; and ten to one it is so scattered about that it has no name at all. At breakfast you will be likely to find me on the door-step with a bowl of bread and milk, while Halicarnassus sits on the bench opposite and brandishes a chicken-bone with the cat mewing furiously for it at his feet. A surreptitious doughnut is sweet and dyspeptic over the morning paper, and gingerbread is always to be had by systematic and intelligent foraging. Consequently this British drill and discipline are thoroughly alarming to me, and I am surprised and grateful to find that we are not individually regulated by a time-table. I expect a drum-beat; — one, incision; two, mastication; three, deglutition; — but what tyranny does one not expect to find under monarchical institutions? Put that into your next volume, intelligent British tourist.

Down the St. Lawrence with millionnaires, and artists, and gay young girls, and sallow-faced invalids, and weary clergymen and men of business who do not know what to do with their unwonted leisure and find pleasuring a most unmitigated bore, and mothers with sick children, dear little unnatural pale faces and heavy eyes, — may your angels bring you health, tiny ones! — and, most interesting of all to me, a party of priests and nuns on their travels. They sit near me, and I can see them without turning my head, and hear them without marked listening. The priests are sleek-headed men, and such as sleep o' nights, ruddy, rotund, robust, with black hair and white hands, well-dressed, well-fed, well-to-do, jolly, gentlemanly, clique-y, sensible, shrewd, *au fait.* The nuns — now I am vexed to look at them. Are nuns expected to be any more dead to the world than priests? Then I should like to know why they must make such frights of themselves, while priests go about like Christians? Why shall a nun walk black, and gaunt, and lank, with a white towel wrapped around her face, all possible beauty and almost all attractiveness despoiled by her hideously unbecoming dress, while priests wear their hair and their hats and their coats and their collars like any other gentleman? Why are the women to be set up as targets, while the men may pass unnoticed and unknown? If the woman's head must be shorn and shaven, why not the man's? It is not fair. I can think of no reason, pretext, or excuse, unless it is to be found in the fact that women are more beautiful than men, and need greater disfigurement to make them ugly. That is a fact which I have long suspected, and observations made on this journey confirm my suspicions, — intensify them into certainty. An ugly woman is handsomer than a handsome man, — if you examine them closely. She is finer-grained, more soft, more delicate. Men are animals more than women. I do not now mean the generic sense in which we are all animals, but specifically and superficially. Men look more like horses and cows. See our brave soldiers returning from the wars — Heaven's blessing rest upon them! — grand, but are they not gruff? A woman's face may be browned, roughened, and reddened by exposure, yet her skin is always skin; but often when a man's face has been sheltered from storm and shine, his skin is hide. His mane is not generally so long and flowing as a horse's, but there it is. Once, in a car, a man in front of me put his arm on the back of his seat and fell asleep. Presently his hand dropped over, and I looked at it, — a mass of broad, brawny vitality, great pipes of veins, great crescents of nails, great furrows at the joints, and you might cut a fine sirloin of beef off the ball of the thumb; and this is a hand! *I* call it an ox. A woman's hand, by hard labor, spreads and cracks, and sprouts bunches at the joints, and becomes tuberous at the ends of the fingers, but you can see that it is a deformity and not nature. It tells a sad story of neglect, of labor, perhaps of heartlessness, cruelty, suffering. But this man's hand was born so. You would not think of pitying him any more than you would pity an elephant for being an elephant instead of an antelope. A woman's hair is silky and soft, and, if not always smooth, susceptible of smoothness. A man's hair is shag. If he tries to make it anything else, he does not mend the matter. Ceasing to be shag, it does not become beauty, but foppishness, effeminacy, Miss Nancyism. A man is a brute by the law of his nature. Let him ape a woman, and he does not cease to be brutal, though he does become ridiculous. The only thing for him to do is to be the best kind of a brute.

In all of which remarks there is nothing derogatory to a man, — nothing at which any one need take offence. I do not say that manhood is not a very excellent kind of creation. Everything is good in its line. I would just as soon have been a beetle as a woman, if I had never been a woman, and did not know what it was. I don't suppose a horse is at all crestfallen because he is a horse. On the contrary, if he is a thorough-bred, blood horse, he is a proud and happy fellow, prancing, spirited, magnificent. So a man may be so magnificently manly that one shall say, Surely this is the monarch of the universe; and hide and shag and mane shall be vitalized with a matchless glory. Let a man make himself grand in his own sphere, and not sit down and moan because he is only a connecting link between a horse and a woman.

I suppose Mother Church is fully cognizant of the true state of affairs, and thinks men already sufficiently Satyric, but woman must be ground down as much as possible, or the world will not be fended off. And ground down they are in body and soul. O Mother Church! as I look upon these nuns, I do not love you. You have done many wise and right deeds. You have been the ark of the testimony, the refuge of the weary, the dispenser of alms, the consoler of the sorrowful, the hope of the dying, the blessing of the dead. You are convenient now, wieldy in an election, effective when a gold ring is missing from the toilette cushion, admirable in your machinery, and astonishing in your persistency and power. But what have you done with these women? In what secret place, in what dungeon of darkness and despair, in what chains of torpidity and oblivion, have you hidden away their souls? They are twenty-five and thirty years old, but they are not women. They are nothing in the world but grown-up children. Their expression, their observation, their interests, are infantile. There is no character in their faces. There are marks of pettishness, but not of passion. Nothing deep, tender, beneficent, maternal, is there. Time has done his part, but life has left no marks. Their smiles and laughter are the merriment of children, beautiful in children, but painful here. Mother Church, you have dwarfed these women, helplessly, hopelessly. You accomplish results, but you deteriorate humanity.

Down the St. Lawrence, the great, melancholy river, grand only in its grandeur, solitary, unapproachable, cut off from the companionship, the activities, and the interests of life by its rocks and rapids; yet calm and conscious, working its work in silent state.

The rapids are bad for traffic, but charming for travellers; and what is a little revenue more or less, to a sensation? There is not danger enough to awaken terror, but there is enough to require vigilance; just enough to exhilarate, to flush the cheek, to brighten the eye, to quicken the breath; just enough for spice and sauce and salt; just enough for you to play at storm and shipwreck, and heroism in danger. The rocking and splashing of the early rapids is mere fun; but when you get on, when the steamer slackens speed, and a skiff puts off from shore, and an Indian pilot comes on board, and mounts to the pilot-house, you begin to feel that matters are getting serious. But the pilot is chatting carelessly with two or three by-standers, so it cannot be much. Ah! this sudden cessation of something! This unnatural quiet. The machinery has stopped. What! the boat is rushing straight on to the banks. H-w-k! A whole shower of spray is dashed into our faces. Little shrieks and laughter, and a sudden hopping up from stools, and a sudden retreat from the railing to the centre of the deck. Staggering, quivering, aghast, the boat reels and careens. Seethe and plunge the angry waters, whirling, foaming, furious. Look at the pilot. No chatting now, no by-standers, but fixed eyes and firm lips, every muscle set, every nerve tense. Yes, it is serious. Serious! close by us, seeming scarcely a yard away, frowns a black rock. The maddened waves dash up its sullen back, the white, passionate surf surges into its wrathful jaws. Here, there, before, behind, black rocks and a wild uproar of waters, through all which Providence and our pilot lead us safely into the still deep beyond, and we look into each other's faces and smile.

And now the sunset reddens on the water, reddens on the bending sky and the beautiful clouds, and men begin to come around with cards and converse of the different hotels in the Montreal that is to be; one tells us that the Prince of Wales beamed royal light upon the St. Lawrence Hall, and we immediately decide to make the balance true by patronizing its rival Donegana, whereupon a man — a mere disinterested spectator of course — informs us in confidence that the Donegana is nothing but ruins; he should not think we would go there; burnt down a few years ago, — a shabby place, kept by a grass widow; but when was American ever scared off by the sound of a ruin? So Donegana it is, the house with the softly flowing Italian name; and then we pass under the arch of the famous Victoria Bridge, whose corner-stone, or cap-stone, or whatever it is that bridges have, was laid by the Prince of Wales. (And to this day I do not know how the flag-staff of our boat cleared the arch. It was ten feet above it, I should think, and I looked at it all the time, and yet it shrivelled under in the most laughable yet baffling manner.) In the mild twilight we disembarked, and were quickly omnibused to the relics of Donegana, which turned out to be very well, very well indeed for ruins, with a smart stone front, and I don't know but stone all the way through, with the usual allowance of lace curtains, and carpets, and gilding in the parlors, notwithstanding flames and conjugal desolation; also a band welcomed us in the gas-lit square adjoining, and we were hospitably entreated and transmitted to the breakfast-table next morning in perfect sight-seeing trim; only the

Anakim was cross, and muttered that they had sent him out in the village to sleep among the hens, and there was a cackling and screaming and chopping off of heads all night long. But the breakfast-table assured us that many a cackle must have been the swan-song of death. Halicarnassus wondered if something might not be invented to consume superfluous noise, as great factories consume their own smoke, but the Anakim said there was no call for any new invention in that line so long as Halicarnassus continued in his present appetite, — with a significant glance at the plump chicken which the latter was vigorously converting into mammalia, and which probably was the very one that disturbed the Anakim's repose. And then we discussed the day's plan of operations. Halicarnassus said he had been diplomatizing for a carriage. The man in the office told him he could have one for five dollars. He thought that was rather high. Man said it was the regular price; could n't get one for any less in the city. Halicarnassus went out and saw one standing idle in the market-place. Asked the price. Three dollars. For how long? Drive you all round the city, Sir; see all the sights. Then he went back and told the man at the office.

"Well," I said, after he had swallowed a wassail-bowl of coffee, and showed no disposition to go on, "what did you do then?"

"Came in to breakfast."

"Did n't you tell the clerk you would not take his carriage?"

"No."

"Did n't you tell the other man you would take his?"

"No."

"What *did* you do?"

"Let it work. Don't be in a hurry. Give a thing time to work."

"And suppose it should work you out of any carriage at all?"

"No danger." And to be sure, when we had finished breakfast, the three-dollar hack was there awaiting our pleasure. Our pleasure was to drive out into the British possessions, first around the mountain, which is quite a mountain for a villa, though nothing to speak of as a mountain, with several handsome residences on its sides, and a good many not so handsome; but the mountain is a pet of Montreal, and, as I said, quite the thing for a cockney mountain. Then we went to the French Cathedral, which is, I believe, the great gun of ecclesiastical North America, but it hung fire with me. It was large, but not great. There was no unity. It was not impressive. It was running over with frippery, — *olla podrida* cropping out everywhere. It confused you. It distracted you. It wearied you. You sighed for somewhat simple, quiet, restful. The pictures were pronounced poor. I don't know whether they were or not. I never can tell a picture as a cook tells her mince-pie meat, by tasting it. One picture is a revealer and one is a daub; but they are alike to me at first glance. For a picture has an individuality all its own. You must woo it with tender ardor, or it will not yield up its heart. The chance look sees only color and contour; but as you gaze the color glows, the contour throbs, the hidden soul heaves the inert canvas with the solemn palpitations of life. Art is dead no longer, but informed with divine vitality. There is no picture but Hope crowned and radiant, or pale and patient Sorrow, or the tender sanctity of Love. The landscape of the artist is neither painting nor nature, but summer fields and rosy sunsets overflooded with his own inward light. Only from her Heaven-anointed monarch, man, can Nature receive her knightly accolade. And shall one detect the false or recognize the true by the minute-hand? I suppose so, since some do. But I cannot. People who live among the divinities may know the goddess, for all her Spartan arms, her naked knee, and knotted robe; but I, earth-born among earth-born, must needs behold the auroral blush, the gliding gait, the flowing vestment, and the divine odor of her purple hair.

In the vestibule of the French Cathedral, I believe it is, you will behold a heart-rending sight in a glass case, namely, a group of children, babies in long clothes and upwards, in a dreadful state of being devoured by cotton-flannel pigs. Their poor little white frocks are stained with blood, and they are knocked about piteously in various stages of mutilation. A label in front informs you that certain innocents in certain localities are subject to this shocking treatment; and you are earnestly conjured to drop your penny or your pound into the box, to rescue them from a fate so terrible. You must be a cannibal if you can withstand this appeal. Suffering that you only hear of, you can forget, but suffering going on right under your eyes is not so easily disposed of.

Leaving the pigs and papooses, we will go to — which of the nunneries? The Gray? Yes. But when you come home, everybody will tell you that you ought to have visited the Black Nunnery. The Gray is not to be mentioned in the same year. Do not, however, flatter yourself that in choosing the Black you will be any more enviable; there will not be wanting myriads who will assure you, that, not having seen the Gray, you might as well have seen nothing at all. To the Gray Nunnery went we, and saw pictures and altars and saints and candlesticks, and little dove-cot floors of galleries jutting out, where a few women crossed, genuflected, and mumbled, and an old woman came out of a door above one of them, and asked the people below not to talk so loud, because they disturbed the worshippers; but the people kept talking, and presently she came out again, and repeated her request, with a little of the Inquisition in her tones and gestures, — no more than was justifiable under the circumstances: but she looked straight at me; and O old woman! it was not I that talked, nor my party. We were noiseless as mice. It was that woman over there in a Gothic bonnet, with a bunch of roses under the roof as big as a cabbage. Presently the great doors opened, and a procession of nuns marched in chanting their gibberish. Of course they wore the disguise of those abominable caps, with gray, uncouth dresses, the skirts taken up in front and pinned behind, after the manner of washerwomen. Yet there were faces among them on which the eye loved to linger, — some not too young for their years, some furtive glances, some demure looks from the yet undeadened youth under those ugly robes, — some faces of struggle and some of victory. O Mother Church, here I do not believe in you! These natures are gnarled, not nurtured. These elaborately reposeful faces are not natural. These downcast eyes and droning voices are not natural. Not one thing here is natural. Whisk off these clinging gray washing-gowns, put these girls into crinoline and Gothic bonnets, and the innocent finery that belongs to them, and send them out into the wholesome daylight to talk and laugh and make merry, — the birthright of their young years. A religion that deprives young girls or old girls of this boon is not the religion of Jesus Christ. Don't tell me!

The nuns pass out, and we wander through the silent yard, cut off by all the gloom of the mediæval times from the din, activity, and good cheer of the street beyond, and are conducted into the Old Men's Department. The floors and furniture are faultlessly and fragrantly clean. The kitchen is neat and susceptible of warmth and comfort, even when the sun's short wooing is over. The beds are ranged along the walls plump and nice; yet I hope that, when I am an old man, I shall not have to sleep on blue calico pillow-cases. Here and there, within and without, old men are basking in the rare sweet warmth of summer, and with their canes and their sunshine seem very well bestowed. Now I like you, Mother Church. You do better by your old men than you do by your young women, — simply because you know more about them. How can you, Papa and Messrs. Cardinals, be expected to understand what is good for a girl? If only you would confine yourself to what you do comprehend, — if only you would apply your admirable organizations to legitimate purposes, and not run mad on machinery, you would do angels' work.

From the old men's quarters we go up-stairs where sewing and knitting and all manner of fancy-work, especially in beads, are taught to long and lank little girls by longer and lanker large girls, companioned by a few old women, with commonplace knitting-work. Everything everywhere is thoroughly neat and comfortable; but I have a desperate pang of home-sickness; for if there is one condition of life more intolerable than any other, it is a state of unvarying, hopeless comfort.

From the Gray Nunnery to the English Church, which I like much better than the French Cathedral. There is a general tone of oakiness, solid, substantial, sincere, like the England of tradition,—set off by a brilliant memorial window and a memorial altar, and other memorial things which I have forgotten, but which I make no doubt the people who put them there have not forgotten. Here also we find, as all along in Canada, vestiges of His Royal Highness, the Prince of Wales. We are shown the Bible which he presented to the Church, and we gaze with becoming reverence upon the august handwriting,—the pew in which he worshipped; and the loyal beadle sees nothing but reverence in our momentary occupation of that consecrated seat. Evidently there is but a very faint line of demarcation in the old man's mind between his heavenly and earthly king; but an old man may have a worse weakness than this,—an unreasoning, blind, faithful fondness and reverence for a blameless prince. God bless the young man, in that he is the son of his father and mother. God help him, in that he is to be King of England.

Chancel and window, altar, and arches and aisles and treasures,—is there anything else? Yes, the apple that Eve ate, transfixed to oak,—hard to be understood, but seeing is believing. And then past Nelson's monument, somewhat battered, like the hero whom it commemorates; past the Champ de Mars, a fine parade-ground, hard and smooth as a floor; past the barracks and the reservoir, to the new Court-House, massive and plain. Then home to dinner and lounging; then travelling-dresses, and the steamer, and a most lovely sunset on the river; and then a night of tranquillity running to fog, and a morning approach to the unique city of North America, — the first and the only walled city *I* ever saw, or you either, I dare say, if you would only be willing to confess it. The aspect of the city, as one first approaches it, is utterly strange and foreign, — a high promontory jutting into the river, with a shelf of squalid, crowded, tall and shaky, or low and squatty tenements at its base, almost standing on the water; and rising behind them, for the back of the shelf, a rough, steep precipice abutted with the solid masonry of wall and citadel. A board fastened somehow about half-way up the rocky cliff, inscribed with the name of Montgomery, marks the spot where a hero, a patriot, a gentleman, met his death. Disembarking, we wind along a stair of a road, up steep ascents, and enter in through the gates into the city, — the walled, upper city, — walls thick, impregnable, gates ponderous, inert, burly. You did well enough in your day, old foes; but with Armstrongs and iron-clads, and

Ericsson still living, where would you be?—answer me that. Quaint, odd, alien old city,—a faint phantasmagoria of past conflicts and forgotten plans, a dingy fragment of *la belle France*, a clinging reminiscence of England, a dim, stone dream of Edinburgh, a little flutter of modern fashion, planted upon a sturdy rampart of antiquity, a little cobweb of commerce and enterprise, netting over a great deal of church and priest and king, with an immovable basis of stolid existence,—that is the Quebec I inferred from the Quebec I saw. Nothing in it was so interesting to me as itself. But passing by itself for the nonce, we prudently took advantage of the fine morning, and drove out to the Falls of Montmorency with staring eyes that wanted to take in all views, before, behind, on this side and that, at once; and because we could not, the joints of my neck at least became so dry with incessant action that they almost creaked. Low stone cottages lined the road-sides, with windows that opened like doors, with an inevitable big black stove whenever your eye got far enough in, with a pleasant stoop in front, with women perpetually washing the floors and the windows, with beautiful and brilliant flowers blooming profusely in every window, and often trailing and climbing about its whole area. Here, I take it, is the home of a real peasantry, a contented class, comfortable and looking for no higher lot. These houses seem durable and ultimate. The roofs of both houses and piazzas are broken, projected, picturesque, and often ornamented. They shelter, they protect, they brood, they embrace. There are little trellises and cornices and fanciful adornments. The solid homeliness is fringed with elegance. The people and the houses do not own each other, but they are married. There is love between them, and pride, and a hearty understanding. I can think of a country where you see little brown or red clapboarded houses that are neither solid nor elegant, that are both slight and awkward, — angular and shingly and dismal. The roofs are intended just to cover the houses, and are scanty at that. The sides are straight, the windows inexorable; and for flowers you have a hollyhock or two, and perhaps an uncomfortably tall sunflower, sovereign for hens. There is no home-look and no home-atmosphere. I love that country better than I like this; but, if you kill me for it, this drive is picturesque. These dumpy little smooth, white, flounced and flowered cottages look like wicker-gates to a happy valley, — born, not built. The cottages of the country, in my thoughts, yes, and in my heart, are neither born nor built, but "put up," — just for convenience, just to lodge in while waiting for something better, or till the corn is grown. Coming man, benefactor of our race, you who shall show us how to be contented without being sluggish, — how to be restful, and yet aspiring, — how to take the goods the gods provide us, without losing out of manly hearts the sweet sense of providing, — how to plant happy feet firmly on the present, and not miss from eager eyes the inspiriting outlook of the future, — how to make a wife of to-day, and not a mistress of to-morrow, — come quickly to a world that sorely needs you, and bring a fresh evangel.

The current of our thoughts is broken in upon by a new and peculiar institution. Every single child, and every group of children on the road, leaves its play as we pass by, and all dart upon us on both sides of the carriage, almost under the wheels, almost under the horses' feet, with outstretched blackened hands, and intense bright black eyes, running, panting, shouting, "*Un sou! un sou! un sou!*" I do not think I am quite in love with this as an institution, but it is very lively as a spectacle; and the little fleet-footed, long-winded beggars show a touching confidence in human nature. There is no servility in their beggary; and when it is glossed over with a thin mercantile veneering, by the brown little paws holding out to you a gorgeous bouquet of one clover-blossom, two dandelions, and a quartette of sorrel-leaves, why, it ceases to be beggarly, and becomes traffic overlaid with grace, the acanthus capital surmounting the fluted shaft. We meet also continual dog-carts, something like the nondescript which "blind Carwell" used to drag. Did you never see it? Well, then, like the cart in which the ark went up to Kirjath-jearim. Now you must know. Stubborn two-wheeled vehicles, with the whole farm loaded into the body, and the whole family on the seat. Here comes one drawn by a cow, not unnatural. Unnatural! It is the key-note of the tune. Everything is cow-y, — slow and sure, firm, but not fast, kindly, sunny, ruminant, heavy, lumbering, basking, content. Calashes also we meet, — a cumbrous, old-fashioned "one-hoss shay," with a yellow body, a suspicion of springlessness, wheels with huge spokes and broad rims, and the driver sitting on the dash-board. Now we are at the Falls of Montmorency. If you would know how they look, go and see them. If you have seen them, you don't need a description; and if you have not seen them, a description would do no good. From the Falls, if you are unsophisticated, you will resume your carriage and return to the city; but if you are *au fait*, you will cross the high-road, cross the pastures, and wind down a damp, mossy wood-path to the steps of Montmorency, — a natural phenomenon, quite as interesting as, and more remarkable than, the Falls, — especially if you go away without seeing it. Any river can fall when it comes to a dam. In fact, there is nothing for it to do but fall; but it is not every river that can carve out in its rage such wonderful stairways as this, — seething and foaming and roaring and leaping through its narrow and narrowing channel, with all the turbulence of its fiery soul unquelled, though the grasp of Time is on its throat, silent, mighty, irresistible.

Montmorency, — Montmorenci, — sweet and storied name! You, too, have received the awful baptism. Blood has mingled with your sacrifices. The song of your wild waves has been lost in the louder thunders of artillery, and the breezes sweeping through these green woods have soothed the agonies of dying men. Into one heart this ancient name, heavy with a weight of disaster and fancied disgrace, sank down like lead, — a burden which only death could cast off, only victory destroy; and death came hand in hand with victory.

Driving home, we take more special note of what interested us aggressively before, — Lord Elgin's residence, — the house occupied by the Duke of Kent when a young man in the army here, long I suppose before the throne of England placed itself at the end of his vista. Did the Prince of Wales, I wonder, visit this place, and, sending away his retinue, walk slowly alone under the shadows of these sombre trees, striving to bring back that far-off past, and some vague outline of the thoughts, the feelings, the fears and fancies of his grandfather, then, like himself, a young man, but, not like himself, a fourth son, poor and an exile, with no foresight probably of the exaltation that awaited his line, — his only child to be not only the lady of his land, but our lady of the world, — a warm-hearted woman worthily seated on the proud throne of Britain, — a noble and great-souled woman, in whose sorrow nations mourn, for whose happiness nations pray, — whose name is never spoken in this far-off Western world but with a silent blessing. Another low-roofed, many-roomed, rambling old house I stand up in the carriage to gaze at lingeringly with longing, misty eyes, — the sometime home of Field Marshal the Marquis de Montcalm. Writing now of this in the felt darkness that pours up from abandoned Fredericksburg, fearing not what the South may do in its exultation, but what the North may do in its despondency, I understand, as I understood not then, nor ever before, what comfort came to the dying hero in the certain thought, "I shall not live to see the surrender of Quebec."

Now again we draw near the city whose thousands of silver (or perhaps tin) roofs dazzle our eyes with their resplendence, and I have an indistinct impression of having been several times packed out and in to see sundry churches, of which I remember nothing except that I looked in vain to see the trophies of captured colors that once hung there, commemorating the exploits of the ancients, — and on the whole, I don't think I care much about churches except on Sundays. Somewhere in Canada — perhaps near Lorette — is some kind of a church, perhaps the oldest, or the first Indian church in Canada, — or may be it was interesting because it was burnt down just before we got there. That is the only definite reminiscence I have of any church in Quebec and its suburbs, and that is not so definite as it might be. I am sure I inspected the church of St. Roque and the church of St. John, because I have entered it in my "Diary"; but if they were all set down on the table before me at this moment, I am sure I could not tell which was which, or that they had not been transported each and all from Boston.

But we ascend the cliff, we enter the citadel, we walk upon the Plains of Abraham, and they overpower you with the intensity of life. The heart beats in labored and painful pulsations with the pressure of the crowding past. Yonder shines the lovely isle of vines that gladdened the eyes of treacherous Cartier, the evil requiter of hospitality. Yonder from Point Levi the laden ships go gayly up the sparkling river, a festive foe. Night drops her mantle, and silently the unsuspected squadron floats down the stealthy waters, and debarks its fateful freight. Silently in the darkness, the long line of armed men writhe up the rugged path. The rising sun reveals a startling sight. The impossible has been attained. Now, too late, the hurried summons sounds. Too late the deadly fire pours in. Too late the thickets flash with murderous rifles. Valor is no substitute for vigilance. Short and sharp the grapple, and victor and vanquished alike lie down in the arms of all-conquering death. Where this little tree ventures forth its tender leaves, Wolfe felt the bullet speeding to his heart. Where this monument stands, his soldier-soul fled, all anguish soothed away by the exultant shout of victory, — fled from passion and pain, from strife and madness, into the eternal calm.

Again and again has this rock under my feet echoed to the tramp of marching men. Again and again has this green and pleasant plain been drenched with blood, this blue, serene sky hung with the black pall of death. This broad level of pasture-land, high up above the rushing waters of the river, but coldly wooed by the faint northern sun, and fiercely swept by the wrathful northern wind, has been the golden bough to many an eager seeker. Against these pitiless cliffs full many a hope has hurtled, full many a heart has broken. Oh the eyes that have looked longingly hither from far Southern homes! Oh the thoughts that have vaguely wandered over these bluffs, searching among the shouting hosts, perhaps breathlessly among the silent sleepers, for household gods! Oh the cold forms that have lain upon these unnoting rocks! Oh the white cheeks that have pressed this springing turf! Oh the dead faces mutely upturned to God!

Struggle, conflict, agony, — how many of earth's Meccas have received their chrism of blood! Thrice and four times hopeless for humanity, if battle is indeed only murder, violence, lust of blood, or power, or revenge,—if in that wild storm of assault and defence and deathly hurt only the fiend and the beast meet incarnate in man. But it cannot be. Battle is the Devil's work, but God is there. When Montgomery cheered his men up their toilsome ascent along this scarcely visible path over the rough rocks, and the treacherous, rugged ice, was he not upborne by an inward power, stronger than brute's, holier than fiend's, higher than man's? When Arnold flung himself against this fortress, when he led his forlorn hope up to these sullen, deadly walls, when, after repulse and loss and bodily suffering and weakness, he could still stand stanch against the foe and exclaim, "I am in the way of my duty, and I know no fear!" was it not the glorious moment of that dishonored life? Battle is of the Devil, but surely God is there. The intoxication of excitement, the sordid thirst for fame and power, the sordid fear of defeat, may have its place; but there, too, stand high resolve, and stern determination,—pure love of country, the immortal longing for glory, ideal aspiration, god-like self-sacrifice, loyalty to soul, to man, to the Highest. The meanest passions of the brute may raven on the battle-field, but the sublimest exaltations of man have found there fit arena.

From the moment of our passing into the citadel enclosure, a young soldier has accompanied us,—whether from caution or courtesy,—and gives us various interesting, and sometimes startling information. He assures us that these guns will fire a ball eight miles, — a long range, but not so long as his bow, I fear. I perceive several gashes or slits in the stone wall of the buildings, and I ask him what they are. "Them are for the soldiers' wives hin the garrison," he replies promptly. I say nothing, but I do not believe they are for the soldiers' wives. A soldier's wife could not get through them. "How many soldiers in a regiment are allowed to have wives?" asks Halicarnassus. "Heighty, sir," is the ready response. I am a little horror-struck, when we leave, to see Halicarnassus hold out his hand as if about to give money to this brave and British soldier, and scarcely less so to see our soldier receive it quietly. But I need not be, for my observation should have taught me that small change — fees I believe it is called — circulates universally in Canada. Out doors and in, it is all one. Everybody takes a fee, and is not ashamed. You fee at the falls, and you fee at the steps. You fee the church, and here we have feed the army; and if we should call on the Governor-General, I suppose one would drop a coin into his outstretched palm, and he would raise his hat and say, "Thank you, sir." I do not know whether there is any connection between this fact and another which I noticed; but if the observation be superficial, and the connection imaginary, I shall be no worse off than other *voyageurs*, so I will hazard the remark, that I saw very few intellectual or elegant looking men and women in Quebec, or, for that matter, in Canada. Everybody looked peasant-y or shoppy, except the soldiers, and they were noticeably healthy, hale, robust, well kept; yet I could not help thinking that it is a poor use to put men to. These soldiers seem simply well-conditioned animals, fat and full-fed; but not nervous, intellectual, sensitive, spiritual. However, if the people of Canada are not intellectual, they are pious. "Great on saints here," says Halicarnassus. "They call their streets St. Genevieve, St. Jean, and so on; and when they have run through the list, and are hard up, they club them and have a Street of All Saints."

Canada seemed to be a kind of Valley of Jehoshaphat for Secessionists. We scented the aroma somewhat at Saratoga; nothing to speak of, nothing to lay hold of; but you were conscious of a chill on your warm loyalty. There were petty smirks and sneers and quips that you could feel, and not see or hear. You *sensed*, to use a rustic expression, the presence of a class that was not palpably treasonable, but rather half cotton. But at Canada it comes out all wool. The hot South opens like a double rose, red and full. The English article is cooler and supercilious. I say nothing, for my *rôle* is to see; but Halicarnassus and the Anakim exchange views with the greatest nonchalance, in spite of pokes and scowls and various subtabular hints.

"What is the news?" says one to the other, who is reading the morning paper.

"Prospect of English intervention," says the other to one.

"Then we are just in season to see Canada for the last time as a British province," says the first.

"And must hurry over to England, if we design to see St. George and the dragon tutelizing Windsor Castle," says the second; whereupon a John Bull yonder looks up from his 'am and heggs, and the very old dragon himself steps down from the banner-folds, and glares out of those irate eyes, and the ubiquitous British tourist, I have no doubt, took out his note-book, and put on his glasses and wrote down for home consumption another instance of the insufferable assurance of these Yankees.

"Where have you been?" I ask Halicarnassus, coming in late to breakfast.

"Only planning the invasion of Canada," says he, coolly, as if it were a mere pre-prandial diversion,—all of which was not only rude, but quite gratuitous, since, apart from the fact that we might not be able to get Canada, I am sure we don't want it. I am disappointed. I suppose I had no right to be. Doubtless it was sheer ignorance, but I had the idea that it was a great country, rich in promise if immature in fact, — a nation to be added to a nation when the clock should strike the hour, — a golden apple to fall into our hands when the fulness of time should come. Such inspection as a few days' observation can give, such inspection as British tourists find sufficient to settle the facts and fate of nations, leads me to infer that it is not golden at all, and not much of an apple; and I cannot think what we should want of it, nor what we should do with it if we had it. The people are radically different from ours. Fancy these dark-eyed beggars and those calm-mouthed, cowy-men in this eager, self-involved republic. They might be annexed to the United States a thousand times and never be united, for I do not believe any process in the world would turn a French peasant into a Yankee farmer. Besides, I cannot see that there is anything of Canada except a broad strip along the St. Lawrence River. It makes a great show on the map, but when you ferret it out, it is nothing but show — and snow and ice and woods and barrenness; and I, for one, hope we shall let Canada alone.

"I think we shall be obliged to leave Quebec to-morrow evening," says Halicarnassus, coming into the hotel parlor on Saturday evening.

"Not at all," I exclaim, promptly laying an embargo on that iniquity.

"Otherwise we shall be compelled to remain till Monday afternoon at four o'clock."

"Which we can very contentedly do."

"But lose a day."

"Keeping the Sabbath holy is never losing a day," replies his guide, philosopher, and friend, sententiously and severely, partly because she thinks so, and partly because she is well content to remain another day in Quebec.

"But as we shall not start till five o'clock," he lamely pleads, "we can go to church twice like saints."

"And begin at five and travel like sinners."

"It will only be clipping off the little end of Sunday."

Now that is a principle the beginning of which is as when one letteth out water, and I will not tolerate it. Short weights are an abomination to the Lord. I would rather steal outright than be mean. A highway robber has some claims upon respect; but a petty, pilfering, tricky Christian is a damning spot on our civilization. Lord Chesterfield asserts that a man's reputation for generosity does not depend so much on what he spends, as on his giving handsomely when it is proper to give at all; and the gay lord builded higher and struck deeper than he knew, or at least said. If a man thinks the Gospel does not require the Sabbath to be strictly kept, I have nothing to say; but if he pretends to keep it, let him keep the whole of it. It takes twenty-four hours to make a day, whether it be the first or the last of the week. I utterly reject the idea of setting off a little nucleus of Sunday, — just a few hours of sermon, and then evaporating into any common day. I want the good of Sunday from beginning to end. I want nothing but Sunday between Saturday and Monday. Week-days filtering in spoil the whole. What is the use of having a Sabbath-day, a rest-day, if Mondays and Tuesdays are to be making continual raids upon it? What good do dinner-party Sundays and travelling Sundays and novel-reading Sundays do? You want your Sunday for a rest, — a change, — a breakwater. It is a day yielded to the poetry, to the aspirations, to the best and highest and holiest part of man. I believe eminently in this world. I have no kind of faith in a system that would push men on to heaven without passing through a novitiate on earth. What may be for us in the future is but vaguely revealed, — just enough to put hope at the bottom of our Pandora's box; but our business is in this world. Right through the thick and thin of this world our path lies. Our strength, our worth, our happiness, our glory, are to be attained through the occupations and advantages of this world. Yet though discipline, and not happiness, is the main staple here, it is not the only product. Six days we must labor and do all work, but the seventh is a holiday. Then we may drop the absorbing now, and revel in anticipated joys, — lift ourselves above the dusty duties, the common pleasures that weary and ensoil, even while they ennoble us, and live for a little while in the bright clear atmosphere of another life, — soothed, comforted, stimulated by the sweetness of celestial harmonies.

> "O day most calm, most bright,
> The fruit of this, the next world's bud,
> The indorsement of Supreme delight,
> Writ by a Friend, and with his blood, —
> The couch of time, care's balm and bay, —
> The week were dark but for thy light,
> Thy torch doth show the way."

He is no friend to man who would abate one jot or tittle of our precious legacy.

Afloat in literature may be found much objurgation concerning the enforced strictures of the old Puritan Sabbath. Perhaps there was a mistake in that direction; but I was brought up on them, and they never hurt me any. At least I was never conscious of any harm, certainly of no suffering. As I look back, I see no awful prisons and chains and gloom, but a pleasant jumble of best clothes, — I remember now their smell when the drawer was opened, — and Sunday-school lessons, and baked beans, and a big red Bible with the tower of Babel in it full of little bells, and a walk to church two miles through the lane, over the bars, through ten-acres, over another pair of bars, through a meadow, over another pair of bars, by Lubber Hill, over a wall, through another meadow, through the woods, over the ridge, by Black Pond, over a fence, across a railroad, over another fence, through a pasture, through the long woods, through a gate, through the low woods, through another gate, out upon the high-road at last. And then there was the long service, during which a child could think her own thoughts, generally ranging no higher than the fine bonnets around her, but never tired, never willing to stay at home; and then Sunday school, and library-books, and gingerbread, and afternoon service, and the long walk home or the longer drive, and catechism in the evening and the never-failing Bible. O Puritan Sabbaths! doubtless you were sometimes stormy without and stormy within; but looking back upon you from afar, I see no clouds, no snow, but perpetual sunshine and blue sky, and ever eager interest and delight, — wild roses blooming under the old stone-wall, wild bees humming among the blackberry-bushes, tremulous sweet columbines skirting the vocal woods, wild geraniums startling their shadowy depths; and I hear now the rustle of dry leaves, bravely stirred by childish feet, just as they used to rustle in the October afternoons of long ago. Sweet Puritan Sabbaths! breathe upon a restless world your calm, still breath, and keep us from the evil!

Somewhat after this fashion I harangued Halicarnassus, who was shamed into silence, but not turned from his purpose; but the next morning he came up from below after breakfast, and informed me, with an air mingled of the condescension of the monarch and the resignation of the martyr, that, as I was so scrupulous about travelling on the Sabbath, he had concluded not to go till Monday afternoon. No, I said, I did not wish to assume the conduct of affairs. I had given my protest, and satisfied my own conscience; but I was not head of the party, and did not choose to assume the responsibility of its movements. I did not think it right to travel on Sunday, but neither do I think it right for one person to compel a whole party to change its plans out of deference to his scruples. So I insisted that I would not cause detention. But Halicarnassus insisted that he would not have my conscience forced. Now it would seem natural that so tender and profound a regard for my scruples would have moved me to a tender and profound gratitude; but nobody understands Halicarnassus except myself. He is a dark lane, full of crooks and turns, — a labyrinth which nobody can thread without the clew. That clew I hold. I know him. I can walk right through him in the darkest night without any lantern. He is fully aware of it. He knows that it is utterly futile for him to attempt to deceive me, and yet, with the infatuation of a lunatic, he is continually producing his flimsy little fictions for me as continually to blow away. For instance, when we were walking down the path to the steps of Montmorency, Grande called out in delight at some new and beautiful white flowers beside the path. What were they? I did not know. What are they, Halicarnassus? "Ah! wax-flowers," says he, coming up, and Grande passed on content, as would ninety-nine out of a hundred; but an indescribable something in his air convinced me that he was not drawing on his botany for his facts. I determined to get at the root of the matter.

"Do you mean," I asked, "that the name of those flowers is wax-flowers?"

"Of course," he replied. "Why not?"

"Do you mean," I persisted, confirmed in my suspicions by his remarkable question, "that you know that they are wax-flowers, or that you do not know that they are not wax-flowers?"

"Why, look at 'em for yourself. Can't you see with your own eyes?" he ejaculated, attempting to walk on.

I planted myself full in front of him. "Halicarnassus, one step further except over my lifeless body you do not go, until you tell me whether those are or are not wax-flowers?"

"Well," he said, brought to bay at last, and sheepishly enough whisking off the heads of a dozen or two with his cane, "if they are not that, they are something else." There!

So when he showed his delicate consideration for my conscience, I was not grateful, but watchful. I detected under the glitter something that was not gold. I made very indifferent and guarded acknowledgments, and silently detached a corps of observation. In five minutes it came out that no train left Quebec on Sunday!

V.

SO we remained over Sunday in Quebec, and in the morning attended service at the French Cathedral; and as we all had the American accomplishments of the "Nonne, a Prioresse," who spoke French

> "ful fayre and fetisly
> After the scole of Stratford atte Bowe,
> The Frenche of Paris was to hire unknowe,"

it may be inferred that we were greatly edified by the service. From the French, as one cannot have too much of a good thing, we proceeded without pause to the English Cathedral,—cathedral by courtesy?—and heard a sermon by a Connecticut bishop, which, however good, was a disappointment, because we wanted the flavor of the soil. And after dinner we walked on the high and sightly Durham terrace, and then went to the Scotch church, joined in Scotch singing, and heard a broad Scotch sermon. So we tried to worship as well as we could; but it is impossible not to be sight-seeing where there are sights to see, and for that matter I don't suppose there is any harm in it. You don't go to a show; but if the church and the people and the minister are all a show, what can you do about it?

As I sat listening in the French Cathedral to a service I but a quarter comprehended, the residual three fourths of me went wandering at its own sweet will, and queried why it is that a battle-ground should so stir the blood, while a church suffers one to pass calmly and coldly out through its portals. I do not believe it is total depravity; for though the church stands for what is good, the battle-field does not stand for all that is bad. The church does indeed represent man's highest aspirations, his longings for holiness and heaven. But the battle-field speaks not, I think, of retrogression. It is in the same line as the church. It stands in the upward path. The church and its influences are the dew and sunshine and spring rains that nourish a gentle, wholesome growth. Battle is the mighty convulsion that marks a geologic era. The fierce throes of battle upheave a continent. The church clothes it with soft alluvium, adorns it with velvet verdure, enriches it with fruits and grains, glorifies it with the beauty of blooms. In the struggle all seems to be chaos and destruction; but after each shock the elevation is greater. Perhaps it is that always the concussion of the shock impresses, while the soft, slow, silent constancy accustoms us and is unheeded; but I think there is another cause. In any church you are not sure of sincerity, of earnestness. Church building and church organization are the outgrowth of man's wants, and mark his upward path ; but you do not know of a certainty whether this individual edifice represents life, or vanity, ostentation, custom, thrift. You look around upon the worshippers in a church, and you are not usually thrilled. You do not see the presence and prevalence of an absorbing, exclusive idea. Devotion does not fix them. They are diffusive, observant, often apparently indifferent, sometimes positively *exhibitive.* They adjust their draperies, whisper to their neighbors, look vacant about the mouth. The beat of a drum or the bleat of a calf outside disturbs and distracts them. An untimely comer dissipates their attention. They are floating, loose, incoherent, at the mercy of trifles. The most inward, vital part of religion does not often show itself in church, though it be nursed and nurtured there. So when we go into an empty church, it is — empty. Hopes, fears, purposes, ambitions, the eager hours of men, do not pervade and penetrate those courts. The walls do not flame with the fire of burning hearts. The white intensity of life may never have glowed within them. No fragrance of intimate, elemental passion lingers still. No fine aroma of being clings through the years and suffuses you with its impalpable sweetness, its subtile strength. You are not awed, because the Awful is not there. But on the battle-field you have no doubt. Imagination roams at will, but in the domains of faith. Realities have been there, and their ghosts walk up and down forever. There men met men in deadly earnest. Right or wrong, they stood face to face with the unseen, the inevitable. The great problem awaited them, and they bent fiery souls to its solution. But one idea moved them all and wholly. They threw themselves body and soul into the raging furnace. All minor distractions were burned out. Every self was fused and lost in one single molten flood, dashing madly against its barrier to whelm in rapturous victory or be broken in sore defeat.

And it is earnestness that utilizes the good. It is sincerity that makes the bad not infernal.

Monday gave us the Indian village, — more Indian-y than village-y, — and the Falls of Lorette. For a description, see the Falls of Montmorency. Lorette is more beautiful, I think, more wild, more varied, more sympathetic, — not so precipitous, not so concentrated, not so forceful, but more picturesque, poetic, sylvan, lovely. The descent is long, broad, and broken. The waters flash and foam over the black rocks like a white lace veil over an Ethiop belle, and then rush on to other woodland scenes.

We left Quebec ignobly, crossing the river in a steamer to which the eminently English adjective *nasty* can fitly apply, — a wheezy, sputtering, black, crazy old craft, muddy enough throughout to have been at the bottom of the river and sucked up again half a dozen times. With care of the luggage, shawls, hackmen, and tickets, we all contrived to become separated, and I found myself crushed into one corner of a little Black Hole of Calcutta, with no chair to sit in, no space to stand in, and no air to breathe, on the sultriest day that Canada had known for years. What windows there were opened by swinging inwards and upwards, which they could not do for the press, and after you had got them up, there was no way to keep them there except to stand and hold them at arm's length. So we waddled across the river. Now we have all read of shipwrecks, and the moral grandeur of resignation and calmness which they have developed. We have read of drowning, and the gorgeous intoxication of the process. But there is neither grandeur nor gorgeousness in drowning in a tub. If you must sink, you at least would like to go down gracefully, in a stately ship, in mid-ocean, in a storm and uproar, bravely, decorously, sublimely, as the soldiers in Ravenshoe, drawn up in line, with their officers at their head, waving to each other calm farewells. I defy anybody to be graceful or heroic in plumping down to the bottom of a city river amid a jam of heated, hurried, panting, angry passengers, mountains of trunks, carpet-bags, and indescribable plunder, and countless stratifications of coagulated, glutinous, or pulverized mud. To the credit of human nature it must be said, that the sufferers kept the peace with each other, though vigorously denouncing the unknown author of all their woes. After an age of suffocation and fusion, there came a stir which was a relief because it was a stir. Nobody seemed to know cause or consequence, but everybody moved; so I moved, and bobbing, fumbling, groping through Egyptian darkness, stumbling over the beams, crawling under the boilers, creeping through the steam-pipes, scalping ourselves against the funnels, we finally came out gasping into the blessed daylight. "Here you are!" exclaimed cheerily the voice of Halicarnassus, as I went winking and blinking in the unaccustomed light. "I began to think I had lost my cane," — he had given it to me when he went to look up the trunks. "Why?" I asked faintly, not yet fully recovered from my long incarceration. "It is so long since I saw you, that I thought you must have fallen overboard," was his gratifying reply. I was still weak, but I gathered up my remaining strength and plunged the head of the cane, a dog's head it was, into his heart. His watch, or his Bible, or something interposed, and rescued him from the fate he merited; and then we rode over the miserable, rickety farther end of the Grand Trunk Railway, and reached Island Pond at midnight, — in time to see the magnificent Northern Lights flashing, flickering, wavering, streaming, and darting over the summer sky; and as the people in the Pond were many and the rooms few, we had plenty of time to enjoy the sight. It was exciting, fascinating, almost bewildering; and feeling the mystic mood, I proposed to write a poem on it, to which Halicarnassus said he had not the smallest objection, provided he should not be held liable to read it, adding, as he offered me his pencil, that it was just the thing, — he wanted some narcotic to counteract the stimulus of the fresh cold air after the long and heated ride, or he should get no sleep for the night.

I do not believe there is in our beautiful but distracted country a single person who is the subject of so cold-blooded, unprovoked, systematic, malignant neglect and abuse on any one point as the writer of these short and simple annals on this. If there is one thing in the whole range of human possibilities on which I pride myself, it is my poetry. I cannot do much at prose. That requires a depth, an equilibrium, a comprehension, a sagacity, a culture, which I do not possess and cannot command. Nor in the domestic drudgery line, nor the parlor ornament line, nor the social philanthropic line, nor the ministering angel line, can I be said to have a determinate value. As an investment, as an economic institution, as an available force, I suppose I must be reckoned a failure; but I do write lovely poetry. That I insist on: and yet, incredible as it may seem, of that one little ewe lamb have I been repeatedly and remorselessly robbed by an unscrupulous public, and a still more unscrupulous private. Whenever I come into the room with a sheet of manuscript in my hand, Halicarnassus glances at it, and if the lines are not all of the same length, he finds at once that he has to go and shovel a path, or bank up the cellar, or get in the wood, unless I have taken the precaution to lock the door and put the key in my pocket. When, by force or fraud, I have compelled a reluctant audience, he is sure to strike in by the time I have got to the second stanza, breaking right into the middle of a figure or a rapture, and asking how much more there is of it. I know of few things better calculated to extinguish the poetic fire than this. I regret to be obliged to say that Halicarnassus, by his persistent hostility, — I believe I may say, persecution, — has disseminated his plebeian prejudices over a very large portion of our joint community, and my muse consequently is held in the smallest esteem. Not but that whenever there is a church to be dedicated, or a centennial to be celebrated, or a picnic to be sung, or a fair to be closed, I am called on to furnish the poetry, which, with that sweetness of disposition which forms a rare but fitting background to poetic genius, I invariably do, to be praised and thanked for a week, and then to be again as before told, upon the slightest provocation, " You better not meddle with verses."

"You stick to prose." "Verses are not your forte." "You can't begin to come up with ——, and ——, and ——."

On that auroral night, crowned with the splendors of the wild mystery of the North, I am sure that the muse awoke and stirred in the depths of my soul, and needed but a word of recognition and encouragement to put on her garland and singing robes, and pour forth a strain which the world would not have willingly let die, and which I would have transferred to these pages. But that word was not spoken. Scorn and sarcasm usurped the throne of gentle cherishing, and the golden moment passed away forever. It is as well. Perhaps it is better; for on second thought, I recollect that the absurd prejudice I have mentioned has extended itself to the editor of this Magazine,* who jerks me down with a pitiless pull whenever I would soar into the empyrean, — ruling out with a rod of iron every shred of poetry from my pages, till I am reduced to the necessity of smuggling it in by writing it in the same form as the rest; when, as he tells poetry only by the capitals and exclamation-points, he thinks it is prose, and lets it go.

Here, if I may be allowed, I should like to make a digression. In an early stage of my journeying, I spoke of the pleasure I had taken in reading "The Betrothal" and "The Espousals." I can-

* The Atlantic Monthly.

not suppose that it is of any consequence to the world whether I think well or ill of a poem, but the only way in which the world will ever come out right is by every one's putting himself right; and I don't wish even my influence to seem to be thrown in favor of so objectionable a book as "Faithful Forever," a continuation of the former poems by the same author. Coventry Patmore's books generally are made up of poetry and prattle, but the poetry makes you forgive the prattle. The tender, strong, wholesome truths they contain steady the frail bark through dangerous waters; but "Faithful Forever" is wrong, false, and pernicious, root and branch, and a thorough misnomer besides. Frederic loves Honoria, who loves and marries Arthur, leaving Frederic out in the cold; whereupon Frederic turns round and marries Jane, knowing all the while that he does not love her and does love Honoria. What kind of a Faithful Forever is this? A man cannot love two women simultaneously, whatever he may do consecutively. If he ceases to love the first, he is surely not faithful forever. If he does not cease to love her, he is false forever to the second, — and worse than false. Marrying from pique or indifference or disappointment is one of the greatest crimes that can be committed, as well as one of the greatest blunders that can be made. The man who can do such a thing is a liar and a perjurer. I can understand that people should give up the people they love, but there is no possible shadow of excuse for their taking people whom they don't love. It is no matter how inferior Jane may be to Frederic. A woman can feel a good many things that she cannot analyze or understand, and there never yet was a woman so stupid that she did not know whether or not her husband loved her, and was not either stricken or savage to find that he did not. No woman ever was born with a heart so small that anything less than the whole of her husband's heart could fill it.

Moreover, apart from unhappy consequences, there is a right and a wrong about it. How dare a man stand up solemnly before God and his fellows with a lie in his right hand? and if he does do it, how dare a poet or a novelist step up and glorify him in it? The man who commits a crime does not do so much mischief as the man who turns the criminal into a hero. Frederic Graham did a weak, wicked, mean, and cowardly deed, not being in his general nature weak, wicked, mean, or cowardly, and was allowed to blunder on to a tolerable sort of something like happiness in the end. No one has a right to complain, for all of us get a great deal more and better than we deserve. We have no right to complain of Providence, but we have a right to complain of the poet who comes up and says not a word in reprobation of the meanness and cowardice, not a word of the cruelty inflicted upon Jane, nor the wrong done to his own soul; but veils the wickedness, excites our sympathy and pity, and in fact makes Frederic out to be a sort of sublime and suffering martyr. He was no martyr at all. Nobody is a martyr, if he cannot help himself. If Frederic had the least spirit of martyrdom, he would have breasted his sorrow manfully and alone. Instead of which, he shuffled himself and his misery upon poor simple Jane, getting all the solace he could from her, and leading her a wretched, almost hopeless life for years. This is what we are to admire! This is the knight without reproach! This is to be Faithful Forever! I suppose Coventry Patmore thinks Frederic is to be commended because he did not break into Honoria's house and run away with her. That is the only thing he could have done worse than he did do, and that I have no doubt he would have done if he could. I have no faith in the honor or the virtue of men or women who will marry where they do not love. I think it is just as sinful — and a thousand times as vile — to marry unlovingly, as to love unlawfully.*

There is this about mountains, — you cannot get away from them. Low country may be beautiful, yet you may be preoccupied and pass through it or by it without consciousness; but the mountains

* Some one just here suggests that it was Jane who was faithful forever, not Frederic. That indeed makes the title appropriate, but does not relieve the atrocity of the plot.

rise, and there is no escape. Representatives of an unseen force, voices from an infinite past, benefactors of the valleys, themselves unblest, almoners of a charity which leaves them in the heights indeed, but the heights of eternal desolation, raised above all sympathies, all tenderness, shining but repellent, grand and cold, mighty and motionless, — we stand before them hushed. They fix us with their immutability. They shroud us with their Egyptian gloom. They sadden. They awe. They overpower. Yet far off how different is the impression! Bright and beautiful, evanescent yet unchanging, lovely as a spirit with their clear, soft outlines and misty resplendence! Exquisitely says Winthrop: "There is nothing so refined as the outline of a distant mountain; even a rose-leaf is stiff-edged and harsh in comparison. Nothing else has that definite indefiniteness, that melting permanence, that evanescing changelessness. [I did not know that I was using his terms.] Clouds in vain strive to imitate it; they are made of slighter stuff; they can be blunt or ragged, but they cannot have that solid positiveness. Even in its cloudy, distant fairness, there is a concise, emphatic reality altogether uncloudlike."

Seeing them from afar, lovely rather than terrible, we feel that though between the mountain and its valley, with much friendly service and continual intercourse, there can be no real communion, still the mountain is not utterly lonely, but has yonder in the east its solace, and in the north a companion, and over toward the west its coterie. Solitary but to the lowly-living, in its own sphere there is immortal companionship, and this vast hall of the heavens, and many a draught of nectar borne by young Ganymede.

The Alpine House seems to be the natural caravansary for Grand Trunk travellers, being accessible from the station without the intervention of so much as an omnibus, and being also within easy reach of many objects of interest. Here, therefore, we lay over awhile to strike out across the mountains and into the valleys, and to gather health and serenity for the weeks that were to come, with their urgent claims for all of both that could be commanded.

Eastern Massachusetts is a very pretty place to live in, and the mutual admiration society is universally agreed by its members to be the very best society on this continent. Nevertheless, by too long and close adherence to that quarter of the globe, one comes to forget how the world was made, and, in fact, that it ever was made. We silently take it for granted. It was always there. Smooth, smiling plains, gentle hills, verdurous slopes, blue, calm streams, and softly wooded banks, — a courteous, well-bred earth it is, and we forget that it has not been so from the beginning. But here among the mountains, Genesis finds exegesis. We stand amid the primeval convulsions of matter, — the first fierce throes of life. Marks of the struggle still linger; nay, the struggle itself is not soothed quite away. No more unexceptionable surfaces, but yawns and fissures, chasms and precipices, deep gashes in the hills, hills bursting up from the plains, rocks torn from their granite beds and tossed hither and thither in some grand storm of Titan wrath, rivers with no equal majesty, but narrow, deep, elfish, rising and falling in wild caprice, playing mad pranks with their uncertain shores, treacherous, reckless, obstreperous. Here we see the changes actually going on. The earth is still a-making. More than one river, scorning its channel, has, within the memory of man, hewn out for itself another, and taken undisputed, if not undisturbed possession. The Peabody River, which rolls modestly enough now, seeming, indeed, a mere thread of brook dancing through a rocky bed by far too large for it, will by and by, when the rains come, rise and roar and rush with such impetuosity that these great water-worn stones, now bleaching quietly in the sun, shall be wrenched up from their resting-places, and whirled down the river with such fury and uproar that the noise of their crashing and rolling shall break in upon your dreams at night. Wild River, a little farther down, you may ford almost dry-shod, and in four hours it shall reach such heights and depths as might upbear our mightiest man-of-war. Many and many a gully, half choked with stones and briers, lurks under the base of an overtopping hill, and shows where a forgotten Undine lived and loved. The hills still bear the scars of their wounds. No soft-springing greenness veils the tortuous processes. Uncompromising and terrible, the marks of their awful rending, the agony of their fiery birth, still remain. Time, the destroyer of man's works, is the perfecter of God's. These ravages are not Time's; they are the doings of an early force, beneficent, but dreadful. It is Time's to soothe and adorn.

We connect the idea of fixity with the mountains, but they seem to me to be continually pirouetting with each other, — exchanging or entirely losing their identity. You are in the Alpine Valley. Around you stand Mount Hayes, so named in honor of a worthy housekeeper; the Imp, sobriquet of a winsome and roguish little girl, who once made the house gay; the Pilot range, — because they pilot the Androscoggin down to the sea, says one to whom I never appeal in vain for facts or reasons; Mount Madison, lifting his shining head beyond an opening niched for him in the woods of a high hill-top by Mr. Hamilton Willis of Boston, whom let all men thank. I thanked him in my heart every morning, noon, and night, looking up from my seat at table to that distant peak, where otherwise I should have seen only a monotonous forest line. Over against the sunset is Mount Moriah, and Carter, and Surprise. You know them well. You can call them all by name. But you have no sooner turned a corner than — where are they? Gone, — all changed. Every line is altered, every contour new. Spurs have become knobs. Peaks are ridges; summits, terraces. Madison probably has disappeared, and some Adams or Jefferson rises before you in unabashed grandeur. Carter and the Imp have hopped around to another point of the compass. All the lesser landmarks, as the old song says,

> "First upon the heel-tap, then upon the toe,
> Wheel about, and turn about, and do just so."

Your topography is entirely dislocated. You must begin your acquaintance anew. Fresh lines and curves, new forms and faces and chameleon tints, thrust you off from the secrets of the Storm-Kings. While you fancy yourself to be battering down the citadel, you are but knocking feebly at the outworks. You have caught a single phase, and their name is legion. Infinite as light, infinite as form, infinite as motion, so infinite are the mountains. Purple and intense against the glowing sunset sky, the Pilot range curves its strong outlines, or shimmers steely-blue in the noonday haze. Day unto day uttereth speech, and night unto night showeth knowledge of their ever-vanishing and ever-returning splendors. New every morning, fresh every evening, we fancy each pageant fairer and finer than the last. Every summer hour, a messenger from heaven, is charged with the waiting landscape, and drapes it with its own garment of woven light, celestial broidery. Sunshine crowns the crests, and stamps their kinship to the skies. Shadows nestle in the dells, flit over the ridges, hide under the overhanging cliffs, to be chased out in gleeful frolic by the slant sunbeams of the mellow afternoon. Clouds and vapors and unseen hands of heaven flood the hills with beauty. They have drunk in the warmth and life of the sun, they quiver beneath his burning glance, they lie steeped in color, gorgeous, tremulous, passionate; rosy red dropping away into pale gold, emeralds dim and sullen where they ripple down towards the darkness, dusky browns and broad reaches of blue-black massiveness, till the silent starlight wraps the scene with blessing, and the earth sitteth still and at rest.

On such an evening, never to be forgotten, we stood alone with the night. Day had gone softly, evening came slowly. There was no speech nor language, only hope and passion and purpose died gently out. Individualities were not, and we stood at one with the universe, hand in hand with the immortals, silent, listening. It was as if the heavens should give up their secret, and smite us with the music of the spheres. Suddenly, unheralded, up over the summit of Mount Moriah came the full moon, a silver disc, a lucent, steady orb, globular and grand, filling the valleys with light, touching all things into a hushed and darkling splendor. To us, standing alone, far from sight of human face or sound of human voice, it seemed the censer of God, swung out to receive the incense of the world.

Multifold mists join hands with the light to play fantastic tricks upon these mighty monarchs. The closing day is tender, bringing sacrifice and oblation; but the day of flitting clouds and frequent showers riots in changing joys. Every subordinate eminence that has arrogated to itself the sublimity of the distant mountain, against whose rocky sides it lay lost, is unmasked by the vapors that gather behind it and reveal its low-lying outlines. Every little dimple of the hills has its chalice of mountain wine. The mist stretches above the ridge, a long, low, level causeway, solid as the mountains themselves, which buttress its farther side, a *via triumpha*, meet highway for the returning chariot of an emperor. It rears itself from the valleys, a dragon rampant and with horrid jaws. It flings itself with smothering caresses about the burly mountains, and stifles them in its close embrace. It trails along the hills, floating in filmy, parting gauze, scattering little flecks of pearl, fringing itself over the hollows, and hustling against a rocky breastwork that bars its onward going. It wreathes upward, curling around the peaks and veiling summits, whose slopes shine white in the unclouded sun. It shuts down gray, dense, sombre, with moody monotone. It opens roguishly one little loop-hole, through which — cloud above, cloud below, cloud on this side and on that — you see a sweet, violet-hued mountain-dome, lying against a background of brilliant blue sky, — just for one heart-beat, and it closes again, gray, sheeted, monotonous.

Leaving the valley, and driving along the Jefferson road, you have the mountains under an entirely new aspect. Before, they stood, as it were, endwise. Now you have them at broadside. Mile after mile you pass under their solid ramparts, but far enough to receive the idea of their height and breadth, their vast material greatness, — far enough to let the broad green levels of the intervale slide between, with here and there a graceful elm, towering and protective, and here and there a brown farm-house. But man's works show puny and mean beside nature, which seems spontaneous as a thought. Man's work is a toil; nature's is a relief. Man labors to attain abundance; nature, to throw off superabundance. The mountain-sides bristle with forests; man drags himself from his valley, and slowly and painfully levels an inch or two for his use; just a little way here and there a green field has crept up into the forest. The mountain-chin has one or two shaven spots; but for the greater part his beard is still unshorn. All along he sends down his boon to men. Everywhere you hear the scurrying feet of little brooks, tumbling pell-mell down the rocks in their frantic haste to reach a goal; — often a pleasant cottage-door, to lighten the burden and cool the brow of toil; often to pour through a hollow log by the wayside, — a never-failing beneficence and joy to the wearied, trusty horses. From the piazza of the Waumbeck House — a quiet, pleasant, home-like little hotel in Jefferson, and the only one, so far as I know, that has had the grace to take to itself one of the old Indian names in which the region abounds, Waumbeck, Waumbek-Methna, Mountains of Snow-Foreheads — a very panorama of magnificence unfolds itself. The whole horizon is rimmed with mountain-ranges. The White Mountain chain stands out bold and firm, sending greeting to his peers afar. Franconia answers clear and bright from the south-west; and from beyond the Connecticut the Green hills make response. Loth to leave, we turn away from these grand out-lying bulwarks to front on our return bulwarks as grand and massive, behind whose impregnable walls we seem shut in from the world forever.

A little lyric in the epos may be found in a side-journey to Bethel, — a village which no one ever heard of, at least I never did, till now; but when we did hear, we heard so much and so well that we at once started on a tour of exploration, and found — as Halicarnassus quotes the Queen of Sheba — there was more of it than we expected.

The ride down in the train, if you are willing and able to stand on the rear platform of the rear car, is of surpassing beauty. The mountains seem to rise and approach in dumb, reluctant farewell. The river bends and insinuates, spreading out to you all its islands of delight. Molten in its depths, golden in its shallows, it meanders through its meadows, a joy forever. Bethel sits on its banks, loveliest of rural villages, and gently unfolds its beauties to your longing eyes. The Bethel House, — a large, old-fashioned conntry-house, with one of those broad, social second-story piazzas, and a well bubbling up in the middle of the dining-room, — think of that, Master Brooke! — a hotel whose landlord welcomes you with lemonade and roses (perhaps he would n't *you!*), — a hotel terrible to evil-doers, but a praise to them that do well, inasmuch as it is conducted on the millennial principle of quietly frightening away disagreeable people with high rates, and fascinating amiable people with reasonable ones, so that, of course, you have the wheat without the chaff, — a hotel where people go to rest and enjoy, and wear morning-dresses all day, and are fine only when they choose — indeed, you can do that anywhere, if you only think so. The idea that you must lug all your best clothes through the wilderness is absurd. A good travelling-dress, admissible of bisection, a muslin spencer for warm evenings, and a velvet bodice when you design to be gorgeous, will take you through with all the honors of war. Besides, there are always sure to be plenty of people in every drawing-room who will be sumptuously attired, and you can feast your eyes luxuriously on them, and gratefully feel that the work is so well done as to need no co-operation of yours, and that you can be comfortable with an easy conscience. Where was I? O, on the top of Paradise Hill, I believe, surveying Paradise, a little indistinct and quavering in the sheen of a summer noon, but clear enough to reveal its Pison, its Gihon, its Hiddekel and Euphrates, compassing the whole land of Havilah; or perhaps I was on Sparrowhawk, beholding Paradise from another point, dotted with homes and church-spires, rich and fertile, fair still, with compassing river and tranquil lake; or, more probable than either, I was driving along the highland that skirts the golden meadows through which the river purls, ruddy in the setting sun, and rejoicing in the beauty amid which he lives and moves and has his being. Lovely Bethel, fairest ornament of the sturdy mountain-land, tender and smiling as if no storm had ever swept, no sin ever marred, — an Arcadia that no one would ever leave but for the magic of the drive back to Gorham through piny woods, under frowning mountains, circled with all the glories of sky and river, — a drive so enticing, that, when you reach Gorham, straight back again you will go to Bethel, and so forever oscillate, unless some stronger magnet interpose.

A rainy day among the mountains is generally considered rather dismal, but I find that I like it. Apart from the fact that you wish, or ought to wish, to see Nature in all her aspects, it is a very beneficent arrangement of Providence, that, when eyes and brain and heart are weary with looking and receiving, an impenetrable barrier is noiselessly let down, and you are forced to rest. Besides, there are many things which it is not absolutely essential to see, but which, nevertheless, are very interesting in the sight. You would not think of turning away from a mountain or a waterfall to visit them, but when you are forcibly shut out from both, you condescend to homelier sights. For instance, I wonder how many frequenters of the Alpine House ever saw or know that there is a dairy in its Plutonian regions. A rainy day discovered it to us, and, with many an injunction touching possible dust, we were bidden into those mysterious precincts. A carpet, laid loose over the steps, forestalled every atom of defilement, and, descending cautiously and fearfully through portals and outer courts, we trod presently the adytum. It was a dark, cool, silent place. The floors were white, spotless, and actually fragrant with cleanliness. The sides of the room were lined with shelves, the shelves begemmed with bright pans, and the bright pans filled with milk, — I don't know how many pans there were, but I should think about a million, — and there was a mound of pails piled up to be washed, and cosey little colonies of butter, pleasant to eyes, nose, and mouth, and a curious machine to work butter over, consisting of something like a table in the shape of the letter V, the flat part a trough, with a wooden handle to push back and forth, and the buttermilk running out at the apex of the V. If the principle on which it is constructed is a secret, I don't believe I have divulged it; but I do not aim to let you know precisely what it is, only that there is such a thing. I hope now that every one will not flock down cellar the moment he alights from the Gorham train. I should be very sorry to divert the stream of travel into Mr. Hitchcock's dairy, for I am sure any great influx of visitors would sorely disconcert the good genius who presides there, and would be an ill requital for her kindness to us; but it was so novel and pleasant a sight that I am sure she will pardon me for speaking of it just this once.

Another mild entertainment during an intermittent rain is a run of about a mile up to the "hennery," which buds and blossoms with the dearest little ducks of ducks, broad-billed, downy, toddling, tumbling in and out of a trough of water, and getting continually lost on the bluff outside; little chickens and turkeys, and great turkeys, not pleasant to the eye, but good for food, and turkey-gobblers, stiffest-mannered of all the feathered creation; and geese, sailing in the creek majestic, or waddling on the grass dumpy; and two or three wild geese, tolled down from the sky, and clipped away from it forever; and guinea-hens, speckled and spheral; and, most magnificent of all, a peacock, who stands in a corner and unfolds the magnificence of his tail. Watching his movements, I could not but reflect upon the superior advantages which a peacock has over a woman. The gorgeousness of his apparel is such that even Solomon in all his glory was not arrayed in the like; yet so admirable is the contrivance for its management that no suspicion of mud or moisture stains its brilliancy. A woman must have recourse to clumsy contrivances of india-rubber and gutta-percha if her silken skirts shall not trail ignobly in the dust. The peacock at will rears his train in a graceful curve, and defies defilement.

Besides abundance of food and parade-ground, these happy fowls have a very agreeable prospect. Their abrupt knoll commands a respectable section of the Androscoggin Valley, — rich meadow-lands, the humanities of church-spire and cottage, the low green sweep of the intervale through which the river croons its quiet way under shadows of rock and tree, answering softly to the hum of bee and song of bird, — answering just as softly to the snort and shriek of its hot-breathed rival, the railroad. Doubtless the railroad, swift, energetic, prompt, gives itself many an air over the slow-going, calm-souled water-way, but let Monsieur

Chemin de Fer look to his laurels, — a thing of yesterday and to-morrow, — a thing of iron and oil and accidents. I, the River, descend from the everlasting mountains. I was born of the perpetual hills. I fear no more the heat o' the sun, nor the furious winter's rages; no obstacle daunts me. Time cannot terrify. My power shall never faint, my foundations never shrink, my fountains never fail.

> "Men may come, and men may go,
> But I go on forever."

And the railroad, pertinacious, intrusive, aggressive, is, after all, the dependent follower, the abject copyist of the river. Toss and scorn as it may, the river is its leader and engineer. Fortunes and ages almost would have been necessary to tunnel those mountains, if indeed tunnelling had been possible, but the river winds at its own sweet will. Without sound of hammer or axe, by force of its own heaven-born instincts, it has levelled its lovely way unerring, and wherever it goes, thither goes the railroad, to its own infinite gain. Railroads are not generally considered picturesque, but from the stand-point of that hennery, and from several other stand-points, I had no fault to find. Unable to go straight on, as the manner of railroads is, it bends to all the wayward little fancies of the river, piercing the wild wood, curling around the base of the granite hills, now let loose a space to shoot across the glade, joyful of the permission to indulge its railroad instinct of straightness; and, amid so much irregularity and headlong wilfulness, a straight line is really refreshing. Up the sides of its embankment wild vines have twisted and climbed, and wild-flowers have budded into bloom.

Berlin Falls is hardly a wet-day resource, but the day on which we saw it changed its mind after we left the hotel, and from clouds and promise of sunshine turned into clouds and certainty of rain. For all that, the drive along the river, within sound of its roaring and gurgling and rippling and laughing overflow of joy, with occasional glimpses of it through the trees, with gray cloud-curtains constantly dropping, then suddenly lifting, and gray sheets of rain fringing down before us, and the thirsty, parched leaves, intoxicated with their much mead of the mountains, slapping us saucily on the cheek, or in mad revel flinging into our faces their goblets of honey-dew, — ah! it was a carnival of tricksy delight, making the blood glow like wine. The falls, which chanced to be indeed no falls, but shower-swollen into rapids, are one of the most wonderful presentations of Nature's masonry that I have ever seen. It is not the water, but the rock, that amazes. The whole Androscoggin River gathers up its strength and plunges through a gorge, — a gateway in the solid rock as regular, as upright, as if man had brought in the whole force of his geometry and gunpowder to the admeasurement and excavation,

— plunges, conscious of imprisonment and the insult to its slighted majesty, — plunges with fierce protest and frenzy of rage, breaks against a grim, unyielding rock to dash itself into a thousand whirling waves; then rushes on to be again imprisoned between the pillars of another gorge, only less regular, not less inexorable, than the first; then, leaping and surging, it beats against its banks, and is hurled wrathfully back in jets of spray and wreaths of foam; or, soothed into gentler mood by the soft touch of mosses on the brown old rocks, it leaps lightly up their dripping sides, and trickles back from the green, wet, overhanging spray, and so, all passion sobbed away, it babbles down to its bed of Lincoln green, where Robin Hood and Maid Marian wait under the oaken boughs.

In the leaden, heavy air the scene was sombre, — tragic. In sunshine and shadows it must have other moods, perhaps a different character; I did not see the sunshine play upon it.

But the day of days you shall give to the mountain. The mountain, Washington, king of all this Atlantic coast, — at least till but just now, when some designing Warwick comes forward to press the claims of an ignoble Carolinian upstart, with, of course, a due and formidable array of feet and figures: but if they have such a mountain, where, I should like to know, has he been all these years? A mountain is not a thing that you can put away in your pocket, or hide under the eaves till an accident reveals its whereabouts. Verily our misguided brethren have much to do to make out a case; and, in the firm belief that I am climbing up the highest point of land this side the Rocky Mountains, I begin my journey.

Time was when the ascent of Mount Washington could be justly considered a difficult and dangerous feat; but the Spirit of the Age, who has many worse things than this to answer for, has struck in and felled and graded and curbed, till now one can ascend the mountain as safely as he goes to market. I consider this road one of the greatest triumphs of that heavily responsible spirit. Loquacious lovers of the "romantic" lament the absence of danger and its excitements, and the road does indeed lie open to that objection. He who in these latter days would earn a reputation for enterprise — and I fancy the love of adventure to be far less common than the love of being thought adventurous — must have recourse to some such forlorn hope as going up the mountain on the ice in midwinter, or coasting down on a hand-sled. But I have no inclination in that direction. I am willing to encounter risks, if there is no other way of attaining objects. But risks in and of themselves are a nuisance. If there is no more excellent way, of course you must clamber along steep, rugged stairways of bridle-paths, where a single misstep will send you plunging upon a cruel and bloody death; but so far as choice goes, one would much more wisely ride over a civilized road, where he can have his whole mind for the mountain, and not be continually hampered with fears and watchfulness for his own personal safety. It is a great mistake to suppose that discomfort is necessarily heroism. Besides, to have opened a carriage-way up the mountain is to have brought the mountain with all its possessions down to the cradle of the young and the crutch of the old, — almost to the couch of the invalid. I saw recorded against one name in the books of the Tip-top House the significant item, "aged eight months." Probably the youngster was not directly much benefited by his excursion, but you are to remember that perhaps his mother could not have come without him, and therein lay the benefit. The day before our ascent, a lady over seventy years old ascended without extreme fatigue or any injury. Several days after, a lady with apparently but a few weeks of earth before her, made the ascent to satisfy the longings of her heart, and gaze upon the expanses of this, before the radiance of another world should burst upon her view. If people insist upon encountering danger, they can find a swift river and ford it, or pile up a heap of stones and climb them, or volunteer to serve their country in the army: meanwhile, let us rejoice that thousands who have been shut away from the feast may now sit down to the table of the Lord.

This road, we were told, was begun about eight years ago, but by disastrous circumstances its completion was delayed until within a year or two. Looking at the country through which it lies, the only wonder is that it ever reached completion. As it is, I believe its proprietors do not consider it quite finished, and are continually working upon its improvement. Good or bad, it seems to me to be much the best road anywhere in the region. The pitches and holes that would fain make coaching on the common roads so precarious are entirely left out here. The ascent is continuous. Not a step but leads upward. The rise was directed never to exceed one foot in six, and it does not; the average is one foot in eight. Of course, to accomplish this there must be a great deal of winding and turning. In one place you can look down upon what seem to be three roads running nearly parallel along a ridge, but what is really the one road twisting to its ascent. Some idea of the skill and science required to engineer it may be gathered by looking into the tangled wilderness and rocky roughness that lie still each side the way. Through such a gnarled, knotted, interlaced jungle of big trees and little trees, and all manner of tangled twining undergrowths, lining the sides of precipices, or hanging with bare roots over them, concealing dangers till the shuddering soul almost plunges into them, the road-men carefully and painfully sought and fought their way. Up on the rocky heights it was comparatively easy, for, as one very expressively phrased it, every stone which they pried up left a hole and made a hole. The stone wrenched from above rolled below, and so lowered the height and raised the depth, and constantly tended to levelness. Besides, there were no huge tree-trunks to be extracted from the unwilling jaws of the mountain by forest-dentists, with much sweat and toil and pain of dentist if not of jaws. Since, also, the rise of one foot in six was considered as great as was compatible with the well-being and well-doing of horses, whenever the way came upon a knob or a breastwork that refused to be brought down within the orthodox dimensions, it must turn. If the knob would not yield, the way must, and, in consequence, its lengthened bitterness is long drawn out. A line that continually doubles on itself is naturally longer than one which goes straight to the mark. Mount Washington is little more than a mile high; the road that creeps up its surly sides is eight miles long. Frost and freshet are constant foes; the one heaves and cracks, and the other tears down through the cracks to undermine and destroy. Twenty-seven new culverts, we were told, had been made, within the space of a mile and a half, since last year; and these culverts are no child's play, but durable works, — aqueducts lined with stone and bridged with plank, large enough for a man to pass through with a wheelbarrow, and laid diagonally across the road, so that the torrents pouring down the gutter shall not have to turn a right angle, which they would gladly evade doing, but a very obtuse one, which they cannot in conscience refuse; and, as the road all the way is built a little higher on the precipice side than on the mountain side, the water naturally runs into the gutter on that side, and so is easily beguiled into leaving the road, which it would delight to destroy, and, roaring through the culvert, tumbles unwarily down the precipice before it knows what it is about.

I have heard it said, that the man who originated this road has since become insane. More likely he was insane at the time. Surely, no man in his senses would ever have projected a scheme so wild and chimerical, so evidently impossible of fulfilment. Projected it was, however, not only in fancy, but in fact, to our great content; and so, tamely but comfortably, an untiring cavalcade, we leave the peaceful glen set at the mountain's base, and wind through the lovely, lively woods, tremulous with sunshine and shadows, musical with the manifold songs of its pregnant solitudes, out from the woods, up from the woods, into the wild, cold, shrieking winds, among the blenched rocks and the pale ghosts of dead forests stiff and stark, up and up among the caverns, and the gorges, and the dreadful chasms, piny ravines black and bottomless, steeps bare and rocky leading down to awful depths; on and on, fighting with the maddened winds and the startled, wrathful wraiths, onward and upward till we stand on the bleak and shivering, the stony and soulless summit.

Desolation of desolations! Desolation of desolations! How terrible is this place! The shining mountain that flashed back to the sun his radiance is become a bald and frowning desert that appalls us with its barrenness. The sweet and sylvan approach gave no sign of such a goal, but the war between life and death was even then begun. The slant sunlight glinted through the jungle and bathed us with its glory of golden-green. The shining boles of the silvery gray birch shot up straight, and the white birch unrolled its patches of dead pallor in the sombre, untrodden depths. The spruces quivered like pure jellies tipped with light, sunshine prisoned in every green crystal. Myrtle-vines ran along the ground, the bunchberry hung out its white banner, and you scarcely saw the trees that lay faint and fallen in the arms of their mates. The damp, soft earth nourished its numerous brood, *Terræ omni parentis alumnos*, its own thirsty soul continually refreshed from springs whose sparkle we could not see, though the gurgle and ripple of their march sung out from so many hiding-places that we seemed to be

"Seated in hearing of a hundred streams."

Whole settlements of the slender, stately brakes

filled the openings, and the mountain-ash drooped in graceful curves over our heads, but gradually the fine tall trees dwindled into dwarfs, chilled to the heart by the silent, pitiless cold. Others battled bravely with the howling winds, which have stripped them bare on one side, while they seem to toss out their arms wildly on the other, imploring protection and aid from the valley-dwellers below. Up and up, and you come suddenly upon the "Silver Forest," a grove of dead white trees, naked of leaf and fruit and bud, bare of color, dry of sap and juice and life, retaining only their form, — cold set outline of their hale and hearty vigor; a skeleton plantation, bleaching in the frosty sun, yet mindful of its past existence, sturdy, and defiant of the woodman's axe; a frost-work mimicry of nature, a phantom forest. On and on, turning to overlook the path you have trodden, at every retrospect the struggle between life and death becomes more and more palpable. The Destroyer has hurled his winds, his frosts, his fires; and gray wastes, broken wastes, black wastes, attest with what signal power. But life follows closely, planting his seeds in the very footprints of death. Where blankness and bleakness seem to reign, a tiny life springs in mosses, rich with promise of better things. Long forked tongues of green are lapping up the dreary wastes, and will presently overpower them with its vivid tints. Even amid the blanched petrifaction of the Silver Grove fresh growths are creeping, and the day is not far distant that shall see those pale statues overtopped, submerged, lost in an emerald sea. Even among the rocks, the strife rages. Some mysterious principle inheres in the insensate rock, whose loss makes this crumbling, discolored, inert *débris*. Up you go, up and up, and life dies out. Chaos and ruin reign supreme. Headlong steeps yawn beside your path, losing their depths in darkness. Great fragments of rock cover all the ground, lie heaped, pile upon pile, jagged, gray, tilted into a thousand sharp angles, refusing a foothold, or offering it treacherously. Wild work has been here; and these gigantic wrecks bear silent witness of the uproar. It seems but a pause, not a peace. Agiocochook, Great Mountain of Spirits, rendezvous of departed souls, clothed with the strength and fired with the passions of the gods, — in what caverns under the cliffs do the wearied Titans rest? From what dungeons of gloom emerging shall they renew their elemental strife? What shall be the sign of their awaking to darken the earth with their missiles and deafen the skies with their thunder? And what daring of man is this to scorn his smiling valleys and adventure up into these realms of storm? No Titan he, yet the truest Titan of all, for he wrestled and overcame. No giant he, yet grander than the giants, since without Pelion or Ossa he has scaled heaven. Through uncounted æons the mountain has been gathering its forces. Frost and snow and ice and the willing winds have been its sworn retainers. Cold and famine and death it flaunted in the face of the besieger. Man is of a day, and the elements are but slippery allies. A spade and a compass are his meagre weapons; yet man has conquered. The struggle was long, with many a reconnoissance and partial triumph, but at length the victory is complete. Man has placed his hand on the monarch's mane. He has pierced leviathan with a hook. The secrets of the mountain are uncovered. His fastnesses conceal no treasures that shall not be spread out to the day. His bolts and bars of ice can no longer press back the foot of the invader. Yon gray and slender ribbon, that floats down his defiles, disappearing now over his ledges to reappear on some lower range, and lie lightly across the plateau, — that is his bridle of submission, his badge of servitude. Obedient to that, he yields up his hoarded wealth and pays tribute, a vassal to his lord. Men and women and little children climb up his rugged sides, and the crown upon his beetling brows is set in the circle of humanity.

In the first depression of abandonment one loses heart, and sees only the abomination of desolation; but gradually the soul lifts itself from the barren earth, and floats out upon the ocean, in which one stands islanded on a gray rock, fixed in seas of sunshine.

Whether you shall have a fair day or a foul is as may be. At the mountain's base they discreetly promise you nothing. It may be sunny and sultry down there, while storms and floods have at it on the peak. But mine was a day of days, — clear, alternating with cloudy. When you had looked long enough to dazzle and weary your eyes, a cloud would come and fold you about with opaqueness, and while you waited in the cloud, lo here! lo there! it flashed apart and shimmered yonder a blue sky, a brilliant landscape, and the distant level of the sea; or slowly its whiteness cleaved and rolled away, revealing a glorified mountain, a lake lying in the shadows, or the simple glen far down from which we came. It was constant change and ever-new delight.

But this going up mountains is a bad thing for the clouds. All their fleecy softness, all their pink and purple and pearly beauty, all the mystery of their unattainableness, is weighed in the balance and found to be fog, and by no means unapproachable. They will never impose upon us again. Never more will they ride through the serene blue, white-stoled cherubs of the sky. Henceforth there is very little sky about them. Sail away, little cloud, little swell, little humbug. Make believe you are away up in the curves of the sky. Not one person in fifty will climb a mountain and find you out. But I have been there, and you are nothing but fog, of the earth, earthy. And when

I sat in the cleft of a rock on the side of Mount Washington, every fibre chilled through with your icy moisture, I could with a good will have sent a sheriff to arrest you for obtaining love under false pretences. O you innocent, child-like cloud! heaving with warmth and passion as we saw, but a gray little imp, cold at the heart, and malignant, and inexorable, as we felt.

Felt it only when we did feel it, after all; for no sooner did it roll slowly away, and, ceasing to be a discomfort, turn into scenery, than all its olden witchery came back. I have had no more than a glimpse of the world from a mountain. The evening and the morning were the first day; and, till time shall be no more, the evening and the morning will be all that there is of the day, æsthetically considered. Yet at noon, — the most unfascinating hour, — and in the early afternoon, though you must needs fail of the twilight and its forerunners, there is an intensity of brilliance and an immensity of breadth, that, it seems to me, must be greater than if the view were broken up by light and shade. You are blinded with a flood of radiance, disturbed, or rather increased, by the flitting cloud-shadows. The mountains deepen in the distance, burning red in the glare of the sun, bristling with pines, mottled with the various tints of oak and maple relieving the soberer evergreens purpling on the slopes through a spiritual hazy glow, delicatest lavender, and pearl, where they lie scarcely pencilling the distant horizon. The clouds come sailing over, flinging their shadows to the plains,—shadows wavering down the mountain-sides with an indescribable sweet tremulousness, scudding over the lower summits, pursued by some frolicsome gale which we do not see, or resting softly in the dells, whose throbbing soothes itself to stillness in the grateful shade. And still, midway between heaven and earth, snatched up from the turmoil of the one into the unspeakable calm of the other, a great peace and rest sink into our souls. All around lies the earth, shining and silent as the sky, rippling in little swells of light, breaking into luminous points, rising into shapely shafts, spreading in limpid, molten silver, and all bathed, transmuted, glorified, with ineffable light, and sacred with eternal silence.

A bubble of home-life adheres to this stern peak. Determination and perseverance have built two stone cottages, rough and squat, where you may, if you have no mercy, eat a fine dinner that has been wearily dragged over eight miles of hillocky, rutty roads, and up eight miles of mountain; and drink without any compunction clear, cold water that the clouds have distilled without any trouble, and the rocks have bottled up in excellent refrigerators and furnish at the shortest notice and on the most reasonable terms, except in very dry weather. Or if a drought drinks up the supply in the natural wells, there is the Lake of the Clouds, humid and dark below, where you may see — I do not know — the angels ascending and descending. The angels of the summit are generally armed with a huge hoop, which supports their brace of buckets as they step cautiously over the cragged rock fragments. If you are ambitious to scale the very highest height, you can easily mount the roof of the most frivolously named Tip-top House, and change your horizon a fraction. If you are gregarious and crave society, you can generally find it in multifarious developments. Hither come artists with sketch-books and greedy eyes. Hither come photographers with instruments, and photograph us all, men, mountains, and rocks. Young ladies come, and find, after all their trouble, that "there is nothing but scenery," and sit and read novels. *Haud ignota loquor.* Young men come, alight from their carriages, enter the house, balance themselves on two legs of their chairs, smoke a cigar, eat a dinner, and record against their names, "Mount Washington is a humbug," — which is quite conclusive as concerning the man, if not concerning the mountain. There is one man in whose fate I feel a lively curiosity. As we were completing our descent, twisted, frowzy, blown to shreds, burnt faces, parched lips, and stringy hair, a solitary horseman might have been seen just commencing his ascent, — the nicest young man that ever was, — daintily gloved, patently booted, oilily curled, snowily wristbanded, with a lovely cambric (*prima facie*) handkerchief bound about his hyacinthine locks and polished hat. What I wish to know is, how did he get along? How did his toilette stand the ascent? Did he, a second Ulysses, tie up all opposing winds in that cambric pocket-handkerchief? or did Auster and Eurus and Notus and Africus vex his fastidious soul?

They say — I do not know who, but somebody — that Mount Washington in past ages towered hundreds of feet above its present summit. Constant wear and tear of frost and heat have brought it down, and its crumbling rock testifies to the still active progress of decay. The mountain will therefore one day flat out, and if we live long enough, Halicarnassus remarks, we may yet see the Tip-top and Summit Houses slowly let down and standing on a rolling prairie. Those, therefore, who prefer mountain to meadow should take warning and make their pilgrimage betimes.

It is likely that you will be the least in the world tired and a good deal sunburnt when you reach the Glen House; and, in defiance of all the physiologies, you will eat a hearty supper and go straight to bed, and it won't hurt you in the least. Nothing ever does among the mountains. The first you will know, you open your eyes and it is morning, and there is Mount Washington coming right in at your window, bearing down upon you with his seamed and shadowy massiveness, and you will forget how rough and rocky he was yesterday, and will pay homage once more to his dignity of imperial purple and his solemn royalty.

The moment you are well awake, you find you are twice as good as new, and after breakfast, if you are sagacious, no one belonging to you will have any peace until you are striking out into the woods again, — the green, murmurous woods, tenanted by innumerable hosts of butterflies in their sunny outskirts, light-winged Psyches hovering in the warm, rich air, stained and spotted and splashed with every bright hue of yellow and scarlet and russet, set off against brilliant blacks and whites; dark, cool woods carpeted with mosses thick, soft, voluptuous with the silent tribute of ages, and in their luxurious depths your willing feet are cushioned, — more blessed than feet of Persian princess crushing her woven lilies and roses; the tender, sweet-scented woods lighted with bright wood-sorrel, and fragrant with dews and damps; — to the Garnet pool, perhaps, first, where the water has rounded out a basin in the rock, and with incessant whirls and eddies has hollowed numerous little sockets, smooth and regular, till you could fancy yourself looking upon the remains of a petrified, sprawling, and half-submerged monster. Where the water is still, it is beautifully colored and shadowed with the surrounding verdancy and flickering light and motion. If you have courage and a firm foothold, if you will not slip on wet rock, and do not mind your hands and knees in climbing up a dry one, if you can coil yourself around a tree that juts out over a path you wish to follow, you can reach points where the action of the water, violent and riotous, can be seen in all its reckless force. But, "Don't hold on by the trees," says Halicarnassus; "you will get your gloves pitchy." This to me, when I was in imminent danger of pitching myself incontinently over the rocks, and down into the whirlpools!

Glen Ellis Falls we found in a random saunter, — a wild, white water-leap, lithe, intent, determined, rousing you far off by the incessant roar of its battle-flood, only to burst upon you as aggressive, as unexpected and momentary, as if no bugle-peal had heralded its onset. Leaning against a tree that juts out over the precipice, clinging by its roots to the earth behind, and affording you only a problematical support, you look down upon a green, translucent pool, lying below rocks thick-set with hardy shrubs and trees, up to the narrow fall that hurls itself down the cleft which it has grooved, concentrated and alert at first, then wavering out with little tremors into the scant sunshine, and meeting the waters beneath to rebound with many a spring of surge and spray. A strange freak of the water-nymphs it is that has fashioned this wild gulf and gorge, softened it with the waving of verdure, and inspirited it with the energy of eager waters.

Unsated we turn in again, thridding the resinous woods to track the shy Naiads hiding in their coverts. Over the brown spines of the pines, soft and perfumed, we loiter, following leisurely the faint warble of waters, till we come to the boiling rapids, where the stream comes hurrying down, and with sudden pique flies apart, on one side going to form the Ellis, on the other the Peabody River, and where in five minutes a stalwart arm could drain the one and double the other. Indeed, the existence of these two rivers seems to be a question of balance and coincidence and hair-breadth escapes. Our driver pointed out to us a tree whose root divides their currents. We pause but a moment on the crazy little bridge, and then climb along to the foot of the "Silver Cascade," farther and higher still, till we can see the little brook murmuring on its mountain way in the cliff above, and look over against it, and down upon it, as it streams through the rock, leaps adown the height, widening and thinning, spreading out over the face of the declivity, transmuting it into crystal, and veiling it with foam, leaping over in a hundred little arcs, lightly bounding to its basin below, then sweeping finely around the base of the projecting rock, and going on its way singing its song of triumph and content. A gentle and beautiful Undine, the worshipping boughs bend to receive its benediction. Venturesome mosses make perpetual little incursions into its lapping tide, and divert numberless little streams to trickle around their darkness, and leap up again in silver jets, clapping their hands for joy.

> "Now thanks to Heaven that of its grace
> Hath led me to this lonely place;
> Joy have I had, and going hence
> I bear away my recompense."

All good and holy thoughts come to these solitudes. Here selfishness dies away, and purity and magnanimity expand, the essence and germ of life. Sitting here in these cool recesses, screened from the sun, moist and musical with the waters, crusts of worldliness and vanity cleave off from the soul. The din dies away, and, with ears attuned to the harmonies of nature, we are soothed to summer quiet. The passion and truth of life flame up into serene but steadfast glow. Every attainment becomes possible. Inflated ambitions shrivel, and we reach after the Infinite. Weak desire is welded into noble purpose. Patience teaches her perfect work, and vindicates her divinity. The unchangeable rocks that face the unstable waters typify to us our struggle and our victory. Day by day the conflict goes on. Day by day the fixed battlements recede and decay before their volatile opponent. Imperceptibly weakness becomes strength, and persistence channels its way. God's work is accomplished slowly, but it is accomplished. Time is not to Him who commands eternity; and man, earth-born, earth-bound, is bosomed in eternity.

One and another has a preference, choosing rather this than that, and claiming the palm for a third; but with you there is no comparison. Each is perfect in his kind. Each bodies his own character and breathes his own expression.

O to lie here through long, long summer days, drenched with coolness and shadow and solitude, cool, cool, cool to the innermost drop of my hot heart's-blood!

Never!

Why do I linger among the mountains? You have seen them all. Nay, verily, I could believe that eyes had never looked upon them before. They were new created for me this summer-day. I plucked the flower of their promise. I touched the vigor of their immortal youth.

But mountains must be read in the original, not in translation. Only their own rugged language, speaking directly to eye and heart, can fully interpret their meaning. What have adjectives, in their wildest outburst, to do with rocks upheaved, furrows ploughed, features chiselled, thousands and thousands of years back in the conjectured past? What is a pen-scratch to a ravine?

For speed and ease cars are, of course, unsurpassed; but for romance, observation, interest, there is nothing like the old-fashioned coach. Cars are city; coaches are country. Cars are the luxurious life of well-born and long-pursed people; coaches are the stirring, eventful career of people who have their own way to make in the world. Cars shoot on independent, thrusting off your sympathy with a snort; coaches admit you to all the little humanities, every jolt harmonizes and adjusts you, till you become a locomotive world, tunefully rolling on in your orbit, independent of the larger world beneath. This is coaching in general. Coaching among the White Mountains is a career by itself, — I mean, of course, if you take it on the outside. How life may look from the inside I am unable to say, having steadfastly avoided that stand-point. When we set out it rained, and I had a battle to fight. First, it was attempted to bestow me inside, to which, if I had been a bale of goods, susceptible of injury by water, I might have assented. But for a living person, with an internal furnace well fed with fuel, in constant operation, to pack himself in a box on account of a shower, is absurd. What if it did rain? I desired to see how things looked in the rain. Besides, it was not incessant; there were continual liftings of cloud and vapor, glimpses of clear sky, and a constant changing of tints, from flashing, dewy splendor, through the softness of shining mists, to the glooms of gray clouds, and the blinding, uncompromising rain, — so that I would have ridden in a cistern rather than have failed to see it. Well, when the outside was seen to be a fixed fact, then I must sit in the middle of the coachman's seat. Why? That by boot, umbrellas, and a man on each side, I might be protected in flank, and rear, and van. I said audibly, that I would rather be set quick i' the earth, and bowled to death with turnips. If my object had been protection, I should have gone inside. This was worse than inside, for it was inside contracted. If I looked in front, there was an umbrella with rare glimpses of a steaming horse; on each side, the exhilarating view of a great coat; behind, a pair of boots. I might as well have been buried alive. No, the upper seat was the only one for a civilized and enlightened being to occupy. There you could be free and look about, and not be crowded; and I am happy to be able to say, that I am not so unused to water as to be afraid of a little more or less of it. So I ceased to argue, planted myself on the upper seat, grasped the railing, and smiled on the angry remonstrants below, — smiled, but *stuck!* "Let her go," said the driver in a savage, whispered growl, — not to me, but a little bird told me, — "let her go. Can't never do nothin' with women. They never know what 's good for 'em. When she 's well wet, then she 'll want to be dried." True, O driver! and thrice that morning you stopped to change horses, and thrice with knightly grace you helped me down from the coach-top, gentle-handed and smooth of brow and tongue, as if no storm had ever lowered on that brow or muttered on that tongue, and thrice I went into the village inns and brooded over the hospitable stoves, and dried my dripping garments; and when once your voice rang through the hostelrie, while yet I was enveloped in clouds of steam, did not the good young woman seize her sizzling flat-iron from the stove, and iron me out on her big table, so that I went not only dry and comfortable, but smooth, uncreased, and respectable, forth into the outer world again?

VI.

THUS I rode, amphibious and happy, on the top of the coach, with only one person sharing the seat with me, and he fortunately a stranger, and therefore sweet-tempered, and a very agreeable and intelligent man, talking sensibly when he talked at all, and talking at all only now and then. Very agreeable and polite; but presently he asked me in courteous phrase if he might smoke, and of course I said yes, and the fragrant white smoke-wreaths mingled with the valley vapors, and as I sat narcotized and rapt, looking, looking, looking into the lovely landscape, and looking it into me, twisting the jagged finger-ends of my gloves around the protruding ends of my fingers, — dreadfully jagged and forlorn the poor gloves looked with their long travel. I don't know how it is, but in all the novels that I ever read, the heroines always have delicate, spotless, exquisite gloves, which are continually lying about in the garden-paths, and which their lovers are constantly picking up and pressing to their hearts and lips, and treasuring in little golden boxes or something, and saying how like the soft glove, pure and sweet, is to the beloved owner; and it is all very pretty, but I cannot think how they manage it. I am sure I should be very sorry to have my lovers go about picking up my gloves. I don't have them a week before they change color; the thumb gapes at its base, the little finger rips away from the next one, and they all burst out at the ends; a stitch drops in the back and slides down to the wrist before you know it has started. You can mend, to be sure, but for every darn yawn twenty holes. I admire a dainty glove as much as any one. I look with enthusiasm not unmingled with despair at these gloves of romance; but such things do not depend entirely upon taste, as male writers seem to think. A pair of gloves cost a dollar and a half, and when you have them, your lovers do not find them in the summer-house. Why not? Because they are lying snugly wrapped in oiled-silk in the upper bureau-drawer, only to be taken out on great occasions. You would as soon think of wearing Victoria's crown for a head-dress, as those gloves on a picnic. So it happens that the gloves your lovers find will be sure to be Lisle-thread, and dingy and battered at that; for how can you pluck flowers and pull vines and tear away mosses without getting them dingy and battered? — and the most fastidious lover in the world cannot expect you to buy a new pair every time. For me, I keep my gloves as long as the backs hold together, and go around for forty-five weeks of the fifty-two with my hands clenched into fists to cover omissions.

Let us not, however, dismiss the subject with this apologetic notice, for there is another side. There is a basis of attack, as well as defence. I not only apologize, but stand up for this much-abused article. Though worn gloves are indeed less beautiful than fresh ones, they have more character. Take one just from the shop, how lank and wan it is, — a perfect monotony of insipidity; but in a day or two it plumps out, it curls over, it wabs up, it wrinkles and bulges and stands alone. All the joints and hollows and curves and motions of your hands speak through its outlines. Twists and rips and scratches and stains bear silent witness of your agitation, your activity, your merry-making. Here breaks through the irrepressible energy of your nature. Let harmless negatives rejoice in their stupid integrity. Genius is expansive and iconoclastic. Enterprise cannot be confined by kid or thread or silk. The life that is in you must have full swing, even if snap go the buttons and gray go the gloves. Truly, if historians had but eyes to see, the record of one's experience might be written out from the bureau-drawer. Happy a thousand times that historians have not eyes to see.

As to mending gloves, after the first attack it is time lost. Let one or two pairs, kept for show and state, be irreproachable; but the rest are for service, and everybody knows that little serving can be done with bandaged hands. You must take hold of things without gloves, or, which amounts to the same thing, with gloves that let your fingers through, or you cannot reasonably expect to take hold of things with any degree of efficiency.

So, as I was saying, I sat on the coach-top twisting my gloves, and I wished in my heart that men would not do such things as that very agreeable gentleman was doing. I do not design to enter on a crusade against tobacco. It is a mooted point in minor morals, in which every one must judge for himself; but I do wish men would not smoke so much. In fact, I should be pleased if they did not smoke at all. I do not believe there is any necessity for it. I believe it is a mere habit of self-indulgence. Women connive at it, because — well, because, in a way, they must. Men are childish, and, as I have said before, animal. I don't think they have nearly the self-restraint, self-denial, high dignity and purity and conscience that women have, — take them in the mass. They give over to habits and pleasures like great boys. People talk about the extravagance of women. But men are equally so, only their extravagance takes a different turn. A woman's is æsthetic; a man's is gross. She buys fine clothes and furniture. He panders to his bodily appetites. Which is worse? Women love men, and wish to be loved by them, and are miserable if they are not. So the wife lets her husband do twenty things which he ought not to do, which it is rude and selfish and wicked for him to do, rather than run the risk of loosening the cords which bind him to her. One can see every day how women manage,— the very word tells the whole story,—*manage* men, by cunning strategy, cajolery, and all manner of indirections, just as if they were elephants. But if men were what they ought to be, there would be no such humiliating necessity. They ought to be so upright, so candid, so just, that it is only necessary to show this is right, this is reasonable, this is wrong, for them to do it, or to refrain from the doing. As it is, men smoke by the hour together, and their wives are thankful it is nothing worse. They would not dare to make a serious attempt to annihilate the pipe. They feel that they hold their own by a tenure so uncertain, that they are forced to ignore minor transgressions for the sake of retaining their throne. I do not say that women are entirely just and upright, but I do think that the womanly nature is *good*-er than the manly nature; I think a very large proportion of female faults are the result of the indirect, but effective wrong training they receive from men; and I think, thirdly, that, take women just as they are, wrong training and all, there is not one in ten hundred thousand million who, if she had a faithful and loving husband, would not be a faithful and loving wife. Men know this, and act upon it. They know that they can commit minor immoralities, and major ones too, and be forgiven. They know it is not necessary for them to keep themselves pure in body and soul lest they alienate their wives. So they yield to their fleshly lusts. What an ado would be made if a woman should form the habit of smoking, or any habit whose deleterious effects extend through her husband's or her father's rooms, cling to his wardrobe, books, and all his especial belongings! Suppose she should even demand an innocent ice-cream as frequently as her husband demands a cigar, — suppose she should spend as much time and money on candy as he spends on tobacco, — would she not be considered an extravagant, selfish, and somewhat vulgar woman? But is it really any worse? Is it less extravagant for a man to tickle his nose, than for a woman to tickle her palate? If a cigar would enfoul the purity of a woman, does it not of a man? Why is it more noble for a man to be the slave of an appetite or a habit, than for a woman? Why is it less impure for a man to saturate his hair, his breath and clothing, with vile, stale odors, than for a woman? What right have men to suppose that they can perfume themselves with stenches, — for whatever may be the fragrance of a burning cigar, the after smell is a stench, — and be any less offensive to a cleanly woman than a woman similarly perfumed is to them? I have never heard that the female sense of smell is less acute than the male. How dare men so presume on womanly sufferance? They dare, because they know they are safe. I can think of a dozen of my own friends who will read this and bring out a fresh box of cigars, and smoke them under my very own face and eyes, and know all the time that I shall keep liking them; and the worst of it is, I know I shall, too. All the same, I do not thoroughly respect a man who has a habit of smoking.

But if men will smoke, as they certainly will, because they are animal and stubborn and self-indulgent and self-willed, let them at least confine their fireworks to their own apartments. If a wife would rather admit her fuliginous husband to her sitting-room than forego his society altogether, — as undoubtedly most women would, for you see it is not a question between a smoky husband and a clear husband, but between a smoky one and none at all, because between his wife and his cigar the man will almost invariably choose the cigar, — I have nothing to say. But don't let a man go into other people's houses and smoke, or, above all things, walk smoking by the side of women. No matter if she does give you permission when you ask it. You should not have asked it. We don't wish you to do it, you may be sure. It is a disrespectful thing. It partakes of the nature of an insult. No matter how grand or learned or distinguished you may be, don't do it. I saw once one of our Cabinet Ministers walking, with his cigar in his mouth, by the side of the wife of the British Minister, and it lowered them both in my opinion, though I don't suppose either of them would take it much to heart if they knew it. If you are walking in the woods or fields, it may be pardonable; but in the public streets no private compact can be of any avail. It is a public mark of disrespect. If you don't regard us enough to throw away or keep away your cigar when you join us, just don't join us. Keep your own side of the street. Nobody wants you; at least I don't. Walk alone if you like, or with whomsoever you can, but if you walk with me, you shall "behave yourself."

But how frightfully hungry these long coach stages make one! especially among the mountains. Famine lurks in that wild air, and is ever springing upon the unwary traveller. The fact was, however, that I had the most dreadful appetite all the way through. "Really," Halicarnassus would say, "it is quite charming to see you in such fine health," being at the same time reduced to a state of extreme disgust at my rapacity. He made an estimate, one day, that I had eaten since we started thirty-one and a half chickens, and I have no doubt I had; for chickens were my *piece de resistance* as well as *entreés;* and then they *were* chickens, not old hens, — little specks of darlings, just giving one hop from the egg-shell to the gridiron, and each time the waiter only brought you one bisegment of the speck, all of whose edible possibilities could easily be salted down in a thimble. I don't say this by way of complaint. A thimbleful of delicacy is better than a "mountain of mummy"; and here let me put in a word in favor of that much-abused institution, hotels. I cannot see why people should go about complaining of them as they do, both in literature and in life. My experience has been almost always favorable. In New York, in Saratoga, in Canada, all through the mountain district, we found ample and adequate entertainment for man and beast. Trollope brings his sledge-hammer down unequivocally. Of course there will be certain viands not cooked precisely according to one's favorite method, and at these prolonged dining-tables you miss the home-feeling of quiet and seclusion; but I should like to know if one does not travel on purpose to miss the home-feeling? If that is what he seeks, it would be so easy to stay at home. One loses half the pleasure and profit of travelling if he must box himself up with his own party. It is a good thing to triturate against other people occasionally. For eating, there are, to be sure, the little oval dishes that have so aroused Trollopian and other ire;

and your mutton, it is true, is brought to you slice-wise, on your plate, instead of the whole sheep set bodily on the table, — the sole presentation appreciated by your true Briton, who, with the traditions of his island home still clinging to him, conceives himself able, I suppose, in no other way to make sure that his meat and maccaroni are not the remnants of somebody else's feast. But let Britannia's son not flatter himself that so he shall escape contamination. His precautions are entirely fruitless. Suppose he does see the whole beast before him, and the very bean-vines, proof positive of first-fruits; cannot the economical landlord gather up heave-shoulder and wave-breast and serve them out to him in next day's mince-pie? Matter revolves, but is never annihilated. Ultimate and penultimate meals mingle in like the colors of shot-silk. Where there is a will, there is a way. If the cook is of a frugal mind, and wills you to eat driblets, driblets you shall eat, under one shape or another. The only way to preserve your peace, is to be content with appearances. Take what is set before you, asking no questions for conscience' sake. If it looks nice, that is enough. Eat and be thankful.

Trollope says he never made a single comfortable meal at an American hotel. The meat was swimming in grease, and the female servants uncivil, impudent, dirty, slow, and provoking. Occasionally they are a little slow, it must be confessed;

but I never met with one, male or female, who was uncivil, impudent, or provoking. If I supposed it possible that my voice should ever reach our late critic, whose good sense and good spirit Americans appreciate, and whose name they would be glad to honor if everything English had not become suspicious to us, the possible synonyme of Pharisaism or stupidity, I should recommend to him Lord Chesterfield's assertion, that a man's own good breeding is the best security against other people's bad manners. For the greasy meats, let him forego meats altogether and take chickens, and he will not find grease enough to soil his best coat, if he should carry the chick away in his pocket. We always found a sufficient variety to enable us to choose a wholesome and a toothsome dinner, with many tempting dainties, and scores of dishes that I never heard of before, and ordered dubiously by way of experiment, and tasted timorously in pursuit of knowledge. As for the corn-cake of the White Hills, if I live a thousand years, I never expect anything in the line of biscuit, loaf, or cakes more utterly satisfactory. It is the very ultimate crystallization of cereals, the poetry and rhythm of bread, brown and golden to the eye, like the lush loveliness of October, crumbling to the touch, unutterable to the taste. It has all the ethereal, evanishing fascination of a spirit. Eve might have set it before Raphael. You scarcely dare touch it lest it disappear and leave you disappointed and desolate. It is melting, insinuating, — a halo, hovering on the border-land of dream and reality, a beautiful but uncertain vision, a dissolving view. I said something of the sort to Halicarnassus one morning, and he said, Yes, it was — on my plate. And yet I have never had as much as I wanted of it, — never. The others were perpetually finishing their breakfast and compelling me, by a kind of moral violence, to finish mine. I made an attempt one morning, the last of my sojourn among the Delectable Mountains, when the opposing elements had left the table prematurely to make arrangements for departure, and startled the waiter by ordering an unlimited supply of corn-cake. Like a thunder-bolt fell on my ear the terrible answer: "There is n't any this morning. It is brown bread." Me miserable!

As we went to dinner, in a large dining-room, upon our arrival at the Glen House, it seemed to me that the guests were the most refined and elegant in their general appearance of any company I had seen since my departure, and I had a pleasant New-English feeling of self-gratulation. But we were drawn up into line directly opposite a row of young girls, who really made me very uncomfortable. They were at an advanced stage of their dinner when we entered, and they devoted themselves to making observations. It was not curiosity, or admiration, or astonishment, or horror. It was simply fixedness. They displayed no emotion whatever, but every time your glance reached within forty-five degrees of them, there they were "staring right on with calm, eternal eyes," and kept at it till the servants created a diversion with the dessert. Now, if there is anything that annoys and disconcerts me, it is to be looked at. Some women would have put them down, but I never can put anybody down. It is as much as I can do to hold my own, — and more, unless I am with well-bred people who always keep their equilibriums. One of these girls was the companion of a venerable and courtly gentleman; and the thought arose, How is it possible for this girl to have possibly that man's blood in her veins, certainly the aroma of his life floating around her, and the faultless model of his demeanor before her, and not be the mirror of every grace? Of how little avail is birth or breeding, if the instinct of politeness be not in the heart. That last remark, however, must "right about face" in order to be just. If the instincts be true, birth and breeding are comparatively of no account, for the heart will dictate to the quick eye and hand and voice the proper course; but where the instincts are wanting, breeding is indispensable to supply the deficiency. What one cannot do by nature he must do by drill. Sometimes it seems to me that young girlhood is intolerable. There is much delightful writing about it, — rose-buds and peach-blossoms and timid fawns; but the timid fawns are scarce in streets and hotels and schools, — or perhaps it is that the fawns who are not timid draw all eyes upon themselves, and make an impression entirely disproportionate to their numbers. I am thinking now, I regret to say, of New England young girls. Where they are charming, they are irresistible; they need yield to nobody in the known world. But I do think that an uninteresting Yankee girl is the most uninteresting of all created objects. Southern girls have almost always tender voices and soft manners. Arrant nonsense comes from their lips with such sweet syllabic flow, such little ripples of pronunciation and musical interludes, that you are attracted and held without the smallest regard to what they are saying. I could sit for hours and hear two of them chattering over a checker-board just for the pleasure of the silvery, tinkling music of their voices. But woe is me for the voices, male and female, that you so often hear in New England, — the harsh, strident voices, the monotonous, cranky, yanky, filing, rasping voices, without modulation, all rise and no fall, a monotonous discord, no soul, no feeling, and no counterfeit of it, loud, positive, angular, and awful. Indeed, I do not see how we New-Englanders are ever to rid ourselves of the reproach of our voices. The number of people who speak well is not large enough materially to influence the rest. Teachers do not teach speaking in school, — they certainly did not in my day, and I have no reason to suppose from results that they do now,—and parents do not teach it at home, for the simple reason, I suppose, that they do not know it themselves. We can all perceive the discord; but how to produce concord, that is the question. This one thing, however, is practicable: if sweetness cannot be increased, volume can be diminished. If you cannot make the right kind of noise, you can at least make as little as possible of the wrong kind. Often the discord extends to manners. Public conveyances and public places produce so many girls who are not gentle, retiring, shady, attractive. They are flingy and sharp and saucy, without being piquant. They take on airs without having the beauty or the brilliancy which alone makes airs delightful. They agonize to make an impression, and they make it, but not always in the line of their intent. Setting out to be picturesque, they become uncouth. They are ridiculous when they mean to be interesting, and silly when they try to be playful. If they would only leave off attitudinizing, one would be appeased. It may not be possible to acquire agreeable manners, any more than a pleasant voice; but it is possible to be quiet. But no suspicion of defect seems ever to have penetrated the bosoms of such girls. They act as if they thought attention was admiration. Levity they mistake for vivacity. Peevishness is elegance. Boldness is dignity. Rudeness is *savoir faire.*

Boisterousness is their vulgate for youthful high spirits.

And what, let me ask just here, is the meaning of the small waists that girls are cramming their lives into? I thought tight-lacing was an effete superstition clean gone forever. But again and again, last summer, I saw this wretched disease, this *cacoethes pectus vinciendi*, breaking out with renewed and increasing virulence; and I heard women — yes, grown-up women, old women — talking about the "Grecian bend," and the tapering line of the slender, willowy waist. Now, girls, when you have laced yourselves into a wand, do not be so infatuated as to suppose that any sensible person looks at you and thinks of willows. Not in the least. Probably he is wondering how you manage to breathe. As for the Grecian bend, you have been told over and over again that no Grecian woman, whether in the flesh or in the stone, ever bent such a figure, — spoiled if it was originally good, made worse if it was originally bad. You wish to be beautiful, and it is a laudable wish; but nothing is beautiful which is not loyal, truthful, natural. You need not take my simple word for it; I do not believe a doctor can anywhere be found who will say that compression is healthful, or a sculptor who will say that it is beautiful. Which now is the higher art, the sculptor's or the mantua-maker's? Which is most likely to be right, the man (or the woman) who devotes his life to the study of beauty and strength, both in essence and expression, or the woman who is concerned only with clipping and trimming? Which do you think takes the more correct view, he who looks upon the human body as God's handiwork, a thing to be reverenced, to be studied, to be obeyed, or one who admires it according as it varies more or less from the standard of a fashion-plate, who considers it as entirely subordinate to the prevailing *mode*, and who hesitates at no devices to bring it down to the desired and utterly arbitrary dimensions? This is what you do; you give yourselves up into the hands, or you yield submissively to the opinions, of people who make no account whatever of the form or the functions of nature; who have never made their profession a liberal one; who never seem to suspect that God had anything to do with the human frame; who, whatever station in life they occupy, have not possessed themselves of the first principles of beauty and grace, while you ignore the opinions, and lay yourself open to the contempt, of those whose natural endowments and whose large and varied culture give them the strongest claim upon your deference. The woman who binds the human frame into such shapes as haunted the hotels last summer, whether she be a dressmaker or a Queen of Fashion, is a woman ignorant alike of the laws of health and beauty; and every woman who submits to such distortion is either ignorant or weak.

The body is fearfully and wonderfully and beautifully made, a glorious possession, a fair and noble edifice, the Temple of the Holy Ghost, beautiful for its symmetry, for its adaptations, for its uses; and they who deform and degrade it by a fashion founded in ignorance, fostered by folly, and fruitful of woe, are working a work which can be forgiven them only when they know not what they do.

If this is not true, then I know not what truth is. If it is not a perfectly plain and patent truth, on the very face of it, then I am utterly incapable of distinguishing between truth and falsehood. Yet, if it is true, how account for the tight-lacing among women who are in a position to be just as intelligent as the doctor and the sculptor are.

Girls, I find a great deal of fault with you, do I not? But I cannot help it. You have been so written and talked and sung and flattered into absurdity and falsehood, that there is nothing left but to stab you with short, sharp words. If I chide you without cause, if I censure that which is not censurable, if I attribute to a class that which belongs only to individuals, if I intimate that ungentle voices, uncultivated language, and unpleasing manners are common when they are really uncommon, if I assume to demand more than every person who loves his country and believes in his countrywomen has a right to demand, on me be all the blame. But for ten persons who will give you flattery and sneers, you will not find one who will tell you wholesome truths. I will tell you what seems to me true and wholesome. Poetasters and cheap sentimentalists will berhyme and beguile you: I cannot help it; but I will at least attempt to administer the corrective of what should be common sense. The Magister was forced to let Von Falterle have a hand in Albano's education, but he "swore to weed as much out of him every day as that other fellow raked in." Dilettanteism prattles pleasant things to you: I want you to *be* everything that is pleasant. Where a fulsome if not a false adulation praises your slender grace, I shall not hesitate to tell you that I see neither slenderness nor grace, but ribs crushed in, a diaphragm flattened down, liver and stomach and spleen and pancreas jammed out of place, out of shape, out of use; and that, if you were born so, humanity would dictate that you should pad liberally, to save beholders from suffering; but of malice aforethought so to contract yourselves is barbarism in the first degree. And all the while I am saying these homely things, I shall have ten thousand times more real regard and veneration for you than your venders of dainty compliments. Regard? Jenny, Lilly, Carry, Hetty, Fanny, and the rest of you, dearly beloved and longed for, — Mary, my queen, my singing-bird, a royal captive, but she shall come to her crown one day, — my two Ellens, graceful and brilliant, — and you, my sweet-mouthed, soft-eyed islander, with your life deep and boundless like the sea that lulled you to baby-slumbers, — knowing you, shall I talk of regard? Knowing you, and from you, all, do I not know what girls can be? Sometimes it seems as if no one knows girls *except* me. If the world did but know you, if it knew what deeps are in you, what strength and salvation for the race lie dormant in your dormant powers, surely it would throw off the deference that masks contempt and give you the right hand of royal fellowship.

And if, in the world just as it is, girls did but know themselves! If they did but know how delightful, how noble and ennobling, how gracious and consoling and helpful, they might be, how wearied eyes might love to rest upon them, how sore hearts might be healed, and weak hearts strengthened, by the fragrance of their unfolding youth! There is not one girl in a thousand, North or South, who might not be lovely and beloved. I do not reckon on a difference of race in North and South, as the manner of some is. The great mass of girls whom one meets in schools and public places are the ones who in the South would be the listless, ragged daughters of poverty. The great mass of Southern girls that we see are the cherished and cultivated upper classes, and answer only to our very best. Like should always be compared with like. And I am not afraid to compare our best, high-born or lowly, with the best of any class or country. They have, besides all that is beautiful, a substantial substratum of sound sense, high principle, practical benevolence, and hidden resources. To behold them, they sparkle like diamonds. To know them, they are beneficent as iron. Let all the others emulate these. Let none be content with being intelligent. Let them determine also to be full of grace.

Among the girls that I saw on my journey who did not please me, there were several who did, — several of whom occasional glimpses promised pleasant things, if only there were opportunity to grasp them, — and two in particular who have left an abiding picture in my gallery. Let me from pure delight linger over the portraiture.

Two sisters taken a-pleasuring by their father, — the younger anywhere from fourteen to eighteen years old, the elder anywhere from sixteen to twenty; — this tall and slender, with a modest, sensitive, quiet, womanly dignity; that animated, unconscious, and entirely girlish; — the one with voice low and soft, the other low and clear. The father was an educated and accomplished Christian gentleman. The relations between the two were most interesting. His demeanor towards them was a charming combination of love and courtesy. Theirs to him was at once confiding and polite. The best rooms, the best seats, the best positions, were not assumed by them or yielded to them with the rude tyranny on one side and mean servility on the other which one too often sees, but pressed upon them with true knightly chivalry, and received, not carelessly as due and usual, but with affectionate deprecation and reluctance. Yet there was not the slightest affectation of affection, than which no affectation is more nauseous. True affection, undoubtedly, does often exist where its expression is caricatured, but the caricature is not less despicable. The pride of the father in his daughters was charming, — it was so natural, so fatherly, so frank, so irresistible, and never offensively exhibited. There was not a taint of show or selfishness in their mutual regard. They had eyes and ears and ready hands for everybody.

And they were admirable travellers. They never had any discomforts. They never found the food bad, or the beds hard, or the servants stupid. They never were tired when anything was to be done, or cross when it had been done, or under any circumstances peevish, or pouty, or "offish." They were ready for everything and content with anything. It was a pleasure to give them a pleasure, because their pleasure was so manifest. They looked eagerly at everything and into everything. The younger one, indeed, was so interested, that she often forgot her feet in her bright, observant eyes, which would lead her right on and on, regardless of the course of others, till she was discovered to be missing, a search instituted, and the wanderer returned smiling, but not disconcerted. They were never restless, uneasy, discontented, wanting to go somewhere else, or stay longer when every one was ready to go, or annoying their friends by rushing into needless danger. They never brought their personal tastes into conflict with the general convenience. They were thoroughly free from affectation. They never seemed to say or do anything with a view to the impression it would make, or even to suspect that they should make an impression. They were just fond enough of dress to array themselves with neatness, freshness, a pretty little touch of youthful ornament, and a very nice sense of fitness. But they were never occupied with their dress, and they had only as much as was necessary, — though that may have been a mother's care, — and what of them was not the result of wise parental care? They did not talk about *gentlemen*. They had evidently been brought up in familiar contact with the thing, so that no glamour hung about the word. They talked of places, people, books, flowers, all simple things, in a simple way. They were interested in music, in pictures, in what they saw and what they did. They sang and played with fresh, natural grace, to the delight and applause of all, and stopped soon enough to make us wish for more, but not soon enough to seem capricious or disobliging or pert.

But my pen fails to picture them to you as I saw them, — the one with her grave, sweet, artless dignity, a perfect Honoria, crowned with the soft glory of a dawning womanhood; the other docile and sprightly, careless, but not thoughtless. The beauty of their characters lay in the perfect balance. Their qualities were set off against each other, and symmetry was the result. They combined opposites into a fascinating harmony. They had all the ease and unconcern of refined association, without the smallest admixture of forwardness. They were neither bold nor bashful. They neither pampered nor neglected themselves, — neither fawned upon nor insulted others. They were everything that they ought to be, and nothing that they ought not to be, and I wished I could put them in a cage, and carry them through the country, and say: "Look, girls, this is what I mean. This is what I wish you to be."

We wound around the mountains, and wandered back and forth through the defiles like the Israelites in the wilderness, seeing everything that was to be seen, and a good deal more. We alighted incessantly, and struck into little wood-paths after cascades and falls, and got them too, sometimes. Of course we penetrated into the dripping Flume, and paddled on the Pool, or the Basin, — I have forgotten which they call it, — for a pool is but a big basin, and a basin a small pool. Of course we sailed and shouted on Echo Lake, and did obeisance to the Old Man of the Mountains and his numerous and nondescript progeny; for he has played pranks up there, and infected the whole surrounding country with a furor of personality. The Old Man himself I acknowledged. That great stone face is clearly and calmly profiled against the sky. His knee, too, is susceptible of proof, for I climbed it. A white horse in the vicinity of Conway is visible to the imaginative eye, and, by a little forcing of vision and conscience, one can make out a turtle, all but the head and legs. But there is a limit to all things, and when Halicarnassus held up both hands in astonishment and admiration, and declared that he saw a kangaroo, and then, in short and rapid succession, a rhinoceros, an armadillo, and a crocodile, I felt, in the words of General Banks, "We have now reached that limit," and shut down the gates upon credulity.

At a little village among the mountains we met our friends, and stopped a week or two, loath to leave the charmed spot. "Where?" Never mind. A place where the sun shines, and lavender-hued clouds whirl in craggy, defiant, thunderous masses around imperturbable mountain-tops; and vapors, pearly and amber-tinted, have not forgotten to float softly among the valleys; and evening skies fling out their pink and purple banner; and stars throb, and glow, and flash, with a radiant life that is not of the earth;—where great rivers have not yet put on the majesty of manhood, but trill over pebbles, curl around rocks, ripple against banks, waltz little eddies, spread dainty pools for gay little trout, dash up saucy spray into the eyes of bending ferns, mock the frantic struggles of lost flowers and twigs, tantalizing them with hope of a rest that never comes, and leap headlong, swirling and singing with a thousand silver tongues, down cranny and ravine in all the wild winsomeness of unchecked youth; — a land flowing with maple-molasses and sugar, and cider apple-sauce, and cheese new and old, and baked beans, and three sermons on Sundays, besides Sabbath school at noon, and no time to go home; and wagons with three seats, [*Mem.* Always choose the back seat, if you wish to secure a reputation for amiability,] three on a seat, two horses, and a colt trotting gravely beside his mother; roads all sand in the hollows and all ruts on the hills, blocked up by snow in the winter, and washed away by thunder-showers in the summer; — a land where carpets are disdained, latches are of wood, thieves unknown, wainscots and wells *au naturel*, women are as busy as bees all day and knit in the chinks, men are invisible till evening, girls braid hats and have beaux, and everybody goes to bed and to sleep at nine o'clock, and gets up nobody knows when, and cooks, eats, and "clears away" breakfast before other people have fairly rubbed their eyes open; where all the town are neighbors for ten miles round, and know your outgoings and incomings without impertinence, gossip without a sting, are intelligent without pretension, sturdy without rudeness, honest without effort, and cherish an orthodoxy true as steel, straight as a pine, unimpeachable in quality, and unlimited in quantity. God bless them! Late may they return to heaven, and never want a man to stand before the Lord forever!

Some people have conscientious scruples about fishing. I respect them. I had them once myself. Wantonly to destroy, for mere sport, the innocent life, in lake and river, seemed to me a cruelty and a shame. But people must fish. Now, then, how shall your theory and practice be harmonized? Practice can't yield. Plainly, theory must. A year ago, I went out on a rock in the Atlantic Ocean, held a line—just to see how it seemed,—and caught eight fishes; and every time a fish came up, a scruple went down. They were n't very large,—the fishes, I mean, not the scruples, though the same adjective might, perhaps, not unjustly be applied to both,—and I don't know that the enormity of the sin depends at all upon the size of the fish; but if it did, so entirely had my success convinced me of man's lawful dominion over the fish of the sea, that I verily believe, if a whale had hooked himself on the end of my line, I should have hauled him up without a pang.

I do not insist that you shall accept my system of ethics. Deplorable results might follow its practical application in every imaginable case. I simply state facts, leaving the "thoughtful reader" to generalize from them whatever code he pleases.

Which facts will partially account for the eagerness with which I, one morning, seconded a proposal to go a-fishing in a river about fourteen miles away. One wanted the scenery, another the drive, a third a chowder, and so on; but I — I may as well confess — wanted the excitement, the fishes, the opportunity of displaying my piscatory prowess. I enjoyed in anticipation the masculine admiration and feminine chagrin that would accompany the beautiful, fat, shining, speckled, prismatic trout into my basket, while other rods waited in vain for a "nibble." I resolved to be magnanimous. Modesty should lend to genius a heightened charm. I would win hearts by my humility, as well as laurels by my dexterity. I would disclaim superior skill, attribute success to fortune, and offer to distribute my spoil among the discomfited. Glory, not pelf, was my object. You may imagine my disgust on finding, at the end of our journey, that there was only one rod for the whole party. Plenty of lines, but no rods. What was to be done? It was proposed to improvise rods from the trees. "No," said the female element. "We don't care. We should n't catch any fish. We 'd just as soon stroll about." I bubbled up, if I did n't boil over. "*We* should n't, should *we?* Pray, speak for yourselves! Did n't I catch eight cod-fishes in the Atlantic Ocean, last summer?

Answer me that!" I was indignant that they should so easily be turned away, by the trivial circumstance of there being no rods, from the noble art of fishing. My spirits rose to the height of the emergency. The story of my exploits makes an impression. There is a marked respect in the tone of their reply. "Let there be no division among us. Go you to the stream, O Nimrod of the waters, since you alone have the prestige of success. We will wander quietly in the woods, build a fire, fry the potatoes, and await your return with the fish." They go to the woods. I hang my prospective trout on my retrospective cod, and march riverward. Halicarnassus, according to the old saw, "leaves this world, and climbs a tree," and, with jackknife, cord, and perseverance, manufactures a fishing-rod, which he courteously offers to me, which I succinctly decline, informing him in no ambiguous phrase that I consider nothing beneath the best as good enough for me. Halicarnassus is convinced by my logic, overpowered by my rhetoric, and meekly yields up the best rod, though the natural man rebels. The bank of the river is rocky, steep, shrubby, and difficult of ascent or descent. Halicarnassus bids me tarry on the bridge, while he descends to reconnoitre. I am acquiescent, and lean over the railing awaiting the result of investigation. Halicarnassus picks his way over the rocks, sidewise and zigzaggy along the bank, and down the river, in search of fish. I grow tired of playing Casabianca, and steal behind the bridge, and pick my way over the rocks, sidewise and zig-zaggy along the bank, and up the river, in search of "fun"; practise irregular and indescribable gymnastics with variable success for half an hour or so. Shout from the bridge. I look up. Too far off to hear the words, but see Halicarnassus gesticulating furiously, and evidently laboring under great excitement. Retrograde as rapidly as circumstances will permit. Halicarnassus makes a speaking-trumpet of his hands, and roars, "I've FOUND — a FISH! LEFT — him for — YOU — to CATCH! Come QUICK!" — and, plunging headlong down the bank, disappears. I am touched to the heart by this sublime instance of self-denial and devotion, and scramble up to the bridge, and plunge down after him. Heel of boot gets entangled in dress every third step, — fishing-line in tree-top every second; progress consequently not so rapid as could be desired. Reach the water at last. Step cautiously from rock to rock to the middle of the stream, — balance on a pebble just large enough to plant both feet on, and just firm enough to make it worth while to run the risk, — drop my line into the spot designated, — a quiet, black little pool in the rushing river, — see no fish, but have faith in Halicarnassus.

"Bite?" asks Halicarnassus, eagerly.

"Not yet," I answer, sweetly. Breathless expectation. Lips compressed. Eyes fixed. Five minutes gone.

"Bite?" calls Halicarnassus, from down the river.

"Not yet," hopefully.

"Lower your line a little. I'll come in a minute." Line is lowered. Arms begin to ache. Rod suddenly bobs down. Snatch it up. Only an old stick. Splash it off contemptuously.

"Bite?" calls Halicarnassus from afar.

"No," faintly responds Marius, amid the ruins of Carthage.

"Perhaps he will by and by," suggests Halicarnassus, encouragingly. Five minutes more. Arms breaking. Knees trembling. Pebble shaky. Brain dizzy. Everything seems to be sailing down the stream. Tempted to give up, but look at the empty basket, think of the expectant party and the eight cod-fish, and possess my soul in patience.

"Bite?" comes the distant voice of Halicarnassus, disappearing by a bend in the river.

"No!" I moan, trying to stand on one foot to rest the other, and ending by standing on neither; for the pebble quivers, convulses, and finally rolls over and expires; and only a vigorous leap and a sudden conversion of the fishing-rod into a balancing-pole save me from an ignominious bath. Weary of the world, and lost to shame, I gather all my remaining strength, wind the line about the rod, poise it on high, hurl it out into the deepest and most unobstructed part of the stream, climb up *pugnis et calcibus* on the back of an old boulder;

coax, threaten, cajole, and intimidate my wet boots to come off; dip my handkerchief in the water, and fold it on my head, to keep from being sunstruck; lie down on the rock, pull my hat over my face, and dream, to the purling of the river, the singing of the birds, and the music of the wind in the trees, (whether in the body I cannot tell, or whether out of the body I cannot tell,) of another river, far, far away, — broad, and deep, and seaward rushing, — now in shadow, now in shine, — now lashed by storm, now calm as a baby's sleep, — bearing on its vast bosom a million crafts, whereof I see only one, — a little pinnace, frail yet buoyant, — tossed hither and thither, yet always keeping her prow to the waves, — washed, but not whelmed. So small and slight a thing, will she not be borne down by the merchant-ships, the ocean steamers, the men-of-war, that ride the waves, reckless in their pride of power? How will she escape the sunken rocks, the treacherous quicksands, the ravening whirlpools, the black and dark night? Lo! yonder, right across her bows, comes one of the Sea-Kings, freighted with death for the frail little bark! Woe! woe! for the lithe little bark! Nay, not death, but life. The Sea-King marks the path of the pinnace. Not death, but life. Signals flash back and forth. She discerns the voice of the Master. He, too, is steering seaward, — not more bravely, not more truly, but in a directer course. He will pilot her past the breakers and the quicksands. He will bring her to the haven where she would be. O brave little bark! Is it Love that watches at the masthead? Is it Wisdom that stands at the helm? Is it Strength that curves the swift keel?——

"Hullo! how many?"

I start up wildly, and knock my hat off into the water. Jump after it, at the imminent risk of going in myself, catch it by one of the strings, and stare at Halicarnassus.

"Asleep, I fancy?" says Halicarnassus, interrogatively.

"Fancy," I echo, dreamily.

"How many fishes?" persists Halicarnassus.

"Fishes?" says the echo.

"Yes, fishes," repeats Halicarnassus, in a louder tone.

"Yes, it must have been the fishes," murmurs the echo.

"Goodness gracious me!" ejaculates Halicarnassus, with the voice of a giant; "how many fishes have you caught?"

"Oh! yes," waking up and hastening to appease his wrath; "eight,—chiefly cod."

Indignation chokes his speech. Meanwhile I wake up still further, and, instead of standing before him like a culprit, beard him like an avenging Fury, and upbraid him with his deception and desertion. He attempts to defend himself, but is overpowered. Conscious guilt dyes his face, and remorse gnaws at the roots of his tongue.

"Sinful heart makes feeble hand."

We walk silently towards the woods. We meet a small boy with a tin pan and thirty-six fishes in it. We accost him.

"Are these fishes for sale?" asks Halicarnassus.

"Bet they be!" says small boy, with energy.

Halicarnassus looks meaningly at me. I look meaningly at Halicarnassus, and both look meaningly at our empty basket.

"Won't you tell?" says Halicarnassus.

"No; won't you?" Halicarnassus whistles, the fishes are transferred from pan to basket, and we walk away as "chirp as a cricket," reach the sylvan party, and are speedily surrounded.

"O what beauties! Who caught them? How many are there?"

"Thirty-six," says Halicarnassus, in a lordly, thoroughbred way. "I caught 'em."

"In a tin pan," I exclaim, disgusted with his self-conceit, and determined to "take him down."

A cry of rage from Halicarnassus, a shout of derision from the party.

"And how many did you catch, pray?" demands he.

"Eight, — all cods," I answer, placidly.

Tolerably satisfied with our aquatic experience, we determined to resume the mountains, but in a milder form; before which, however, it became necessary to do a little shopping. An individual —one of the party, whose name I will not divulge, and whose identity you never can conjecture, so it is n't worth while to exhaust yourself with guessing—found one day, while she was in the country, that she had walked a hole through the bottom of her boots. How she discovered this fact is of no moment; but, upon investigating the subject, she ascertained that it could scarcely be said with propriety that there was a hole in her boots, but, to use a term which savors of the street, though I employ it literally, there *was n't anything else.* Now the fact of itself is not worthy of remark. That the integrity of a pair of boots should yield to the continued solicitations of time, toil, bone, and muscle, is too nearly a matter of everyday occurrence to excite alarm. The "irrepressible conflict" between leather and land has, so far as I know, been suspended but once since

"Adam delved and Eve span,"

and that was only an amnesty of forty years while the Israelites were wandering in the wilderness. But when you are deep in the heart of the country, scouring woods, climbing mountains, and fording rivers, having with your usual improvidence neglected to furnish yourself with stout boots, then a "horrid chasm," or series of chasms, yawning in the only pair that are of any use to you, presents a spectacle which no reflective mind can contemplate without dismay.

It was, in fact, with a good deal of dismay that the individual in question sat down, one morning, on "Webster's Unabridged,"—that being the only available seat in an apartment not over-capacious, —and went into a committee of the whole on the state of her boots. The prospect was not inviting. Heels frightfully wrenched and askew, and showing indubitable symptoms of a precipitate secession; binding frayed, ravelled, evidently stubborn in resistance, but at length overpowered and rent into innumerable fissures; buttons dislocated, dragged up by the roots, yet clinging to a forlorn hope with a courage and constancy worthy of a better cause; upper-leather (glove-kid), once black, now "the ashen hue of age," gray, purple, flayed, scratched, and generally lacerated; soles, ah! the soles! There the process of disintegration culminated. Curled, crisped, jagged, gaping, stratified, laminated, torn by internal convulsions, upheaved by external forces, they might have belonged to some pre-Adamic era, and certainly presented a series of dissolving views, deeply interesting, but not, it must be confessed, highly entertaining.

After arranging these boots in every possible combination, — side by side, heel to heel, toe to toe, — and finding that the result of each and every combination was that

> "No light, but rather darkness visible,
> Served only to discover sights of woe,"

the Individual at length, with a sigh, placed them, keel upwards, on the floor in front of her, and, resting her head in her hands, gazed at them with such a fixedness and rigidity that she might have been taken for an old Ouate, absorbed in the exercise of his legitimate calling. (The old Druidical order were divided into three classes, Druids, Bards, and Ouates. The Druids philosophized and theologized, the Bards harped and sang, and the Ouates divined and *contemplated the nature of things.* I thought I would tell you, as you might not know. I execrate the self-conceited way some people have of tossing off their erudite items and allusions in a careless, familiar style, as if it is such A B C to them that they don't for a moment think of any one's not understanding it. Worse still is it to have some jagged brickbat, dug up from a heap of Patagonian rubbish, flung at you with a "we have all heard of"; or to be turned off, just as your ears are wide open to listen to an old pre-Thautic myth, with "the story of —— is too familiar to need repetition." You have not the most distant conception what the story is, yet you don't like to say so, because it seems to be intimated that every intelligent person ought to know it; so you hold your peace. My dear, don't do it. Don't hold your peace. Don't let yourself be put down in that way. Don't be deceived. Half the time these people never knew it themselves, I dare say, more than a week beforehand, and have been puzzling their brains ever since for a chance to get it in.)

The Individual came at length to the conclusion that something must be done. Masterly inactivity must give way to the exigencies of the case. She had recourse to the "oldest inhabitant." A series of questions disclosed the important fact that —

"Well, there was a store at Sonose, about fourteen miles away; and Mr. Williams, he kept candy, and slate-pencils, and sich — "

"Do you suppose he keeps good thick boots?"

"O la! no."

"Do you suppose he keeps any kind of boots? You see I have worn mine out, and what am I to do?"

"Well, now, I thinks likely you can get 'em mended."

Individual brightens up. "O, do you?"

"Yes, there 's Mr. Jacobs, lives right out there, under the hill; he makes men's boots. I do' know as he could do yours, but you might try. Thinks likely he ain't got the tools, nor the stuff to do that sort of work with."

I did n't care for the tools or the stuff. All I wanted was the shoemaker; if I could find *him*, I had little doubt that all the rest would follow naturally from the premises. So I arranged my "sandal shoon and scallop-shell," and departed on my pilgrimage. The way had been carefully pointed out to me, but I never can remember such things more than one turn, or street, ahead; so I made a point of inquiring of every one I met, where Mr. Jacobs lived. Every one, by the way, consisted of a little girl with a basket of potatoes, and a man carrying the United States mail on his arm.

At length the Individual found the house as directed, and found also that it was no house, but a barn, and the shoemaker's shop was up-stairs, and the stairs were on the outside. If they were firm and strong, their looks were against them. Neither step nor balustrade invited confidence. The Individual stood on the lower one in a meditative mood for a while, and then gave a jump by way of test, thinking it best to go through the one nearest the ground, if she must go through any. An ominous creaking and swaying and cracking followed, but no actual rupture. The second step was tested with the same result; then the third and fourth; and, reflecting that appearances are deceitful, and recollecting the rocking-stone at Gloucester, Massachusetts, and the tower of Pisa, &c., the Individual shook off her fears, and ascended rapidly. Being somewhat unfamiliar with the etiquette of shoemaker's shops, she hesitated whether to knock or plunge at once into the middle of things, but decided to err on the safe side, and gave a very moderate and conservative rap. Silence. A louder knock. The door rattled.

Louder still. The whole building shook. Knuckles filed a caveat. Applied the heel of the dilapidated boot in her hand. Suffocated with a cloud of dust thence ensuing. Contemplated the nature of things for a while. Heard a voice. A man called from a neighboring turnip-field, "Arter Jake?"

"Yes, sir, — if he is a shoemaker" (to make sure of identity).

"Yes, well, he ain't to home."

"Oh."

"He 's gone to Sonose."

"When will he be back, if you please?"

"Wall, I can't say for sartain. Next week or week after, — leastwise 'fore the fair. Got a job?"

"Yes, sir, but I can't very well wait so long. Do you know of any shoemakers anywhere about?"

"Wall, ma'am, I do' know as I do. Folks is mostly farmers here. There 's Fuller, just moved, though. Come up from Exton yesterday. P'r'aps he 'll give you a lift. That 's his house right down there. 'T aint more 'n half a mile."

"Yes, sir, I see it. Thank you."

Individual descends from her precarious elevation, and marches to the attack of Fuller. A fresh-faced, good-natured-looking man is just coming out at the gate. His pleasant countenance captivates her at once, and, with a silent but intense hope that he may be the shoemaker, she asks if "Mr. Fuller lives here."

"Well," replies the man, in an easy, drawling tone, that harmonizes admirably with his face, "when a fellow is moving, he can't be said to live anywhere. I guess he 'll live here, though, as soon as the stove gets up."

I reciprocated his frankness with an engaging smile, and asked, in a confidential tone, "Do you suppose he would mend a shoe for me?"

I thought I would begin with a shoe, and, if I found him acquiescent, I would mount gradually to a boot, then to a pair. But my little subterfuge was water spilled on the ground.

"I don't know whether he would or not, but I know one thing."

"Well?"

"Could n't if he wanted to. Ain't got his tools here. They ain't come up yet."

"Oh! is that all?"

"*All?*"

"Yes; because, if you know how, I should n't think it would make so much difference about the tools. Could n't you borrow a gimlet or something from the neighbors?"

"A GIMLET?"

"Yes, or whatever you want, to make shoes with."

"An awl, you mean."

"Well, yes, an awl. Could n't you borrow an awl?"

"Nary awl."

"When will your tools come?"

"Well, I don't know; you see I don't hurry 'em up, because it's haying, and I and my men, we'd just as lieves work out of doors a part of the time as not. We don't mend shoes much. We make 'em mostly."

"Oh! that's better still; would you make me a pair?"

"Well, we don't do that kind of work. We work for the dealers. We make the shoes that they send down South for the niggers. We ain't got the lasts that would do for you."

Individual goes home, as Chaucèr says, "in doleful dumps," and determines to take the boots under her own supervision. First, she inks over all the gray parts. Then she takes some sealing-wax, and sticks down all the bits of cuticle torn up. Then, in lieu of anything better, she takes some white flannel-silk, — not embroidery-silk, you understand, but flannel-silk, harder twisted and stronger, such as is to be found, so far as I have tried, only in Boston, — and therewith endeavors to sew down the curled sole to its appropriate sphere, or rather plane. It is not the easiest or the most agreeable work in the world. How people manage to *make* shoes I cannot divine, for of all awkward things to get hold of, and to handle and manage after you have hold, I think a shoe is the worst. The place where you put a needle in does not seem to hold the most distant relation to the place where it comes out. You set it where you wish it to go, and then proceed *vi et armis et* thimble, but it resists your armed intervention. Then you rest the head of the needle against the window-sill, and push. You feel something move. Everything is going on and in delightfully. Mind asserts its control over matter. You pause to examine. In? Yes, head deep in the pine-wood, but the point not an inch further in the shoe. You pull out. The shoe comes off the needle, but the needle does not come out of the window-sill. You pull the silk, and break it, and then work the needle out as well as you can, and then begin again, — destroying three needles, getting your fingers "exquisitely pricked," and keeping your temper — if you can.

By some such process did the Individual, a passage of whose biography I am now giving you, endeavor to repair the ravages of time and toil. In so far as she succeeded in making the crooked places straight and the rough places plain, her efforts may be said to have been crowned with success. It is but fair to add, however, that the result did not inspire her with so much confidence but that she determined to lay by the boots for a while, reserving them for such times as they should be most needed, with a vague hope also that rest might exercise some wonderful recuperative power.

About five days after this, they were again

brought out, to do duty on a long walk. The event was most mournful. The flannel-silk gave way at the first fire. The soles rolled themselves up again in a most uncomfortable manner. At every step, the foot had to be put forward, placed lightly on the ground, and then drawn back. The walk was an agony. It so happened that on our return, without any intention, we came out of the woods in the immediate vicinity of the shoemaker's aforesaid, and the Individual was quite sure she heard the sound of his hammer. She remembered that, when she was young and at school, she was familiar with a certain "wardrobe," which was generally so bulging-full of clothes, that the doors could not, by any fair, straightforward means, be shut; but if you sprang upon them suddenly, taking them unawares, as it were, and when they were off their guard, you could sometimes effect a closure. She determined to try this plan on the shoemaker. So she bade the rest of the party go on, while she turned off in the direction of the hammering. She went straight into the shop, without knocking, the door being ajar. There he was at it, sure enough.

"Your tools have come!" she exclaimed, with ill-concealed exultation. "Now, will you mend my shoes?"

"Well, I don't know as I can, hardly. I'm pretty much in a hurry. What with moving and haying, I've got a little behindhand."

"Oh! but you must mend them, because I am going up on the mountain to-morrow, and I have no others to wear, and I am afraid of the snakes; so you see, you must."

"Got 'em here?"

Individual furtively works off the best one, and picks it up, — while his eyes are bent on his work, — as if she had only dropped it, and hands it to him. He takes it, turns it over, pulls it, knocks it, with an evident intention of understanding the subject thoroughly.

"Rather a haggard-looking boot," he remarks, after his close survey.

"Yes, but — "

"Other a'n't so bad, I suppose?"

"Well — I — don't know — that is — "

"Both bad enough."

"Yes, indeed," with an uneasy laugh.

"Let 's see the other one." The other one is produced, and examined in silence.

"Are *you* going to wear them boots up the mountain?" with a tone that said very plainly, "Of course you 're not."

"Why, yes, I *was* going to wear them. Don't you think they will do?"

"I would n't trust *my* feet in 'em."

"O—h! *Are* there snakes? Do you think snakes could bite through them?"

A shake of the head, and a little, low, plaintive whistle, is the only reply, but they speak in thunder tones of boa-constrictors, anacondas, and cobra di capellos.

"They were very good and stout when I had them. I called them very stout shoes."

"O yes, they 're made of good material, but you see they 're worn out. I don't believe I could mend them worth while. The stitches would tear right out."

"But could n't you, somehow, glue on a pair of soles? any way to make them stick. I 'll pay you anything, if you 'll only make them last till I go home, or even till I get down the mountain. Now, I am sure you can do it, if you will only think so. Don't you know Kossuth says, 'Nothing is difficult to him who wills'?"

He was evidently moved by the earnestness of the appeal. "I suppose they 'd be worth more to you now than half a dozen pair when you get home."

"Worth! why, they would be of inestimable value. Think of the snakes! I don't care how you do them, nor how you make them look. If you will only glue on, or sew on, or nail on, or rivet on, something that is thick and will stick, I will pay you, and be grateful to you through the remainder of my natural life."

"Well, — you leave 'em, and come over again this afternoon, and if I can do anything, I 'll do it by that time."

"Oh! I am so much obliged to you"; and I

went away in high spirits, just putting my head back through the door to say, "Now you persevere, and I am sure you will succeed."

I was as happy as a queen. To be sure, I had to walk home without any shoes; but the grass was as soft as velvet, and the dust as clean as sand, and it did not hurt me in the least. To be sure, he had not promised to mend them; but I had faith in him, and how did it turn out? Verily, I should not have known the boots, if I had seen only the soles. They were clipped, and shaved, and underpinned, and smoothed, and looked as if they had taken out "a new lease of life."

"I don't suppose they will last you as long as I have been doing them," he remarked, with unprofessional frankness. I did not believe him, and indeed his prophecy was not true, for they are in existence yet, and I never disposed of "a quarter" in my life with more satisfaction than I dropped it that day into his benevolent hand.

A thousand years hence, when New Hampshire shall have become as populous as Babylon, this sketch may become the foundation of some "Tale of Beowulf" or other. At any rate here it is ready.

Of all the White Mountains, the one of which you hear least said is Agamenticus, and perhaps justly, for it is not one of the White Mountains, but an isolated peak by itself. My information concerning it is founded partly on observation, partly on testimony, and partly on memory, supported where she is weak by conjecture. These three sources, however, mingle their waters together somewhat too intricately for accurate analysis, and I shall, therefore, waive distinctions, and plant myself on the broad basis of assertion, warning the future historian and antiquary not to take this paper as conclusive without extraneous props.

Agamenticus is a huge rock rising abruptly from a level country along New Hampshire's half-yard of sea-shore. As it is the only large rock on the eastern coast of the United States, it is an invaluable beacon to mariners. The first city ever built on the American continent was laid out at its base, and the remains are now visible from its summit; but, as funds failed, and the founders were killed by the Indians, it was never completed, in fact was never begun, only laid out. To the east I was certain I saw Boar's Head and a steamer steaming towards it, till I was assured that in such case the steamer must have been steaming over the corn-fields, because, unlike Ænon near to Salim, there was no water there. So I suppose it must have been

"A painted ship upon a painted ocean."

The ascent to Agamenticus is sidling and uncertain so long as you hug your carriage; but, leaving that, and confiding yourself to Mother Earth, you gather both strength and equipoise from the touch, and, with a little boy to guide you through the woods and over the rocks, you will find the ascent quite pleasant and safe, if you are careful not to slip down, which you will be sure to do on your descent, whether you are careful or not. At the summit of the mountain is a fine and flourishing growth of muskmelons, sugar, and currant-wine. At least we found them there in profusion.

Agamenticus has its legend. Many years ago, the Indians, to avert the plague, drove twenty thousand cattle to the top of the mountain, and there sacrificed them to the Great Spirit. We could still discern traces of the sacrifice, — burnt stones, bits of green-black glass, and charred pine branches. Then we came home.

Perthes says, "That part of a journey which remains after the travelling is the journey." What remains of my journey, for me, for you? Will any live over again a pleasant past and look more cheerily into a lowering future for these wayward words of mine? Are there clouded lives that will find a little sunshine; pent-up souls that will catch a breath of blooms in my rambling record? Are there lips that will relax their tightness; eyes that will lose for a moment the shadow of remembered pain? Then, indeed, the best part of my journey is yet to come.

A Call

to my Countrywomen.

A

Call to my Countrywomen.

IN the newspapers and magazines you shall see many poems and papers — written by women who meekly term themselves weak, and modestly profess to represent only the weak among their sex — discussing the duties which the weak owe to their country in days like these. The invariable conclusion is, that, though they cannot fight, because they are not men, — or go down to nurse the sick and wounded, because they have children to take care of, — or write effectively, because they do not know how, — or do any great and heroic thing, because they have not the ability, — they can pray; and they generally do close with a melodious and beautiful prayer. Now praying is a good thing. It is, in fact, the very best thing in the world to do, and there is no danger of our having too much of it; but if women, weak or strong, consider that praying is all they can or ought to do for their country, and so settle down contented with that, they make as great a mistake as if they did not pray at all. True, women cannot fight, and there is no call for any great number of female nurses; notwithstanding this, the issue of this war depends quite as much upon American women as upon American men, — and depends, too, not upon the few who write, but upon the many who do not. The women of the Revolution were not only Mrs. Adams, Mrs. Reed, and Mrs. Schuyler, but the wives of the farmers and shoemakers and blacksmiths everywhere. It is not Mrs. Stowe, or Mrs. Howe, or Miss Stevenson, or Miss Dix, alone, who is to save the country, but the thousands upon thousands who are at this moment darning stockings, tending babies, sweeping floors. It is to them I speak. It is they whom I wish to get hold of; for in their hands lies slumbering the future of this nation.

Shall I say that the women of to-day have not come up to the level of to-day, — that they do not stand abreast with its issues, — they do not rise to the height of its great argument? I do not forget what you have done. I have beheld, O Dorcases, with admiration and gratitude, the coats and garments, the lint and bandages, which you have made. If you could have finished the war with your needles, it would have been finished long ago; but stitching does not crush rebellion, does not annihilate treason, or hew traitors in pieces before the Lord. Excellent as far as it goes, it stops fearfully short of the goal. This ought ye to do, but there are other things which you ought not to leave undone. The war cannot be finished by sheets and pillow-cases. Sometimes I am tempted to believe that it cannot be finished till we have flung them all away. When I read of the rebels fighting bare-headed, bare-footed, haggard, and unshorn, in rags and filth, — fighting bravely, heroically, successfully, — I am ready to make a burnt-offering of our stacks of clothing. I feel and fear that we must come down, as they have done, to a recklessness of all incidentals, down to the rough and rugged fastnesses of life, down to the very gates of death itself, before we shall be ready and worthy to win victories. Yet it is not so, for the hardest fights the earth has ever known have been made by the delicate-handed and purple-robed. So, in the ultimate analysis, it is neither gold-lace nor rags that overpower obstacles, but the fiery soul that consumes both in the intensity of its furnace-heat, bending impossibilities to the ends of its passionate purpose.

This soul of fire is what I wish to see kindled in our women, — burning white and strong and steady, through all weakness, timidity, vacillation, treachery in church or state or press or parlor, scorching, blasting, annihilating whatsoever loveth and maketh a lie, — extinguished by no tempest of defeat, no drizzle of delay, but glowing on its steadfast path till it shall have cleared through the abomination of our desolation a highway for the Prince of Peace.

O my countrywomen, I long to see you stand under the time and bear it up in your strong hearts, and not need to be borne up through it. I wish you to stimulate, and not crave stimulants from others. I wish you to be the consolers, the encouragers, the sustainers, and not tremble in perpetual need of consolation and encouragement. When men's brains are knotted and their brows corrugated with fearful looking for and hearing of financial crises, military disasters, and any and every form of national calamity consequent upon the war, come you out to meet them, serene and smiling and unafraid. And let your smile be no formal distortion of your lips, but a bright ray from the sunshine in your heart. Take not acquiescently, but joyfully, the spoiling of your goods. Not only look poverty in the face with high disdain, but embrace it with gladness and welcome. The loss is but for a moment; the gain is for all time. Go further than this. Consecrate to a holy cause not only the incidentals of life, but life itself. Father, husband, child, — I do not say, Give them up to toil, exposure, suffering, death, without a murmur; — that implies reluctance. I rather say, Urge them to the offering; fill them with sacred fury; fire them with irresistible desire; strengthen them to heroic will. Look not on details, the present, the trivial, the fleeting aspects of our conflict, but fix your ardent gaze on its eternal side. Be not resigned, but rejoicing. Be spontaneous and exultant. Be large and lofty. Count it all joy that you are reckoned worthy to suffer in a grand and righteous cause. Give thanks evermore that you were born in this time; and *because* it is dark, be you the light of the world.

And follow the soldier to the battle-field with your spirit. The great army of letters that marches southward with every morning sun is a powerful engine of war. Fill them with tears and sighs, lament separation and suffering, dwell on your loneliness and fears, mourn over the dishonesty of contractors and the incompetency of leaders, doubt if the South will ever be conquered, and foresee financial ruin, and you will damp the powder and dull the swords that ought to deal death upon the foe. Write as tenderly as you will. In camp, the roughest man idealizes his far-off home, and every word of love uplifts him to a lover. But let your tenderness unfold its sunny side, and keep the shadows for His pity who knows the end from the beginning, and whom no fore-boding can dishearten. Glory in your tribulation. Show your soldier that his unflinching courage, his undying fortitude, are your crown of rejoicing. Incite him to enthusiasm by your inspiration. Make a mock of your discomforts. Be unwearying in details of the little interests of home. Fill your letters with kittens and canaries, with baby's shoes, and Johnny's sled, and the old cloak which you have turned into a handsome gown. Keep him posted in all the village-gossip, the lectures, the courtings, the sleigh-rides, and the singing-schools. Bring out the good points of the world in strong relief. Tell every piquant and pleasant and funny story you can think of. Show him that you clearly apprehend that all this warfare means peace, and that a dastardly peace would pave the way for speedy, incessant, and more appalling warfare. Help him to bear his burdens by showing him how elastic you are under yours. Hearten him, enliven him, tone him up to the true hero-pitch. Hush your plaintive *Miserere*, accept the nation's pain for penance, and commission every Northern breeze to bear a *Te Deum laudamus*.

It fell to me once to read the record of a young life laid early on our country's altar. I saw noble words traced by the still hand, — words of duty and honor and love and trust that thrilled my heart and brought back once more the virtue of the Golden Age, — nay, rather revealed the virgin gold of this; but through all his letters and his life shone, half concealed, yet wholly revealed, a silver thread of light, woven in by a woman's hand. Rest and courage and hope, patience in the weariness of disease, strength that nerved his arm for shock and onset, and for the last grand charge that laid his young head low, — all flowed in upon him through the tones of one brave, sweet voice far off. A gentle, fragile, soft-eyed woman, what could such a delicate flower do against the "thunder-storm of battle"? What *did* she do? Poured her own great heart and her own high spirit into the patriot's heart and soul, and so did all. Now as she goes to and fro in her daily life, soft-eyed still and serene, she seems to me no longer a beautiful girl, but a saint wrapped around already with the radiance of immortality.

Under God, the only question, as to whether this war shall be conducted to a shameful or an honorable close, is not of men or money or material resource. In these our superiority is unquestioned. As Wellington phrased it, there is hard pounding; but we shall pound the longest, if only our hearts do not fail us. Women need not beat their pewter spoons into bullets, for there are plenty of bullets without them. It is not whether our soldiers shall fight a good fight; they have played the man on a hundred battle-fields. It is not whether officers are or are not competent; generals have blundered nations into victory since the world began. It is whether this people shall have virtue to endure to the end, — to endure, not starving, not cold, but the pangs of hope deferred, of disappointment and uncertainty, of commerce deranged and outward prosperity checked. Will our vigilance to detect treachery and our perseverance to punish it hold out? If we stand firm, we shall be saved, though so as by fire. If we do not, we shall fall, and shall richly deserve to fall; and may God sweep us off from the face of the earth, and plant in our stead a nation with the hearts of men!

O women, here you may stand powerful, invincible, I had almost said omnipotent. Rise now to the heights of a sublime courage, — for the hour has need of you. When the first ball smote the rocky sides of Sumter, the rebound thrilled from shore to shore, and waked the slumbering hero in every human soul. Then every eye flamed, every lip was touched with a live coal from the sacred altar, every form dilated to the stature of the Golden Age. Then we felt in our veins the pulse of immortal youth. Then all the chivalry of the ancient days, all the heroism, all the self-sacrifice that shaped itself into noble living, came back to us, poured over us, swept away the dross of selfishness and deception and petty scheming, and Patriotism rose from the swelling wave stately as a goddess. Patriotism, that had been to us but a dingy and meaningless antiquity, took on a new form, a new mien, a countenance divinely fair and forever young, and received once more the homage of our hearts. Was that a childish outburst of excitement, or the glow of an aroused principle? Was it a puerile anger, or a manly indignation? Did we spring up startled pygmies, or girded giants? If the former, let us veil our faces, and march swiftly (and silently) to merciful forgetfulness. If the latter, shall we not lay aside every weight, and this besetting sin of despondency, and run with patience the race set before us?

A true philosophy and a true religion make the way possible to us. The Most High ruleth in the kingdom of men, and giveth it to whomsoever He will; and he never yet willed that a nation strong in means, and battling for the right, should be given over to a nation weak and battling for the wrong. Nations have their future — reward and penalty — in this world; and it is as certain as God lives, that Providence *and* the heaviest battalions will prevail. We have had reverses, but no misfortune hath happened unto us but such as is common unto nations. Country has been sacrificed to partisanship. Early love has fallen away, and lukewarmness has taken its place. Unlimited enthusiasm has given place to limited stolidity. Disloyalty, overawed at first into quietude, has lifted its head among us, and waxes wroth and ravening. There are dissensions at home worse than the guns of our foes. Some that did run well have faltered; some signal-lights have gone shamefully out, and some are lurid with a baleful glare. But unto this end were we born, and for this cause came we into the world. When shall greatness of soul stand forth, if not in evil times?

When the skies are fair and the seas smooth, all ships sail festively. But the clouds lower, the winds shriek, the waves boil, and immediately each craft shows its quality. The deep is strown with broken masts, parted keels, floating wrecks; but here and there a ship rides the raging sea, and flings defiance to the wind. She overlives the sea because she is sea-worthy. Not our eighty years of peace alone, but our two years of war, are the touchstone of our character. We have rolled our Democracy as a sweet morsel under our tongue; we have gloried in the prosperity which it brought to the individual; but if the comforts of men minister to the degradation of man, if Democracy levels down and does not level up, if our era of peace and plenty leaves us so feeble and frivolous, so childish, so impatient, so deaf to all that calls to us from the past, and entreats us in the future, that we faint and fail under the stress of our one short effort, then indeed is our Democracy our shame and curse. Let us show now what manner of people we are. Let us be clear-sighted and far-sighted to see how great is the issue that hangs upon the occasion. It is not a mere military reputation that is at stake, not the decay of a generation's commerce, not the determination of this or that party to power. It is the question of the world that we have been set to answer. In the great conflict of ages, the long strife between right and wrong, between progress and sluggardy, through the providence of God we are placed in the vanguard. Three hundred years ago a world was unfolded for the battle-ground. Choice spirits came hither to level and intrench. Swords clashed and blood flowed, and the great reconnoisance was successfully made. Since then both sides have been gathering strength, marshalling forces, planting batteries, and to-day we stand in the thick of the fray. Shall we fail? Men and women of America, will you fail? Shall the cause go by default? When a great idea, that has been uplifted on the shoulders of generations, comes now to its Thermopylæ, its glory-gate, and needs only stout hearts for its strong hands, — when the eyes of a great multitude are turned upon you, and the fates of dumb millions in the silent future rest with you, — when the suffering and sorrowful, the lowly, whose immortal hunger for justice gnaws at their hearts, who blindly see, but keenly feel, by their God-given instincts, that somehow you are working out their salvation, and the high-born, monarchs in the domain of mind, who, standing far off, see with prophetic eye the two courses that lie before you, one to the Uplands of vindicated Right, one to the Valley of the Shadow of Death, alike fasten upon you their hopes, their prayers, their tears, — will you, for a moment's bodily comfort and rest and repose, grind all these expectations and hopes between the upper and nether millstone? Will you fail the world in this fateful hour by your faint-heartedness? Will you fail yourself, and put the knife to your own throat? For the peace which you so dearly buy shall bring to you neither ease nor rest. You will but have spread a bed of thorns. Failure will write disgrace upon the brow of this generation, and shame will outlast the age. It is not with us as with the South. She can surrender without dishonor. She is the weaker power, and her success will be against the nature of things. Her dishonor lay in her attempt, not in its relinquishment. But we shall fail, not because of mechanics and mathematics, but because our manhood and womanhood weighed in the balance are found wanting. There are few who will not share in the sin. There are none who will not share in the shame. Wives, would you hold back your husbands? Mothers, would you keep your sons? From what? for what? From the doing of the grandest duty that ever ennobled man, to the grief of the greatest infamy that ever crushed him down. You would hold him back from prizes before which Olympian laurels fade, for a fate before which a Helot slave might cower. His country in the agony of her death-struggle calls to him for succor. All the blood in all the ages, poured out for liberty, poured out for him, cries unto him from the ground. All that life has of noble, of heroic, beckons him forward. Death itself wears for him a golden crown. Ever since the world swung free from God's hand, men have died, — obeying the blind fiat of Nature; but only once in a generation comes the sacrificial year, the year of jubilee, when men march lovingly to meet their fate and die for a nation's life. Holding back, we transmit to those that shall come after us a blackened waste. The little one that lies in his cradle will be accursed for our sakes. Every child will be base-born, springing from ignoble blood. We inherited a fair fame, and bays from a glorious battle; but for him is no background, no standpoint. His country will be a burden on his shoulders, a blush upon his cheek, a chain about his feet. There is no career for the future, but a weary effort, a long, a painful, a heavy-hearted struggle to lift the land out of its slough of degradation and set it once more upon a dry place.

Therefore let us have done at once and forever with paltry considerations, with talk of despondency and darkness. Let compromise, submission, and every form of dishonorable peace be not so much as named among us. Tolerate no coward's voice or pen or eye. Wherever the serpent's head is raised, strike it down. Measure every man by the standard of manhood. Measure country's price by country's worth, and country's worth by country's integrity. Let a cold, clear breeze sweep down from the mountains of life, and drive out these miasmas that befog and beguile the unwary. Around every hearthstone let sunshine gleam. In every home let fatherland have its altar and its fortress. From every household let words of cheer and resolve and high-heartiness ring out, till the whole land is shining and resonant in the bloom of its awakening spring.

A Spasm of Sense.

A Spasm of Sense.

THE conjunction of amiability and sense in the same individual renders that individual's position in a world like this very disagreeable. Amiability without sense, or sense without amiability, runs along smoothly enough. The former takes things as they are. It receives all glitter as pure gold, and does not see that it is custom alone which varnishes wrong with a shiny coat of respectability, and glorifies selfishness with the aureole of sacrifice. It sets down all collisions as foreordained, and never observes that they occur because people will not smooth off their angles, but sharpen them, and not only sharpen them, but run them into you. It forgets that the Lord made man upright, but he hath sought out many inventions. It attributes all the confusion and inaptitude which it finds to the nature of things, and never suspects that the Devil goes around in the night, thrusting the square men into the round places, and the round men into the square places. It never notices that the reason why the rope does not unwind easily is because one strand is a world too large, and another a world too small, and so it sticks where it ought to roll, and rolls where it ought to stick. It makes sweet, faint efforts, with tender fingers and palpitating heart to oil the wheels and polish up the machine, and does not for a moment imagine that the hitch is owing to original incompatibility of parts and purposes, that the whole machine must be pulled to pieces and made over, and that nothing will be done by standing patiently by, trying to soothe away the creaking and wheezing and groaning of the laboring, lumbering thing, by laying on a little drop of sweet oil with a pin-feather. As it does not see any of these things that are happening before its eyes, of course it is shallowly happy. And on the other hand, he who does see them, and is not amiable, is grimly and Grendally happy. He likes to say disagreeable things, and all this dismay and disaster scatter disagreeable things broadcast along his path, so that all he has to do is to pick them up and say them. Therefore this world is his paradise. He would not know what to do with himself in a world where matters were sorted and folded and laid away ready for you when you should want them. He likes to see human affairs mixing themselves up in irretrievable confusion. If he detects a symptom of straightening, it shall go hard but he will thrust in his own fingers and snarl a thread or two. He is delighted to find dogged duty and eager desire butting each other. All the irresistible forces crashing against all the immovable bodies give him no shock, only a pleasant titillation. He is never so happy as when men are taking hold of things by the blade, and cutting their hands, and losing blood. He tells them of it, but not in order to relieve so much as to "aggravate" them; and he does aggravate them, and is satisfied. O, but he is an aggravating person!

It is you, you who combine the heart of a seraph with the head of a cherub, who know what trouble is. You see where the shoe pinches, but your whole soul relucts from pointing out the tender place. You see why things go wrong, and how they might be set right; but you have a mortal dread of being thought meddlesome and impertinent, or cold and cruel, or restless and arrogant, if you attempt to demolish the wrong or rebel against the custom. When you draw your bow at an abuse, people think you are trying to bring down religion and propriety and humanity. But your conscience will not let you see the abuse raving to and fro over the earth without taking aim; so, either way, you are cut to the heart.

I love men. I adore women. I value their good opinion. There is much in them to applaud and imitate. There is much in them to elicit faith and reverence. If, only, one could see their good qualities alone, or, seeing their vapid and vicious ones, could contemplate them with no touch of tenderness for the owner, life might indeed be lovely. As it is, while I am at one moment rapt in enthusiastic admiration of the strength and grace, the power and pathos, the hidden resources, the profound capabilities of my race, at another, I could wish, Nero-like, that all mankind were concentrated in one person, and all womankind in another, that I might take them, after the fashion of rural schoolmasters, and shake their heads together. Condemnation and reproach are not in my line; but there is so much in the world that merits condemnation and reproach, and receives indifference and even reward, there is so much acquiescence in wrong doing and wrong thinking, so much letting things jolt along in the same rut wherein we and they were born, without inquiring whether, lifted into another groove, they might not run more easily, that, if one who does see the difficulty holds his peace, the very stones will cry out. However gladly one would lie on a bed of roses and glide silken-sailed down the stream of life, how exquisitely painful soever it may be to say what you fear and feel may give pain, it is only a Sybarite who sets ease above righteousness, only a coward who misses victory through dread of defeat.

There are many false ideas afloat regarding womanly duties. I do not design now to open anew any vulgar, worn-out, woman's-rightsy question. Every remark that could be made on that theme has been made — but one, and that I will take the liberty to make now in a single sentence, and close the discussion. It is this: the man who gave rubber-boots to women did more to elevate woman than all the theorizers, male or female, that ever were born.

But without any suspicious lunges into that dubious region which lies outside of woman's universally acknowledged "sphere," (a blight rest upon the word!) there is within the pale, within the boundary-line which the most conservative never dreamed of questioning, room for a great divergence of ideas. Now divergence of ideas does not necessarily imply fighting at short range. People may adopt a course of conduct which you do not approve; yet you may feel it your duty to make no open animadversion. Circumstances may have suggested such a course to them, or forced it upon them; and perhaps, considering all things, it is the best they can do. But when, encouraged by your silence, they publish it to the world, not only as relatively, but intrinsically, the best and most desirable, — when, not content with swallowing it themselves as medicine, they insist on ramming it down your throat as food, — it is time to buckle on your armor, and have at them.

A little book, published by the Tract Society, called "The Mother and her Work," has been doing just this thing. It is a modest little book.

It makes no pretensions to literary or other superiority. It has much excellent counsel, pious reflection, and comfortable suggestion. Being a little book, it costs but little, and it will console, refresh, and instruct weary, conscientious mothers, and so have a large circulation, a wide influence, and do an immense amount of mischief. For the Evil One in his senses never sends out poison labelled "POISON." He mixes it in with great quantities of innocent and nutritive flour and sugar. He shapes it in cunning shapes of pigs and lambs and hearts and birds and braids. He tints it with gay hues of green and pink and rose, and puts it in the confectioner's glass windows, where you buy — what? Poison? No, indeed! Candy, at prices to suit the purchasers. So this good and pious little book has such a preponderance of goodness and piety that the poison in it will not be detected, except by chemical analysis. It will go down sweetly, like grapes of Beulah. Nobody will suspect he is poisoned; but just so far as it reaches and touches, the social dyspepsia will be aggravated.

I submit a few atoms of the poison revealed by careful examination.

"The mother's is a *most honorable* calling. 'What a pity that one so gifted should be so tied down!' remarks a superficial observer, as she looks upon the mother of a young and increasing family. The pale, thin face and feeble step, bespeaking the multiplied and wearying cares of domestic life, elicit an earnest sympathy from the many, thoughtlessly flitting across her pathway, and the remark passes from mouth to mouth, 'How I pity her! What a shame it is! She is completely worn down with so many children.' It may be, however, that this young mother is one who needs and asks no pity," etc.

"But the *true mother* yields herself uncomplainingly, yea, cheerfully, to the wholesome privation, solitude, and self-denial allotted her. . . . . . Was she fond of travelling, of visiting the wonderful in Nature and in Art, of mingling in new and often-varying scenes? Now she has found 'an abiding city,' and no allurements are strong enough to tempt her thence. Had society charms for her, and in the social circle and the festive throng were her chief delights? Now she stays at home, and the gorgeous saloon and brilliant assemblage give place to the nursery and the baby. Was she devoted to literary pursuits? Now the library is seldom visited, the cherished studies are neglected, the rattle and the doll are substituted for the pen. Her piano is silent, while she chants softly and sweetly the soothing lullaby. Her dress can last another season now, and the hat — oh, she does not care, if it is not in the latest mode, for she has a baby to look after, and has no time for herself. Even the ride and the walk are given up, perhaps too often, with the excuse, 'Baby-tending is exercise enough for me.' Her whole life is reversed."

The assumption is, that all this is just as it should be. The thoughtless person may fancy that it is a pity; but it is not a pity. This is a model mother and a model state of things. It is not simply to be submitted to, not simply to be patiently borne; it is to be aspired to as the noblest and holiest state.

That is the strychnine. You may counsel people to take joyfully the spoiling of their goods, and comfort, encourage, and strengthen them by so doing; but when you tell them that to be robbed and plundered is of itself a priceless blessing, the highest stage of human development, you do them harm; because, in general, falsehood is always harmful, and because, in particular, so far as you influence them at all, you prevent them from taking measures to stop the wrong-doing. You ought to counsel them to bear with Christian resignation what they cannot help; but you ought with equal fervor to counsel them to look around and see if there are not many things which they can help, and if there are, by all means to help them. What is inevitable comes to us from God, no matter how many hands it passes through; but submission to unnecessary evils is cowardice or laziness; and extolling of the evil as good is sheer ignorance, or perversity, or servility. Even the ills that must be borne, should be borne under protest, lest patience degenerate into slavery. Christian character is never formed by acquiescence in, or apotheosis of wrong.

The principle that underlies these extracts, and makes them ministrative of evil, is the principle that a woman can benefit her children by sacrificing herself. It teaches, that pale, thin faces and feeble steps are excellent things in young mothers, — provided they are gained by maternal duties. We infer that it is meet, right, and the bounden duty of such to give up society, reading, riding, music, and become indifferent to dress, cultivation, recreation, to everything, in short, except taking care of the children. It is all just as wrong as it can be. It is wrong morally; it is wrong socially; wrong in principle, wrong in practice. It is a blunder as well as a crime, for it works woe. It is a wrong means to accomplish an end; and it does not accomplish the end, after all, but demolishes it.

On the contrary, the duty and dignity of a mother require that she should never subordinate herself to her children. When she does so, she does it to their manifest injury and her own. Of course, if illness or accident demand unusual care, she does well to grow thin and pale in bestowing unusual care. But when a mother in the ordinary routine of life grows thin and pale, gives up riding, reading, and the amusements and occupations of life, there is a wrong somewhere, and her children shall reap the fruits of it. The father and mother are the head of the family, the most comely and the most honorable part. They cannot benefit their children by descending from their Heaven-appointed places, and becoming perpetual and exclusive feet and hands. This is the great fault of American mothers. They swamp themselves in a slough of self-sacrifice. They are smothered in their own sweetness. They dash into domesticity with an impetus and abandonment that annihilate themselves. They sink into their families like a light in a poisonous well, and are extinguished.

One hears much complaint of the direction and character of female education. It is dolefully affirmed that young ladies learn how to sing operas, but not how to keep house, — that they can conjugate Greek verbs, but cannot make bread, — that they are good for pretty toying, but not for homely using. Doubtless there is foundation for this remark, or it would never have been made. But I have been in the East and the West, and the North and the South; I know that I have seen the best society, and I am sure I have seen very bad, if not the worst; and I never met a woman whose superior education, whose piano, whose pencil, whose German, or French, or any school-accomplishments, or even whose novels, clashed with her domestic duties. I have read of them in books; I did hear of one once; but I never met one, — not one. I have seen women, through love of gossip, through indolence, through sheer famine of mental *pabulum*, leave undone things that ought to be done, — rush to the assembly, the lecture-room, the sewing-circle, or vegetate in squalid, shabby, unwholesome homes ; but I never saw education run to ruin. So it seems to me that we are needlessly alarmed in that direction.

But I have seen scores and scores of women leave school, leave their piano and drawing and fancy-work, and all manner of pretty and pleasant things, and marry and bury themselves. You hear of them about six times in ten years, and there is a baby each time. They crawl out of the farther end of the ten years, sallow and wrinkled and lank, — teeth gone, hair gone, roses gone, plumpness gone, — freshness, and vivacity, and sparkle, everything that is dewy, and springing, and spontaneous, gone, gone, gone forever. This our Tract-Society book puts very prettily. "She wraps herself in the robes of infantile simplicity, and, burying her womanly nature in the tomb of childhood, patiently awaits the sure-coming resurrection in the form of a noble, high-minded, world-stirring son, or a virtuous, lovely daughter. The nursery is the mother's chrysalis. Let her abide for a little season, and she shall emerge triumphantly, with ethereal wings and a happy flight."

But the nursery has no business to be the mother's chrysalis. God never intended her to wind herself up into a cocoon. If he had, he would have made her a caterpillar. She has no right to bury her womanly nature in the tomb of childhood. It will surely be required at her hands. It was given her to sun itself in the broad, bright day, to root itself fast and firm in the earth, to spread itself wide to the sky, that her children in their infancy and youth and maturity, that her husband in his strength and his weakness, that her kinsfolk and neighbors and the poor of the land, the halt and the blind and all Christ's little ones, may sit under its shadow with great delight. No woman has a right to sacrifice her own soul to problematical, high-minded, world-stirring sons, and virtuous, lovely daughters. To be the mother of such, one might perhaps pour out one's life in draughts so copious that the fountain should run dry; but world-stirring people are extremely rare. One in a century is a liberal allowance. The overwhelming probabilities are, that her sons will be lawyers and shoemakers and farmers and commission-merchants, her daughters nice, "smart," pretty girls, all good, honest, kind-hearted, commonplace people, not at all world-stirring, not at all the people one would glory to merge one's self in. If the mother is not satisfied with this, if she wants them otherwise, she must be otherwise. The surest way to have high-minded children is to be high-minded yourself. A man cannot burrow in his counting-room for ten or twenty of the best years of his life, and come out as much of a man and as little of a mole as he went in. But the twenty years should have ministered to his manhood, instead of trampling on it. Still less can a woman bury herself in her nursery, and come out without harm. But the years should have done her great good. This world is not made for a tomb, but a garden. You are to be a seed, not a death. Plant yourself, and you will sprout. Bury yourself, and you can only decay. For a dead opportunity there is no resurrection. The only enjoyment, the only use to be attained in this world, must be attained on the wing. Each day brings its own happiness, its own benefit; but it has none to spare. What escapes to-day is escaped forever. To-morrow has no overflow to atone for the lost yesterdays.

Few things are more painful to look upon than the self-renunciation, the self-abnegation of mothers, — painful both for its testimony and its prophecy. Its testimony is of over-care, over-work, over-weariness, the abuse of capacities that were bestowed for most sacred uses, an utter waste of most pure and life-giving waters. Its prophecy is of early decline and decadence, forfeiture of position and power, and worst, perhaps, of all, irreparable loss and grievous wrong to the children for whom all is sacrificed.

God gives to the mother supremacy in her family. It belongs to her to maintain it. This cannot be done without exertion. The temptation to come down from her throne, and become a mere hewer of wood and drawer of water is very strong. It is so much easier to work with the hands than with the head. One can chop sticks all day serenely unperplexed. But to administer a government demands observation and knowledge and judgment and resolution and inexhaustible patience. Yet, however uneasy lies the head that wears the crown of womanhood, that crown cannot be bartered away for any baser wreath without infinite harm. In both cases there must be sacrifice; but in the one case it is unto death, in the other unto life. If the mother stands on high ground, she brings her children up to her own level; if she sinks, they sink with her.

To maintain her rank, no exertion is too great, no means too small. Dress is one of the most obvious things to a child. If the mother wears cheap or shabby or ill-assorted clothes, while the children's are fine and harmonious, it is impossible that they should not receive the impression that they are of more consequence than their mother. Therefore, for her children's sake, if not for her own, the mother should always be well-dressed. Her baby, so far as it is concerned in the matter, instead of being an excuse for a faded bonnet, should be an inducement for a fresh one. It is not a question of riches or poverty; it is a thing of relations. It is simply that the mother's dress — her morning and evening and street and church dress — should be quite as good as, and if there is any difference, better than her child's. It is of no manner of consequence how a child is clad, provided only its health be not injured, its taste corrupted, or its self-respect wounded. Children look prettier in the cheapest and simplest materials than in the richest and most elaborate. But how common is it to see the children gayly caparisoned in silk and feathers and flounces, while the mother is enveloped in an atmosphere of cottony fadiness! One would take the child to be mistress, and the mother a servant. "But," the mother says, "I do not care for dress, and Caroline does. She, poor child, would be mortified not to be dressed like the other children." Then do you teach her better. Plant in her mind a higher standard of self-respect. Don't tell her you cannot afford to do for her thus and thus; that will scatter premature thorns along her path; but say that you do not approve of it; it is proper for her to dress in such and such a way. And be so nobly and grandly a woman that she shall have faith in you.

It is essential also that the mother have sense, intelligence, comprehension. As much as she can add of education and accomplishments will increase her stock in trade. Her reading and riding and music, instead of being neglected for her children's sake, should for their sake be scrupulously cultivated. Of the two things, it is a thousand times better that they should be attended by a nursery-maid in their infancy than by a feeble, timid, inefficient matron in their youth. The mother can oversee half a dozen children with a nurse; but she needs all her strength, all her mind, her own eyes, and ears, and quick perceptions, and delicate intuition, and calm self-possession, when her sturdy boys and wild young girls are leaping and bounding and careering into their lusty life. All manner of novel temptations beset them, — perils by night and perils by day, — perils in the house and by the way. Their fierce and hungry young souls, rioting in awakening consciousness, ravening for pleasure, strong and tumultuous, snatch eagerly at every bait. They want then a mother able to curb, and guide, and rule them; and only a mother who commands their respect can do this. Let them see her sought for her social worth, — let them see that she is familiar with all the conditions of their life, — that her vision is at once broader and keener than theirs, — that her feet have travelled along the paths they are just beginning to explore, — that she knows all the phases alike of their strength and their weakness, — and her influence over them is unbounded. Let them see her uncertain, uncomfortable, hesitating, fearful without discrimination, leaning where she ought to support, interfering without power of suggesting, counselling, but not controlling, with no presence, no bearing, no experience, no prestige, and they will carry matters with a high hand. They will overrule her decisions, and their love will not be unmingled with contempt. It will be strong enough to prick them when they have done wrong, but not strong enough to keep them from doing wrong.

Nothing gives a young girl such vantage-ground in society and in life as a mother, — a sensible, amiable, brilliant, and commanding woman. Under the shelter of such a mother's wing, the neophyte is safe. This mother will attract to herself the wittiest and the wisest. The young girl can see society in its best phases, without being herself drawn out into its glare. She forms her own style on the purest models. She gains confidence, without losing modesty. Familiar with wisdom, she will not be dazed by folly. Having the opportunity to make observations before she begins to be observed, she does not become the prey of the weak and the wicked. Her taste is strengthened and refined, her standard elevates itself, her judgment acquires a firm basis. But cast upon her own resources, her own blank inexperience, at her first entrance into the world, with nothing to stand between her and what is openly vapid and covertly vicious, with no clear eye to detect for her the false and distinguish the true, no strong, firm, judicious hand to guide tenderly and undeviatingly, to repress without irritating and encourage without emboldening, what wonder that the peach-bloom loses its delicacy, deepening into *rouge* or hardening into brass, and the happy young life is stranded on a cruel shore?

Hence it follows that our social gatherings consist, to so lamentable an extent, of pert youngsters, or faded oldsters. Thence come those abominable "young people's parties," where a score or two or three of boys and girls meet and manage after their own hearts. Thence it happens that conversation seems to be taking its place among the Lost Arts, and the smallest of small talk reigns in its stead. Society, instead of giving its tone to the children, takes it from them, and since it cannot be juvenile, becomes insipid, and because it is too old to prattle, jabbers. Talkers are everywhere, but where are the men that say things? Where are the people that can be listened to and quoted? Where are the flinty people whose contact strikes fire? Where are the electric people who thrill a whole circle with sudden vitality? Where are the strong people who hedge themselves around with their individuality, and will be roused by no prince's kiss, but taken only by storm, yet once captured, are sweeter than the dews of Hymettus? Where are the seers, the prophets, the Magi, who shall unfold for us the secrets of the sky and the seas, and the mystery of human hearts?

Yet fathers and mothers not only acquiesce in this state of things, they approve of it. They foster it. They are forward to annihilate themselves. They are careful to let their darlings go out alone, lest they be a restraint upon them, — as if that were not what parents were made for. If they were what they ought to be, the restraint would be not only wholesome, but impalpable. The relation between parents and children should be such that pleasure shall not be quite perfect, unless shared by both. Parents ought to take such a tender, proud, intellectual interest in the pursuits and amusements of their children that the children shall feel the glory of the victory dimmed, unless their parents are there to witness it. If the presence of a sensible mother is felt as a restraint, it shows conclusively that restraint is needed.

A woman also needs self-cultivation, both physical and mental, in order to self-respect. Undoubtedly Diogenes glorified himself in his tub. But people in general, and women in universal, — except the geniuses, — need the pomp of circumstance. A slouchy garb is both effect and cause of a slouchy mind. A woman who lets go her hold upon dress, literature, music, amusement, will almost inevitably slide down into a bog of muggy moral indolence. She will lose her spirit, and when the spirit is gone out of a woman, there is not much left of her. When she cheapens herself, she diminishes her value. Especially when the evanescent charms of mere youth are gone, when the responsibilities of life have left their mark upon her, is it indispensable that she attend to all the fitnesses of externals, and strengthen and polish all her mental and social qualities. By this I do not mean that women should allow themselves to lose their beauty as they increase in years. Men grow handsomer as they grow older. There is no reason, there ought to be no reason, why women should not. They will have a different kind of beauty, but it will be just as truly beauty and more impressive and attractive than the beauty of sixteen. It is absurd to suppose that God has made women so that their glory passes away in half a dozen years. It is absurd to suppose that thought and feeling and passion and purpose, all holy instincts and impulses, can chisel away on a woman's face for thirty, forty, fifty years, and leave that face at the end worse than they found it. They found it a negative, — mere skin and bone, blood and muscle and fat. They can but leave their mark upon it, and the mark of good is good. Pity does not have the same finger-touch as revenge. Love does not hold the same brush as hatred. Sympathy and gratitude and benevolence have a different sign-manual from cruelty and carelessness and deceit. All these busy little sprites draw their fine lines, lay on their fine colors; the face lights up under their tiny hands; the prisoned soul shines clearer and clearer through, and there is the consecration and the poet's dream.

But such beauty is made, not born. Care and weariness and despondency come of themselves, and groove their own furrows. Hope and intelligence and interest and buoyancy must be wooed for their gentle and genial touch. A mother must battle against the tendencies that drag her downward. She must take pains to grow, or she will not grow. She must sedulously cultivate her mind and heart, or her old age will be ungraceful; and if she lose freshness without acquiring ripeness, she is indeed in an evil case. The first, the most important trust which God has given to any one is himself. To secure this trust, He has made us so that in no possible way can we benefit the world so much as by making the most of ourselves. Indulging our whims, or, inordinately, our just tastes, is not developing ourselves; but neither is leaving our own fields to grow thorns and thistles, that we may plant somebody else's garden-plot, keeping our charge. Even were it possible for a mother to work well to her children in thus working ill to herself, I do not think she would be justified in doing it. Her account is not complete when she says, "Here are they whom thou hast given me." She must first say, "Here am I." But when it is seen that suicide is also child-murder, it must appear that she is under doubly heavy bonds for herself.

Husbands, moreover, have claims, though wives often ignore them. It is the commonest thing in the world to see parents tender of their children's feelings, alive to their wants, indulgent to their tastes, kind, considerate, and forbearing; but to each other hasty, careless, and cold. Conjugal love often seems to die out before parental love. It ought not so to be. Husband and wife should each stand first in the other's estimation. They have no right to forget each other's comfort, convenience, sensitiveness, tastes, or happiness, in those of their children. Nothing can discharge them from the obligations which they are under to each other. But if a woman lets herself become shabby, drudgy, and commonplace as a wife, in her efforts to be perfect as a mother, can she expect to retain the consideration that is due to the wife? Not a man in the world but would rather see his wife tidy, neat, and elegant in her attire, easy and assured in her bearing, intelligent and vivacious in her talk, than the contrary; and if she neglect these things, ought she to be surprised if he turns to fresh woods and pastures new for the diversion and entertainment which he seeks in vain at home? This is quaky ground, but I know where I am, and I am not afraid. I don't expect men or women to say that they agree with me, but I am right for all that. Let us bring our common sense to bear on this point, and not be fooled by reiteration. Cause and effect obtain here as elsewhere. If you add two and two, the result is four, however much you may try to blink it. People do not always tell lies, when they are telling what is not the truth; but falsehood is still disastrous. Men and women think they believe a thousand things which they do not believe; but as long as they think so, it is just as bad as if it were so. Men talk — and women listen and echo — about the overpowering loveliness and charm of a young mother surrounded by her blooming family, ministering to their wants and absorbed in their welfare, self-denying and self-forgetful; and she is lovely and charming; but if this is all, it is little more than the charm and loveliness of a picture. It is not magnetic and irresistible. It has the semblance, but not the smell of life. It is pretty to look at, but it is not vigorous for command. Her husband will have a certain kind of admiration and love. Her wish will be law within a certain very limited sphere; but beyond that he will not take her into his counsels and confidence. A woman must make herself obvious to her husband, or he will drift out beyond her horizon. She will be to him very nearly what she wills and works to be. If she adapts herself to her children, and does not adapt herself to her husband, he will fall into the arrangement, and the two will fall apart. I do not mean that they will quarrel, but they will lead separate lives. They will be no longer husband and wife. There will be a domestic alliance, but no marriage. A predominant interest in the same objects binds them together after a fashion; but marriage is something beyond that. If a woman wishes and purposes to be the friend of her husband, — if she would be valuable to him, not simply as the nurse of his children and the directress of his household, but as a woman fresh and fair and fascinating, — to him intrinsically lovely and attractive, — she should make an effort for it. It is not by any means a thing that comes of itself, or that can be left to itself. She must read, and observe, and think, and rest up to it. Men, as a general thing, will not tell you so. They talk about having the slippers ready, and enjoin women to be domestic. But men are blockheads, — dear, and affectionate, and generous blockheads, — benevolent, large-hearted, and chivalrous, — kind, and patient, and hard-working, — but stupid where women are concerned. Indispensable and delightful as they are in real life, — pleasant and comfortable as women actually find them, — not one in ten thousand but makes a dunce of himself the moment he opens his mouth to theorize about women. Besides, they have "an axe to grind." The pretty things they inculcate — slippers, and coffee, and care, and courtesy — ought indeed to be done, but the others ought not to be left undone. And to the former women seldom need to be exhorted. They take to them naturally. A great many more women fret boorish husbands with fond little attentions than wound appreciative ones by neglect. Women domesticate themselves to death already. What they want is cultivation. They need to be stimulated to develop a large, comprehensive, catholic life, in which their domestic duties shall have an appropriate niche, and not dwindle down to a narrow and servile one, over which those duties shall spread and occupy the whole space.

This mistake is the foundation of a world of wretchedness and ruin. I can see Satan standing at the mother's elbow. He follows her around into the nursery and the kitchen. He tosses up the babies and the omelets, delivers dutiful harangues about the inappropriateness of the piano and the library, and grins fiendishly in his sleeve at the wreck he is making, — a wreck not necessarily of character, but of happiness; for I suppose Satan has so bad a disposition, that, if he cannot do all the harm he would wish, he will still do all he can. It is true that there are thousands of noble men married to fond and foolish women, and they are both happy. Well, the fond and foolish women are very fortunate. They have fallen into hands that will entreat them tenderly, and they will not perceive any lack. Nor are the noble men wholly unfortunate, in that they have not taken to their hearts shrews. But this is not marriage.

There are women less foolish. They see their husbands attracted in other directions more often and more easily than in theirs. They have too much sterling worth and profound faith to be vulgarly jealous. They fear nothing like shame or crime; but they feel the fact that their own preoccupation with homely household duties precludes real companionship, the interchange of emotions, thoughts, sentiments, — a living, and palpable, and vivid contact of mind with mind, of heart with heart. They see others whose leisure ministers to grace, accomplishments, piquancy, and attractiveness, and the moth flies towards the light by his own nature. Because he is a wise, and virtuous, and honorable moth, he does not dart into the flame. He does not even scorch his wings. He never thinks of such a thing. He merely circles around the pleasant light, sunning himself in it without much thought one way or another, only feeling that it is pleasant; but meanwhile Mrs. Moth sits at home in darkness, mending the children's clothes, which is not exhilarating. Many a woman who feels that she possesses her husband's affection misses something. She does not secure his fervor, his admiration. His love is honest and solid, but a little dormant, and therefore dull. It does not brace, and tone, and stimulate. She wants not the love only, but the keenness, and edge, and flavor of the love; and she suffers untold pangs. I know it, for I have seen it. It is not a thing to be uttered. Most women do not admit it even to themselves; but it is revealed by a lift of the eyelash, by a quiver of the eye, by a tone of the voice, by a trick of the finger.

But what is the good of saying all this, if a

woman cannot help herself? The children must be seen to, and the work must be done, and after that she has no time left. The "mother of a young and increasing family," with her "pale, thin face and feeble step," and her "multiplied and wearying cares," is "completely worn down with so many children." She has neither time nor spirit for self-culture, beyond what she may obtain in the nursery. What satisfaction is there in proving that she is far below where she ought to be, if inexorable circumstance prevent her from climbing higher? What use is there in telling her that she will alienate her husband and injure her children by her course, when there is no other course for her to pursue? What can she do about it?

There is one thing that she need not do. She need not sit down and write a book, affirming that it is the most glorious and desirable condition imaginable. She need not lift up her voice and declare that "she lives above the ills and disquietudes of her condition, in an atmosphere of love and peace and pleasure far beyond the storms and conflicts of this material life." Who ever heard of the mother of a young and increasing family living in an atmosphere of peace, not to say pleasure, above conflicts and storms? Who does not know that the private history of families with the ordinary allowance of brains is a record of recurring internecine warfare? If she said less, we might believe her. When she says so much, we cannot help suspecting. To make the best of anything, it is not necessary to declare that it is the best thing. Children must be taken care of, but it is altogether probable that there are too many of them. Some people think that opinion several times more atrocious than murder in the first degree; but I see no atrocity in it. I think there is an immense quantity of nonsense about, regarding this thing. I believe in Malthus, — a great deal more than Malthus did himself. The prosperity of a country is often measured by its population; but quite likely it should be taken in inverse ratio. I certainly do not see why the mere multiplication of the species is so indicative of prosperity. Mobs are not so altogether lovely that one should desire their indefinite increase. A village is honorable, not according to the number, but the character of its residents. The drunkards and the paupers and the thieves and the idiots rather diminish than increase its respectability. It seems to me that the world would be greatly benefited by thinning out. Most of the places that I have seen would be much improved by being decimated, not to say quinqueted or bisected. If people are stubborn and rebellious, stiff-necked and uncircumcised in heart and ears, the fewer of them the better. A small population, trained to honor and virtue, to liberality of culture and breadth of view, to self-reliance and self-respect, is a thousand times better than an over-crowded one with everything at loose ends. As with the village, so with the family. There ought to be no more children than can be healthily and thoroughly reared, as regards the moral, physical, and intellectual nature both of themselves and their parents. All beyond this is wrong and disastrous. I know of no greater crime than to give life to souls, and then degrade them, or suffer them to be degraded. Children are the poor man's blessing and Cornelia's jewels, just so long as Cornelia and the poor man can make adequate provision for them. But the ragged, filthy, squalid, unearthly little wretches that wallow before the poor man's shanty-door are the poor man's shame and curse. The sickly, sallow, sorrowful little ones, shadowed too early by life's cares, are something other than a blessing. When Cornelia finds her children too many for her, when her step trembles and her cheek fades, when the sparkle dies out of her wine of life and her salt has lost its savor, her jewels are Tarpeian jewels. One child educated by healthy and happy parents is better than seven dragging their mother into the grave, notwithstanding the unmeasured reprobation of our little book. Of course, if they can stand seven, very well. Seven and seventy times seven, if you like, only let them be buds, not blights. If we obeyed the laws of God, children would be like spring blossoms. They would impart as much freshness and strength as they abstract. They are a natural institution, and Nature is eminently healthy. But when they "come crowding into the home-nest," as our book daintily says, they are unnatural. God never meant the home-nest to be crowded. There is room enough and elbow-room enough in the world for everything that ought to be in it. The moment there is crowding, you may be sure something wrong is going on. Either a bad thing is happening, or too much of a good thing, which counts up just the same. The parents begin to repair the evil by a greater one. They attempt to patch their own rents by dilapidating their children. They recruit their own exhausted energies by laying hold of the young energies around them, and older children are wearied, and fretted, and deformed in figure and temper by the care of younger children. This is horrible. Some care and task and responsibility are good for a child's own development; but care and toil and labor laid upon children beyond what is best for their own character is intolerable and inexcusable oppression. Parents have no right to lighten their own burdens by imposing them upon the children. The poor things had nothing to do with being born. They came into the world without any volition of their own. Their existence began only to serve the pleasure or the pride of others. It was a culpable cruelty, in the first place, to introduce them into a sphere where no adequate provision could be made for their comfort and culture; but to shoulder them, after they get here, with the load which belongs to their parents is outrageous. Earth is not a paradise at best, and at worst it is very near the other place. The least we can do is to make the way as smooth as possible for the new-comers. There is not the least danger that it will be too smooth. If you stagger under the weight which you have imprudently assumed, stagger. But don't be such an unutterable coward as to illumine your own life by darkening the young lives which sprang from yours. I often wonder that children do not open their mouths and curse the father that begat and the mother that bore them. I often wonder that parents do not tremble lest the cry of the children whom they oppress go up into the ears of the Lord of Sabaoth, and bring down wrath upon their guilty heads. It was well that God planted filial affection and reverence as an instinct in the human breast. If it depended upon reason, it would have but a precarious existence.

I wish women would have the sense and courage, — I will not say, to say what they think, for that is not always desirable, — but to think according to the facts. They have a strong desire to please men, which is quite right and natural; but in their eagerness to do this, they sometimes forget what is due to themselves. To think namby-pambyism for the sake of pleasing men is running benevolence into the ground. Not that women consciously do this, but they do it. They don't mean to pander to false masculine notions, but they do. They don't know that they are pandering to them, but they are. Men say silly things, partly because they don't know any better, and partly because they don't want any better. They are strong, and can generally make shift to bear their end of the pole without being crushed. So they are tolerably content. They are not very much to blame. People cannot be expected to start on a crusade against ills of which they have but a vague and cloudy conception. The edge does not cut them, and so they think it is not much of a sword after all. But women have, or ought to have, a more subtile and intimate acquaintance with realities. They ought to know what is fact and what is fol-de-rol. They ought to distinguish between the really noble and the simply physical, not to say faulty. If men do not, it is women's duty to help them. I think, if women would only not be quite so afraid of being thought unwomanly, they would be a great deal more womanly than they are. To be brave, and single-minded, and discriminating, and judicious, and clear-sighted, and self-reliant, and decisive, that is pure womanly. To be womanish is not to be womanly. To be flabby, and plastic, and weak, and acquiescent, and insipid, is not womanly. And I could wish sometimes that women would not be quite so patient. They often exhibit a degree of long-suffering entirely unwarrantable. There is no use in suffering, unless you cannot help it; and a good, stout, resolute protest would often be a great deal more wise, and Christian, and beneficial on all sides, than so much patient endurance. A little spirit and "spunk" would go a great way towards setting the world right. It is not necessary to be a termagant. The firmest will and the stoutest heart may be combined with the gentlest delicacy. Tameness is not the stuff that the finest women are made of. Nobody can be more kind, considerate, or sympathizing towards weakness or weariness than men, if they only know it exists; and it is a wrong to them to go on bolstering them up in their bungling opinions, when a few sensible ideas, wisely administered, would do so much to enlighten them, and reveal the path which needs only to be revealed to secure their unhesitating entrance upon it. It is absurd to suppose that unvarying acquiescence is necessary to secure and retain their esteem, and that a frank avowal of differing opinions, even if they were wrong, would work its forfeiture. A respect held on so frail a tenure were little worth. But it is not so. I believe that manhood and womanhood are too truly harmonious to need iron bands, too truly noble to require the props of falsehood. Truth, simple and sincere, without partiality and without hypocrisy, is the best food for both. If any are to be found on either side too weak to administer or digest it, the remedy is not to mix it with folly or falsehood, for they are poisons, but to strengthen the organisms with wholesome tonics, — not undiluted, perhaps, but certainly unadulterated.

O Edmund Sparkler, you builded better than you knew, when you reared eulogiums upon the woman with no nonsense about her.

Camilla's Concert.

Camilla's Concert.

I, WHO labor under the suspicion of not knowing the difference between "Old Hundred" and "Old Dan Tucker," — I, whose every attempt at music, though only the humming of a simple household melody, has, from my earliest childhood, been regarded as a premonitory symptom of epilepsy, or, at the very least, hysterics, to be treated with cold water, the bellows, and an unmerciful beating between my shoulders, — I, who can but with much difficulty and many a retrogression make my way among the olden mazes of tenor, alto, treble, bass, and who stand "clean daft" in the resounding confusion of andante, soprano, falsetto, palmetto, pianissimo, akimbo, l'allegro, and il penseroso, — *I* was bidden to Camilla's concert, and, like a sheep to the slaughter, I went.

He bears a great loss and sorrow who has "no ear for music." Into one great garden of delights he may not go. There needs no flaming sword to bar the way, since for him there is no gate called Beautiful which he should seek to enter. Blunted and stolid he stumps through life for whom its harp-strings vainly quiver. Yet, on the other hand, what does he not gain? He loses the concord of sweet sounds, but he is spared the discord of harsh noises. For the surges of bewildering harmony and the depths of dissonant disgust, he stands on the levels of perpetual peace. You are distressed, because in yonder well-trained orchestra a single voice is pitched one sixteenth of a note too high. For me, I lean out of my window on summer nights enraptured over the organ-man who turns poor lost Lilian Dale round and round with his inexorable crank. It does not disturb me that his organ wheezes and sputters and grunts. Indeed, there is for me absolutely no wheeze, no sputter, no grunt. I only see dark eyes of Italy, her olive face, and her gemmed and lustrous hair. You mutter maledictions on the infernal noise and caterwauling. I hear no caterwauling, but the river-god of Arno ripples soft songs in the summer-tide to the lilies that bend above him. It is the guitar of the cantatrice that murmurs through the scented, dewy air, — the cantatrice with the laurel yet green on her brow, gliding over the molten moonlit water-ways of Venice, and dreamily chiming her well-pleased lute with the plash of the oars of the gondolier. It is the chant of the flower-girl with large eyes shining under the palm-branches in the market-place of Milan; and with the distant echoing notes come the sweet breath of her violets and the unquenchable odors of her crushed geraniums borne on many a white sail from the glorified Adriatic. Bronzed cheek and swart brow under my window, I shall by and by throw you a paltry nickel cent for your tropical dreams; meanwhile tell me, did the sun of Dante's Florence give your blood its fierce flow and the tawny hue to your bared and brawny breast? Is it the rage of Tasso's madness that burns in your uplifted eyes? Do you take shelter from the fervid noon under the cypresses of Monte Mario? Will you meet queenly Marguerite with myrtle wreath and myrtle fragrance, as she wanders through the chestnut vales? Will you sleep to-night between the colonnades under the golden moon of Napoli? Go back, O child of the Mid-land Sea! Go out from this cold shore, that yields but crabbed harvests for your threefold vintages of Italy. Go, suck the sunshine from Seville oranges under the elms of Posilippo. Go, watch the shadows of the vines swaying in the mulberry-trees from Epomeo's gales. Bind the ivy in a triple crown above Bianca's comely hair, and pipe not so wailingly to the Vikings of this frigid Norse-land.

But Italy, remember, my frigid Norseland has a heart of fire in her bosom beneath its overlying snows, before which yours dies like the white sick hearth-flame before the noonday sun. Passion, but not compassion, is here "cooled a long age in the deep-delved earth." We lure our choristers with honeyed words and gentle ways: you lay your sweetest songsters on the gridiron. Our orchards ring with the full-throated happiness of a thousand birds: your pomegranate groves are silent, and your miserable cannibal kitchens would tell the reason why, if outraged spits could speak. Go away, therefore, from my window, Giuseppe; the air is growing damp and chilly, and I do not sleep in the shadows of broken temples.

Yet I love music; not as you love it, my friend, with intelligence, discrimination, and delicacy, but in a dull, woodeny way, as the "gouty oaks" loved it, when they felt in their fibrous frames the stir of Amphion's lyre, and "floundered into hornpipes"; as the gray, stupid rocks loved it, when they came rolling heavily to his feet to listen; in a great, coarse, clumsy, ichthyosaurian way, as the rivers loved sad Orpheus's wailing tones, stopping in their mighty courses, and the thick-hided hippopotamus dragged himself up from the unheeded pause of the waves, dimly thrilled with a vague ecstasy. The confession is sad, yet only in such beastly fashion come sweetest voices to me, — not in the fulness of all their vibrations, but sounding dimly through many an earthly layer. Music I do not so much hear as feel. All the exquisite nerves that bear to your soul these tidings of heaven in me lie torpid or dead. No beatitude travels to my heart over that road. But as sometimes an invalid, unable through mortal sickness to swallow his needed nutriment, is yet kept alive many days by being immersed in a bath of wine and milk, which somehow, through unwonted courses, penetrates to the sources of vitality, — so I, though the natural avenues of sweet sounds have been hermetically sealed, do yet receive the fine flow of the musical ether. I feel the flood of harmony pouring around me. An inward, palpable, measured tremulousness of the subtile secret essence of life attests the presence of some sweet disturbing cause, and, borne on unseen wings, I mount to loftier heights and diviner airs.

So I was comforted for my waxed ears and Camilla's concert.

There is one other advantage in being possessed with a deaf-and-dumb devil, which, now that I am on the subject of compensation, I may as well mention. You are left out of the arena of fierce discussion and debate. You do not enter upon the lists wherefrom you would be sure to come off discomfited. Of all reputations, a musical reputation seems the most shifting and uncertain; and of all rivalries, musical rivalries are the most prolific of heart-burnings and discomfort. Now, if I should sing or play, I should wish to sing and play well. But what is well? Nancie in the village "singing-seats" stands head and shoulders above the rest, and wears her honors tranquilly, — an authority at all rehearsals and serenades. But Anabella comes up from the town to spend Thanksgiving, and, without the least mitigation or remorse of voice, absolutely drowns out poor Nancie, who goes under, giving many signs. Yet she dies not unavenged, for Harriette sweeps down from the city, and immediately suspends the victorious Anabella from her aduncate nose, and carries all before her. Mysterious is the arrangement of the world. The last round of the ladder is not yet reached. To Madame Morlot, Harriette is a savage, *une bête*, without cultivation. "Oh, the dismal little fright! a thousand years of study would be useless; go, scour the floors; she has positively no voice." No voice, Madame Morlot? Harriette, no voice, — who burst every ear-drum in the room last night with her howling and hooting, and made the stoutest heart tremble with fearful forebodings of what might come next? But Madame Morlot is not infallible, for Herr Driesbach sits shivering at the dreadful noises which Madame Morlot extorts from his sensitive and suffering piano, and at the necessity which lies upon him to go and congratulate her upon her performance. Ah! if his tortured conscience might but congratulate her and himself upon its close! And so the scale ascends. Hills on hills and Alps on Alps arise, and who shall mount the ultimate peak till all the world shall say, "Here reigns the

Excellence"? I listen with pleasure to untutored Nancie till Anabella takes all the wind from her sails. I think the force of music can no further go than Madame Morlot, and, behold, Herr Driesbach has knocked out that underpinning. I am bewildered, and I say, helplessly, "What shall I admire and be *à la mode?*" But if it is so disheartening to me, who am only a passive listener, what must be the agonies of the *dramatis personæ?* "Hang it!" says Charles Lamb, "how I like to be liked, and what I do to be liked!" And do Nancie, Harriette, and Herr Driesbach like it any less? What shall avenge them for their *spretæ injuria formæ?* What can repay the hapless performer, who has performed her very best, for learning by terrible, indisputable indirections that her cherished and boasted Cremona is but a very second fiddle?

So, standing on the high ground of certain immunity from criticism and hostile judgment, I do not so much console myself as I do not stand in need of consolation. I rather give thanks for my mute and necessarily unoffending lips, and I shall go in great good-humor to Camilla's concert.

There are many different ways of going to a concert. You can be one of a party of fashionable people to whom music is a diversion, a pastime, an agreeable change from the assembly or the theatre. They applaud, they condemn, they criticise. They know all about it. Into such company as this, even I, whose poor old head is always getting itself wedged in where it has no business to be, have chanced to be thrown. This is torture. My cue is to turn into the Irishman's echo, which always returned for his "How d' ye do?" a "Pretty well, thank you." I cling to the skirts of that member of the party who is agreed to have the best taste and echo his responses an octave higher. If he sighs at the end of a song, I bring out my pocket-handkerchief. If he says "charming," I murmur "delicious." If he thinks it "exquisite," I pronounce it "enchanting." Where he is rapt in admiration, I go into a trance, and so shamble through the performances, miserable impostor that I am, and ten to one nobody finds out that I am a dunce, fit for treason, stratagem, and spoils. It is a great strain upon the mental powers, but it is wonderful to see how much may be accomplished, and what skill may be attained, by long practice.

Also one may go to a concert as a conductor with a single musical friend. By conductor I do not mean escort, but a magnetic conductor, rapture conductor, a fit medium through which to convey away his delight, so that he shall not become surcharged and explode. He does not take you for your pleasure, nor for his own, but for use. He desires some one to whom he can from time to time express his opinions and his enthusiasm, sure of an attentive listener, — since nothing is so pleasant as to see one's views welcomed. Now you cannot pretend that in such a case your listening is thoroughly honest. You are receptive of theories, criticisms, and reminiscences; but you would not like to be obliged to pass an examination on them afterwards. You do, it must be confessed, sometimes, in the midst of eloquent dissertations, strike out into little flowery by-paths of your own, quite foreign to the grand paved-ways along which your friend supposes he is so kind as to be leading you. But however digressive your mind may be, do not suffer your eyes to digress. Whatever may be the intensity of your *ennui*, endeavor to preserve an animated expression, and your success is complete. This is all that is necessary. You will never be called upon for notes or comments. Your little escapades will never be detected. It is not your opinions that were sought, nor your education that was to be furthered. You were only an escape-pipe, and your mission ceased when the soul of song fled and the gas was turned off. This, too, is all that can justly be demanded. Minister, lecturer, singer, no one has any right to ask of his audience anything more than opportunity, — the externals of attention. All the rest is his own look-out. If you prepossess your mind with a theme, you do not give him an even chance. You must offer him in the beginning a *tabula rasa*, — a fair field, and then it is his business to go in and win your attention; and if he cannot, let him pay the costs, for the fault is his own.

This also is torture, but its name is Zoar, a little one.

There is yet another way. You may go with one or many who believe in individuality. They go to the concert for love of music, — negatively for its rest and refreshment, positively for its embodied delights. They take you for your enjoyment, which they permit you to compass after your own fashion. They force from you no comment. They demand no criticism. They do not require censure as your certificate of taste. They do not trouble themselves with your demeanor. If you choose to talk in the pauses, they are receptive and cordial. If you choose to be silent, it is just as well. If you go to sleep, they will not mind, — unless, under the spell of the genius of the place, your sleep becomes vocal, and you involuntarily join the concert in the undesirable *rôle* of De Trop. If you go into raptures, it is all the same; you are not watched and made a note of. They leave you at the top of your bent. Whether you shall be amused, delighted, or disgusted, they respect your decisions and allow you to remain free.

How did I go to my concert? Can I tell for the eyes that made "a sunshine in the shady place"? Was I not veiled with the beautiful hair, and blinded with the lily's white splendor? So went I with the Fairy Queen in her golden coach drawn by six white mice, and, behold, I was in Camilla's concert-room.

It is to be a fiddle affair. Now I am free to say, if there is anything I hate, it is a fiddle. Hide it away under as many Italian coatings as you choose, viol, violin, viola, violone, violoncello, violoncellettissimo, at bottom it is all one, a fiddle; in its best estate, a whirligig, without dignity, sentiment, or power; and at worst a rubbing, rasping, squeaking, woolleny, noisy nuisance, that it sets my teeth on edge to think of. I shudder at the mere memory of the reluctant bow dragging its slow length across the whining strings. And here I am, in my sober senses, come to hear a fiddle!

But it is Camilla's. Do you remember a little girl who, a few years ago, became famous for her wonderful performance on the violin? At six years of age she went to a great concert, and of all the fine instruments there, the unseen spirit within her made choice, "Papa, I should like to learn the violin." So she learned it and loved it, and when ten years old delighted foreign and American audiences with her marvellous genius. It was the little Camilla who now, after ten years of silence, tuned her beloved instrument once more.

As she walks softly and quietly in, I am conscious of a disappointment. I had unwittingly framed for her an æsthetic violin, with the essential strings and bridge and bow indeed, but submerged and forgot in such Orient splendors as befit her glorious genius. Barbaric pearl and gold, finest carved work, flashing gems from Indian watercourses, the delicatest pink sea-shell, a bubble-prism caught and crystallized, — of all rare and curious substances wrought with dainty device, fantastic as a dream, and resplendent as the light, should her instrument be fashioned. Only in "something rich and strange" should the mystic soul lie sleeping for whom her lips shall break the spell of slumber, and her young fingers unbar the sacred gates. And, oh me! it is, after all, the very same old red fiddle! Dee, dee!

But she neither glides nor trips nor treads, as heroines invariably do, but walks in like a good Christian woman. She steps upon the stage and faces the audience that gives her hearty greeting and waits the prelude. There is time for cool survey. I am angry still about the red fiddle, and I look scrutinizingly at her dress, and think how ugly is the mode. The skirt is white silk, — a brocade, I believe, — at any rate, stiff, and, though probably full to overflowing in the hands of the seamstress, who must compress it within prescribed limits about the waist, looks scanty and straight. Why should she not, she who comes before us to-night, not as a fashion, but an inspiration, — why should she not assume that immortal classic drapery whose graceful falls and folds the sculptor vainly tries to imitate, the painter vainly seeks to limn? When Corinne tuned her lyre at the Capitol, when she knelt to be crowned with her laurel crown at the hands of a Roman senator, is it possible to conceive her swollen out with crinoline? And yet I remember, that, though *sa robe était blanche, et son costume était très pittoresque*, it was *sans s'écarter cependant assez des usages reçus pour que l'on pût y trouver de l'affectation;* and I suppose, if one should now suddenly collapse from conventional rotundity to antique statuesqueness, the great "*on*" would very readily "*y trouver de l'affectation.*" Nevertheless, though one must dress in Rome as Romans do, and though the Roman way of dressing is, taking all things into the account, as good as any, and, if not more graceful, a thousand times more convenient, wholesome, comfortable, and manageable than Helen's, still it does seem that, when one steps out of the ordinary area of Roman life and assumes an abnormal position, one might, without violence, assume temporarily an abnormal dress, and refresh our dilated eyes once more with flowing, wavy outlines. Music is one of the eternities: why should not its accessories be? Why should a discord disturb the eye, when only concords delight the ear?

But I lift my eyes from Camilla's unpliant drapery to the red red rose in her hair, and thence, naturally, to her silent face, and in that instant ugly dress and red red rose fade out of my sight. What is it that I see, with tearful tenderness and a nameless pain at the heart? A young face deepened and drawn with suffering; dark, large eyes, whose natural laughing light has been quenched in tears, yet shining still with a distant gleam caught from the eternal fires. O still, pathetic face! A sterner form than Time has passed and left his vestige there. Happy little girl, playing among the flickering shadows of the Rhine-land, who could not foresee the darker shadows that should settle and never lift nor flicker from her heavy heart? Large, lambent eyes, that might have been sweet, but now are only steadfast, — that may yet be sweet, when they look to-night into a baby's cradle, but gazing now upon a waiting audience, are only steadfast. Ah! so it is. Life has such hard conditions, that every dear and precious gift, every rare virtue, every pleasant facility, every genial endowment, love, hope, joy, wit, sprightliness, benevolence, must sometimes be cast into the crucible to distil the one elixir, patience. Large, lambent eyes, in which days and nights of tears are petrified, steadfast eyes that are neither mournful nor hopeful nor anxious, but with such unvoiced sadness in their depths that the hot tears well up in my heart, what do you see in the waiting audience? Not censure, nor pity, nor forgiveness, for you do not need them, — but surely a warm human sympathy, since heart can speak to heart, though the thin, fixed lips have sealed their secret well. Sad mother, whose rose of life was crushed before it had budded, tender young lips that had drunk the cup of sorrow to the dregs, while their cup of bliss should hardly yet be brimmed for life's sweet spring-time, your crumbling fanes and broken arches and prostrate columns lie not among the ruins of Time. Be comforted of that. They bear witness of a more pitiless Destroyer, and by this token I know there shall dawn a brighter day. The God of the fatherless and the widow, of the worse than widowed and fatherless, the Avenger of the Slaughter of the Innocents, be with you, and shield and shelter and bless!

But the overture wavers to its close, and her soul hears far off the voice of the coming Spirit. A deeper light shines in the strangely introverted eyes, — the look as of one listening intently to a distant melody which no one else can hear, — the look of one to whom the room and the people and the presence are but a dream, and past and future centre on the far-off song. Slowly she raises her instrument. I almost shudder to see the tawny wood touching her white shoulder; yet that cannot be common or unclean which she so loves and carries with almost a caress. Still intent, she raises the bow with a slow sweep, as if it were a wand of divination. Nearer and nearer comes the heavenly voice, pouring around her a flood of mystic melody. And now at last it breaks upon our ears, — softly at first, only a sweet faint echo from that other sphere, but deepening, strengthening, conquering, — now rising on the swells of a controlling passion, now sinking into the depths with its low wail of pain; exultant, scornful, furious, in the glad outburst of opening joy and the fierce onslaught of strength; crowned, sceptred, glorious in garland and singing-robes, throned in the high realms of its inheritance, a kingdom of boundless scope and ever new delights: then sweeping down through the lower world with diminishing rapture, rapture lessening into astonishment, astonishment dying into despair, it gathers up the passion and the pain, the blight and woe and agony; all garnered joys are scattered. Evil supplants the good. Hope dies, love pales, and faith is faint and wan. But every death has its moaning ghost, pale spectre of vanished loves. Oh, fearful revenge of the outraged soul! The mysterious, uncomprehended, incomprehensible soul! The irrepressible, unquenchable, immortal soul, whose every mark is everlasting! Every secret sin committed against it cries out from the house-tops. Cunning may strive to conceal, will may determine to smother, love may fondly whisper, "It does not hurt"; but the soul will not *be* outraged. Somewhere, somehow, when and where you least expect, unconscious, perhaps, to its owner, unrecognized by the many, visible only to the clear vision, somewhere, somehow, the soul bursts asunder its bonds. It is but a little song, a tripping of the fingers over the keys, a drawing of the bow across the strings,—only that! Only that? It is the protest of the wronged and ignored soul. It is the outburst of the pent and prisoned soul. All the ache and agony, all the secret wrong and silent endurance, all the rejected love and wounded trust and slighted truth, all the riches wasted, all the youth poisoned, all the hope trampled, all the light darkened, — all meet and mingle in a mad whirl of waters. They surge and lash and rage, a wild storm of harmony. Barriers are broken. Circumstance is not. The soul! the soul! the soul! the wronged and fettered soul! the freed and royal soul! It alone is king. Lift up your heads, O ye gates, and be ye lift up, ye everlasting doors, and the King of Glory shall come in! Tremble, O Tyrant, in your mountain-fastness! Tremble, Deceiver, in your cavern under the sea! Your victim is your accuser. Your sin has found you out. Your crime cries to Heaven. You have condemned and killed the just. You have murdered the innocent in secret places, and in the noonday sun the voice of their blood crieth unto God from the ground. There is no speech nor language. There is no will nor design. The seal of silence is unbroken. But unconscious, entranced, inspired, the god has lashed his Sibyl on. The vital instinct of the soul, its heaven-born, up-springing life, flings back the silver veil, and reveals the hidden things to him who hath eyes to see.

The storm sobs and soothes itself to silence.

There is a hush, and then an enthusiasm of delight. The small head slightly bows, the still face scarcely smiles, the slight form disappears, — and after all, it was only a fiddle.

"When Music, heavenly maid, was young," begins the ode; but Music, heavenly maid, seems to me still so young, so very young, as scarcely to have made her power felt. Her language is as yet unlearned. When a baby of a month is hungry or in pain, he contrives to make the fact understood. If he is at peace with himself and his surroundings, he leaves no doubt on the subject. To precisely this degree of intelligibility has the Heavenly Maid attained among us. When Beethoven sat down to the composition of one of his grand harmonies, there was undoubtedly in his mind as distinct a conception of that which he wished to express, of that within him which clamored for expression, as ever rises before a painter's eye, or sings in a poet's brain. Thought, emotion, passion, hope, fear, joy, sorrow, each had its life and law. The painter paints you this. This the poet sings you. You stand before a picture, and to your loving, searching gaze its truths unfold. You read the poem with the understanding, and catch its concealed meanings. But what do you know of what was in Beethoven's soul? Who grasps his conception? Who faithfully renders, who even thoroughly knows his idea? Here and there to some patient night-watcher the lofty gates are unbarred, "on golden hinges turning." But, for the greater part, the musician who would tell so much speaks to unheeding ears. We comprehend him but infinitesimally. It is the Battle of Prague. Adrianus sits down to the piano, and Dion stands by his side, music-sheet in hand, acting as showman. "The cannon," says Dion, at the proper place, and you imagine you recognize reverberation. "Charge," continues Dion, and with a violent effort you fancy the ground trembles. "Groans of the wounded," and you are partly horror-struck and partly incredulous. But what lame representation is this! As if one should tie a paper around the ankle of the Belvedere Apollo, with the inscription, "This is the ankle." A collar declares, "This is the neck." A bandeau locates his "forehead." A bracelet indicates the "arm." Is the sculpture thus significant? Hardly more does our music yet signify to us. You hear an unfamiliar air. You like it or dislike it, or are indifferent. You can tell that it is slow and plaintive, or brisk and lively, or perhaps even that it is defiant or stirring; but how insensible you are to the delicate shades of its meaning! How hidden is the song in the heart of the composer till he gives you the key! You hear as though you heard not. You hear the thunder, and the cataract, and the crash of the avalanche; but the song of the nightingale, the chirp of the katydid, the murmur of the waterfall never reach you. This cannot be the ultimatum. Music must hold in its own bosom its own interpretation, and man must have in his its corresponding susceptibilities. Music is language, and language implies a people who employ and understand it. But music, even by its professor, is as yet faintly understood. Its meanings go on crutches. They must be helped out by words. What does this piece say to you? Interpret it. You cannot. You must be taught much before you can know all. It must be translated from music into speech before you can entirely assimilate it. Musicians do not trust alone to notes for moods. Their light shines only through a glass darkly. But in some other sphere, in some happier time, in a world where gross wants shall have disappeared, and therefore the grossness of words shall be no longer necessary, where hunger and thirst and cold and care and passion have no more admittance, and only love and faith and hope and admiration and aspiration shall crave utterance, in that blessed unseen world shall not music be the every-day speech, conveying meaning not only with a sweetness, but with an accuracy, delicacy, and distinctness, of which we have now but a faint conception? Here words are not only rough, but ambiguous. There harmonies shall be minutely intelligible. Speak with what directness we can, be as explanatory, emphatic, illustrative as we may, there are mistakes, misunderstandings, many and grievous, and consequent missteps and catastrophes. But in that other world language shall be exactly coexistent with life; music shall be precisely adequate to meaning. There shall be no hidden corners, no bungling incompatibilities, but the searching sound penetrates into the secret sources of the soul, all-pervading. Not a nook, not a crevice, no maze so intricate, but the sound floats in to gather up the fragrant aroma, to bear it yonder to another waiting soul, and deposit it as deftly by unerring magnetisms in the corresponding clefts.

Toot away, then, fifer-fellow! Turn your slow crank, inexorable Italian! Thrum your thrums, Miss Laura, for Signor Bernadotti! You are a long way off, but your footprints point the right way. With many a yawn and sigh subjective, with, I greatly fear me, many a malediction objective, you are "learning the language of another world." To us, huddled together in our little ant-hill, one is "*une bête*," and one is "*mon ange*"; but from that fixed star we are all so far as to have no parallax.

But I come down from the golden stars, for the white-robed one has raised her wand again, and we float away through the glowing gates of the sunrise, over the purple waves, over the vine-lands of sunny France, in among the shadows of the storied Pyrenees. Sorrow and sighing have fled away. Tragedy no longer "in sceptred pall comes sweeping by"; but young lambs leap in wild frolic, silken-fleeced sheep lie on the slopes of the hills, and shepherd calls to shepherd from his mountain-peak. Peaceful hamlets lie far down the valley, and every gentle height blooms with a happy home. Dark-eyed Basque girls dance through the fruitful orchards. I see the gleam of their scarlet scarfs wound in with their bold black hair. I hear their rich voices trilling the lays of their land, and ringing with happy laughter. But I mount higher and yet higher, till gleam and voice are lost. Here the freshening air sweeps down, and the low gurgle of living water purling out from cool, dark chasms, mingles with the shepherd's flute. Here the young shepherd himself climbs, leaping from rock to rock, supple, strong, brave, and free as the soul of his race, — the same iron in his sinews, and the same fire in his blood that dealt the "dolorous rout" to Charlemagne a thousand years ago. Sweetly across the path of Roncesvalles blow the evening gales, wafting tender messages to the listening girls below. Green grows the grass and gay the flowers that spring from the blood of princely paladins, the flower of chivalry. No bugle-blast can bring old Roland back, though it wind long and loud through the echoing woods. Lads and lasses, worthy scions of valiant stems, may sit on happy evenings in the shadow of the vines, or group themselves on the greensward in the pauses of the dance, and sing their songs of battle and victory, — the olden legends of their heroic sires; but the strain that floats down from the darkening slopes into their heart of hearts, the song that reddens in their glowing cheeks, and throbs in their throbbing breasts, and shines in their dewy eyes, is not the shock of deadly onset, glorious though it be. It is the sweet old song, — old, yet ever new, — whose burden is,

"Come live with me and be my love," —

old, yet always new, — sweet and tender, and not to be gainsaid, whether it be piped to a shepherdess in Arcadia, or whether a princess hears it from princely lips in her palace on the sea.

But the mountain shadows stretch down the valleys and wrap the meadows in twilight. Farther and farther the notes recede as the flutesman gathers his quiet flock along the winding paths. Smooth and far in the tranquil evening-air fall the receding notes, a clear, silvery sweetness; farther and farther in the hushed evening air, lessening and lowering, as you bend to listen, till the vanishing strain just cleaves, a single thread of pearl-pure melody, finer, finer, finer, through the dewy twilight, and — you hear only your own heart-beats. It is not dead, but risen. It never ceased. It knew no pause. It has gone up the heights to mingle with the songs of the angels. You rouse yourself with a start, and gaze at your neighbor half bewildered. What is it? Where are we? Oh, my remorseful heart! There is no shepherd, no mountain, no girl with scarlet ribbon and black braids bound on her beautiful temples. It was only a fiddle on a platform!

Now you need not tell me that. I know better. I have lived among fiddles all my life, — embryotic, Silurian fiddles, splintered from cornstalks, that blessed me in the golden afternoons of green summers waving in the sunshine of long ago, — sympathetic fiddles that did me yeomen's service once, when I fell off a bag of corn up garret and broke my head, and the frightened fiddles, not knowing what else to do, came and fiddled to me lying on the settee, with such boundless, extravagant flourish that nobody heard the doctor's gig rolling by, and so *sinciput* and *occiput* were left overnight to compose their own quarrels, whereby I was naturally all right before the doctor had a chance at me, suffering only the slight disadvantage of going broken-headed through life. What I might have been with a whole skull, I don't know; but I will say, that, good or bad, and even in fragments, my head is the best part of me.

Yes, I think I may dare affirm that whatever there is to know about a fiddle I know, and I can give my affidavit that it is no fiddle that takes you up on its broad wings, outstripping the "wondrous horse of brass," which required

> "the space of a day natural,
> This is to sayn, four and twenty houres,
> Wher so you list, in drought or elles showres,

To beren your body into every place
To which your herte willeth for to pace,
Withouten wemme of you, thurgh foule or faire," —

since it bears you, "withouten" even so much as your "herte's" will, in a moment's time, over the seas and above the stars.

A fiddle, is it? Do not for one moment believe it. — A poet walked through Southern woods, and the Dryads opened their hearts to him. They unfolded the secrets that dwell in the depths of forests. They sang to him under the starlight the songs of their green, rustling land. They whispered the loves of the trees sentient to poets: —

"The sayling pine; the cedar, proud and tall;
The vine-propt elme; the poplar, never dry;
The builder oake, sole king of forrests all;
The aspine, good for staves; the cypresse funerall;
The lawrell, meed of mightie conquerours
And poets sage; the firre, that weepeth stille;
The willow, worne of forlorne paramours;
The eugh, obedient to the benders will;
The birch, for shaftes; the sallow, for the mill;
The mirrhe, sweete-bleeding in the bitter wounde;
The warlike beech; the ash, for nothing ill;
The fruitful olive; and the platane round;
The carver holme; the maple, seldom inward sound."

They sang to him with their lutes. They danced before him with sunny, subtile grace, wreathing him with strange loveliness. They brought him honey and wine in the white cups of lilies, till his brain was drunk with delight; and they kept watch by his moss pillow, while he slept.

In the dew of the morning, he arose and felled the kindly tree that had sheltered him, not knowing it was the home of Arborine, fairest of the wood-nymphs. But he did it not for cruelty, but tenderness, to carve a memorial of his most memorable night, and so pulled down no thunders on his head. For Arborine loved him, and, like her sister Undine in the North, found her soul in loving him. Unseen, the beautiful nymph guided his hand as he fashioned the sounding viol, not knowing he was fashioning a palace for a soul new-born. He wrought skilfully, strung the intense chords, and smote them with the sympathetic bow. What burst of music flooded the still air! What new song trembled among the mermaiden tresses of the oaks! What new presence quivered in every listening harebell and every fearful windflower? The forest felt a change, for tricksy nymph had proved a mortal love, and put off her fairy phantasms for the deep consciousness of humanity. The wood heard, bewildered. A shudder as of sorrow thrilled through it. A breeze that was almost sad swept down the shady aisles as the Poet passed out into the sunshine and the world.

But Nature knows no pain, though Arborines appear never more. A balm springs up in every wound. Over the hills, and far away beyond their utmost purple rim, and deep into the dying day, the happy love-born one followed her love, happy to exchange her sylvan immortality for the spasm of mortal life, — happy, in her human self-abnegation, to lie close on his heart and whisper close in his ear, though he knew only the loving voice and never the loving lips. Through the world they passed, the Poet and his mystic viol. It gathered to itself the melodies that fluttered over sea and land, — songs of the mountains, and songs of the valleys, — murmurs of love, and the trumpet-tones of war, — bugle-blast of huntsman on the track of the chamois, and mother's lullaby to the baby at her breast. All that earth had of sweetness the nymph drew into her viol-home, and poured it forth anew in strains of more than mortal harmony. The fire and fervor of human hearts, the quiet ripple of inland waters, the anthem of the stormy sea, the voices of the flowers and the birds, lent their melody to the song of her who knew them all.

The Poet died. Died, too, sweet Arborine, swooning away in the fierce grasp of this stranger Sorrow, to enter by the black gate of death into the full presence and recognition of him by loving whom she had learned to be.

The viol passed into strange hands, and wandered down the centuries, but its olden echoes linger still. Fragrance of Southern woods, coolness of shaded waters, inspiration of mountain-breezes, all the secret forces of Nature that the wood-nymph knew, and the joy, the passion, and the pain that throb only in a woman's heart, lie still, silent under the silent strings, but wakening into life at the touch of a royal hand.

Do you not believe my story? But I have seen the viol and the royal hand!

CHERI.

CHERI.

CHERI is the Canary-bird, — a yellow bird with a white tail, when the cat leaves him any tail at all. He came as a gift, and I welcomed him, but without gratitude. For a gift is nothing. Always behind the gift stands the giver, and under the gift lies the motive. The gift itself has no character. It may be a blunder, a bribe, an offering, according to the nature and design of the giver; and you are outraged, or magnanimous, or grateful. Cheri came to me with no love-token under his soft wings, — only the "good riddance" of his heartless master. Those little black eyes had twinkled, those shining silken feathers had gleamed, that round throat had waved with melody in vain. He had worn his welcome out. Even the virtues which should have throbbed, tender and all-embracing, under priestly vestments, had no tenderness, no embrace for him, — only a mockery and a prophecy, a cold and cynical prediction that I should soon tire of his shrill voice. Yes, Cheri, your sweet silver trills, your rippling June-brook warbles, were to him only a shrew's scolding. I took the bird wrathfully, his name had been Cherry, and rechristened him on the spot Cheri, in anticipation of the new life that was to dawn upon him, no longer despised Cherry, but Cheri, my cherished one.

He has been with me now nearly a year, and every trick of his voice and head and tail is just as fresh, graceful, and charming as on the first day of his arrival. He is a constant recreation and delight. I put him in my own room, and went up to look at him two or three times the first evening. Every time I looked he would be quite still, but his little black beads of eyes shone wide open in the candle-light, and I recalled how Chaucer's

> "Smale foules maken melodie
> That slepen alle night with open eye,"

and reflected that Cheri certainly made melodie enough in the daytime to be ranked with the poetic tribe; but one night, after he had been here long enough to have worn away his nervous excitement, I happened to go into the room very softly, and the black beads had disappeared. The tiny head had disappeared too, and only a little round ball of feathers was balanced on his perch. Then I remembered that chickens have a way of putting their heads in their pockets when they go to sleep, and poetry yielded to poultry, Cheri stepped out of Chaucer, and took his place in the hencoop.

He has had an eventful life since he came to me. In the summer I hung him on a hook under the piazza for the merry company of robins and bluebirds, which he enjoyed excessively. One day, in the midst of a most successful concert, an envious gust swept down the cage, up went the door, and out flew the frightened bird. I could have borne to lose him, but I was sure he would lose himself, — a tender little *dilettante*, served like a prince all the days of his life, never having to lift a finger to help himself, or knowing a want unsatisfied. Now, thrown suddenly upon his own resources, homeless, friendless, forlorn, how could he ever make his fortune in this bleak New England, for all he has, according to Cuvier, more brains in his head in proportion to his size than any other created being? I saw him already in midsummer, drenched with cold rains, chilled and perishing; but sharper eyes than mine had marked his flight, and a pair of swift hands plunged after him into the long grass that tangled his wings and kept him back from headlong destruction.

Amicable relations between Cheri and the cat are on a most precarious footing. The cat was established in the house before Cheri came, — a lovely, frolicsome kitten, that sat in my lap, purred up in my face, rubbed her nose against my book, and grew up, to my horror, out of all possibility of caresses, into a great, ugly, fierce, fighting animal, that comes into the house drenched and dripping from the mud-puddle in which she has been rolling in a deadly struggle with every Tom Hyer and Bill Sayers of the cat kind that make night hideous through the village. This cat seems to be possessed with a devil every time she looks at Cheri. Her green eyes bulge out of her head, her whole feline soul rushes into them, and glares with a hot, greeny-yellow fire and fury of unquenchable desire. One evening I had put the cage on a chair, and was quietly reading in the room below, when a great slam and bang startled the house. "The bird!" shrieked a voice, mine or another's. I rushed up-stairs. The moonlight shone in, revealing the cage upturned on the floor, the water running, the seeds scattered about, and a feather here and there. The cat had managed to elude observation and glide in, and she now managed to elude observation and glide out. Cheri was alive, but his enemy had attacked him in the flank, and turned his left wing, which was pretty much gone, according to all appearances. He could not mount his perch, and for three days, crouching on the floor of his cage, life seemed to have lost its charm. His spirits drooped, his appetite failed, and his song was hushed. Then his feathers grew out again, his spirit returned to him with his appetite, and he hopped about as good as new. To think that cat should have been able to thrust her villanous claw in far enough to clutch a handful of feathers out of him before she upset the cage! I have heard that canaries sometimes die of fright. If so, I think Cheri would have been justified in doing it. To have a great overgrown monster, with burning globes of eyes as big as your head and claws as sharp as daggers, come glaring on you in the darkness, overturn your house, and grab half your side with one huge paw, is a thing well calculated to alarm a person of delicate organization.

Then I said to myself, this cat thinks she has struck a placer, and a hundred to one she will be driving her pick in here again directly. So I removed the cage immediately, and set it on a high bureau, with a "whisking-stick" close by it. Sure enough I was awakened the next morning before day by a prolonged and mournful "maeouw" of disappointment from the old dragon at not finding the prey where she had expected. Before she had time to push her researches to success, she and I and the stick were not letting the grass grow under our feet on the stairs. Long after, when the fright and flurry had been forgotten, the cage was again left in a rocking-chair in the upper front entry, where I had been sitting in the sunshine all the afternoon with Cheri, who thinks me, though far inferior to a robin or a finch, still better than no company at all. In the course of the evening I happened to open the lower entry door, when the cat suddenly appeared on the lower stair. I should have supposed she had come from the sitting-room with me, but for a certain elaborate and enforced *nonchalance* in her demeanor, a jaunty air of *insouciance*, as far removed, on the one hand, from the calm equilibrium of dignity which almost imperceptibly soothes and reassures you, as from the guileless gayety of infantile ignorance, which perforce "medicines your weariness," on the other, — a demeanor which at once disgusts and alarms you. I felt confident that some underhand work was going on. I went upstairs. There was Cheri again, this time with his right wing gone, and a modicum of his tail. The cage had retained its position, but the Evil One had made her grip at him; and the same routine of weariness, silence, loss of appetite and spirits was to be gone through with again, followed by re-pluming and recuperating. But every time I think of it, I am lost in wonder at the skill and sagacity of that cat. It was something to carry on the campaign in a rocking-chair, without disturbing the base of operations so as to make a noise and create a diversion in favor of the bird; but the cunning and self-control which, as soon as I opened the door, made her leave the bird, and come purring about my feet, and tossing her innocent head to disarm suspicion, was wonderful. I look at her sometimes, when we have been sitting together a long while, and say, with steadfast gaze, "Cat-soul, what are you? Where are you? Whence come you? Whither go you?" But she only flirts her whiskers, and gives me no satisfaction.

But I saw at once that I must make a different disposition of Cheri. It would never do to have him thus mauled. To be sure, I suppose the cat might be educationally mauled into letting him alone; but why should I beat the beast for simply acting after her kind? Has not the Manciple, with as much philosophy as poetry, bidden,—

"Let take a cat, and foster hire with milke
And tendre flesh, and make hire couche of silke,
And let hire see a mous go by the wall,
Anon she weiveth milke and flesh, and all,
And every deintee that is in that hous,
Swich appetit hath she to ete the mous
Lo, here hath kind hire domination,
And appetit flemeth discretion"?

Accordingly I respected the "domination" of "kind," took the cage into the parlor and hung it up in the folds of the window-curtain, where there is always sunshine, wrapping a strip of brown paper around the lower part of the cage, so that he should not scatter his seeds over the carpet. What is the result? Perversely he forsakes his cup of seed, nicely mixed to suit his royal taste; forsakes his conch-shell, nicely fastened within easy reach: forsakes the bright sand that lies whitely strewn beneath his feet, and pecks, pecks, pecks away at that stiff, raw, coarse brown paper, jagging great gaps in it from hour to hour. I do not mind the waste of paper, even at its present high prices; but suppose there should be an ornithological dyspepsia; or a congestion of the gizzard, or some internal derangement? The possibility of such a thing gave me infinite uneasiness at first; but he has now been at it so long without suffering perceptible harm, that I begin to think Nature knows what she is about, and brown paper agrees with birds. I am confident, however, that he would devour it all the same, whether it were salutary or otherwise, for he is a mule-headed fellow. I let him loose on the flower-stand yesterday, hoping he might deal death to a horde of insects who had suddenly squatted on the soil of the money-plant. He scarcely so much as looked at the insects, but hopped up to the adjoining rose-bush, and proceeded to gorge himself with tender young leaves. I tilted him away from that, and he fluttered across the money-plant over to the geranium opposite. Disturbed there, he flashed to the other side of the stand, and, quick as thought, gave one mighty dab at a delicate little fuchsia that is just "picking up" from the effects of transplanting and a long winter journey. Seeing he was bent on making himself disagreeable, I put him into his cage again, first having to chase him all about the room to catch him, and prying him up at last from between a picture and the wall, where he had flown and settled down in his struggle to get out. For my Cheri is not in the least tame. He is an entirely uneducated bird. I have seen canaries sit on people's fingers and eat from their tongues, but Cheri flies around like a madman at the first approach of fingers. Indeed, he quite provokes me by his want of trust. He ought to know by this time that I am his friend, yet he goes off into violent hysterics the moment I touch him. He does not even show fight. There is no outcry of anger or alarm, but one "Yang!" of utter despair. He gives up at once. Life is a burden, his "Yang!" says. "Everything is going to ruin. There is no use in trying. I wish I never was born. Yang!" Little old croaker, what are you Yang-ing for? Nobody wishes to harm you. It is your little cowardly heart that sees lions and hyenas in a well-meaning forefinger and thumb. Be sensible.

Another opportunity for the exhibition of his perversity is furnished by his bathing. His personal habits are exquisite. He has a gentleman's liking for cold water and the appliances of cleanliness; but if I spread a newspaper on the floor, and prepare everything for a comfortable and convenient bath, the little imp clings to his perch immovable. It is not only a bath that he wishes, but fun. Mischief is his *sine qua non* of enjoyment. "What is the good of bathing, if you cannot spoil anything?" says he. "If you will put the bath-tub in the window, where I can splash and spatter the glass and the curtains and the furniture, very well, but if not, why —" he sits incorrigible, with eyes half closed, pretending to be sleepy, and not see water anywhere, the rogue!

One day I heard a great "to-do" in the cage, and found that half the blind was shut, and helped Cheri to a reflection of himself, which he evidently thought was another bird, and he was in high feather. He hopped about from perch to perch, sidled from one side of the cage to the other, bowed and bobbed and courtesied to himself, sung and swelled and smirked, and became thoroughly frantic with delight. "Poor thing!" I said, "you are lonely, no wonder." I had given him a new and shining cage, a green curtain, a sunny window; but of what avail are these to a desolate heart? Who does not know that the soul may starve in splendor? "Solitude," says Balzac, I think, "is a fine thing; but it is also a fine thing to have some one to whom you can say, from time to time, that solitude is a fine thing." I know that I am but a poor substitute for a canary-bird, — a gross and sorry companion for one of ethereal mould. I can supply seed and water and conch-shells, but what do I know of finchy loves and hopes? What sympathy have I to offer in his joyous or sorrowful moods? How can I respond to his enthusiasms? How can I compare notes with him as to the sunshine and the trees and the curtain and views of life? It is not sunshine, but sympathy, that lights up houses into homes. Companionship is what he needs, alike for his higher aspirations and his every-day experiences, — somebody to whom he can observe that "The sand is rather gritty to-day, is n't it?"

"Very much as usual, my dear."

"Here is a remarkably plump seed, my dear; won't you have it?"

"No, thank you, dear, nothing more. Trol-la-la-r-r-r!"

"Do let me help you to a bit of this hemp. It is quite a marvel of ripeness."

"Thank you. Just a snip. Plenty."

"My dear, I think you are stopping in the bath-tub too long this morning. I fancied you were a trifle hoarse yesterday."

"It was the company, pet. I strained my voice slightly in that last duet."

"We shall have to be furnished with a new shell before long. This old one is getting to be rather the last peas of the picking."

"Yes, I nearly broke my beak over it yesterday. I was quite ashamed of it when the ladies were staring at you so admiringly."

"Little one, I have a great mind to try that swing. It has tempted me this long while."

"My love, I beg you will do no such thing. You will inevitably break your neck."

Instead of this pleasant conjugal chit-chat, what has he? Nothing. He stands looking out at the window till his eyes ache, and then he turns around and looks at me. If any one comes in and begins to talk, and he delightedly joins, he gets a handkerchief thrown over his cage. Sometimes the cat creeps in, — very seldom, for I do not trust her, even with the height of the room between them, and punish her whenever I find her on forbidden ground, by taking her up-stairs and putting her out on the porch-roof, where she has her choice to stay and starve or jump off. This satisfies my conscience while giving a good lesson to the cat, who is not fond of saltatory feats, now that she is getting into years. If it is after her kind to prey upon birds, and she must therefore not be beaten, it is also after her kind to leap from anywhere and come down on her feet, and therefore the thing does not harm her. Whenever she does stealthily worm herself in, Cheri gives the pitch the moment he sets eyes on her. Cat looks up steadily at him for five minutes. Cheri, confident, strikes out in a very tempting way. Cat describes a semicircle around the window, back and forth, back and forth, keeping ever her back to the room and her front to the foe, glaring and mewing and licking her chaps. O, what a delicious tit-bit, if one could but get at it! Cheri sings relentlessly. Like Shirley with Louis Moore in her clutches, he will not subdue one of his charms in compassion.

> "Certes it is *not* of herte, all that he sings."

She leaps into a chair. Not a quarter high enough.

She jumps to the window-seat, and walks to and fro, managing the turning-points with much difficulty. Impossible. She goes over to the other window. Still worse. She takes up position on the sofa, and her whole soul exhales into one want.

She mews and licks her chaps alternately. Cheri "pitilessly sweet" sings with unsparing insolence at the top of his voice, and looks indifferently over her head.

That is the extent of his society. "It is too bad," I said one day, and scoured the country for a canary-bird. Everybody had had one, but it was sold. Then I remembered Barnum's Happy Family, and went out to the hen-pen, and brought in a little auburn chicken, with white breast, and wings just budding; a size and a half larger than Cheri, it is true, but the smallest of the lot, and very soft and small for a chicken, the prettiest wee, waddling tot you ever saw, a Minnie Warren of a little duck, and put him in the cage. A tempest in a tea-pot! Cheri went immediately into fits and furies. He hopped about convulsively. You might have supposed him attacked simultaneously with St. Anthony's fire, St. Vitus's dance, and delirium tremens. He shrieked, he writhed, he yelled, he raved. The chicken was stupid. If he had exerted himself a little to be agreeable, if he had only shown the smallest symptom of interest or curiosity or desire to cultivate an acquaintance, I have no doubt something might have been accomplished; but he just huddled down in one corner of the cage, half frightened to death, like a logy, lumpy, country bumpkin as he was, and I swept him back to his native coop in disgust. Relieved from the lout's presence, Cheri gradually laid aside his tantrums, smoothed down his ruffled plumes, and resumed the manners of a gentleman.

My attempt at happy families was nipped in the bud, decidedly.

By and by I went to the market-town, and, having sold my butter and eggs, hunted up a bird-fancier. He had plenty of heliotropes, verbenas, and japonicas, and *had* had plenty of birds, but of course they were every one gone. Nobody wanted them. He had just about given them away, for a quarter of a dollar or so, and since then ever so many had been to buy them. Could he tell me where I might find one? Yes, he sold one to the barber last week, down near the depot. Did n't believe but what he would sell it. Was it a female bird? For my ambition had grown by what it fed on, and, instead of contenting myself simply with a companion for Cheri, I was now planning for a whole brood of canaries, with all the interests of housekeeping, baby-tending, and the manifold small cares incident upon domestic life. In short, I was launching out upon an entirely new career, setting a new world a-spinning in that small wire cage. Yes, it was a female bird. A good bird? For I could not understand the marvellously low price. Yes 'm, prime. Had eight young ones last year. Eight young ones! I rather caught my breath. I wanted a brood, but I thought three was the regular number, and I must confess I could hardly look with fortitude on such a sudden and enormous accession of responsibility. Besides, the cage was not half large enough. And how could they all bathe? And how could I take proper care of so many? And, dear me, eight young ones! And eight more next year is sixteen. And the grandchildren! And the great-grandchildren! Hills on hills and Alps on Alps! I shall be pecked out of house and home. I walked up the street musingly, and finally concluded not to call on the barber just yet.

It was very well I did so, for just afterwards Cheri's matins and vespers waxed fainter and fainter, and finally ceased altogether. In great anxiety I called in the highest medical science, which announced that he was only shedding his feathers. This opinion was corroborated by numerous little angelic soft fine feathers scattered about in localities that precluded the cat. Cheri is a proud youngster, and I suppose he thought if he must lose his good looks, there was no use in keeping up his voice; therefore he moped and pouted for several months, and would have appeared to very great disadvantage in case I had introduced a stranger to his good graces.

So Cheri is still alone in the world, but when my ship comes home from sea and brings an additional hour to my day, and a few golden eagles to my purse, he is going to have his mate, eight young ones and all, and I shall buy him a new cage, a trifle smaller than Noah's ark, and a cask of canary-seed and a South Sea turtle-shell, and just put them in the cage and let them colonize. If they increase and multiply beyond all possibility of provision, why, I shall by that time, perhaps, have become world-encrusted and hard-hearted, and shall turn the cat in upon them for an hour or two, which will no doubt have the effect of at once thinning them down to wieldy proportions.

Sweet little Cheri. My heart smites me to see you chirping there so innocent and affectionate while I sit here plotting treason against you. Bright as is the day and dazzling as the sunlit snow, you turn away from it all, so strong is your craving for sympathy, and bend your tiny head towards me to pour out the fulness of your song.

And what a song it is! All the bloom of his beautiful islands sheds its fragrance there. The hum of his honey-bees roving through beds of spices, the loveliness of dark-eyed maidens treading the wine-press with ruddy feet, the laughter of young boys swinging in the vines and stained with the scented grapes, — all the music that rings through his orange-groves, all the sunshine of the tropics caught in the glow of fruit and flower, in the blue of sky and sea, in the blinding whiteness of the shore and the amethystine evening, — all come quivering over the western wave in the falls of his tuneful voice. You shall hear it while the day is yet dark in the folds of the morning twilight, — a weak, faint, preliminary "whoo! whoo!" uncertain and tentative, then a trill or two of awakened assurance, and then, with a confident, courageous gush and glory of soul, he flings aside all minor considerations, and dashes *con amore* into the very middle of things. I am not musical, and cannot give you his notes in technical hieroglyphs, but in exact and intelligible lines such as all may understand, whether musical or not, his song is like this, — and you may rely upon its accuracy, for I wrote it down from his own lips this morning: —

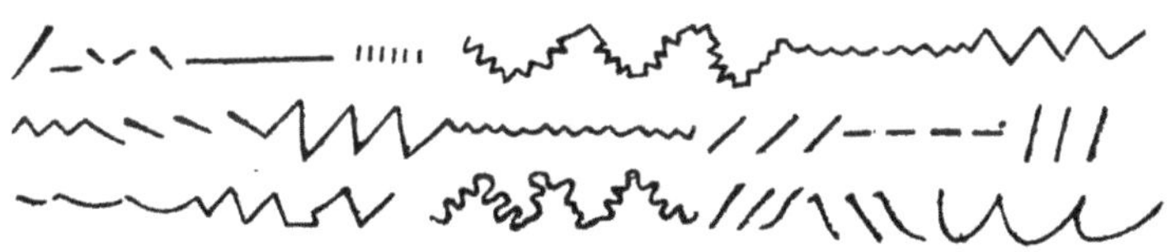

Side-Glances

at

Harvard Class-Day.

SIDE-GLANCES AT HARVARD CLASS-DAY.

IT happened to me once to "assist" at the celebration of Class-Day at Harvard University. Class-Day is the peculiar institution of the Senior Class, and marks its completion of College study and release from College rules.

Harvard has set up her Lares and Penates in a fine old grove, or a fine old grove and green have sprouted up around her, as the case may be, — most probably the latter, if one may judge from the appearance of the buildings which constitute the homes of the students, and which seem to have been built, and to be now sustained, without the remotest reference to taste or influence, but solely to furnish shelter, — angular, formal, stiff, windowy, bricky, and worse within than without. Why, I pray to know, as the first inquiry suggested by Class-Day, why is it that a boys' school should be placed beyond the pale of civilization? Do boys take so naturally to the amenities of life, that they can safely dispense with the conditions of amenity? Have boys so strong a predisposition to grace, that society can afford to take them away from home and its influences, and turn them loose with dozens of other boys into a bare and battered boarding-house, with its wood-work dingy, unpainted, gashed, scratched; windows dingy and dim; walls dingy and gray and smoked; everything narrow and rickety, unhomelike and unattractive?

America boasts of having the finest educational system in the world. Harvard is, if not the most distinguished, certainly among the first institutions in the country; but it is necessary only to stand upon the threshold of the first Harvard house which I entered, to pass through its mean entry and climb up its uncouth staircase, to be assured that our educational system has not yet found its key-stone. It has all the necessary materials, but it is incomplete. At its base it is falling every day more and more into shape and symmetry, but towards the top it is still only a pile of pebbles and boulders, and no arch. We have Primary Schools, Grammar Schools, High Schools, in which, first, boys and girls are educated together, as it seems impossible not to believe that God meant them to be; in which, secondly, home life and school life come together, and correct each other; in which, thirdly, comfortable and comely arrangements throughout minister to self-respect. But the moment you rise as high as a college, nature is violated. First, boys go off by themselves to their own destruction; secondly, home influences are withdrawn; and, thirdly, — at Harvard, which is the only college I ever visited, — the thorough comeliness which is found in the lower grades of schools does not appear. The separation of boys and girls in school is a subject which has been much talked about, but has not yet come to its adequate discussion. But the achievements of the past are the surest guaranties of the future. When we remember that, sixty years ago, the lowest district public schools were open to boys only, and that since that time girls have flocked into every grade of school below a college, it is difficult to believe that college doors will forever stand closed to them. *I* believe that the time will come when any system framed for boys alone or for girls alone will be looked upon in the same light in which we now regard a monastery or a nunnery. Precisely the same course will not be prescribed to both sexes, but they will be associated in their education to the inestimable advantage of both.

This, however, I do not purpose now to discuss further. Neither shall I speak of the second deficiency, — that of home influences, — any further than it is connected with the third, namely, a culpable neglect of circumstances which minister directly to character. I design to speak only of those evils which lie on the surface, patent to the most casual observer, and which may be removed without any change in the structure of society. And among the first of these I reckon the mean and meagre homes provided for the college students. If the State were poor, if the question were between mere rude shelter and no college education, we should do well to choose the former, and our choice would be our glory. It would be worth while even to live in such a house as Thoreau suggests, a tool-box with a few augur-holes bored in it to admit air, and a hook to hook down the lid at night. But we are not poor. Society has money enough to do everything it wishes to do; and it has provided no better homes for its young men because it has not come to the point of believing that better homes are necessary. Sometimes it affects to maintain that this way of living is beneficial, and talks of the disciplinary power of soldiers' fare. It is true that a soldier, living on a crust of bread and lying on the ground for love of country or of duty, is ennobled by it; but it is also true, that a miser doing the same things for love of stocks and gold is degraded; and a dreamer doing it serenely unconscious is neither ennobled nor degraded, but is simply laying the foundation for dyspepsia. To despise the elegances of life when they interfere with its duties is the part of a hero. To be indifferent to them when they stand in the way of knowledge is the attribute of a philosopher. To disregard them when they would contribute to both character and culture is neither the one nor the other. It was very well to cultivate the muses on a little oatmeal, when resources were so scanty that a bequest of seven hundred and seventy-nine pounds seventeen shillings and two pence was a gift munificent enough to confer upon the donor the honor of giving his name to the College so endowed; when a tax of one peck of corn, or twelve pence a year, from each family was all that could reasonably be levied for the maintenance of poor scholars at the College; when the Pilgrims — hardly escaped from persecution, and plunged into the midst of perils by Indian warfare, perils by frost and famine and disease, but filled with the love of liberty, and fired with the conviction that only fortified by learning could it be a blessing — gave of their scanty stock and their warm hearts, one man his sheep, another his nine shillings' worth of cotton cloth, a third his pewter flagon, and so on down to the fruit-dish, the sugar-spoon, the silver-tipt jug, and the trencher-salt; but a generation that is not astonished when a man pays six thousand dollars for a few feet of land to bury himself in, is without excuse in not providing for its sons a dignified and respectable home during the four years of their college life, — years generally when they are most susceptible of impressions, most impatient of restraints, most removed from society, and most need to be surrounded by every inducement to a courteous and Christian life. What was a large-minded liberality then may be but niggardliness or narrowness now. If indeed there be a principle in the case, the principle that this arrangement is better adapted to a generous growth than a more ornate one, then let it be carried out. Let all public edifices and private houses be reduced to a scale of Spartan simplicity; let camel's-hair and leathern girdles take the place of broadcloth, and meat be locusts and wild honey. But so long as treasures of art and treasures of wealth are lavished on churches, and court-houses, and capitols, and private dwellings, so long as earth and sea are forced to give up the riches which are in them for the adornment of the person and the enjoyment of the palate, we cannot consistently bring forward either principles or practice to defend our neglect withal. If the experiment of a rough and primitive life is to be tried, let it be tried at home, where community of interests, and diversity of tastes, and the refinements of family and social life, will prevent it from degenerating into a fatal failure; but do not let a horde of boys colonize in a base and shabby dwelling, unless you are willing to admit the corollary that they may to that extent become base and shabby. If they do become so, they are scarcely blameworthy; if they do not, it is no thanks to the system, but because other causes come in to deflect its conclusions. But why set down a weight at one end of the lever because there is a power at the other? Why not wait until, in the natural course of things, the lever comes to an obstacle, and then let the power bear down with all its might to remove it?

Doubtless those who look back upon their college days through the luminous mist of years, see no gray walls or rough floors, and count it only less than sacrilege to find spot or wrinkle or any such thing on the garments of their *alma mater*. But awful is the gift of the gods that we can become used to things; awful, since, by becoming used to them, we become insensible to their faults and tolerant of their defects. Harvard is beloved of her sons: would she be any less beloved if she were also beautiful to outside barbarians? Would her fame be less fair, or her name less dear, if those who come up to her solemn feasts, filled with the idea of her greatness, could not only tell her towers, but consider her palaces, without being forced to bury their admiration and reverence under the first threshold which they cross? O, be sure the true princess is not yet found, for the king's daughter is all glorious within.

Deficiency takes shelter under antiquity and

associations: associations may, indeed, festoon unlovely places, but would they cluster any less richly around walls that were stately and adequate? Is it not fitter that associations should adorn, than that they should conceal? If here and there a relic of the olden time is cherished because it is olden, — a house, a book, a dress, — shall we then live only in the houses, read only the books, and wear the dresses of our ancestors? If here and there some ship has breasted the billows of time, and sails the seas to-day because of its own inherent grace and strength, shall we, therefore, cling to crazy old crafts that can with difficulty be towed out of harbor, and must be kept afloat by constant application of tar and oakum? As I read the Bible and the world, gray hairs are a crown unto a man only when they are found in the way of righteousness. Laden with guilt and heavy woes, behold the *aged sinner* goes. A seemly old age is fair and beautiful, and to be had in honor by all people; but an old age squalid and pinched is of all things most pitiful.

After the Oration and Poem, which, having nothing distinctive, I pass over, comes the "Collation." The members of the Senior Class prepare a banquet, — sometimes separately and sometimes in clubs, at an expense varying from fifty to five hundred dollars, — to which they invite as many friends as they choose, or as are available. The banquet is quite as rich, varied, and elegant as you find at evening parties, and the occasion is a merry and pleasant one. But it occurred to me that there may be unpleasant things connected with this custom. In a class of seventy-five, in a country like America, it is probable that a certain proportion are ill able to meet the expense which such a custom necessitates. Some have fought their own way through college. Some must have been fought through by their parents. To them I should think this elaborate and considerable outlay must be a very sensible inconvenience. The mere expense of books and board, tuition and clothing, cannot be met without strict economy, and much parental and family sacrifice. And at the end of it all, when every nerve has been strained, and must be strained harder still before the man can be considered fairly on his feet and able to run his own race in life, comes this new call for entirely uncollegiate disbursements. Of course it is only a custom. There is no college by-law, I suppose, which prescribes a valedictory *symposium*. Probably it grew up gradually from small ice-cream beginnings to its present formidable proportions; but a custom is as rigid as a chain. I wondered whether the moral character of the young men was generally strong enough, by the time they were in their fourth collegiate year, to enable them to go counter to the custom, if it involved personal sacrifice at home, — whether there was generally sufficient courtliness, not to say Christianity, in the class, — whether there was sufficient courtesy, chivalry, high-breeding, — to make the omission of this party-giving unnoticeable, or not unpleasant. I by no means say, that the inability of a portion of the students to entertain their friends sumptuously should prevent those who are able from doing so. As the world is, some will be rich and some will be poor. This is a fact which they have to face the moment they go out into the world; and the sooner they grapple with it, and find out its real bearings and worth, or worthlessness, the better. Boys are usually old enough by the time they are graduated to understand and take philosophically such a distinction. Nor do I admit that poor people have any right to be sore on the subject of their poverty. The one sensitiveness which I cannot comprehend, with which I have no sympathy, for which I have no pity, and of which I have no tolerance, is sensitiveness about poverty. It is an essentially vulgar feeling. I cannot conceive how a man who has any real elevation of character, any self-respect, can for a moment experience so ignoble a shame. One may be annoyed at the inconveniences, and impatient of the restraints of poverty; but to be ashamed to be called poor or to be thought poor, to resort to shifts, not for the sake of being comfortable or elegant, but of seeming to be above the necessity of shifts, is an indication of an inferior mind, whether it dwell in prince or in peasant. The man who does it shows that he has not in his own opinion character enough to stand alone. He must be supported by adventitious circumstances, or he must fall. Nobody, therefore, need ever expect to receive sympathy from me in recounting the social pangs or slights of poverty. You never can be slighted, if you do not slight yourself. People may attempt to do it, but their shafts have no barb. You turn it all into natural history. It is a psychological phenomenon, a study, something to be analyzed, classified, reasoned from, and bent to your own convenience, but not to be taken to heart. It amuses you; it interests you; it adds to your stock of facts; it makes life curious and valuable: but if you suffer from it, it is because you have not basis, stamina; and probably you deserve to be slighted. This, however, is true only when people have become somewhat concentrated. Children know nothing of it. They live chiefly from without, not from within. Only gradually as they approach maturity do they cut loose from the scaffolding, and depend upon their own centre of gravity. Appearances are very strong in school. Money and prodigality have great weight there, notwithstanding the democracy of attainments and abilities. Have the students self-poise enough to refrain from these festive expenses without suffering mortification? Have they virtue enough to refrain from them with the certainty of incurring such suffering? Have they nobility, and generosity, and largeness of soul enough, while abstaining themselves for conscience' sake, to share in the plans, and sympathize without servility in the pleasures of their rich comrades? to look on with friendly interest, without cynicism or concealed malice, at the preparations in which they do not join? Or do they yield to selfishness, and gratify their own vanity, weakness, self-indulgence, and love of pleasure, at whatever cost to their parents? Or is there such a state of public opinion and usage in College, that this custom is equally honored in the breach and in the observance?

When the feasting was over, the most picturesque part of the day began. The College green put off suddenly its antique gravity, and became

> "Embrouded . . . . . as it were a mede
> Alle ful of fresshe floures, white and rede," —

"floures" which to their gay hues and graceful outlines added the rare charm of fluttering in perpetual motion. It was a kaleidoscope without angles. To me, niched in the embrasure of an old upper window, the scene, it seemed, might have stepped out of the Oriental splendor of Arabian Nights. I never saw so many well-dressed people together in my life before. That seems a rather tame fact to buttress Arabian Nights withal, but it implies much. The distance was a little too great for one to note personal and individual beauty; but since I have heard that Boston is famous for its ugly women, perhaps that was an advantage, as diminishing likewise individual ugliness. If no one was strikingly handsome, no one was strikingly plain. And though you could not mark the delicacies of faces, you could have the full effect of costume, — rich, majestic, floating, gossamery, impalpable. Everything was fresh, spotless, and in tune. It scarcely needed music to resolve all the incessant waver and shimmer into a dance; but the music came, and, like sand-grains under the magnet, the beautiful atoms swept into stately shapes and tremulous measured activity, —

> " A fine, sweet earthquake gently moved
> By the soft wind of whispering silks."

Then it seemed like a German festival, and came back to me the Fatherland, the lovely season of the Blossoming, the short, sweet bliss-month among the Blumenbühl Mountains.

Nothing can be more appropriate, more harmonious, than dancing on the green. Youth, and gayety, and beauty — and in summer we are all young, and gay, and beautiful — mingle well with the eternal youth of blue sky, and velvet sward, and the light breezes toying in the tree-tops. Youth and Nature kiss each other in the bright, clear purity of the happy summer-tide. Whatever objections lie against dancing elsewhere must veil their faces there.

If only men would not dance! It is the most unbecoming exercise which they can adopt. In women you have the sweep and wave of drapery, gentle undulations, summer-cloud floatings, soft, sinuous movements, fluency of pliant forms, the willowy bend and rebound of lithe and lovely suppleness. It is grace generic, — the sublime, the evanescent mysticism of motion, without use, without aim, except its own overflowing and all-sufficing fascination. But when a man dances, it reminds me of that amusing French book called "Le Diable Boiteux," which has been free-thinkingly translated, "The Devil on Two Sticks." A woman's dancing is gliding, swaying, serpentine. A man's is jerks, hops, convulsions, and acute angles. The woman is light, airy, indistinctly defined. Airy movements are in keeping. The man is sombre in hue, grave in tone, distinctly outlined; and nothing is more incongruous, to my thinking, than his dancing. The feminine drapery conceals processes and gives results. The masculine absence of drapery reveals processes, and thereby destroys results.

Once upon a time, long before the Flood, the clergyman of a country-village, possessed with such a zeal as Paul bore record of concerning Israel, conceived it his duty to "make a note" of sundry young members of his flock who had met for a drive and a supper, with a dance fringed upon the outskirts. The fame thereof being noised abroad, a sturdy old farmer, with a good deal of shrewd sense and mother-wit in his brains, and a fine, indirect way of hitting the nail on the head with a side-stroke, was questioned in a neighboring village as to the facts of the case. "Yes," he said, surlily, "the young folks had a party, and got up a dance, and the minister was mad, — and I don't blame him, — he thinks nobody has any business to dance, unless he knows how better than they did!" It was a rather different *casus belli* from that which the worthy clergyman would have preferred before a council; but it "meets my views" precisely as to the validity of the objections urged against dancing. I would have women dance, and women only, because it is the most beautiful thing in the world. And I think my views are Scriptural, for I find that it was the *virgins* of Israel that were to go forth in the dances of them that make merry. It was the *daughters* of Shiloh that went out to dance in dances at the feast of the Lord on the south of Lebonah.

From my window overlooking the green, I was led away into some one or other of the several halls to see the "round dances"; and it was like going from Paradise to Pandemonium. From the pure and healthy lawn, all the purer for the pure and peaceful people pleasantly walking up and down in the sunshine and shade, or grouped in the numerous windows, like bouquets of rare tropical flowers, — from the green, rainbowed in vivid splendor, and alive with soft, tranquil motion, fair forms, and the flutter of beautiful and brilliant colors, — from the green, sanctified already by the pale faces of sick, and wounded, and maimed soldiers who had gone out from the shadows of those sheltering trees to draw the sword for country, and returned white wraiths of their vigorous youth, the sad vanguard of that great army of blessed martyrs who shall keep forever in the mind of this generation how costly and precious a thing is liberty, who shall lift our worldly age out of the slough of its material prosperity into the sublimity of suffering and sacrifice, — from suggestions, and fancies, and dreamy musing, and "phantasms sweet," into the hall, where, for flower-scented summer air were thick clouds of fine, penetrating dust; and for lightly trooping fairies, a jam of heated human beings, so that you shall hardly come nigh the dancers for the press; and when you have, with difficulty, and many contortions, and much apologizing, threaded the solid mass, piercing through the forest of fans, — what? An enclosure, but no more illusion.

Waltzing is a profane and vicious dance. When it is prosecuted in the centre of a great crowd, in a dusty hall, on a warm midsummer day, it is also a disgusting dance. Night is its only appropriate time. The blinding, dazzling gas-light throws a grateful glare over the salient points of its indecency, and blends the whole into a wild whirl that dizzies and dazes one ; but the uncompromising afternoon, pouring in through manifold windows, tears away every illusion, and reveals the whole coarseness and commonness and all the repulsive details of this most alien and unmaidenly revel. The very *pose* of the dance is profanity. Attitudes which are the instinctive expression of intimate emotions, glowing rosy-red in the auroral time of tenderness, and justified in unabashed freedom only by a long and faithful habitude of unselfish devotion, are here openly, deliberately, and carelessly assumed by people who have but a casual and partial society-acquaintance. This I reckon profanity. This is levity the most culpable. This is a guilty and wanton waste of delicacy. That it is practised by good girls and tolerated by good mothers does not prove that it is good. Custom blunts the edge of many perceptions. A good thing soiled may be redeemed by good people ; but waltz as many as you may, spotless maidens, you will only smut yourselves, and not cleanse the waltz. It is of itself unclean.

There were, besides, peculiar *désagréments* on this occasion. As I said, there was no illusion, — not a particle. It was no Vale of Tempe, with Nymphs and Apollos. The boys were boys, young, full of healthful promise, but too much in the husk for exhibition, and not entirely at ease in their situation, — indeed, very much *not* at ease, — unmistakably warm, nervous, and uncomfortable. The girls were pretty enough girls, I dare say, under ordinary circumstances, — one was really lovely, with soft cheeks, long eyelashes, eyes deep and liquid, and Tasso's gold in her hair, though of a bad figure, ill set off by a bad dress, — but Venus herself could not have been seen to advantage in such evil plight as they, panting, perspiring, ruffled, frowzy, — puff-balls revolving through an atmosphere of dust, — a maze of steaming, reeking human couples, inhumanly heated and simmering together with a more than Spartan fortitude.

It was remarkable, and at the same time amusing, to observe the difference in the demeanor of the two sexes. The lions and the fawns seemed to have changed hearts, — perhaps they had. It was the boys that were nervous. The girls were unquailing. The boys were, however, heroic. They tried bravely to hide the fox and his gnawings; but traces were visible. They made desperate feint of being at the height of enjoyment and unconscious of spectators; but they had much modesty, for all that. The girls threw themselves into it *pugnis et calcibus*, — unshrinking, indefatigable. Did I say that it was amusing? I should rather say that it was painful. Can it be anything but painful to see young girls exhibiting the hardihood of the "professional" without the extenuating necessity?

There is another thing which girls and their mothers do not seem to consider. The present mode of dress renders waltzing almost as objectionable in a large room as the boldest feats of a French ballet-dancer.

If the title of my article do not sufficiently indicate the depth and breadth of knowledge on which my opinions assume to be based, let me, that I may not seem to claim confidence upon false pretences, confess that I have never seen, either in this country or abroad, any ballet-dancer or any dancer on any stage. I do not suppose that I have ever been at any assembly where waltzing was a part of the amusements half a dozen times in my life, and never in the daytime, until upon this occasion. I also admit that the sensations with which one would look upon this performance at Harvard would depend very much upon whether one went to it from that end of society which begins at the Jardin Mabille, or that which begins at a New England farm-house. I speak from the stand-point of the New England farm-house. Whether that or the Jardin Mabille is nearer the stand-point of the Bible, every one must decide for himself. When I say "this is right, this is wrong," I do not wish to be understood as settling the question for others, but as expressing my own strongest conviction. When

I say that the present mode of dress renders waltzing almost as objectionable in a large room as the boldest feats of a French ballet-dancer, I mean that, from what I have heard and read of ballet-dancers, I judge that these girls gyrating in the centre of their gyrating and unmanageable hoops, cannot avoid, or do not know how to avoid, at any rate do not avoid, the exposure which the short skirts of the ballet-dancer are intended to make, and which, taking to myself all the shame of both the prudery and the coarseness if I am wrong, I call an indecent exposure. In the glare and glamour of gas-light, it is flash and clouds and indistinctness. In the broad and honest daylight it is not. Indeed, I do not know that I will say "almost." Anything which tends to remove from woman her sanctity is not only almost, but altogether objectionable. Questionable action is often consecrated by holy motive, and there, even mistake is not fatal; but in this thing is no noble principle to neutralize practical error.

I do not speak thus about waltzing because I like to say it; but ye have compelled me. If one member suffers, all the members suffer with it. I respect and revere woman, and I cannot see her destroying or debasing the impalpable fragrance and delicacy of her nature without feeling the shame and shudder in my own heart. Great is my boldness of speech towards you, because great is my glorying of you. Though I speak as a fool, yet as a fool receive me. My opinions may be rustic. They are at least honest; and may it not be that the first fresh impressions of an unprejudiced and uninfluenced observer are as likely to be natural and correct views as those which are the result of many after-thoughts, long use, and an experience of multifold fascinations, combined with the original producing cause? My opinions may be wrong, but they will do no harm; the penalty will rest alone on me: while, if they are right, they may serve as a nail or two to be fastened by the masters of assemblies.

O girls, I implore you to believe me! They are not your true friends who would persuade you that you can permit this thing with impunity. It is not they who best know your strength, your power, your possibilities. It is not they who pay you the truest homage. Believe *me*, for it is not possible that I can have any but the highest motive. If the evil of foreign customs is to be incorporated into American society, if foul freedom of manners is to defile our pure freedom of life, if the robes of our refinement are to be white only when relieved against the dark background revealed by the polluted stage of a corrupt metropolis, on you will fall the burden of the consequences. Believe *me*, for your weal and mine are one. Your glory is my glory. Your degradation is mine. There are honeyed words whose very essence is insult. There are bold and bitter words whose roots lie in the deepest reverence. Beware of the leaven of the Pharisees and of the Sadducees. Beware of the honor which is dishonor.

I hear that the ground is taken that the affairs of Class-Day are not a legitimate subject of public comment; that it is a private matter of the Senior Class, of which one has no more right to speak in print than one has so to speak of a house in Beacon Street to which one might be invited. Is it indeed so? I have no right to go into Mr. Smith's house in Beacon Street, — I use the term Smith as simply generic, not meaning to imply for a moment that so plebeian a name ever marred a Beacon Street door-plate, — and subsequently print that I was hospitably entreated, or that the chair-covers were faded and the conversation brilliant. Neither have I any right to go into Master Jones's room, in Hollis Hall, and inform the public that he keeps wine in his cigar-box, and that he entertained his friends awkwardly or gracefully. But suppose all the Beacon Street families have a custom of devoting one day of every year to festivities, in which festivities all Boston, and all the friends, and the friends' friends, whom each Beacon Street family chooses to invite, are invited to partake. The Common, and the State-House, and the Music-Hall, &c. are set apart for dancing, the houses are given up to feasting, — and this occurs year after year. Is it a strictly private affair?

I have still no right to denounce or applaud or in any way characterize Mr. Smith's special arrangements; but have I not a right to discuss in the most public manner the general features of the custom? May I not say that I consider the feasting a possible danger, and the dancing a certain evil, and assign my reasons for these opinions?

I have spoken of the condition of some of the College buildings. I find in the College records repeated instances of the College authorities appealing to the public concerning this very thing. So early as 1651, the Rev. Henry Dunster, President of the College, represented to the Commissioners of the United Colonies the decaying condition of the College buildings, and the necessity of their repair and enlargement: and the Commissioners reply, that they will recommend to the Colonies to give some yearly help, by pecks, half-bushels, and bushels of wheat. Is a subject that is brought before Congress improper to be brought before the public in a magazine?

I have spoken of the banqueting arranged by the Senior Class. Is that private? I find in a book regularly printed and published, a book written by a former President of the College, — a man whom no words of mine can affect, yet whom I cannot pass without laying at his feet my tribute of gratitude and reverence; a man who lives to receive from his contemporaries the honors which are generally awarded only by posterity, — I find in this book accounts of votes passed by the Corporation and Overseers, prohibiting Commencers from "preparing or providing either plum-cake, or roasted, boiled, or baked meats, or pies of any kind"; and afterwards, if any one should do anything contrary to this act, or "go about to evade it by plain cake, they shall not be admitted to their degree"; and also, "that commons be of better quality, have more variety, clean table-cloths of convenient length and breadth twice a week, and that plates be allowed." Now if the plum-cake and pies of the "Commencers" are spread before the public, how shall one know that the plum-cake and pies of an occasion at least equally public, and only a month beforehand, must not be mentioned? If any family in Beacon Street should publish its housekeeping rules and items in this unhesitating manner, I think a very pardonable confusion of ideas might exist as to what was legitimately public, and what must be held private. If it be said that these items concern a period from which the many years that have since elapsed remove the seal of silence, I have but to turn to the Boston Daily Advertiser, a journal whose taste and judgment are unquestionable, and find in its issue of July 18, 1863, eight closely printed columns devoted to a minute description of what they said, and what they did, at the College festival arranged by the Association of the Alumni, in which description may be read such eminently private incidents as that — by some unfortunate mistake, which would have been a death-blow to any Beacon Street housekeeper — there were one hundred more guests than there were plates, and — what it might be hoped would be quite unnecessary to state — that the unlucky *De trop* "bore the disappointment with the most admirable good-breeding, *and retired from the hall without noise or disturbance.*" (Noble army of martyrs! Let a monument more durable than brass rise in the hearts of their countrymen to commemorate their heroism, and let it be graven all over, in characters of living light, with the old-time query, "Why did n't Jack eat his supper?")

I find also in the same issue of the same paper the Commencement Dinner, its guests, its quantity and quality, its talk, its singing of songs, and giving of gifts, spread before the public. If, now, the festivities of Commencement and of the Alumni Association are public, by what token shall one know that the festivities of Class-Day, which have every appearance of being just as public, are in reality a family affair, and strictly private?

I have spoken of waltzing. The propriety of my speaking must stand or fall with the previous count. But in the book to which I have before referred is recorded a vote passed by the Overseers, "To restrain unsuitable and unseasonable dancing in the College." If a rule of the College is published throughout the land, is not the land in some measure appealed to, and may it not speak when it thinks it sees a custom in open and systematic violation of the rule?

But, independent of this special rule, Harvard College was founded in the early days of the Colony. It was the pet and pride and hope of the colonists. They gave to it of their abundance and their poverty. To what end? "Dreading to leave an illiterate ministry to the churches," says the author of "New England First-Fruits." The first Constitution of the College declares one of its objects to be "to make and establish all such orders, statutes, and constitutions as they shall see necessary for the instituting, guiding, and furthering of the said College, and the several members thereof, from time to time, in piety, morality, and learning." Later, its objects are said to be "the advancement of all good literature, arts, and sciences," and "the education of the English and Indian youth of this country in knowledge and godliness." Of the rules of the College, "Let every student be earnestly pressed to consider well the main end of his life and studies is, to know God and Jesus Christ, which is eternal life, and, therefore, to lay Christ in the bottom, as the only foundation of all sound knowledge and learning." Quincy says that to the Congregational clergy the "institution is perhaps more indebted than to any other class of men for early support, if not for existence." That it has not avowedly turned aside from its original object is indicated by the motto which it still bears, *Christo et Ecclesiæ.* Now I wish to know if the official sanction of this College, founded by statesmen-clergy for the promotion of piety and learning, to further the welfare of the State, consecrated to Christ and the Church, is to be given to a practice which no one will maintain positively conduces to either piety and learning, but which many believe to be positively detrimental to both, and which an overwhelming majority of the Congregational clergy who founded, and of their ecclesiastical descendants at the present day, would, I am confident, condemn, and yet it is not to be publicly spoken of, because it is a private affair! Has it any right to privacy? Does the College belong to a Senior Class, or to the State? Have the many donations been given, and the appropriations been made, for the pleasure or even profit of any one class, or for the whole Commonwealth? Has any class any right to introduce in any College hall, or anywhere, as a College class, with the sanction of the Faculty, a custom which is entirely disconnected with either learning or piety, a custom of doubtful propriety, not to say morality, inasmuch as many believe it to be wrong, and a custom, therefore, whose tendency is to weaken confidence in the College, and consequently to restrict its beneficence? And is the discussion of this thing a violation of the rites of hospitality?

These are my counts against "Class-Day," as it is now conducted. It contains much that is calculated to promote neither learning nor godliness, but to retard both. Neither literary nor moral excellence seems to enter as an element into its standard. In point of notoriety and popular interest it seems to me to reach, if not to overtop, Commencement-Day, and therefore it tends to subordinate scholarship to other and infinitely less important matters. It in a manner necessitates an expenditure which many are ill able to bear, and under which, I have reason to believe, many parents do groan, being burdened. It has not the pleasure and warmth of reunion to recommend it, for it precedes separation. The expense is not incurred by men who are masters of their own career, who know where they stand and what they can do; but chiefly by boys who are dependent upon others, and whose knowledge of ways and means is limited, while their knowledge of wants is deep and pressing and aggressive. It is an extraordinary and unnecessary expense, coming in the midst of ordinary and necessary expense, while the question of reimbursement is still entirely in abeyance. It launches young men at the outset of their career into extravagance and display, — limited indeed in range, but rampant within that range, — and thereby throws the influence of highest authority in favor of, rather than against, that reckless profusion, display, and dissipation which is the weakness and the bane of our social life. It signalizes in a marked and public manner the completion of the most varied and complete course of study in the country, and the commencement of a career which should be the most noble and beneficial, not by peculiar and appropriate ceremonies, but by the commonest rites of the lecture-room and ball-room; and I cannot but think that, especially at this period of our history, when no treasure is esteemed too precious for sacrifice, and the land is red with the blood of her best and bravest, — when Harvard herself mourns for her children lost, but glories in her heroes fallen, — that the most obvious and prominent customs of Class-Day would be more honored in the breach than in the observance.

I look upon the violation of hospitality as one of the seven deadly sins, — a sin for which no punishment is too great; but this sin I have not consciously, and I do not think I have actually, committed. I cannot but suspect, that, if I had employed the language of exclusive eulogy, — such language as is employed at and concerning the Commencement dinners and the Alumni dinners, — I might have described the celebration of Class-

Day with much more minuteness than I have attempted to do, and should have heard no complaints of violated hospitality. This I would gladly have done, had it been possible. As it was not, I have pointed out those features which seemed to me objectionable, — certainly with no design so ridiculous as that of setting up myself against Harvard University, but equally certainly with no heart so craven as to shrink from denouncing what seemed to me wrong because it would be setting myself against Harvard University. Opinions must be judged by their own weight, not by the weight of the persons who utter them. The fair fame of Harvard is the possession of every son and daughter of Massachusetts, and the least stain that mars her escutcheon is the sorrow of all. But Harvard is not the Ark of the Covenant, to be touched only by consecrated hands, upon penalty of instant death. She is honorable, but not sacred; wise, but not infallible. To *Christo et Ecclesiæ*, she has a right; to *Noli me tangere*, she has none. A very small hand may hurl an arrow. If it is heaven-directed, it may pierce in between the joints of the armor. If not, it may rebound upon the archer. I make the venture, promising that I shall not follow the example of that President of Harvard who died of a broken heart, because, according to Cotton Mather, he "*fell under the displeasure of certain good men who made a figure in that neighborhood.*"

As it may never again happen to me to be writing about colleges, I desire to say in this paper everything I have to say on the subject, and therefore take this opportunity to refer to the practice of "hazing," although it is but remotely connected with Class-Day. If we should find it among hinds, a remnant of the barbarisms of the Dark Ages, blindly handed down by such slow-growing people as go to mill with their meal on one side of the saddle and a stone on the other to balance, as their fathers did, because it never occurred to them to divide the meal into two parcels and make it balance itself, we should not be surprised; but "hazing" occurs among boys who have been accustomed to the circulation of ideas, boys old enough and intelligent enough to understand the difference between brutality and frolic, old enough to know what honor and courage mean, and therefore I cannot conceive how they should countenance a practice which entirely ignores and defies honor, and which has not a single redeeming feature. It has neither wisdom nor wit, no spirit, no genius, no impulsiveness, scarcely boyish mirth. A narrow range of stale practical jokes, lighted up by no gleam of originality, seems to be transmitted from year to year with as much fidelity as the Hebrew Bible, and not half the latitude allowed to clergymen of the English Established Church. But besides its platitude, its one overpowering and fatal characteristic is its intense and essential cowardice. Cowardice is its head and front and bones and blood. One boy does not single out another boy of his own weight, and take his chances in a fair stand-up fight. But a party of Sophomores club together in such numbers as to render opposition useless, and pounce upon their victim unawares, as Brooks and his minions pounced upon Sumner, and as the Southern chivalry is given to doing. For sweet pity's sake, let this mode of warfare be monopolized by the Southern chivalry.

The lame excuse is offered, that it does the Freshmen good, — takes the conceit out of them. But if there is any Class in College so divested of conceit as to be justified in throwing stones, it is surely not the Sophomore Class. Moreover, whatever good it may do the sufferers, it does harm, and only harm, to the perpetrators; and neither the Law nor the Gospel requires a man to improve other people's characters at the expense of his own. Nobody can do a wrong without injuring himself; and no young man can do a mean, cowardly wrong like this without suffering severest injury. It is the very spirit of the slaveholder, a dastardly and detestable, a tyrannical and cruel spirit. If young men are so blinded by custom and habit that a meanness is not to them a meanness because it has been practised for years, so much the worse for the young men, and so much the worse for our country, whose sweat of blood attests the bale and blast which this evil spirit has wrought. If uprightness, if courage, if humanity and rectitude and the mind conscious to itself of right are anything more than a name, let the young men who mean to make time minister to life scorn this debasing and stupid practice.

Why, as one resource against this, as well as for its own intrinsic importance, should there not be a military department to every college, as well as a mathematical department? Why might not every college be a military normal school, so that the exuberance and riot of animal spirits, the young, adventurous strength and joy in being, might not only be kept from striking out as now in illegitimate, unworthy, and hurtful directions, but might become the very basis and groundwork of useful purposes. Such exercise would be so promotive of health and discipline, it would so train and *limber* the physical powers, that the superior quality of study would, I doubt not, more than atone for whatever deficiency in quantity might result. And even suppose a little less attention should be given to Euclid and Homer, which is of the greater importance now-a-days, an ear that can detect a false quantity in a Greek verse, or an eye that can sight a Rebel nine hundred yards off, and a hand that can pull a trigger and shoot him? Knowledge is power; but knowledge must sharpen its edges and polish its points, if it would be greatliest available in days like these. The knowledge that can plant batteries and plan campaigns, that is fertile in expedients and wise to baffle the foe, is just now the strongest power. Diagrams and first-aorists are good, and they who have fed on such meat have grown great, and done the state service in their generation; but these times demand new measures and new men. It is conceded that we shall probably be for many years a military nation. At least a generation of vigilance shall be the price of our liberty. And even of peace we can have no stronger assurance than a wise and wieldy readiness for war. Now the education of our unwarlike days is not adequate to the emergencies of this martial hour. We must be seasoned with something stronger than Attic salt, or we shall be cast out and trodden under foot of men. True, all education is worthy. Everything that exercises the mind fits it for its work; but professional education is indispensable to professional men. And the profession, *par excellence*, of every man of this generation is war. Country overrides all personal considerations. Lawyer, minister, what not, a man's first duty is the salvation of his country. When she calls, he must go; and before she calls, let him, if possible, prepare himself to serve her in the best manner. As things are now at Harvard, college boys are scarcely better than cow-boys for the army. Their costly education runs greatly to waste. It gives them no direct advantage over the clod who stumbles against a trisyllable. So far as it makes them better men, of course they are better soldiers; but for all of military education which their college gives them, they are fit only for privates, whose sole duty is to obey. They know nothing of military drill or tactics or strategy. The State cannot afford this waste. She cannot afford to lose the fruits of mental toil and discipline. She needs trained mind even more than trained muscle. It is harder to find brains than to find hands. The average mental endowment may be no higher in college than out; but granting it to be as high, the culture which it receives gives it immense advantage. The fruits of that culture, readiness, resources, comprehensiveness, should all be held in the service of the State. Military knowledge and practice should be imparted and enforced to utilize ability, and make it the instrument, not only of personal, but of national welfare. That education which gives men the advantage over others in the race of life should be so directed as to convey that advantage to country, when she stands in need. Every college might and should be made a nursery of athletes in mind and body, clear-eyed, stout-hearted, strong-limbed, cool-brained, — a nursery of soldiers, quick, self-possessed, brave and cautious and wary, ready in invention, skilful to command men and evolve from a mob an army, — a nursery of gentlemen, reminiscent of no lawless revels, midnight orgies, brutal outrages, launching out already attainted into an attainting world, but with many a memory of adventure, wild, it may be, and not over-wise, yet pure as a breeze from the hills, — banded and sworn

> " To serve as model for the mighty world,
> To break the heathen and uphold the Christ,
> To ride abroad redressing human wrongs,
> To speak no slander, no, nor listen to it,
> To lead sweet lives in purest chastity,
> Not only to keep down the base in man,
> But teach high thought, and amiable words,
> And courtliness, and the desire of fame,
> And love of truth, and all that makes a man."

SUCCESS IN LIFE.

SUCCESS IN LIFE.

THE SUCCESSFUL.

THERE are successes more melancholy than any failure. There are failures more noble than success. The man who began life as a ploughboy, who went from his father's farm to the great city with his wardrobe tied up in his handkerchief, and one dollar in his pocket, and who by application, economy, and forecast has amassed a fortune, is not necessarily a successful man. If his object was to amass a fortune, he is so far successful; but it is a mean and miserable object, and his life would be a contemptible, if it were not a terrible, failure. We do not keep this sufficiently in mind. American society, and perhaps all society, is too apt to do homage to material prosperity; but material prosperity may be obtained by the sacrifice of moral grandeur; and so obtained, it is an apple of Sodom. A man may call out his whole energy, wield all his power, and wealth follow as one of the results.

This is well. Wealth may even be an object, if it be a subordinate object, — the servant of a higher power. Wealth may minister to the noblest part of man, — but only minister, not master. Only as a minister it deserves regard. When it usurps the throne and becomes monarch, it is of all things most pitiful and abject. The man who sets out with the determination to be rich as an end, sets out with a very ignoble determination; and he who seeks or values wealth for the respect which it secures and the position it gives, is not very much higher in the scale; yet such people are often held up to the admiration and imitation of American youth; and oftener still have those men been held up for imitation who, whether by determination or drift, had become rich, and whose sole claim to distinction was that they had become rich. Again and again I have seen "success" which seemed to me to be the brand of ignominy rather than the stamp of worth, — the epitaph of culture, if not of character. I look on with a profound and regretful pity. You successful, — *you!* with half your powers lying dormant, — you, with your imagination stifled, your conscience unfaithful, your chivalry deadened into shrewdness, your religion a thing of tithes and forms; — you successful, in whom romance has died out; to whom fidelity and constancy and aspiration are nothing but a voice; who remember love and heroism and self-sacrifice only as the vaporings of youth; who measure principles by your purse, utility by your using; who see nothing glorious this side of honesty; nothing terrible in the surrender of faith; nothing degrading that is not amenable to the law; nothing in your birthright that may not be sold for a mess of pottage, if only the mess be large enough, and the pottage savory; — you successful? Is this success? Then, indeed, humanity is a base and bitter failure.

It is not necessary that a man should be a robber or a murderer, in order to degrade himself. Without defrauding his neighbor of a cent, without laying himself open to a single accusation of illegality or violence, a man may destroy himself. A moral suicide, he kills out all that belongs to his highest nature, and leaves but a bare and battered wreck where the temple of the Holy Ghost should rise.

> "Measure not the work
> Until the day 's out, and the labor done;
> Then bring your gauges."

Is that man successful who trades on his country's necessities? He, not a politician, nor a horse-jockey, nor a footpad, but a man who talks of honor and integrity, — a man of standing and influence, whose virtue is not tempted by hunger, whose life has been such that he may be supposed intelligently to comprehend the interests which are at stake, and the measures which should be taken to secure them, — is he successful because he obtains in a few months, by the perquisites — not illegal, but strained to the extreme verge of legal

— of an office, — not illegal, but accidental, not in the line of promotion, — a sum of money which the greatest merit and the highest office in the land cannot claim for years? He is shrewd. He understands his business. He knows the inns and outs. He can manage the sharpers. He can turn an honest penny, and a good many of them. He need not refuse to do himself a good turn with his left hand, while he is doing his country a good turn with his right. It is all fair and aboveboard. He does the business assigned him, and does it well. He takes no more compensation than the law allows. The money may as well go to him as to shoddy contractors, Shylock sutlers, and the legion of plebeian rascals. But it was a good stroke. It was a great chance. It was a rare success.

O wretched failure! O pitiful abortion! O accursed hunger for gold! When the nation struggles in a death-agony, when her life-blood is poured out from hundreds of noble hearts, when men and women and children are sending up to the Lord the incense of daily sacrifice in her behalf, and we know not yet whether prayer and effort, whether faith and works, shall avail, — whether our lost birthright, sought carefully, and with tears, shall be restored to us once more, — in this solemn and awful hour, a man can close his eyes and ears to the fearful sights and great signs in the heavens, and, stooping earthward, delve with his muck-rake in the gutter for the paltry pennies!

A man? A MAN! Is this manhood? Is this manliness? Is this the race that our institutions engender? Is this the best production which we have a right to expect? Is this the result which Christianity and civilization combine to offer? Is this the advantage which the nineteenth century claims over its predecessors? Is this the flower of all the ages, — earth's last, best gift to heaven?

No, — no, — no, — this is a changeling, and no child. The true brother's blood cries to us from Baltimore. It rings out from the East where Winthrop fell. It swells up from the West with Lyon's dirge. And all along, from hill and valley and river-depths, where the soil is drenched, and the waters are reddened, and nameless graves are scattered, — cleaving clearly through the rattle of musketry, mingling grandly with the "diapason of the cannonade," or floating softly up under the silent stars, — "the thrilling, solemn, proud, pathetic voice" ceases not to cry unto us day and night; its echoes linger tenderly and tearfully around every hearth-stone, and vibrate with a royal resonance from mountain to sea-shore. The mother bends to it in her silent watches. The soldier, tempest-tost, hears it through the creaking cordage, and every true heart knows its brother, and takes up the magnificent strain, — victorious, triumphant, exultant, —

"Dulce et decorum est pro patria mori."

Sweet and honorable is it for country to die.

THE UNSUCCESSFUL.

THE unsuccessful men are all around us; and among them are those who confound all distinctions set up by society, and illustrate the great law of compensation set up by God, cutting society at right angles, and obtuse angles, and acute angles, unnoticed, or but flippantly mentioned by the careless, but giving food for intimate reflections to those for whom things suggest thoughts.

Have you not seen them, — these unsuccessful men? — men who seem not to have found their niche, but are always on somebody's hands for settlement, or, if settled, never at rest? If they are poor, their neighbors say, Why does he not learn a trade? or, Why does he not stick to his trade? He might be well off, if he were not so flighty. He has a good head-piece, but he potters rhymes; he tricks out toy-engines and knick-knacks; he roams about the woods gathering snakes and toads; and meanwhile he is out at the elbows. If he is rich, they say, Why does he not make a career? He has great resources. His brain is inexhaustible. He is equipped for any emergency. There is nothing which he might not attain, if he would only apply himself, but he fritters himself away. He sticks to nothing. He touches on this, that, and the other, and falls off.

True, O Philosophers, he does stick to nothing,

but condemn him not too harshly. It is the old difficulty of the square man in the round hole, and the round man in the square hole. They never did rest easy there since time began, and never will. Many — perhaps the greater number — of people have no overmastering inclination for any employment. They are farmers because their fathers were before them, and that road was graded for them, — or shoemakers, or lawyers, or ministers, for the same reason. If circumstances had impelled them in a different direction, they would have gone in a different direction, and been content. It is not easy for them to conceive that a man is an indifferent lawyer, because his raw material should have been worked up into a practical engineer; or an unthrifty shoemaker, because he is a statesman nipped in the bud. Yet such things are. Sometimes these men are gay, giddy, rollicking fellows. Sometimes their faces are known at the gaming-houses and the gin-palaces. Sometimes they go down quickly to a dishonored grave, over which Love stands bewildered, and weeps her unavailing tears. Sometimes, on the other hand, they are gloomy, sad, silent. Perhaps they are morose. Worse still, they are whining, fretful, complaining. You would even call them sour. Often they are cynical and disagreeable. But be not too hasty, too sweeping, too clear-cut. I have seen such men who were the reverse of the Pharisees. Their faces were a tombstone. The portals of their soul were guarded by lions scarcely chained. But though their temple had no Beautiful Gate, it was none the less a temple, consecrated to the Most High. Within it, day and night, the sacred fire burned, the sacred Presence rested. There, honor, justice, devotion, and all heroic virtues dwelt. Thence falsehood, impurity, profanity, — whatsoever loveth and maketh a lie, — were excluded. They are unsuccessful, because they will not lower the standard which their youth unfurled. Its folds float high above them, out of reach, but not out of sight, nor out of desire. With constant feet they are climbing up to grasp it. You do not see it; no, and you never will. You need not strain your aching eyes; but they see it, and comfort their weary hearts withal.

These men may receive sympathy, but they do not need pity. They are a thousand times more blessed than the vulgarly successful. The shell is wrinkled, and gray, and ugly; but within, the meat is sweet and succulent. Perhaps they will never make a figure in the world, but

> "True happiness abides with him alone
> Who in the silent hour of inward thought
> Can still suspect and still revere himself
> In lowliness of mind."

And it is even better never to be happy than to be sordidly happy. It is better to be nobly dissatisfied than meanly content. A splendid sadness is better than a vile enjoyment.

I hear of people that never failed in anything they undertook. I do not believe in them. In the first place, however, I do not believe this testimony is true. It is the honest false-witness, it is the benevolent slander of their affectionate and admiring friends. But if it were in any case true, I should not believe in the man of whom it was affirmed. It is difficult to conceive that a person of elevated character should not attempt many things too high for him. He finds himself set down in the midst of life. Earth, air, and water, his own mind and heart, the whole mental, moral, and physical world, teem with mysteries. He is surrounded with problems incapable of mortal solution. He must grasp many of them and be foiled. He must attack many foes and be repulsed. He may be stupidly blind, or selfish, or cowardly, and make no endeavor, — in which case he will of course endure no defeat. If he sets out with small aims, he may accomplish them; but it is not a thing to boast of. It is better to fall below a high standard than to come up to a low one, — to try great things and fail, than to try only small ones and succeed. For he who attempts grandly will achieve much, while he whose very desires are small will make but small acquisitions. Of course, I am not speaking now of definite, mensurable matters of fact, in which the reverse is the case. Of course, it is better to build a small house and pay for it, than to build a palace and involve yourself in debt. It is wiser to set yourself a reasonable task and perform it, than a prodigious one and do nothing. I am endeavoring to present only one side of a truth which is many-sided, — and that side is, that great deeds are done by those who aspire greatly. You may not attain perfection, but if you strive to be perfect, you will be better than if you were content to be as good as your neighbors. You are not, perhaps, the world's coming man; but if you aim at the completest possible self-development, you will be a far greater man than if your only aim is to keep out of the poor-house. "I have taken all knowledge to be my province," said Lord Bacon. He did not conquer; he could not even overrun his whole province; but he made vast inroads, — vaster by far than if he had designed only to occupy a garden-plot in the Delectable Land. True greatness is a growth, and not an accident. The bud, brought into light and warmth, may burst suddenly into flower; but the seed must have been planted, and the kindly soil must have wrapped it about, and shade and shine and shower must have wrought down into the darkness, and nursed and nurtured the tiny germ. The touch of circumstance may reveal, may even quicken, but cannot create, nobility.

This I reckon to be success in life, — fitness, — perfect adaptation. I hold him successful, and him only, who has found or conquered a position in which he can bring himself into full play. Success is perfect or partial, according as it comes up to, or falls below, this standard. But entire success is rare in this world. Success in business, success in ambition, is not success in life, though it may be comprehended in it. Very few are the symmetrical lives. Very few of us are working at the top of our bent. One may give scope to his mechanical invention, but his poetry is cramped. One has his intellect at high pressure, but the fires are out under his heart. One is the bond-servant of love, and Pegasus becomes a dray-horse, Apollo must keep the pot boiling, and Minerva is hurried with the fall sewing. So we go, and above us the sun shines, and the stars throb; and beneath us the snows, and the flowers, and the blind, instinctive earth; and over all, and in all, God blessed forever.

Now, then, success being the best thing, we do well to strive for it; but success being difficult to attain, if not unattainable, it remains for us to wring from our failures all the sap and sustenance and succor that are in them, if so be we may grow thereby to a finer and fuller richness, and hear one day the rapturous voice bid us come up higher.

And be it remembered, what a man is, not what a man does, is the measure of success. The deed is but the outflow of the soul. By their fruits ye shall know *them*. The outward act has its inward significance, though we may not always interpret it aright, and its moral aspect depends upon the agent. "In vain," says Sir Thomas Browne, "we admire the lustre of anything seen; that which is truly glorious is invisible." Character, not condition, is the trust of life. A man's own self is God's most valuable deposit with him. This is not egotism, but the broadest benevolence. A man can do no good to the world beyond himself. A stream can rise no higher than its fountain. A corrupt tree cannot bring forth good fruit. If a man's soul is stunted and gnarled and dwarfed, his actions will be. If his soul is corrupt and base and petty, so will his actions be. Faith is the basis of works. Essence underlies influence. If a man beget an hundred children, and live many years, and his soul be not filled with good, I say that an untimely birth is better than he.

When I see, as I sometimes do see, those whom the world calls unsuccessful, furnished with every virtue and adorned with every grace, made considerate through suffering, sympathetic by isolation, spiritedly patient, meek, yet defiant, calm and contemptuous, tender even of the sorrows and tolerant of the joys which they despise, enduring the sympathy and accepting the companionship of weakness because it is kindly offered, though it be a burden to be dropped just inside the door, and not a treasure to be taken into the heart's chamber, — I am ready to say, Blessed are the unsuccessful.

Blessed *are* the unsuccessful, the men who have nobly striven and nobly failed. He alone is in an evil case who has set his heart on false or selfish or trivial ends. Whether he secure them or not, he is alike unsuccessful. But he who "loves high" is king in his own right, though he "live low." His plans may be abortive, but himself is sure. God may overrule his desires, and thwart his hopes, and baffle his purposes, but all things shall work together for his good. Though he fall, he shall rise again. Every defeat shall be a victory. Every calamity shall drop down blessing. Inward disappointment shall minister to enduring joy. From the grapes of sorrow he shall press the wine of life.

Theodore Winthrop died in the bud of his promise. As I write that name, hallowed from our olden time, and now baptized anew for the generations that are to follow, comes back again that warm, bright, midsummer morning, freighted with woe, — that dark, sad summer morning that wrenched him away from sweet life, and left silence for song, ashes for beauty, — only cold, impassive clay, where glowing, vigorous vitality had throbbed and surged.

Scarcely had his fame risen to illumine that early grave, but, one by one, from his silent desk came those brilliant books, speaking to all who had ears to hear words of grand resolve and faith, — words of higher import than their sound, — keywords to a noble life; for all the bravery and purity and trust and truth and tenderness that gleam in golden setting throughout his books must have been matched with bravery and purity and trust and truth and tenderness in the soul from which they sprang. Looking at what might have been accomplished with endowments so rare, culture so careful, and patience so untiring, our lament for the dead is not untinged with bitterness. A mind so well poised, so self-confident, so eager in its honorable desire for honorable fame, that, without the stimulus of publication, it could produce work after work, compact and finished, studded with gems of wit and wisdom, white and radiant with inward purity,—could polish away roughness, and toil on alone, pursuing ideal perfection, and attaining a rare excellence,—surely, here was promise of great things for the future; but it seemed otherwise to God. A poor little drummer-boy, not knowing what he did, sped a bullet straightway to as noble a heart as ever beat, and quenched a royal life.

I have spoken of Winthrop, but a thousand hearts will supply each its own name wreathed with cypress and laurel. Were these lives failures? Is not the grandeur of the sacrifice its offset? The choice of life or death is in no man's hands. The choice is only and occasionally in the manner. All must die. To a few, and only a few, is granted the opportunity of dying martyrs. They rush on to meet the King of Terrors. They wrest the crown from his awful brow, and set it on their own triumphant. They die, not from inevitable age or irresistible disease, but in the full flush of manhood, in the very prime and zenith of life, in that glorious transition-hour when hope is culminating in fruition. They die of set purpose, with unflinching will, for God and the right. O thrice and four times happy these who bulwark liberty with their own breasts! No common urn enshrines their sacred dust. No vulgar marble emblazons their hero-deeds. Every place which their life has touched becomes at once and forever holy ground. A nation's gratitude embalms their memory. In the generations which are to come, when we are lying in undistinguished earth, mothers shall lead their little children by the hand, and say: "Here he was born. This is the blue sky that bent over his baby head. Here he fell, fighting for his country. Here his ashes lie"; — and the path thither shall be well worn, and for many and many a year there shall be hushed voices, and trembling lips, and tear-dimmed eyes. Everywhere there shall be death, — yours and mine, — but only here and there immortality, — and it is his.

So the young soldier's passing away is not untimely. The longest life can accomplish only benefaction and fame, and the life that has accomplished these has reached life's ultimatum. It is a fair and decorous fate to devote length of days to humanity, but he who gathers up his life with all its beauty and happiness and hope, and lays it on the altar of sacrifice, — he has done all. A century of earthly existence only scatters its benefits one by one. The martyr binds his in a single bundle of life, and the offering is complete. To all noble minds fame is sweet and desirable, and threescore years and ten are all too few to carve the monument more durable than brass; but when such men as Winthrop die such death as his, we seize the tools that fall from their dying grasp, and complete the fragmentary structure, in shape more graceful, it may be, in height more majestic, in colors more lovely, than their own hands could have wrought. We attribute to them, not simply what they did, but all that they might have done. Had Winthrop lived, failing health, adverse circumstance, might have blasted his promise in the bud; but now nothing of that can ever mar his fame. We surround him with his aspirations. We glorify him with his possibilities. He is not only the knight without fear and without reproach, but the author immortal as the brightest auspices could have made his strong and growing powers. A century could not have left him greater than the love and hope and sorrow of his countrymen, building on the little that is known of his short and beautiful life, have made him.

O men and women everywhere who are following on to know the Lord, faint yet pursuing; men and women who are troubled, toiling, doubting, hoping, watching, struggling; whose attainments "through the long green days, worn bare of grass and sunshine," lag hopelessly behind your aspirations; who are haunted evermore by the ghosts of your young purposes; who see far off the shining hills your feet are fain to tread; who work your work with dumb, assiduous energy, but with perpetual protest, — I bid you good luck in the name of the Lord.

HAPPIEST DAYS.

HAPPIEST DAYS.

LONG ago, when you were a little boy or a little girl, — perhaps not so very long ago, either, — were you never interrupted in your play by being called in to have your face washed, your hair combed, and your soiled apron exchanged for a clean one, preparatory to an introduction to Mrs. Smith, or Dr. Jones, or Aunt Judkins, your mother's early friend? And after being ushered into that august presence, and made to face a battery of questions which were either above or below your capacity, and which you consequently despised as trash or resented as insult, did you not, as you were gleefully vanishing, hear a soft sigh breathed out upon the air, — "Dear child, he is seeing his happiest days"? In the concrete, it was Mrs. Smith or Dr. Jones speaking of you. But going back to general principles, it was Commonplacedom expressing its opinion of childhood.

There never was a greater piece of absurdity

in the world. I thought so when I was a child, and now I know it; and I desire here to brand it as at once a platitude and a falsehood. How the idea gained currency, that childhood is the happiest period of life, I cannot conceive. How, once started, it kept afloat, is equally incomprehensible. I should have supposed that the experience of every sane person would have given the lie to it. I should have supposed that every soul, as it burst into flower, would have hurled off the imputation. I can only account for it by recurring to Lady Mary Wortley Montague's statistics, and concluding that the fools *are* three out of four in every person's acquaintance.

I for one lift up my voice emphatically against the assertion, and do affirm that I think childhood is the most undesirable portion of human life, and I am thankful to be well out of it. I look upon it as no better than a mitigated form of slavery. There is not a child in the land that can call his soul, or his body, or his jacket his own. A little soft lump of clay he comes into the world, and is moulded into a vessel of honor or a vessel of dishonor long before he can put in a word about the matter. He has no voice as to his education or his training, what he shall eat, what he shall drink, or wherewithal he shall be clothed. He has to wait upon the wisdom, the whims, and often the wickedness of other people. Imagine, my six-foot friend, how you would feel, to be obliged to wear your woollen mittens when you desire to bloom out in straw-colored kids, or to be buttoned into your black waistcoat when your taste leads you to select your white, or to be forced under your Kossuth hat when you had set your heart on your black beaver: yet this is what children are perpetually called on to undergo. Their wills are just as strong as ours, and their tastes are stronger, yet they have to bend the one and sacrifice the other; and they do it under pressure of necessity. Their reason is not convinced; they are forced to yield to superior power; and, of all disagreeable things in the world, the most disagreeable is not to have your own way. When you are grown up, you wear a print frock because you cannot afford a silk, or because a silk would be out of place, — you wear India-rubber overshoes because your polished patent-leather would be ruined by the mud; and your self-denial is amply compensated by the reflection of superior fitness or economy. But a child has no such reflection to console him. He puts on his battered, gray old shoes because you make him; he hangs up his new trousers and goes back into his detestable girl's-frock because he will be punished if he does not, and it is intolerable.

It is of no use to say that this is their discipline, and is all necessary to their welfare. It is a repulsive condition of life in which such degrading *surveillance* is necessary. You may affirm that an absolute despotism is the only government fit for Dahomey, and I may not disallow it; but when you go on and say that Dahomey is the happiest country in the world, why — I refer you to Dogberry. Now the parents of a child are, from the nature of the case, absolute despots. They may be wise, and gentle, and doting despots, and the chain may be satin-smooth and golden-strong; but if it be of rusty iron, parting every now and then and letting the poor prisoner violently loose, and again suddenly caught hold of, bringing him up with a jerk, galling his tender limbs and irretrievably ruining his temper, — it is all the same; there is no help for it. And really, to look around the world and see the people that are its fathers and mothers is appalling, — the narrow-minded, prejudiced, ignorant, ill-tempered, fretful, peevish, passionate, careworn, harassed men and women. Even we grown people, independent of them and capable of self-defence, have as much as we can do to keep the peace. Where is there a city, or a town, or a village, in which are no bickerings, no jealousies, no angers, no petty or swollen spites? Then fancy yourself, instead of the neighbor and occasional visitor of these poor human beings, their children, subject to their absolute control, with no power of protest against their folly, no refuge from their injustice, but living on through thick and thin right under their guns.

"Oh!" but you say, "this is a very one-sided view. You leave out entirely the natural tenderness that comes in to temper the matter. Without that, a child's situation would of course be intolerable; but the love that is born with him makes all things smooth."

No, it does not make all things smooth. It does wonders, to be sure, but it does not make cross people pleasant, nor violent people calm, nor fretful people easy, nor obstinate people reasonable, nor foolish people wise,—that is, it may do so spasmodically, but it does not hold them to it and keep them at it. A great deal of beautiful moonshine is written about the sanctities of home and the sacraments of marriage and birth. I do not mean to say that there is no sanctity and no sacrament. Moonshine is not nothing. It is light,—real, honest light,—just as truly as the sunshine. It is sunshine at second-hand. It illuminates, but indistinctly. It beautifies, but it does not vivify or fructify. It comes indeed from the sun, but in too roundabout a way to do the sun's work. So, if a woman is pretty nearly sanctified before she is married, wifehood and motherhood may accomplish the work; but there is not one man in ten thousand of the writers aforesaid who would marry a vixen, trusting to the sanctifying influences of marriage to tone her down to sweetness. A thoughtful, gentle, pure, and elevated woman, who has been accustomed to stand face to face with the eternities, will see in her child a soul. If the circumstances of her life leave her leisure and adequate repose, that soul will be to her a solemn trust, a sacred charge, for which she will give her own soul's life in pledge. But how many such women do you suppose there are in your village? Heaven forbid that I should even appear to be depreciating woman! Do I not know too well their strength, and their virtue which is their strength? But, stepping out of idyls and novels, and stepping into American kitchens, is it not true that the larger part of the mothers see in their babies, or act as if they saw, only babies? And if there are three or four or half a dozen of them, as there generally are, so much the more do they see babies whose bodies monopolize the mother's time to the disadvantage of their souls. She loves them, and she works for them day and night; but when they are ranting and ramping and quarrelling, and torturing her over-tense nerves, she forgets the infinite, and applies herself energetically to the finite, by sending Harry with a round scolding into one corner, and Susy into another, with no light thrown upon the point in dispute, no principle settled as a guide in future difficulties, and little discrimination as to the relative guilt of the offenders. But there is no court of appeal before which Harry and Susy can lay their case in these charming "happiest days"!

Then there are parents who love their children like wild beasts. It is a passionate, blind, instinctive, unreasoning love. They have no more intelligent discernment, when an outside difficulty arises with respect to their children, than a she-bear. They wax furious over the most richly deserved punishment, if inflicted by a teacher's hand; they take the part of their child against legal authority; but observe, this does not prevent them from laying their own hands heavily on their children. The same obstinate ignorance and narrowness that are exhibited without exist within also. Folly is folly, abroad or at home. A man does not play the fool out-doors and act the sage in the house. When the poor child becomes obnoxious, the same unreasoning rage falls upon him. The object of a ferocious love is the object of an equally ferocious anger. It is only he who loves wisely that loves well.

The manner in which children's tastes are disregarded, their feelings ignored, and their instincts violated, is enough to disaffect one with childhood. They are expected to kiss all flesh that asks them to do so. They are jerked up into the laps of people whom they abhor. They say, "Yes, ma'am," under pain of bread and water for a week, when their unerring nature prompts them to hurl out emphatically, "No." They are sent out of the room whenever a fascinating bit of scandal is to be rehearsed, packed off to bed just as everybody is settled down for a charming evening, bothered about their lessons when their play is but fairly under way, and hedged and hampered on every side. It is true, that all this may be for their good, but what of that? So everything is for the good of grown-up people; but does that make us contented? It is doubtless for our good in the long run that we lose our pocket-books, and break our arms, and catch a fever, and have our brothers defraud a bank, and our houses burn down, and people steal our umbrellas, and borrow our books and never return them. In fact, we know that upon certain conditions all things work together for our good, but, notwithstanding, we find some things very unpleasant; and we may talk to our children of discipline and health by the hour together, and it will never be anything but an intolerable nuisance to them to be swooped off to bed by a dingy old nurse just as the people are beginning to come, and shining silk, and floating lace, and odorous, faint flowers are taking their ecstatic young souls back into the golden days of the good Haroun al Raschid.

Even in this very point lies one of the miseries of childhood, that no philosophy comes to temper their sorrow. We do not know why we are troubled, but we know there *is* some good, grand reason for it. The poor little children do not know even that. They find trouble utterly inconsequent and unreasonable. The problem of evil is to them absolutely incapable of solution. We know that beyond our horizon stretches the infinite universe. We grasp only one link of a chain whose beginning and end is eternity. So we readily adjust ourselves to mystery, and are content. We apply to everything inexplicable the test of partial view, and maintain our tranquillity. We fall into the ranks, and march on, acquiescent, if not jubilant. We hear the roar of cannon and the rattle of musketry. Stalwart forms fall by our side, and brawny arms are stricken. Our own hopes bite the dust, our own hearts bury their dead; but we know that law is inexorable. Effect must follow cause, and there is no happening without causation. So, knowing ourselves to be only one small brigade of the army of the Lord, we defile through the passes of this narrow world, bearing aloft on our banner, and writing ever on our hearts, the divine consolation, "What thou knowest not now thou shalt know hereafter." This is an unspeakable tranquillizer and comforter, of which, woe is me! the little ones know nothing. They have no underlying generalities on which to stand. Law and logic and eternity are nothing to them. They only know that it rains, and they will have to wait another week before they go a-fishing; and why could n't it have rained Friday just as well as Saturday? and it always does rain or something when I want to go anywhere, — so, there! And the frantic flood of tears comes up from outraged justice as well as from disappointed hope. It is the flimsiest of all possible arguments to say that their sorrows are trifling, to talk about their little cares and trials. These little things are great to little men and women. A pine bucket full is just as full as a hogshead. The ant has to tug just as hard to carry a grain of corn as the Irishman does to carry a hod of bricks. You can see the bran running out of Fanny's doll's arm, or the cat putting her foot through Tom's new kite, without losing your equanimity; but their hearts feel the pang of hopeless sorrow, or foiled ambition, or bitter disappointment, — and the emotion is the thing in question, not the event that caused it.

It is an additional disadvantage to children in their troubles, that they can never estimate the relations of things. They have no perspective. All things are at equal distances from the point of sight. Life presents to them neither foreground nor background, principal figure nor subordinates, but only a plain spread of canvas, on which one thing stands out just as big and just as black as another. You classify your *désagréments*. This is a mere temporary annoyance, and receives but a passing thought. This is a life-long sorrow, but it is superficial; it will drop off from you at the grave, be folded away with your cerements, and leave no scar on your spirit. This thrusts its lancet into the secret place where your soul abideth, but you know that it tortures only to heal; it is recuperative, not destructive, and you will rise from it to newness of life. But when little ones see a ripple in the current of their joy, they do not know, they cannot tell, that it is only a pebble breaking softly in upon the summer flow, to toss a cool spray up into the white bosom of the lilies, or to bathe the bending violets upon the green and grateful bank. It seems to them as if the whole strong tide is thrust fiercely and violently back, and hurled into a new channel, chasmed in the rough, rent granite. It is impossible to calculate the waste of grief and pathos which this incapacity causes. Fanny's doll aforesaid is left too near the fire, and waxy tears roll down her ruddy cheeks, to the utter ruin of her pretty face and her gay frock; and anon poor Fanny breaks her little heart in moans and sobs and sore lamentations. It is Rachel weeping for her children. I went on a tramp one May morning to buy a tissue-paper wreath of flowers for a little girl to wear to a May-party, where all the other little girls were expected to appear similarly crowned. After a long and weary search, I was forced to return without it. Scarcely had I pulled the bell, when I heard the quick pattering of little feet in the entry.

Never in all my life shall I lose the memory of those wistful eyes, that did not so much as look up to my face, but levelled themselves to my hand, and filmed with disappointment to find it empty. *I* could see that the wreath was a very insignificant matter. I knew that every little beggar in the street had garlanded herself with sixpenny róses, and I should have preferred that my darling should be content with her own silky brown hair; but my taste availed her nothing, and the iron entered into her soul. Once a little boy, who could just stretch himself up as high as his papa's knee, climbed surreptitiously into the store-closet and upset the milk-pitcher. Terrified, he crept behind the flour-barrel, and there Nemesis found him, and he looked so charming and so guilty that two or three others were called to come and enjoy the sight. But he, unhappy midget, did not know that he looked charming; he did not know that his guilty consciousness only made him the more interesting; he did not know that he seemed an epitome of humanity, a Liliputian miniature of the great world; and his large, blue, solemn eyes were filled with remorse. As he stood there silent, with his grave, utterly mournful face, he had robbed a bank, he had forged a note, he had committed a murder, he was guilty of treason. All the horror of conscience, all the shame of discovery, all the unavailing regret of a detected, atrocious, but not utterly hardened pirate, tore his poor little innocent heart. Yet children are seeing their happiest days!

These people — the aforesaid three fourths of our acquaintance — lay great stress on the fact that children are free from care, as if freedom from care were one of the beatitudes of Paradise; but I should like to know if freedom from care is any blessing to beings who don't know what care is. You who are careful and troubled about many things may dwell on it with great satisfaction, but children don't find it delightful by any means. On the contrary, they are never so happy as when they can get a little care, or cheat themselves into the belief that they have it. You can make them proud for a day by sending them on some responsible errand. If you will not place care upon them, they will make it for themselves. You shall see a whole family of dolls stricken down simultaneously with malignant measles, or a restive horse evoked from a passive parlor-chair. They are a great deal more eager to assume care, than you are to throw it off. To be sure, they may be quite as eager to be rid of it after a while; but while this does not prove that care is delightful, it certainly does prove that freedom from care is not.

Now I should like, Herr Narr, to have you look at the other side for a moment: for there is a positive and a negative pole. Children not only have their full share of misery, but they do not have their full share of happiness; at least, they miss many sources of happiness to which we have access. They have no consciousness. They have sensations, but no perceptions. We look longingly upon them, because they are so graceful, and simple, and natural, and frank, and artless; but though this may make us happy, it does not make them happy, because they don't know anything about it. It never occurs to them that they are graceful. No child is ever artless to himself. The only difference he sees between you and himself is, that you are grown-up and he is little. Sometimes I think he does have a dim perception that when he is ill, it is because he has eaten too much, and he must take medicine, and feed on heartless dry toast, while, when you are ill, you have the dyspepsia, and go to Europe. But the beauty and sweetness of children are entirely wasted on themselves, and their frankness is a source of infinite annoyance to each other. A man enjoys *himself*. If he is handsome, or wise, or witty, he generally knows it, and takes great satisfaction in it; but a child does not. He loses half his happiness because he does not know that he is happy. If he ever has any consciousness, it is an isolated, momentary thing, with no relation to anything antecedent or subsequent. It lays hold on nothing. Not only have they no perception of themselves, but they have no perception of anything. They never recognize an exigency.

They do not salute greatness. Has not the Autocrat told us of some lady who remembered a certain momentous event in our Revolutionary War, and remembered it only by and because of the regret she experienced at leaving her doll behind when her family was forced to fly from home? What humiliation is this! What an utter failure to appreciate the issues of life! For her there was no revolution, no upheaval of world-old theories, no struggle for freedom, no great combat of the heroisms. All the passion and pain, the mortal throes of error, the glory of sacrifice, the victory of an idea, the triumph of right, the dawn of a new era, — all, all were hidden from her behind a lump of wax. And what was true of her is true of all her class. Having eyes, they see not; with their ears they do not hear. The din of arms, the waving of banners, the gleam of swords, fearful sights and great signs in the heavens, or the still, small voice that thrills when wind and fire and earthquake have swept by, may proclaim the coming of the Lord, and they stumble along, munching bread-and-butter. Out in the solitudes Nature speaks with her many-toned voices, and they are deaf. They have a blind sensational enjoyment, such as a squirrel or a chicken may have, but they can in no wise interpret the Mighty Mother, nor even hear her words. The ocean moans his secret to unheeding ears. The agony of the underworld finds no speech in the mountain-peaks, bare and grand. The old oaks stretch out their arms in vain. Grove whispers to grove, and the robin stops to listen, but the child plays on. He bruises the happy buttercups, he crushes the quivering anemone, and his cruel fingers are stained with the harebell's purple blood. Rippling waterfall and rolling river, the majesty of sombre woods, the wild waste of wilderness, the fairy spirits of sunshine, the sparkling wine of June, and the golden languor of October, the child passes by, and a dipper of blackberries, or a pocketful of chestnuts, fills and satisfies his horrible little soul. And in face of all this people say, — there are people who *dare* to say, — that childhood's are the "happiest days."

I may have been peculiarly unfortunate in my surroundings, but the children of poetry and novels were very infrequent in my day. The innocent cherubs never studied in my school-house, nor played puss-in-the-corner in our back-yard. Childhood, when I was young, had rosy cheeks and bright eyes, as I remember, but it was also extremely given to quarrelling. It used frequently to "get mad." It made nothing of twitching away books and balls. It often pouted. Sometimes it would bite. If it wore a fine frock, it would strut. It told lies, — "whoppers" at that. It took the larger half of the apple. It was not, as a general thing, magnanimous, but "aggravating." It may have been fun to you who looked on, but it was death to us who were in the midst.

This whole way of viewing childhood, this regretful retrospect of its vanished joys, this infatuated apotheosis of doughiness and rank unfinish, this fearful looking-for of dread old age, is low, gross, material, utterly unworthy of a sublime manhood, utterly false to Christian truth. Childhood is pre-eminently the animal stage of existence. The baby is a beast, — a very soft, tender, caressive beast, — a beast full of promise, — a beast with the germ of an angel, — but a beast still. A week-old baby gives no more sign of intelligence, of love, or ambition, or hope, or fear, or passion, or purpose, than a week-old monkey, and is not half so frisky and funny. In fact, it is a puling, scowling, wretched, dismal, desperate-looking animal. It is only as it grows old that the beast gives way and the angel-wings bud, and all along through infancy and childhood the beast gives way and gives way and the angel-wings bud and bud; and yet we entertain our angel so unawares, that we look back regretfully to the time when the angel was in abeyance and the beast raved regnant.

The only advantage which childhood has over manhood is the absence of foreboding, and this indeed is much. A large part of our suffering is anticipatory, much of which children are spared. The present happiness is clouded for them by no shadowy possibility; but for this small indemnity shall we offset the glory of our manly years? Because their narrowness cannot take in the contingencies that threaten peace, are they blessed above all others? Does not the same narrowness cut them off from the bright certainty that underlies all doubts and fears? If ignorance is bliss, man stands at the summit of mortal misery, and the scale of happiness is a descending one. We must go down into the ocean-depths, where, for the scintillant soul, a dim, twilight instinct lights up gelatinous lives. If childhood is indeed the happiest period, then the mysterious God-breathed breath was no boon, and the Deity is cruel. Immortality were well exchanged for the blank of annihilation.

We hear of the dissipated illusions of youth, the paling of bright, young dreams. Life, it is said, turns out to be different from what was pictured. The rosy-hued morning fades away into the gray and livid evening, the black and ghastly night. In especial cases it may be so, but I do not believe it is the general experience. It surely need not be. It should not be. I have found things a great deal better than I expected. I am but one; but with all my oneness, with all that there is of me, I protest against such generalities. I think they are slanderous of Him who ordained life, its processes and its vicissitudes. He never made our dreams to outstrip our realizations. Every conception, brain-born, has its execution, hand-wrought. Life is not a paltry tin cup which the child drains dry, leaving the man to go weary and hopeless, quaffing at it in vain with black, parched lips. It is a fountain ever springing. It is a great deep, which the wisest has never bounded, the grandest never fathomed.

It is not only idle, but stupid, to lament the departure of childhood's joys. It is as if something precious and valued had been forcibly torn from us, and we go sorrowing for lost treasure. But these things fall off from us naturally; we do not give them up. We are never called upon to give them up. There is no pang, no sorrow, no wrenching away of a part of our lives. The baby lies in his cradle and plays with his fingers and toes. There comes an hour when his fingers and toes no longer afford him amusement. He has attained to the dignity of a rattle, a whip, a ball. Has he suffered a loss? Has he not rather made a great gain? When he passed from his toes to his toys, did he do it mournfully? Does he look at his little feet and hands with a sigh for the joys that once loitered there, but are now forever gone? Does he not rather feel a little ashamed, when you remind him of those days? Does he not feel that it trenches somewhat on his dignity? Yet the regret of maturity for its past joys amounts to nothing less than this. Such regret is regret that we cannot lie in the sunshine and play with our toes, — that we are no longer but one remove, or but few removes, from the idiot. Away with such folly! Every season of life has its distinctive and appropriate enjoyments, which bud and blossom and ripen and fall off as the season glides on to its close, to be succeeded by others better and brighter. There is no consciousness of loss, for there is no loss. There is only a growing up, and out of, and beyond.

Life does turn out differently from what was anticipated. It is an infinitely higher and holier and nobler thing than our childhood fancied. The world that lay before us then was but a tinsel toy to the world which our firm feet tread. We have entered into the undiscovered land. We have explored its ways of pleasantness, its depths of dole, its mountains of difficulty, its valleys of delight, and, behold! it is very good. Storms have swept fiercely, but they swept to purify. We have heard in its thunders the Voice that woke once the echoes of the Garden. Its lightnings have riven a path for the Angel of Peace.

Manhood discovers what childhood can never divine, — that the sorrows of life are superficial, and the happiness of life structural; and this knowledge alone is enough to give a peace which passeth understanding.

Yes, the dreams of youth were dreams, but the waking was more glorious than they. They were only dreams, — fitful, flitting, fragmentary visions of the coming day. The shallow joys, the capricious pleasures, the wavering sunshine of infancy, have deepened into virtues, graces, heroisms. We have the bold outlook of calm, self-confident courage, the strong fortitude of endurance, the imperial magnificence of self-denial. Our hearts expand with benevolence, our lives broaden with beneficence. We cease our perpetual skirmishing at the outposts, and go inward to the citadel. Down into the secret places of life we descend. Down among the beautiful ones, in the cool and quiet shadows, on the sunny summer levels, we walk securely, and the hidden fountains are unsealed.

For those people who do nothing, for those to whom Christianity brings no revelation, for those who see no eternity in time, no infinity in life, for those to whom opportunity is but the handmaid of selfishness, to whom smallness is informed by no greatness, for whom the lowly is never lifted up by indwelling love to the heights of divine performance, — for them, indeed, each hurrying year may well be a King of Terrors. To pass out from the flooding light of the morning, to feel all the dewiness drunk up by the thirsty, insatiate sun, to see the shadows slowly and swiftly gathering, and no starlight to break the gloom, and no home beyond the gloom for the unhoused, startled, shivering soul, — ah! this indeed is terrible. The "confusions of a wasted youth" strew thick confusions of a dreary age. Where youth garners up only such power as beauty or strength may bestow, where youth is but the revel of physical or frivolous delight, where youth aspires only with paltry and ignoble ambitions, where youth presses the wine of life into the cup of variety, there indeed Age comes, a thrice unwelcome guest. Put him off. Thrust him back. Weep for the early days: you have found no happiness to replace their joys. Mourn for the trifles that were innocent, since the trifles of your manhood are heavy with guilt. Fight to the last. Retreat inch by inch. With every step you lose. Every day robs you of treasure. Every hour passes you over to insignificance; and at the end stands Death. The bare and desolate decline drops suddenly into the hopeless, dreadful grave, the black and yawning grave, the foul and loathsome grave.

But why those who are Christians and not Pagans, who believe that death is not an eternal sleep, who wrest from life its uses and gather from life its beauty, — why they should dally along the road, and cling frantically to the old landmarks, and shrink fearfully from the approaching future, I cannot tell. You are getting into years. True. But you are getting out again. The bowed frame, the tottering step, the unsteady hand, the failing eye, the heavy ear, the tremulous voice, they will all be yours. The grasshopper will become a burden, and desire shall fail. The fire shall be smothered in your heart, and for passion you shall have only peace. This is not pleasant. It is never pleasant to feel the inevitable passing away of priceless possessions. If this were to be the culmination of your fate, you might indeed take up the wail for your lost youth. But this is only for a moment. The infirmities of age come gradually. Gently we are led down into the valley. Slowly, and not without a soft loveliness, the shadows lengthen. At the worst these weaknesses are but the stepping-stones in the river, passing over which you shall come to immortal vigor, immortal fire, immortal beauty. All along the western sky flames and glows the auroral light of another life. The banner of victory waves right over your dungeon of defeat. By the golden gateway of the sunsetting,

"Through the dear might of Him who walked the waves,"

you shall pass into the "cloud-land, gorgeous land," whose splendor is unveiled only to the eyes of the Immortals. Would you loiter to your inheritance?

You are "getting into years." Yes, but the years are getting into you, — the ripe, rich years, the genial, mellow years, the lusty, luscious years. One by one the crudities of your youth are falling off from you, — the vanity, the egotism, the isolation, the bewilderment, the uncertainty. Nearer and nearer you are approaching yourself. You are consolidating your forces. You are becoming master of the situation. Every wrong road into which you have wandered has brought you, by the knowledge of that mistake, so much closer to the truth. You no longer draw your bow at a venture, but shoot straight at the mark. Your purposes concentrate, and your path is cleared. On the ruins of shattered plans you find your vantage-ground. Your broken hopes, your thwarted purposes, your defeated aspirations, become a staff of strength with which you mount to sublimer heights. With self-possession and self-command return the possession and the command of all things. The title-deed of creation, forfeited, is reclaimed. The king has come to his own again. Earth and sea and sky pour out their largess of love. All the past crowds down to lay its treasures at your feet. Patriotism stands once more in the breach at Thermopylæ, — bears down the serried hosts of Bannockburn, — lays its calm hand in the fire, still, as if it felt the pressure of a mother's lips, — gathers to its heart the points of opposing spears, to make a way for the avenging feet behind. All that the ages have of greatness and glory your hand may pluck, and every year adds to the purple vintage. Every year comes laden with the riches of the lives that were lavished on it. Every year brings to you softness and sweetness and strength. Every year evokes order from confusion, till all things find scope and adjustment. Every year sweeps a broader circle for your horizon, grooves a deeper channel for your experience. Through sun and shade and shower you ripen to a large and liberal life.

Yours is the deep joy, the unspoken fervor, the sacred fury of the fight. Yours is the power to redress wrong, to defend the weak, to succor the needy, to relieve the suffering, to confound the oppressor. While vigor leaps in great tidal pulses along your veins, you stand in the thickest of the fray, and broadsword and battle-axe come crashing down through helmet and visor. When force has spent itself, you withdraw from the field, your weapons pass into younger hands, you rest under your laurels, and your works do follow you. Your badges are the scars of your honorable wounds. Your life finds its vindication in the deeds which you have wrought. The possible to-morrow has become the secure yesterday. Above the tumult and the turbulence, above the struggle and the doubt, you sit in the serene evening, awaiting your promotion.

Come, then, O dreaded years! Your brows are awful, but not with frowns. I hear your resonant tramp far off, but it is sweet as the May-maidens' song. In your grave prophetic eyes I read a golden promise. I know that you bear in your bosom the fulness of my life. Veiled monarchs of the future, shining dim and beautiful, you shall become my vassals, swift-footed to bear my messages, swift-handed to work my will. Nourished by the nectar which you will pour in passing from your crystal cups, Death shall have no dominion over me, but I shall go on from strength to strength and from glory to glory.

CPSIA information can be obtained
at www.ICGtesting.com
Printed in the USA
LVHW040351110522
718423LV00001B/201

9 783375 006921